# Onaedo

## THE BLACKSMITH'S DAUGHTER

A NOVEL

NGOZI ACHEBE

MANDAC-GOLDBERG
PUBLISHING

Published by
MANDAC-GOLDBERG PUBLISHING,
Olympia, Washington

First paperback edition originally published by
MANDAC-GOLDBERG PUBLISHING
in March 2010.

This is a work of fiction. While the literary perceptions may be based
on experience, all names, characters, places and incidents are products
of the author's imagination or are used fictitiously. Any resemblance to
actual persons, living or dead is entirely coincidental.

Library of Congress Cataloging-in-Publication Data – on file

Achebe, Ngozi
Onaedo-The Blacksmith's Daughter:
a novel by Ngozi Achebe – 1st ed.
Fiction


ISBN-13: 978-0-9826473-0-1 (Hardcover)
ISBN-13: 978-0-9826473-1-8 (Paperback)

www.mandacgoldberg.com

Cover credits: (Main woman) iStock©Lumigraphics, (Woman,
lower left) iStock©_moriarty_, (map) iStock©nicoolay, (ship)
photoexpress©Cambo, (texture) RD Studio Microstock.
Photomanipulation by Michael Rohani. Author photography by
Valerie Bowlick-Terrell.

The Fell Types (body text and ornaments) are
digitally reproduced by Igino Marini. www.iginomarini.com.

Book design by DesignForBooks.com

Printed in the United States of America.

✣

*For my parents*
*Augustine Ndubisi Achebe*
*and*
*Matilda Chikodili Achebe*
*without whom I would not be.*

✣

# Prologue

S HE STOOD AT THE DOOR and saw it blinking in the dark like a red-eyed monster; there were messages. Her fingers hesitated on the switch near the door. This was an upscale neighborhood in Philadelphia where bad things didn't happen, but one could never be too careful. And she was alone tonight.

Maxine turned on the light and her eyes adjusted from the previous gloom. Satisfied that there were no intruders lurking, she walked in. The décor of the entrance hall was calculated to give an aura of wealth that was important when one lived in a place like this, especially since they were the only African American couple that lived in the cul-de-sac. They made sure to do nothing that might scare their neighbors—no loud music, no noisy parties and even as her marriage to Darren had crumbled, she had smiled brightly at Claire every day from across the street, talked about the weather, the children's school and everything else but what was going on inside this house.

She quickly pushed all thoughts of Darren out of her mind in the manner she'd perfected in the two years since their divorce. There were things that she had to do now, like getting ready for her father's visit. She hoped Esmeralda, the cleaning lady who came in twice a week, had made up the guest room. She stopped by the dark-wood side-table that was pushed against the wall underneath a large, ornate entrance mirror. She looked into the mirror as she did each time she passed it and saw the same thing—her father's face looking back at her. She wasn't surprised; she had begun to see more and more of him in herself. After so many years of separation—exactly thirty-three years since he went back to Africa—he had begun to appear to her in the brown cocoa of her skin, the darkness of her eyes and the fullness of her lips. Sometimes when she looked closely enough, she also saw traces of her mother's blonde Nordic and Irish forbears, the features that had always been subtle in Maxine and had become even less obvious as she grew older.

She inclined her head and touched her curly, dark-brown hair. She had tried to straighten it with a perm last week but it had sprung back to its natural curls, defying any attempt to deny where *that* had come from. She sighed and pulled it back in a twisted bun as she walked to the window and parted the curtains lightly. As in most affluent neighborhoods, the streets of Chestnut Hill were usually empty at this time of night. She looked at the mansions of the cul-de-sac she had called home for the twelve years she'd been married to Darren and for the two after the divorce, fourteen years in all. A lone jogger who could have been either a man or a woman ran past and she made a mental note to resume the early morning runs that had not seemed as important as writing the book that had taken over her days. Running wasn't the only thing that she'd neglected. When the girls returned, she'd start doing things with them again. She sighed and turned away from the empty street. She had to prepare the spare room for her father's arrival tomorrow. She paused, thinking about his visit. She had to admit that anxiety nibbled at her guts. It had been so long since he'd left; she'd felt the loss for years.

She had been about five or six then and cried for nights until her mother had told her to pull herself together, that Daddy had gone to fight in a war in his homeland and would come back for them when it was over. Only he hadn't come back. Not then, and not for thirty years after.

She gave herself a mental shake. She wasn't going to let thoughts from the past spoil this reunion. It had been a long time in the making and the time for regrets was long past, so was yearning for things that might have been. She was a grown woman with her own family now, even if she had joined the divorce statistics.

She walked towards the still-blinking answer-machine and hit playback. She always thought of it as a creature, its electronic numbers were its eyes and now it counted down as each message played out. The first ones were fast talking salesmen who pitched easy credit and timeshare vacations, then it was her mother reminding her not to forget her promise to speak at the women's shelter later that week, the next was her daughters' school reminding her of the upcoming parent-teacher meetings. She made a mental note to remind Darren about it when she called him later to ask what time he would bring the girls back tomorrow.

As she turned and walked to the kitchen, her feet caught in the tangle of paper that had spilled to the floor from the fax machine. Junk mail. She bent to pick them up and shook her head. She didn't have to look closely to see what they were: bogus invitations from Nigerian businessmen inviting her to open bank accounts for some retired military dictator's wife. The rewards would be substantial, and one of the pages even had 'Central Bank of Nigeria' written in bold letters to lend authenticity.

As she fed the pages into the shredder, Maxine wondered what kind of fool they must take her for to fall for such an obvious scam. In the past, when faxes were still a novelty, she'd been convinced that someone had figured out that she was half Nigerian and targeted her for that reason. It was later that she learned that almost everyone with a fax machine in America received similar messages.

What would her father think of this country now, she wondered, in 1999 at the threshold of a new millennium? It was indeed a very different place from the one that he'd left it in 1967. He had left for Nigeria—actually a much smaller country within it called Biafra, which no longer existed—to fight in a war.

She thought back to that cold fall day years before when he announced suddenly that he had to leave to return to his home, to fight in a war alongside his people. She remembered his tears and hers, then, as if by telepathy she heard his voice. It took her a moment to realize that it was the answering machine. She stopped to listen. The one thing that had not stuck in her memory was the way he sounded. Did he sound different or did she just not remember? She tried to concentrate on the message. He would be on the KLM flight from Lagos to Amsterdam and then to arrive in Philadelphia at 9 pm tomorrow. He paused, said that he couldn't wait to see her and then he hung up.

She could sense his anxiety; it mirrored her own. They would be like two strangers. After he'd left he had sent smuggled letters that told of the dire situation in the warzone, the lack of food and the starving and dying. Her mother had tirelessly organized donation drives with friends, going door to door, collecting children's clothes, books, cans of food and shoes for the starving 'Biafran Children'. When his letters had stopped, they thought he had died, but then he wrote one day to say that he now had another life, that they couldn't come see him and he wouldn't be back. Wars did that to people.

Her mother had agreed to a divorce; she had grown tired of waiting. He had written letters to Maxine reminding her that she was his first daughter, his *ada*, and that gave her a special place in the family; he would come back for her someday, he promised, but she never wrote back and soon his letters dwindled to once yearly, as they'd been for the past twenty years.

Maxine closed her eyes and stood still, waiting for the surge of anger that had kept her from him for over thirty years, but it wasn't there anymore.

She was pleased that she'd at last laid it to rest, she thought, as she opened her eyes and continued walking toward the kitchen. The box that she'd expected sat on the countertop. Esmeralda, the cleaning lady, must have brought it in from the mailbox Maxine thought as she picked up a knife and cut the binding tape. She wrinkled her nose to suppress a sneeze at the strong smell of lemons that still lingered in the air. She had long ago given up on asking Esmeralda not to saturate the place with citrus cleaner. She pulled open the box flaps and saw six hardcover books stacked face down. She lifted the top book and opened it to see her picture, two years younger, with a short biography below saying that said she lived in Philadelphia with her two daughters. She turned it. Under the title was her name *Maxine Adeze Chinando*. She studied it thoughtfully. She'd decided to use her maiden name, her African name, to acknowledge her father and the narrative that was African. Her daughters had objected.

"Nobody will know it's your book, Mom; nobody knows you by that name," Adrianne had declared with all the wisdom of her fifteen years and Cee-cee had agreed as she did with most things her older sister said.

She held it for a while, reliving the journey that had brought her here. The inspiration for the book had been the result of two serendipitous events a year ago—a bunch of old diaries picked up at a garage sale in Sag Harbor and running into Travis Johnston.

She and Darren vacationed most summers at Sag Harbor, a Long Island town on the shore. They'd gone even before they were married and when the children came along it had become became a firm family tradition. A year ago she'd gone back there alone, a decision she'd regretted almost as soon as she set foot in their rented house. Everything about Sag Harbor was the same, but somehow it had all felt different. Even the old house that belonged to the two elderly African American sisters two blocks down the street was up for sale. It was true that Maxine had only a passing acquaintance with them, waving good-morning or good-afternoon as they made their way to the beach or downtown to the shops. Nevertheless, she'd still be sorry to see the house without Jacinta and Nathalia Gomez Wyatt, especially since she was determined to continue to come here with the children, divorced or not.

There had been a sign in front of the house advertising the sisters' final garage sale, and judging by the number of people streaming into the yard, it seemed that there was an interesting collection for sale. Out of curiosity she'd followed the crowd. There were bargain hunters taking a break from kicking up the warm beach sand to mill around the tables laden with plates and glasses, pewter cups and vases, old cut-glass wine decanters and racks of old clothing, velvet window dressings and boxes of old books. She had looked around and found nothing of interest, and would have left if she hadn't seen Travis, a freelance journalist with the *Philadelphia News Chronicle* whom she vaguely remembered from a party a few months before. They had greeted each other like old friends and he told her he was in Sag Harbor to research the role Africans had played, when they'd arrived in the seaside town a long time before to hunt whales with the native Manhasset, Montauk, and Shinnecock Indians.

Maxine's interest had been piqued and she remembered thinking how good looking he was with his well groomed dreadlocks and neat, tan Dockers even as she cautioned herself that she was not ready to date just yet. Nevertheless she'd been drawn to him and was curious about his research; it was he who had encouraged her to take the old books that Nathalia had offered to sell to her. The old lady had approached them, carrying a box that looked heavy.

"I'll carry that for you, Ms. Wyatt," Travis had said, taking the box from her.

"Oh, thank you, Travis," the old lady said looking curiously at Maxine. "Your husband's not with you this year?"

"Not this year," Maxine had replied not wanting to elaborate but the old lady had looked at her like she knew anyway.

"I want you to buy this," she said gesturing towards the box. "It's only a dollar, the whole thing, but it's all in Portuguese. I was telling Travis that my family is originally from Brazil," she said, fixing Maxine again with a steady gaze. Her hair was a thick, iron-gray and blended well with her purple chiffon dress that billowed with the smell of lavender each time she moved. It was difficult to guess her age, but Travis had said later she was around eighty-five.

"I don't think you can go wrong with a dollar for a box of books," Travis had whispered to Maxine, his eyes teasing. "Moreover, I'll carry it to your car for you if you want." Maxine knew that it was an excuse, a way to reinforce the dinner invitation he'd made earlier. She smiled and dug into her purse for the money. She nodded her acceptance of the invitation without more persuasion; anything was better than going back to the loneliness of her rented seafront house in Eastville.

"I've never had them translated, but maybe you will," Ms Wyatt added as she took the proffered dollar, slipping it into a shiny, patent leather handbag already overflowing with bills from the sale.

Maxine had nodded again politely and looked at the cardboard box. It seemed as though its green color might be from moss grow-ing inside. She exchanged another glance with Travis. She knew the transaction was just an excuse for the old lady to get rid of her junk but they all played along. She could always throw it into the trash later when she got back home to Philadelphia.

"Shame I can't find the other box," Ms Wyatt said looking around distractedly. "I haven't seen it for years. Maybe you can come back later for it," she added.

Maxine had thanked her and hastily made her escape. One box was bad enough.

"Her sister, Jacinta died a few months ago," Travis told her as they walked to the car. "They both moved here over fifty years ago to open a small hotel for African American tourists—middle class types from Harlem that spent summer vacations here in Sag Harbor. They sold it later to a hotel chain and made money buying and sell-ing land too. But now with Jacinta's death, Nathalia is moving back to Rhode Island."

"I didn't know her sister died," Maxine said.

"She died a few months ago so Nathalia is going back to Providence to stay with family. Their great grandfather was from Brazil. Did you know there are a lot of Brazilian immigrants, both black and white, that settled in Rhode Island and other New England states? It will be an interesting topic for my next research."

When they got to the car, Travis had packed the box into the trunk of her Mercedes and she'd promptly forgotten it until weeks later when she was back in Philadelphia. Travis had called, reminding her about it and offering to send the manuscripts to a translator. He'd invited her to dinner to discuss it. Weeks later, at their now-customary weekly dinner-date at the *Blue Raider* he told her excitedly what a monumental find the moldy books really were.

The manuscripts, it turned out, were the four-hundred-year-old diaries of a Brazilian slave who'd learned to write in Portuguese and detailed the lives and events of the time.

Travis had used his journalistic connections in the media to publicize the manuscripts' discovery in the local media and Maxine had reluctantly become a minor celebrity as the finder of such a rare treasure. She'd done interviews for local radio stations and newspapers and explained that history had been her major in college, with special emphasis on Africans in Renaissance Europe, although she'd not used her bachelor degree for anything after; she had married a busy obstetrician and had kept her own career on hold while supporting his.

She'd gone back to Sag Harbor with a small television crew to find Nathalia Wyatt. The diaries had come from her mother's side of the family she'd said. When the interview was over, Nathalia had leaned toward Maxine with a conspiratorial wink and whispered, "I knew somehow that you should have those books, dear. You should tell the whole story. You know, the untold part."

Maxine had agreed, although she was not really sure to what she'd agreed.

One television affiliate in particular had wanted a more in-depth interview and Maxine had agreed. It was around then—and Maxine wasn't even quite sure when it had happened—that the conversation had turned to her father. The earnest brunette from KAVA TV had asked if it were true that her father was African and from the same tribe as the author of the dairies, and if it was also true that her father had abandoned his family and gone back to Africa. How difficult had it been growing up as a biracial child in 1960s America?

Maxine had been caught off-guard. She hadn't expected questions about her father but had quickly replied that, yes, her father was from Nigeria and that, yes, he was Igbo from the same ethnic group as the diarist under discussion. No, her father had not abandoned her but rather had gone back in 1967 to fight for his country—for Biafra.

"Biafra?" the interviewer had asked in surprise. It was obvious her producer had somehow dropped the ball. "Where is that? In Africa?"

"It doesn't exist anymore," Maxine had replied, enjoying her inquisitor's discomfiture. "But it used to be small nation in Nigeria," she added.

"A country inside a country? Like Senegal and the Gambia?"

She knew her Africa, Maxine had thought admiringly. "A bit more complicated than that," Maxine had replied.

"So what happened to this country—to Biafra?" the interviewer asked.

"There was talk of secession, of war crimes and genocide," Maxine replied sounding vague. The fact was that she hadn't thought about any of this in years and was sorry that she'd brought it up at all. She remembered the things that her father had talked about and the little that she had subsequently read while in college. She thought back to when the name Biafra had come up in a talk by a speaker from Medicins Sans Frontiers who had mentioned that their organization was created in response to the situation in Biafra. The word Biafra and memories of her father were like a tangled web in the depths of her psyche, where angry thoughts were spiders that gobbled up the trapped flies that were her memories. Out of curiosity, she had researched it in the newspaper archives of the college library, hoping for the elusive catharsis. That was nearly two decades ago.

"Really? Genocide?" The lady from KAVA TV had asked, sensing a fresh angle to the diary interviews as the memories raced through Maxine's mind. "You mean like Rwanda?" she pressed.

"Well, yes, but this was long before Rwanda—back in 1967," Maxine replied, and hoped that the interviewer wouldn't ask for more details.

"Oh I see," the reporter had said, probably sensing Maxine's discomfort with the topic. "Well I hope you can come back and talk to us more about this. I can see that it was an important event in your life."

Maxine had breathed a sigh of relief; she wanted to talk about her discovery, not the estrangement from her father whom she had not seen and barely heard from in thirty years, or an extinct country she never really knew and scarcely remembered.

Weeks later, after she had walked out of the studio and the diaries had been donated to the African-American museum in Philadelphia courtesy of Nathalia Gomez Wyatt and her late sister, Maxine had started toying with the idea of writing a book based on the discovered diaries. Strangely, writing a book about a culture she knew little about was not as daunting as perhaps it should have been. There was no doubt that she'd always yearned to write *something*. But marriage to Darren and looking after the children had left very little time for much else. She'd been the busy doctor's wife, supporting his career and making the required rounds of social events until the divorce, followed by a journey of self discovery; to find herself, just like all the self-help books she'd read had asked her to do. Thanks to a generous divorce settlement, now she could.

But wanting to write was one thing; doing it was a different matter. The charge to Maxine by Ms. Wyatt to tell a four-hundred-year-old story was not going to be easy. The question was, how did one write about something one knew so little about? Maxine's only claim to authenticity was that her father was an Igbo and, therefore, from the same area in Africa as the diarist, but she had no special knowledge of his world or the culture that had nurtured him.

She had been determined to learn, to write, and to use any help she could find. Travis, as usual, had been an invaluable resource. He smoothed a path for her to the campus of the University of Philadelphia where a Nigerian professor of Africana studies became her mentor and teacher. She showed Maxine ancient stories still told by people along the West African coast, and the riverine areas of the Niger Delta. She had helped Maxine search museums for ancient ships' logs, and diaries of sailors and priests. They'd pored over records documenting centuries of Portuguese pioneers, their sea explorations, slave trade and burgeoning empire. After a year of investigation and threading together leads, the fabric of a four-hundred-year-old tale was firmly woven and a story was ready to be told.

The paper shredder wheezed to a halt. Maxine returned to the present. She bent to slide another sheet into its serrated teeth. She saw the faded sepia-photograph peeking out of the drawer that she'd removed from an old album a few days ago. In it was a tall black man with a little girl on his lap sitting beside a smiling, blonde woman. It was 1965 and they were her parents. How old had she been then? Four? Maybe five? She wasn't sure.

This was how she remembered him, tall and dark, giving her rides to playgrounds on broad shoulders, to birthday parties and school. She was young, but not too young to remember the surreptitious stares of other mothers and fathers.

His funny tortoise-stories had made her and her mother laugh. He was the son of a well-to-do businessman until the war had left him destitute, and stranded him in a strange land without funds. He had told her she was a remaking of his mother who had died the first year he left home. "Adeze, you have her eyes, you know," he would say, pulling at Maxine's nose playfully. That was his name for her; he said it meant Princess. "And you have her mouth, too. You are my mother, come back to me, an exact reincarnation." People never really died but came back to live through beloved grandchildren he told her.

Her mother Olivia was white, a New York debutante from a wealthy family who had been estranged from her family when she had married the student from Africa against their wishes. She had rebelled and gone to live in Philadelphia. Later, when the marriage fell apart she had remarried, reconciled with her family, and gradually returned to the wealthy life of 'the ladies that lunched,' met at expensive restaurants and donated to charities. She hadn't discouraged Maxine, who remained her only child, from keeping in touch with her father in Nigeria but Maxine had pretended to lose interest, angry that he never came back for them.

And back then, Maxine had put all the blame on one word. Biafra. It had changed everything and she'd hated it as much as she'd hated the other word she'd heard from her father. Genocide. Biafra and Genocide—two words she did not understand, but both of which were seared into every memory she had of her father. Mention of either had brought him either joy or despair and had cast a pall over her later childhood.

"This is genocide, Olivia," he'd said often as he paced around the living room of their crowded, one-bedroom apartment in South Philly from which he'd commuted daily to Temple University. He'd religiously subscribed to the *New York Times* although they could hardly afford it on his meager allowance and Olivia's tips as a waitress, the job she'd taken when she'd dropped out of college.

"We have to work hard to stop the genocide," he'd told her quietly as he anxiously read the newspaper. "My people have been annihilated." Maxine would sit in her corner watching him silently as he searched for news of Biafra and genocide in between pages of Martin Luther King's stirring speeches and reports of a war in another place called Vietnam. He had told her how people marched in a place called Selma, in Alabama, to bring about change. "That's why nobody can hear us; there's a lot going on here and in the rest of the world," he said, turning to her as he talked about things she barely understood. "Our struggle is in a faraway corner of the world that nobody's interested in, so we have to do it ourselves because nobody else will help." And the way he'd said *we* made her wonder what she could do to help.

That was a long time ago. To Maxine it hadn't meant much then but all that had changed with the years. When she was older, she'd heard of Rwanda and Bosnia and whatever was about to happen in Sudan. Now, she forgave him for leaving; now she knew better. That was why she had reached out to him. It was time.

The rattle of ice broke the silence as it dropped into the ice tray inside the refrigerator. She filled a glass with water, picked up one of the books and returned to the couch in the living room. She sank her tired feet into the beige carpet as she sat on a sofa. Her eyes swept over the tan leather sectional arranged in a half-moon around a glass-topped table on which rested a bowl of red and green wooden apples. They looked real enough to eat. The gold-embroidered throw cushions were lined up on the couch in a precise row, the way Esmeralda had arranged them earlier. Soon the girls would be home with their untidy schoolbags, scattered books, and soccer cleats and she would welcome the chaos.

The table clock made a grating sound startling her; she jumped and then smiled. It was an hour late; she'd forgotten to change the batteries again. She switched on the lamp and opened the book and then turned to the page where the story she knew so well began.

ᗰᗰᗰᗰᗰᗰᗰᗰᗰ

## WEST AFRICA

## 16ᵗʰ CENTURY

# CHAPTER

# I

O naedo hoped that her brother Udemezue would leave soon and go drinking with his friends. She was walking behind him alongside her friend, Adanma. It was a clear night, the kind that the moon lights so brightly that the night thinks it's day. As they drew nearer to their destination, they heard dozens of voices rise in a tide of happiness until it was dampened by the brooding silence of the surrounding trees.

Udemezue stopped to let them catch up.

"I don't want to have to worry about looking for both of you when I get back," he warned. "I promised Ugodi that you'll be with me all the time."

Onaedo knew he was trying to look stern but it was too dark to tell for sure. Despite the bright silvery light of the moon that hid more than it revealed, the girls were able to exchange knowing looks. Onaedo smiled to herself. They were both fifteen and Udemezue was only five years older although he acted like an old man, especially since his marriage about a year ago. He seemed to think that it gave him all kinds of authority and Onaedo played along most of the time because he was really a good brother.

Moreover, tonight was too important to waste on an argument with Udemezue. In fact, it was in her interest to be extra nice to him so he would leave them in peace. So she nodded with all the docility she could muster and fixed him with a look of submission that she hoped wouldn't seem too suspicious, if he could see it.

"We'll be here when you come back, don't worry." It was Adanma who spoke up.

"Adanma, it's not you I'm worried about," Udemezue replied, "but my sister." He sounded stern but Onaedo sensed that he wouldn't be able to maintain his strict demeanor. He never could.

"I have already promised that I will not be any trouble," Onaedo replied. She hoped that now that he'd said his piece he would move along and find his drinking mates. She was fond of him, not only because they were the only two from the same mother but also because he was more lenient than most other older brothers.

Like tonight. He had compelled their mother Ugodi, against her better judgment, to allow her to stay out late at night. Earlier, their mother had complained about how young women of marriage-able age should not be out so late, especially where there were many unattached young men. Onaedo wanted to retort that that was how young women found husbands—amongst unattached young men, but she knew that it wasn't a winning argument with her mother, or at least wouldn't have been in the mood she'd been in.

So she'd tried compromise instead. "Nothing will happen," she'd said in her most wheedling voice. "Udemezue will take care of us," she added, bringing up her brother's name as a reliable ally.

That had raised even more suspicion. "Us?" Ugodi had asked. "Who is us?" Her voice had taken on a quiet, dangerously calm qual-ity that meant she was going to pass an irrevocable decree.

"Adanma. She's coming with me," Onaedo had said desperately, wondering when Udemezue was going to show up as planned to rescue her from this impending disaster. "Her mother has already given her permission, provided Udemezue accompanies us."

"Oh, of course," Ugodi had replied sarcastically, warming to the subject. "How did I forget Adanma, your partner in all wrong-doing? So her mother said she could go with you, did she? I hope that you told her mother what both of you will be doing because I know you haven't told me and I know you two well; it won't be anything good. Your words are always sweet when you want something." Ugodi had glared at her. "But you don't fool me. I know you and Adanma are like morning and chewing stick; one is never without the other and it's the same way with any mischief the two of you cook up."

"I promise that we'll behave," Onaedo said again. She didn't relish the direction of the conversation; a few more moments of this and Ugodi would forbid her to go altogether. That would be disastrous for her plans for tonight. It was then, right on cue, that Udemezue had walked in from his compound to save the day.

"Don't worry I'll take care of them," Udemezue had announced authoritatively. Then without missing a beat or waiting for their mother's acquiescence he had turned to Onaedo. "*Ngwa*. Hurry up. Let's go and get Adanma."

Onaedo had held her breath wondering what their mother would say but Ugodi had retreated, pursing her lips. She muttered something about the fact that Udemezue should be spending more time with his new wife and baby instead of frittering away the night with unmarried young people.

Onaedo was relieved; before his marriage, Ugodi would never have let Udemezue do something like this, but he was a responsible married man now.

Onaedo looked at him with gratitude. They looked alike—everybody said so—both tall and light-skinned like the color of muddy earth after a heavy rain. And they looked more like their father Eneda than Ugodi. Onaedo was the only one that had inherited their father's strange eyes—the peculiar color of dry and fresh leaves mixed together. People said it made Eneda a great blacksmith; it gave him the inner vision to see beauty in things in a way that ordinary men could not. Some even said that it gave him supernatural powers.

Tonight, Onaedo was not thinking about the cosmic importance of her eye color. She was anxious to escape her mother's scrutiny and get on with the business of the night.

She hurried into the inner room of the red and white, square mud house she shared with her mother. Each of Eneda's three wives had their own quarters and each had its own little compound.

Onaedo changed into the new outfit that she planned to wear with Adanma tonight. She secured the blue and white cloth around her waist leaving her chest bare before she slipped three small snake-like strings of red and black discs over her head. They rested snuggly on her waist. She picked up the leg brass rings, the *nja* her mother had bought for her when her monthly *iso ezi,* had begun, marking her transition into marriageable womanhood. Every young woman had a stack of such rings; they were things of pride but, tonight, she decided she didn't want to wear them. They jangled and tinkled in harmony when one walked, which could be a noisy giveaway; *not the kind of attention that I want to draw to myself where I'm going tonight* she thought as she put them down again. She ran a hand over the amulet that hung on a string around her neck. She was ready.

Her mother looked her up and down when she reappeared, but said nothing more.

Relieved, brother and sister left and made their way to Adanma's compound.

"I will wait out here," Udemezue said, stopping when they got to the gate. "You go in and get Adanma."

Onaedo nodded and went in. Adanma was her closest friend and she did nothing without her. They were only a few months apart in age and belonged to the same age grade.

Adanma was already waiting. Onaedo told her about the scene with Ugodi "My mother was just as difficult to convince," Adanma said brushing past Onaedo. "Let's hurry before she changes her mind." She yelled out her goodbyes and said she was leaving.

Adanma was slightly shorter and darker than Onaedo with more rounded breasts and a fuller figure. She liked to show it off by swinging her waist in an exaggerated manner much to Onaedo's constant amusement and young men's admiring stares. However she knew Adanma had eyes for only one man and that was Udemezue.

Even in the semi-darkness, Onaedo could feel Adanma relax when she saw Udemezue. She had been secretly in love with him since girlhood and had been disappointed the previous year when Udemezue had married someone else. But Adanma was nothing if not persistent and she entertained hopes of becoming his second wife someday soon. Onaedo had artfully learned to use this promise of a closer relationship with her brother to get Adanma to do things for her that her friend would not otherwise do. Like tonight.

It was already late and Onaedo was fretting—if Udemezue didn't hurry and leave them to join his own friends, all her plans could unravel. As if reading her mind, Udemezue announced that he was leaving. At last.

"Both of you had better be here when I return," he said looking from his sister to Adanma. "I don't want any scandalous behavior, do you hear me?"

As soon as Udemezue left, Onaedo grabbed Adanma by the arm and pulled her aside. "Listen. I'm going to meet somebody and I need you to help me," she said breathless with excitement. "I've lost my heart to him and this time it's real."

She sensed Adanma's skepticism but ignored it. She knew Adanma had good reason to be unimpressed. She'd said similar things in the past about others only to lose interest within a few weeks.

"This time it's different," she said again. "Come with me." She led a reluctant Adanma through the crowd of people strolling leisurely or standing in groups laughing and teasing each other. They wove a path towards one end of the square until they reached the wider path that led away from it. The tall palms, acacias, and ancient irokos reached indifferently into the night sky in scenes like this that had probably played out since the beginning of time.

Onaedo stopped. She glanced at the moon. As a child, she usually spent hours gazing up at it and wondering what exactly it was. It had not entirely lost its fascination for her and seemed to give the nighttime a temporary magic that made ordinary jokes more hilarious, absurdities more profound, and the mundane an enticing mystery.

"Wait for me here," she said turning to Adanma. "You must distract Udemezue if he returns early."

"Are you going to disobey your mother? She warned us to stay close to Udemezue."

"She won't know if nobody tells her," Onaedo answered, sounding irritated. "And I know you won't tell her," she added.

"She'll find out anyway; Ugodi has a way of finding out everything," Adanma said with an air of fatalism that did nothing except further annoy Onaedo. She was exasperated. Adanma could be quite tiresome and almost as tedious as her mother was when she disapproved of something, but she decided to cajole her friend. "I swear to you Adanma, this isn't like before. This time is different."

"That's what you said the last time," Adanma retorted. "If you're caught this time, my hand is not in it, Onaedo. I helped with your schemes the last time and was nearly discovered myself. If my mother or your mother discovers us now, they'll cut off both our ears and give them to us to hold."

"Whoever heard of anybody's ears being cut off," Onaedo replied, mocking her friend good-naturedly although she realized that it wouldn't do to antagonize her further. She knew however, that Adanma would eventually come round to her way of thinking. She just needed a little more convincing. "Adanma, you always exaggerate and that's why I don't tell you anything. Nobody will find out if you keep your mouth shut."

"I always keep my mouth shut." Onaedo could hear her bristling and decided to proceed slowly. She knew that she had to deal with Adanma's cautious nature, which dampened things like water poured on a fire. Adanma knew how to steal pleasure from any adventure, she thought. They were so different; Onaedo was wild, at times impulsive and always adventurous, while Adanma was deliberate and cautious but could be acerbic if she needed to. Their natures combined and worked harmoniously most times.

Onaedo knew in her heart that Adanma had reason to be wary of her latest escapade but that was because she didn't know Dualo, the new object of her affection, Onaedo thought. He was special and different from the other young men who had showed an interest in her in the past. She knew that at first contemplation, Dualo seemed an unlikely match for her because he had no money. His father had died early and he lacked a concerned father figure that was willing to give him the money he needed to get started. In fact, the only uncle that had shown an interest was a wood worker, and had turned around and indentured Dualo to his service so that the young man was beholden to him in perpetuity, or so it seemed, for there appeared to be no end to his apprenticeship.

The whole situation irked Onaedo who wanted to marry him as soon as possible. Her time was running out. After her *iso ezi*, she was expected to accept a suitor right away. Six months had already passed and her mother was beginning to fret as every month came and went and she had not decided who she wanted to marry.

Onaedo came from one of the most famous and influential families in Abonani. She was the daughter of Eneda the wealthy, high-ranking elder and blacksmith in Abonani and probably the most talented in the whole of *Olu n'Igbo*—that was the known universe of all people. She was expected to marry a man that could at least fend for himself, and Dualo was clearly not that man.

Onaedo put an arm across Adanma's shoulder. "I'll repay you for this, I promise," she said casually knowing Adanma would not hold her to it.

"How are you going to repay me?" Adanma replied sounding a little annoyed.

Just then one of the other girls approached. Nonye was a notorious gossip and her eyes glittered like still water in the moonlight as she weighed the situation. "What are you two whispering about?" she asked. "I saw both of you leave and knew something important must be going on."

"Nothing," both girls said in unison. "Go ahead; we're coming behind you," Onaedo added.

Nonye hesitated and looked from Onaedo to Adanma, trying to read the situation. When she failed to find what she was looking for, she decided to move on.

Adanma turned to Onaedo. "I hope you're not going to stay long. The last time I had to lie to put Udemezue off. I can't tell good lies."

"Stop worrying yourself. I'll be back before you know it," Onaedo said, trying to quiet her impatience. "How do I look?" She made a half pirouette and looked back at her friend.

Adanma looked her over. "*Imaka.* You always look beautiful," Adanma said.

Onaedo nodded. She was used to people telling her that she was beautiful but she was not vain. She had inherited the best features of both her parents; her father's tall frame, his eyes and complexion, and her mother's engaging smile. Tonight she wanted to look beautiful.

"Just don't stay too long," Adanma repeated.

"I won't."

She saw Nonye coming towards them, as she turned to leave and moved away faster. Adanma would find a convincing lie to tell their meddlesome friend. She slipped into the pathway that led away from the square.

෨෧

Onaedo knew the meeting place. Dualo had picked it because it was removed from the square but not so far out as to make it unsafe. The leaves shivered in a balmy breeze, allowing the light to dapple the path below. A thousand flowers scented the air, mingling with the forest smell of plant and animal decay. The noise from the square grew faint as she walked away. She hoped Dualo was nearby.

She tried not to think of dwarf night-hunters or the will-o'-the-wisp that populated her nightmares on dark nights. She nudged her mind to more pleasant things, like her love for Dualo. It was real and she had known it from the first time she saw him. At first, he'd been cool and kept a safe distance from her. He told her later that he had regarded her as unattainable because every young man talked about her and tried to win her attention.

"I heard that you lead every man who wants you on a wild dance in dry season," he had teased her later. "And that you're the daughter of Eneda the most powerful man in Abonani aside from the Ezeigwe himself. How can a poor indentured woodworker like me afford to marry someone like you?"

Onaedo had brushed aside his concerns. She told him that she loved him and that was all that mattered. She had charmed and pursued him relentlessly until he succumbed and served up utter devotion.

These clandestine meetings were a risky breach of etiquette since there had been no formal approach of her people and they both indulged in impractical dreams of acquiring sudden wealth and solving their problem. When they caressed in the dark nights they wove long romantic intrigues about how they were going to overcome their poverty.

She heard a night bird caw nearby and stopped briefly to check her bearings. She saw the clearing ahead and walked briskly towards it. Suddenly, a shadow joined hers, startling her. A pair of arms grabbed her wrists from behind and she screamed in fright.

She was relieved to see who it was but annoyed to see it was Oguebie and not Dualo. She had not expected to see Oguebie out here. "What do you think you're doing?"

"I should ask you the same question, Onaedo daughter of Eneda. What are you doing here?" Oguebie countered.

Onaedo tried to pull her hand away. It was pure bad luck meeting Oguebie of all people out here. He was the Ezeigwe's brother, an arrogant man that strutted about like it was he and not his brother who was the actual ruler of Abonani. He was a rich man that Onaedo did not particularly like, although a lot of women in Abonani considered him very desirable. It annoyed Onaedo that he often acted as though the mere fact of being from the ruling family entitled him to everything and every woman.

A few months ago, he had brought a gourd of palm-wine to
Eneda and asked Onaedo to marry him. He did not bother to find
out first if she liked him, as most other men would have done. If he
had, he could have saved himself the embarrassment of her refusal.
Afterwards, she had *even* refused to return the empty gourd of palm-
wine as was customary. But that not-so-subtle refusal had not daunted
him. Oguebie asked Eneda to pressure her to accept his proposal but
Onaedo had declined him again. There was something about him and
she sensed it, a ruthless streak in Oguebie that made her uncomfortable. Moreover, she didn't like his household; some of his younger
wives acted high and mighty just because their husband was rich.
There was no doubt he was a shrewd businessman who had made good
early in life and had become wealthy at a young age. He had also married his first wife quite early so that he had daughters that were, in
fact, around Onaedo's age. He was highly ambitious and traded in the
Delta City with the white man, although many in Abonani believed
that he was involved in some questionable businesses too.

Now Oguebie looked down on her smiling. His expensive blue
and white cotton cloth passed under one arm and was knotted over
the opposite shoulder as he held her prisoner in his hands in the
middle of the night in a deserted pathway. She tried again to pull
from his grip. *What was he doing out here?* she thought. Although he
was not so old, Oguebie was among the clan's titleholders and that
exalted position made it unseemly for him to be out with young
people this late at night.

Oguebie pulled her closer and she could smell the tobacco
snuff and the white man's alcoholic spirit on his warm breath.
Only the wealthy in Abonani could afford the luxuries that traders
brought back doing business with the Portuguese merchants that
came to the Delta City.

"You shouldn't be out alone at this time, Onaedo," he said in a
low tone, his cloth rubbing her face as he pulled her closer. "What
will your family say if they discover that you're here all by yourself,
eh?" He loosened his hold slightly but did not release her.

"Udemezue knows that I'm here," she said as her heart settled back into her chest.

"I'm sure that your brother thinks that you're in the square and not wandering about dangerous paths in the middle of the night."

"Please, leave me alone," she said with as much authority as she could muster.

"Onaedo, you are a very beautiful and spirited young woman and I like that," Oguebie said pulling her even closer. "But you should be wary because beauty is really worthless by itself. I hear that you can be stubborn but I like that—a woman who knows her mind. You will fit perfectly into my household."

"I'm not ready to marry yet," Onaedo said.

"You? Don't you know that you're growing old, already? Your family has already held your coming out feast," he said, jerking her closer. "And I don't believe you. Someone is keeping you from me. Tell me who it is."

Onaedo's head swam with the muskiness of the scented night air and the rush of her earlier fright. She had to escape from Oguebie as quickly as possible; Dualo might appear any minute to look for her.

"I don't know what you are talking about. Please let me go."

"Listen to me, little woman. The winged termite will eventually lose its wings and fall prey to the patient frog." Oguebie laughed aloud at his own joke and in the quiet night his mirth had a sinister edge.

Onaedo saw his head turn into a giant frog and return to human form again, and she shook her head to clear her overactive imagination. In the lunar half-light, he looked fierce but his appearance hid a certain weakness of character. She knew him well from the people that came to her father's *obi* to complain about him. Oguebie was a problem not just to his brother the Ezeigwe and the ruling family, but also to the clan as a whole. He was constantly involved in one shady escapade or another and he had been fined several times by the town elders for unscrupulous behavior such as failure to honor agreements and other dishonorable deeds not befitting an *ozo* titleholder. Each time, he managed to wriggle his way out of trouble.

"Which lover are you meeting so late?" Oguebie asked her.

Onaedo wished the ordeal would end. There was no way of escape. "No one. I left something under one of those trees earlier in the day. I'm just going to collect it." She hoped that he believed her but her story sounded weak even to her own ears and she couldn't think of a more convincing lie.

"I'll go with you," he said, adopting a friendly tone. "We don't want something to jump from these bushes and carry you away. It's not impossible these days or maybe you haven't heard." He lowered his voice in a conspiratorial whisper that sounded more like a threat. Onaedo knew what he meant.

Recently, there had been an attempted kidnapping in one of the neighboring towns and, in fact, Onaedo had overheard her father say that Oguebie's name had been mentioned during the investigations of the incident when a delegation from that town had arrived at Abonani. They had demanded that the perpetuator be surrendered to them for justice.

To pacify them, the Abonani elders had promised to investigate the allegation but there was no real proof of Oguebie's involvement. The case against him soon fell apart and the other side was eventually placated and persuaded that neither Oguebie nor anyone from Abonani was involved.

Later, the elders of Abonani had expressed their anger privately. The incident was a serious matter that could have led to a war with a peaceful neighbor and many of them remained unconvinced of Oguebie's innocence.

"That Oguebie is a bad one," Onaedo overheard them complaining. The titled men and elders met in Eneda's house and, as she served them kola-nuts and smoked meat, she tried to listen unobtrusively. "Sooner or later his bad ways will catch up with him. Kidnapping, even of strangers, is an offense against Ani the land goddess. It is *nso* Ani and such behavior does not go unpunished. She's the strongest deity next to Chukwu and she can be vengeful if wronged."

But as far as Onaedo could see, nothing seemed to happen to Oguebie; instead, he prospered and continued to live a life that seemed as charmed as it was flawed.

"Go on, I'm coming with you," Oguebie said to her.

"I don't need a guard following me around," Onaedo replied. If Oguebie saw her with Dualo, her father would know, and that was the last thing that she wanted. She felt Oguebie's eyes narrow speculatively as he looked her over. He reached out to stroke the braids on her head and she jerked away. She almost broke away from him.

"I'll let you go now but be careful; don't be out too late," he admonished, wagging a paternal finger before he finally released her. She breathed a sigh of relief and walked away, praying that he would not follow as she fought the urge to look back.

ന്ദ

When she left Oguebie she increased her pace, detesting the wetness of the undergrowth brushing against her legs. She almost stumbled into the two strong arms that suddenly encircled her, pulling her into the nearby clearing and making her shriek again. She wondered briefly if Oguebie had managed to sneak ahead of her again by some feat of magic. It was Dualo this time.

"Why did you startle me like that?" she scolded.

"I'm sorry," he apologized, letting her go. "I thought that you saw me. I didn't mean to scare you."

She relented. "This is the second time tonight that someone has grabbed me," she said, placing a steadying hand against him as she brushed the leaves from her legs. She told him about her encounter with Oguebie.

"Be careful, Onaedo," Dualo said, with concern. "He's a powerful and dangerous man. He feuds even with his own brother, the Ezeigwe."

"I know. My father says he's a troublemaker. Nobody knows what to do about him because he's as cunning as a tortoise. Nobody ever catches him doing anything wrong."

"Well, let us talk about something else," Dualo said. "I have good news," he said trying hard to suppress the excitement in his voice. "My apprenticeship is going to end in a few months. My uncle has finally agreed to set me up with money of my own."

"Do you trust him to do it this time?" Onaedo asked. She was hopeful, but knew that the man was a notorious miser; he had not kept any of the promises he'd made to his nephew. He claimed that Dualo was his most talented worker and he could not do without him, but in fact he was loath to allow Dualo to set up his own woodcarving enterprise even though there was enough work to keep everyone busy in Abonani and the surrounding towns.

"I think he means it this time," Dualo said, sounding a little doubtful himself. "He has no reason not to. I've served him well since my father's death."

She pulled back and looked into his face. His eyes were dark and unfathomable lakes and his brows were branches that overhung it. She tenderly touched the two faint linear scars on his cheekbones. They were meant to ward off evil. She had similar scars on her back, on both shoulders.

"Do you think that he'll support us if he knows that we want to marry?" she asked.

He shrugged. "I don't know. He might think that I'm presumptuous for going after Eneda's daughter. 'Did you not see any other girl more within your reach? A dwarf should hang his bag where he can reach it.'" Dualo mimicked his uncle and Onaedo laughed because the improvisation was hilarious and perfectly delivered.

Dualo was silent.

"What is it?" Onaedo asked.

"Before I met you, I was satisfied to keep serving my uncle until he allowed me to go. I have been everywhere with him, two years in the southern countries and another two in the Delta City. I have learned all there is to know. I hope he keeps his word this time because I've paid my debts." Dualo looked closely into her face as he spoke. "You have a beautiful name—Onaedo—Golden Jewel. You are now my Golden Jewel, and all that I do now is so that I can be with you." He stopped and pulled her close. "Let's pretend that we're married already and you have come home to cook my meal."

"What foolish talk," she said laughing. But she was pleased all the same. The game was her invention to keep her occupied on days when she only had her imagination for company.

"I like this charm," Dualo said, catching the amulet around her neck. He turned it in his hands. Two tiny metal sticks had been stuck across one another with a blood red stone anchoring both in the middle. "You told me before that your father gave it to you. Did he make it himself?"

"No. It belonged to one of his ancestors from long ago but he put the medicine in it. It wards off malicious spirits that made me sick as a child."

"It is very unusual," Dualo said, handling it in the semi-darkness. "I have seen something like it before. The white people wear similar ornaments."

Onaedo placed her hands over his rough workman's hands to examine the amulet with him. "You may be right. It belonged to one of my father's female ancestors who originally came from the Delta," she explained.

"How did she come all that way to marry an Abonani man?" Dualo asked, a smile in his voice. The Delta Kingdom was about four days' travel—a market week—down south, across the Great River. Abonani men had gone there to trade from ancient times but it was a foreign country to most Abonani people. The culture and language were different and most had never travelled that far, although everybody had heard stories of the splendid city by the coast where the white man anchored his ships to do business. Abonani traders took mainly red-tailed pepper and ivory to trade there. "It is a long way to go to marry," he added.

"It is a long story," Onaedo said. "She was the daughter of a nobleman at the king's court but something scandalous happened. She was married off by her father to an Igbo trader from Abonani as punishment."

"What did she do exactly to get punished in this way?" Dualo asked, trying to conceal the laughter in his voice. "And when did marrying an Abonani man become punishment?"

"When you're the daughter of a nobleman in the Delta court, I suppose," Onaedo replied laughing, finding the story funny too. "They generally regard we Igbos as backward, inferior people. She had no choice. But she was already pregnant when she came here. That was part of the scandal. She had fallen in love with a white man, a young merchant sailor that came to trade at the Delta City from the white man's country. He had lived in the Delta City with the priests and teachers. She wanted to follow him back to his country and, because of him, she'd declined the chance to marry the heir to the Delta king. Her father was furious because her marriage to the heir would have given him power at the court and an opportunity to ally their family with the ruling royals. But his daughter chose instead to be with a visitor. Her infuriated father forced her to marry my ances-tor and made him take her away. That's how she came here. Since she was already pregnant, her unborn child now belonged to her new hus-band, as is the custom. She also brought the white man's religion with her, a strange practice that nobody in Abonani understood or was interested in for that matter, not even her own children. When she died, her strange rituals died with her; only these charms were left," Onaedo said, fingering the amulet. "There are a few others around."

"That's a sad story," Dualo said, hugging her again. "But we'll do better than she did. I will walk you to the edge of the square to make sure that you're safe."

They agreed to meet again. She walked back towards the sound of voices. If she were lucky, Udemezue would be tipsy enough not to care if she hugged a hunchback in the middle of the square.

ରେ

"What took you so long?" Adanma complained. "Udemezue has already come here once to look for you. I had to find a way to send him away."

"I'm getting married," Onaedo said, barely able to suppress her exuberance.

"Married? To whom?"

"Who else? To Dualo, of course," Onaedo replied, a little deflated and annoyed.

"You must be jesting. He has no money."

"How do you know that?" This was not going well. If Adanma could not be convinced that Dualo was a suitable husband for her, neither would anybody else.

"Wasn't he at the Delta for a while as an apprentice with his uncle or something like that?" Adanma asked. "From what I hear, he still has no money, at least not enough to marry."

Onaedo saw Udemezue approach and made a gesture for Adanma to change the topic.

"So what have you two been doing?" Udemezue asked, smiling amiably in a way that told Onaedo that palm-wine had made him mellow.

"Why do you always think that we're doing something bad?" Onaedo complained.

"Because you usually are," Udemezue said. "*Ngwa*. Get ready. It's time to go home."

He turned his smile at Adanma, who'd been dumbstruck since he appeared, treating her in his casual platonic way.

"It's time to go home," he said again, turning to lead the way into the flood of people ebbing out of the square and back into town.

ను

They walked Adanma back to her mother's house first, and then brother and sister continued home. Onaedo was restless. She wanted to confide is somebody else aside from Adanma whose total experience in love was limited to her long-running infatuation for

Udemezue. Onaedo had older half-sisters, daughters from her father's other wives, but they were a lot older than she was and had married men in faraway towns so that she hardly ever saw them. There was her mother Ugodi, but telling her something like this was out of the question. She would be rightfully scandalized by her daughter's clandestine activities. Her aunt Aku was another potential confidant, but she would tell Ugodi because they did not keep secrets from one another; telling one was like telling the other.

She looked at Udemezue who was humming a low tune under his breath. They had always been close. When they were children, he was like a hero to her, and she followed him like a shadow everywhere he went. He told her boys' secrets, like what happened during the secret initiation that was called 'Knowing the Spirits'. It was a ceremony forbidden to girls. "Pour palm-wine down an ant hole and slap a palm frond across it. That will summon the spirits and they will surely appear as masquerades," he had said.

"Is that what you do at the secret masquerade house?," she asked.

"Of course," he'd replied, laughing, and although she hadn't been sure whether to believe him or not, she'd never had the courage to try it.

But this was different. Even Udemezue, for all his brotherly affection for her, might not approve of this affair with Dualo.

Still, what was there to lose? He never stayed angry with her for long and he sometimes had good advice. Just then, Udemezue burst into a loud song at the top of his voice and at the end started laughing at some private joke. Onaedo looked at him and decided that maybe he was too drunk tonight for a serious discussion.

They turned onto the path that led to the large compound that Eneda shared with his wives, including their mother. Udemezue's own *obi* was further down the road and he lived there with his new wife and daughter.

"When next will you be traveling to the Great River market?" Onaedo asked, stopping briefly as they reached the outer walls of the compound.

Udemezue shook his head. "I'm not sure. The markets are not so good these days and I'm even thinking of not continuing with that trade. The middlemen have been finding fault with all our merchandise of late. They complain about everything—the kola-nuts are not fresh, the pepper is not ripe or not hot, too dry, or the animal skins are not the right color, as if we have any influence over that."

"Why don't you cross the Great River and take your goods into the city and trade directly with the white man?"

"The middlemen will never allow that. It cuts into their profit."

"But Oguebie trades in the city," Onaedo persisted, remembering her encounter with him earlier. "How is he able to do that and you cannot?"

"Oguebie has a lot of connections at the Delta City. He has friends within the royal family and they have given him permission to do business there," Udemezue sounded gloomy. "Maybe I should have listened to Eneda and followed him into the blacksmith business like our two older half-brothers. They make a good living even if they are not as talented as our father is."

"That's your fault. Eneda said that you had a lot of talent and tried to persuade you, but you refused."

"You were the gifted one, if I remember," Udemezue retorted. "He said that you had an eye for the craft."

"I'm a girl," Onaedo replied laughing. "Women do not become blacksmiths."

"I don't like the heat of the furnace," Udemezue confessed. "I prefer to be outside—hunting, trading, or even farming." He opened the gate for her to pass through. "Let the dawn bring light, my sister."

"May the dawn bring light for you too," Onaedo replied and watched as he shut the gate, humming as he made his way to his own *obi* a short walk away.

# CHAPTER

# 2

Oguebie was not pleased to find that Onaedo was meeting with Dualo. He had stayed back to watch her and couldn't believe that Onaedo had rejected him in favor of a mere apprentice woodcarver at his own brother's palace.

*"What a fool that girl is,"* he muttered to himself, as a slow anger darkened his mood. *"The daughter of Eneda, the great blacksmith, meeting with a nobody."*

There was nothing he could do about it at the moment. He knew firsthand how stubborn Onaedo could be. She had rejected his marriage proposal months ago and furthermore, her father spoiled her. Any other father would have compelled her to marry Oguebie; after all, he came with a cache of privileges as the Ezeigwe's brother. But not Eneda. He had acted as if it were all up to Onaedo and pretended that he had no say in the matter. Oguebie had been annoyed by the whole situation. In his opinion, Eneda and his kinsmen were brazen to the core; they drank his palm-wine and then turned around to tell him that Onaedo had said no to his request. Whoever heard of a daughter having a choice in such matters? To add insult to injury, he had had to send for his empty palm-wine gourd that Onaedo should have returned to him. In these situations, one sometimes needed to count one's own teeth with his tongue to arrive at the truth. The rejection was not by Onaedo, for Oguebie knew Eneda could make her do his bidding. No. The rejection was by Eneda himself. Oguebie suspected Eneda did not want him for an in-law.

The problem with Eneda, Oguebie thought, was that he believed he was more progressive than other men in Abonani. It was unfortunate that the blacksmith was quite important in Abonani. He was the chief adviser to his brother, the Ezeigwe, and the way he always sought out Eneda's counsel, one would think it was Eneda that was the ruler and not the Ezeigwe. That state of affairs irritated Oguebie to no end.

He tried to dismiss the incident from his mind. He had to hurry home because he was going south to the coast in a few weeks and had to prepare for the business he had to do in the Delta City.

The voices from the square were louder. He hesitated briefly, debating whether to join in the merriment. He decided against it. If he were ten years younger, he thought regretfully, then maybe. There would be nobody his age there now and the youngsters would think him pathetic for trying to reclaim his youth.

Oguebie went on the road that led back into town and his thoughts turned to the new business scheme he was about to embark upon in the Delta City. His business partner down there was a man by the name of Ideheno, a prince of the Delta court who had opened doors for him. They had a foolproof plan in the making that could earn them untold riches. Just what he wanted now, with all the trouble he was having here in Abonani where he was not appreciated. If their plans paid off, Abonani musicians would put his name in song for generations to come, extolling his achievements in the manner in which greatness was immortalized. Perhaps he might even take the next higher *ozo* title just to show his detractors that he was now a force to be reckoned with. His critics would be silenced once and for all, especially if he went on to take the highest title—*Eze* or King. But he knew that was an impossible task. Nobody in living memory had ever ascended that far by the strength of his hand alone and moreover it would put him in direct conflict with his brother who was already an Eze albeit with limited powers—the only type of kingship to which the Abonani people had agreed.

If he had his way, things were going to change in Abonani soon. There were subtle and effective ways of wresting power and he was going to be the patient, enduring fisherman that waits out the big fish.

He thought about how lucky he was to have Ideheno for a friend. They were similar in many respects—both loved to live ostentatiously and they both had powerful half-brothers whose power they coveted and wanted to take. For some time, they had both made empty plans and dreamed of the impossible, feeling powerless in their respective palaces to institute a power coup.

Until now. Their opportunity had come in the form of two Portuguese merchants. They had opened an unexpected business avenue just as Oguebie and Ideheno were beginning to lose hope of ever bringing their plans of insurrection to fruition.

Oguebie relived the excited optimism he felt upon meeting the two white men. He nearly fell as he stumbled on a mound on the road and cursed loudly. A cloud had covered the moon's face making it darker. He bent to make sure that he had not cut his foot. He knew what he needed, he thought, straightening up and continuing his walk—one of those contraptions the Portuguese traders and a few high ranking courtiers in the Delta court wore on their feet. He'd seen a few traded in court and he had wanted to buy a pair, but the only drawback he heard was that after a while it made one's feet so soft that it was difficult to revert to walking barefoot. He had once considered such indulgences a foolish excess but given the important role he planned for himself in the future of Abonani, he would do well to acquaint himself with the things that would set him apart from ordinary, less travelled men.

The moon was uncovered once more and Oguebie was near the *obi eze*, which was his brother's palace. Oguebie regarded the dark, silent building awash in moonlight. The sight of it made his stomach burn with irritation. Why did his brother insist on everything being so utilitarian? Compared to what he had seen down south in the Delta Kingdom, this was like living in a hovel. Even his own *obi* here in Abonani was grander than this poor excuse of a building. Whenever he complained about it, people looked at him with exasperation and told him that they had more important things to think about than putting up buildings just for the sake of it. If he didn't like the way they did things in Abonani, why didn't he just go to the Delta City and stay there?

"One of these days I'm going to," he muttered, as he continued his walk. But that was easier said than done because he wasn't very popular down there either. They disliked it when he boasted of turning Abonani into a more splendid kingdom than the Delta City. Some called him an uncultured and an uncouth Igbo man when they thought he couldn't hear, but he didn't care much about that. He had his own agenda.

He reviewed the latest business plan in his mind. It would be easy money, at least that's what Ideheno had said when he took him to meet the two white men just before Oguebie left for Abonani. Ideheno said that the Portuguese merchants were interested in a new kind of trade and Oguebie was keen to find out what they wanted. His interest had been stirred because he had never earned the kind of money Ideheno told him they were going to make; he was excited and cautious.

"They're going to sell guns to us for the first time," Ideheno said with contagious optimism. "Their king in Portugal has prohibited such sales before. Can you imagine what power we'll have now with guns? You can fight and defeat your brother and I will do the same here. Our two kingdoms will flourish, side by side."

Oguebie had agreed that it was an excellent idea but he had wanted to know more details. "What exactly does the white man want in return for his guns?" It sounded too good to be true. Also, he was anxious that they might not have enough commodities to trade for the guns, which he knew would be costly. Even if they cornered the entire ivory market, and pepper and skins, it still might not be enough. Being the fast strategist that he was, he was already thinking ahead and formulating a plan.

Oguebie remembered uneasily that Ideheno had been a little evasive and short on details about the nature of the new trade. "Don't worry, we'll get more information when we talk to my friend Alvarez, the white man," he had said, trying to reassure Oguebie.

He remembered the meeting clearly because he knew at the time it would change his life. The white man, Alvarez, had brought a friend, another white man to meet with them in the small shack just outside of the Delta City, as far from palace spies as possible. The square mud shack with its rotting timber roof had been a church built by a Portuguese priest. That was before he had succumbed to the fever and bad air from the surrounding swamps that the white men called *mal' aria*. The locals sang songs that marveled at how the white man who appeared so strong in other ways seemed to succumb like babies to any small bout of fever. The white men's graveyards were small mounds around the church and Ideheno told him that a small congregation of resilient local converts still gathered most mornings to recite mass in Latin. Otherwise, it stood empty most days.

On that day as the two white men finalized plans with Ideheno, who spoke fluent Portuguese, Oguebie had been busy planning how he would corner the market on red-tailed peppers and ivory tusks by buying all the supplies in Abonani and the surrounding towns. He would be the only trader with merchandise to sell to the Portuguese for their guns. He would trust Ideheno's judgment on this. After all he was the one that spoke Portuguese having attended the palace school from when he was a boy. For Oguebie, it was more pleasant to think about the money he would make and how he would lord it over the Abonani elders. They had tried and failed over the years to send him into exile for what he considered minor infractions including the last incident when all he was doing was collecting on a debt before things had suddenly got out of hand. He had fought off their constant accusations by the sheer strength of his will, but he knew that sooner or later his enemies would prevail, especially when there

were men like Eneda who always acted as though they were more
morally principled than everybody else.

He wished again that Onaedo had said yes to his proposal. That
would have neutralized some of Eneda's antagonism towards him.
He sighed with frustration. He hoped that with a bit of luck, soon
none of that would matter; he would have enough money to silence
any opposition, even Eneda.

Walking along the lonesome Abonani road, thoughts of rebel-
lion made Oguebie tremble in anticipation. This kind of thought
energized him no end. It was even better than having a desirable
young woman like Onaedo.

By now he could see his *obi* as he turned the corner. Pride welled
inside him whenever he saw the impressive building he had constructed based on what he had seen at the Delta City. He had built
into what was usually a simple structure for most men in Abonani, a
complex warren of rooms and corridors that ended up being a rather
poor imitation of the Delta King's palace, but admittedly the most
imposing house in Abonani.

His thoughts went back to Onaedo. He could get any woman he
wanted, he thought with some smugness, and in the past had even
persuaded a couple of married women to risk clandestine affairs with
him. So why was he bothered with the unruly daughter of Eneda,
the blacksmith?

In his heart, he knew why. He liked to have his way and didn't
take kindly to rejection. He resolved to do something about it. In
fact, he was going to pay a certain woodcarver's uncle a visit and
make him an offer Oguebie was sure that he wouldn't refuse.

Thoughts about scheming swirled about in his head and light-
ened his mood by the time he crossed the threshold into his inner
room. He was met with the vision of a beautiful woman lying on his
bed, waiting.

"Where have you been?" she asked, sleepily, her long arms
stretched over her head. Her naked breasts sat firmly on her chest

and remained so even when she turned on her side. "I've been wait-ing for you," she added yawning.

It was his youngest wife. He had invited her to be with him in his *obi* tonight as though he knew he would need to exorcise the thoughts of another woman from his mind. Thoughts of Onaedo would wait for another day.

The naked light from the wick oil-lamp in the corner flickered leisurely, its light licking the nude woman's body, throwing dancing shadows on the wall behind her. His eyes swept over her again. She was beautiful, and beautiful women were his weakness. He felt desire stir in him.

"I'm here now," he said sitting down on the bed.

"I've been waiting for you," she whispered again into his ear as he slipped in beside her on the wooden bed. It creaked loudly beneath them.

CHAPTER

3

"Where is Onaedo?"

It was Aku, Onaedo's aunt, asking her sister Ugodi. Aku was also regarded as Onaedo's second mother and was Ugodi's only living sibling. She only had sons and so was inordinately fond of Onaedo. She was a midwife and so had been there when Onaedo was born. It was she who ensured that Onaedo's first contact with the outside world was with the Earth goddess Ani, when Ugodi pushed her out into the world, wet and slippery, onto a banana leaf.

Aku had shared her sister Ugodi's anxieties about Onaedo's early frailties but she was a practical woman. Instead of just worrying she consulted with *dibias* to protect her young niece with powerful medicines. Now Onaedo was a strong, tough girl.

Aku was helping her sister with the yearly restoration of the buildings. It was something that every woman did to prevent holes and fine cracks from growing into deep rifts that could take the whole house down if ignored. They used wet mud from a small pit they had squished with their feet.

When it was time for a break they washed their hands and sat on two dwarf stools in Ugodi's front yard while Ugodi gave her a small drinking gourd that she'd filled with palm-wine.

"Onaedo isn't home," Ugodi said. "She went to see Adanma. I overhead them say that they were going to a coming-of-age ceremony for one of their friends today. Young women today have it so easy," she added. "You remember when we were their age? Our mother would never let us go anywhere without a chaperone."

Aku took a sip before returning it. "Mmm, I don't recall anybody restricting us that much. Even if it was so, you still managed to slip away whenever you could. You were quite rebellious, as I remember."

"Me?" Ugodi replied, feigning innocence. "I don't think so; at least not more than you."

Aku clicked her tongue in disagreement. "Onaedo is just like you; the one that every man wants."

Ugodi looked at her uncertainly but Aku smiled at her reassuringly as she took another sip from the gourd. In the early years, there had been a rivalry between them and Aku had nursed a mild resentment towards her because Ugodi was younger, prettier, and everyone's favorite. Now that they were adults Aku could agree that Ugodi was the more attractive one—her skin was dark and flawless and her dark lashes and evenly flared nose was nicely proportioned over her full lips. Onaedo was a younger image of her mother only slightly fairer and taller. Aku was smaller and naturally thin. 'You never look well-fed,' their mother would often complain when she was alive 'Anybody that looks at you would think we starve you.' It was as though they had come from opposite sides of the same womb. Aku's skin was the same reddish-brown color as her hair—not unlike the dull copper wires both women wore around their ankles. But Aku's fragile appearance was deceptive because beneath it was an iron will and a sharp tongue that sometimes rubbed people the wrong way, especially if they did not know her well.

With time, however, any feelings of sibling rivalry had faded between them. It was replaced instead by a fierce loyalty and devotion to each other that even their husbands and children had come to respect.

The late afternoon air was heavy and languid with fresh, unfermented palm-wine. The women surveyed their nearly finished work. "This palm-wine is so clean and sweet," Ugodi said, pouring more for both of them. "It is like the white of a baby's eyes."

"It's going to my head too," Aku said. "We should finish the job after this."

"This is the last one."

"I like the way they did your hair," Aku said, reaching over to run a hand over Ugodi's short beautifully patterned hair that meandered over her scalp. She narrowed her eyes as she studied her sister. "Where did all this gray hair come from? I thought you are the *nwa* and I'm the old one."

"I know," Ugodi said, fingering the string of blue beads around her neck. "We are neither of us, young antelopes anymore."

"Speak for yourself," Aku responded half-smiling. "Anyway, I haven't asked about the soap business. Is it still making you money?"

Ugodi nodded. "It's become profitable since I started making large quantities." She pointed to the corner of the yard where piles of black, round balls of soap were heaped up on a mat. "The women will collect them for the market tomorrow."

"I'm glad that our mother left you the business," Aku said, nodding. "I couldn't have done it, breathing the ash every day." She shrugged. "But you're better at it than anybody I know. Your soap foams more and cleans better than anything on the market. I'm glad that you hired people to help you, as long as they don't steal your secrets."

Ugodi sighed. "I'm getting tired of it now. It was supposed to be a side-business to my farming; I prefer that."

"It's made you one of the richest women in Abonani, so don't give it up."

"I'm not rich," Ugodi said.

"If you say so, I'll agree with you. You are poor," Aku said. They looked at each other and laughed. Afterwards they both sat in silence taking turns to sip more of the palm-wine.

"Talking about mother, I see you have expanded her *chi* shrine," Aku said, looking at a small collection of mud cones and bits of earthenware. Surviving daughters venerated their female ancestors in this way.

"She was a great woman so she must not be forgotten. It was Onaedo that helped me put in the new things," Ugodi said.

"Onaedo is a good daughter," Aku said. "You can rest assured that when you're gone you will not be forgotten as long as she is alive."

"That's why we pray for daughters."

"That's true," Aku nodded in agreement. "By the way, has she said anything about any young man in whom she's interested?"

Ugodi looked at her, a slight frown pulling her eyebrows together. "I didn't know she was interested in anybody."

"I haven't heard anything either," Aku replied quickly. "I was just asking." There were rumors but it would serve no purpose to rile her sister, Aku thought.

It was too late. Ugodi had all the opening she needed to talk about her favorite topic of late. "I don't really know what Onaedo is waiting for," she said, launching into a litany of complaints about suitors Onaedo had turned down. "My sister, let me tell you now, my patience is running out. If she refuses one more young man, I will prevail on Eneda to force her to marry somebody of our own choosing. Young women have too much freedom these days and don't know how to use it."

"I don't remember anybody choosing your own husband for you," Aku retorted. "*Biko*, leave her alone."

"Why should I leave her alone? What good is a woman who doesn't have the common sense to marry early? I know this is the doing of Eneda's other wives. They're jealous of my success and have started their malevolent spells. They're laughing at me already. They'll laugh more if my only daughter ends up an old, unmarried woman. Aku, please help me talk some sense into her. She listens to you."

"Why the hurry?" Aku asked with a slight frown. "She's still a child. She only formed breasts the other day. Aren't you going to allow her to emerge from the womb before you marry her off? Leave her alone. Please."

"One is never too young to get married. Many girls much younger than she is are already betrothed."

"But Abonani has decreed that we do not like that custom," Aku pointed out. "A young girl must be old enough to agree first before she is married off."

"I'm just saying it the way I feel. That's all."

Aku sighed. Ugodi's constant nagging about Onaedo could be wearisome. In the past, Ugodi would accuse her of being too casual about the issue. "It's because you have only sons that you don't understand what I'm going through, Aku. If you had a daughter who took sleep from your eyes at night due to worry, you would think differently."

Aku didn't want to fight today. "Listen, Ugodi, I'll talk to Onaedo again if you want me to. Let's return to work; I'm tired of this conversation," Aku said standing up.

The walls were smooth and shiny with the bits of glassy sand in the mud. They added lines and jagged patterns in red, white and black.

The water in the earthenware pot turned ochre red as they rinsed their hands in it.

"I have to go," Aku said, collecting her work tools into a long basket. "It's my turn to cook the evening meal."

Onaedo entered as she arrived at the gate.

"Are you leaving already?" Onaedo asked. "I would have come home earlier, if I knew you were here."

"I was helping your mother," Aku replied. "I have something to discuss with you but it will have to wait for another day. Greet your father for me. I didn't have time to go into his *obi* today, but I know that he doesn't like to be disturbed when he's working anyway." She hugged Onaedo goodbye and hurried out in the direction of the falling sun.

രരാ

Onaedo opened the door to her father's yam barn and looked around carefully. The dwarf kola-nut tree waved its leaves in a slow breeze, its trunk studded with large gray pods. She picked up the two that had fallen to the ground and threw them into her basket.

Her father had many tenant farmers who paid their rent in kind. Inside the barn, the yams were tied in vertical rows on numerous bamboo stakes and the tubers protruded from the poles like pregnant bellies. Onaedo looked around again before she stepped in. Yesterday she had stepped on a resting snake and was lucky she had not been bitten. The startled snake had slithered away with an angry hiss as she ran screaming back into the yard. Ugodi had asked her afterwards to remind Udemezue to send for Ochuagwo, the snake exterminator to search the whole compound. Not that anyone believed that the exorbitant fees he charged were merited, Onaedo thought, as she untied a yam tuber and dropped it into the basket. But she had to admit that whatever it was that he left behind kept the dangerous reptiles away for a long time afterwards. Each time, as he left, he would say "Call me if you see anything," as though he was not going to charge a new fee for coming back.

Back in the yard, she peeled the yam and placed it into the water that boiled over on the fire. Her mother was busy dissolving cups of ash powder into a pot of hot water as she prepared to make a batch of soap. She lifted the boiling paste and poured it into another container that was half-full of palm oil heating over a small fire. This was the important part.

"Let me help you stir," Onaedo offered, picking up a wooden spatula.

"Quick! Help me take it off the fire," Ugodi called out to her. The mixture was starting to thicken into a gelatinous mass.

Onaedo was prepared. This stage was always unpredictable. She grabbed a couple of thick raffia pads and held each side of the pot.

"Let's lift it together," Ugodi instructed. They removed it from the flames and placed it next to another container whose contents had already cooled.

Onaedo sat down again to tend to the boiling yam while Ugodi took a big, wooden spoon and dug into the cold, thick, black bituminous soap. She would mold it into round, black balls when it hardened some more.

Ugodi rolled a small portion between her fingers to test its texture. Satisfied, she looked at Onaedo. "By the way, I was talking to Aku today and she said that you might be interested in some young man. Who is it?"

"Nobody," Onaedo said feigning nonchalance. "I have to check on the *egusi* that I shelled yesterday." She stood and started walking towards the back wall where the shelled pumpkin seeds were drying on mats.

"That can wait," Ugodi called out, but Onaedo pretended she was too far away to hear.

ဢ

Eneda was winding down for the night when Onaedo came in with his evening meal. His workshop was a large room attached to his *obi* through a wide archway.

"Your food is here," Onaedo said, placing two wooden bowls on a ledge.

"Thank you," he said without looking up. He disliked any disturbance even if it was at the end of a workday.

Onaedo liked the ordered chaos of Eneda's workshop at the end of the day. The kiln, the heart of all the activity, was stoked to high heat by an endless supply of firewood and charcoal by Eneda's workers and apprentices who rushed about as if stopping for one moment would root them to a spot. They took great care; everything was so dangerously hot that a careless mistake could cost a deep festering burn that might never heal.

The finished products were pulled from the fire and left to cool. This was her favorite part and she sat down to watch Eneda, the master craftsman put the finishing touches to his work. The heat of the dying fire made him glisten with sweat.

He stood slowly, took a finished vase in his hands, and carried it across the room. He was tall and lanky and he moved with deliberate, economical steps, picking his way leisurely between the hot obstacles strewn across the room. His talent was legendary in all of *Olu n'Igbo*, and his work priceless.

Eneda always pretended to be unaware of her presence. They had played this game for as long as she could remember. If she kept quiet, he let her stay. As she grew older, she learned to keep secrets; things others divulged to Eneda in confidence that could never be heard outside the four walls of his *obi*. That was how she became a custodian of memories.

It was here that she had learned the story of the founding of Abonani from her father. Nine men had journeyed from a faraway kingdom to settle the present land in a time before time; she knew all by name, they were committed to heart.

Sometimes she thought that maybe Eneda sought her opinion but he asked for it in that abstract way that people have of talking aloud to themselves, not really inviting a response. As the chief adviser to the Ezeigwe, people often told Eneda things that they wanted only him to know and it was here that she had come to learn about Oguebie. She had become wary of him when she learned all that he was capable of doing.

She looked around the workshop and sighed. If she were a man, she would have become a blacksmith like her father. He looked up at her, distracted by the noise.

"Are you ready to eat yet?" she asked. "The food will grow cold and Ugodi will be upset."

Eneda frowned as he put the finishing touches on a bronze jar. "I'm not hungry yet."

Somebody accidentally dropped a vase, shattering the quiet. Eneda looked at the offender for an interminably long time before turning away in disgust. He was known for being temperamental when it came to his work and it was best to keep quiet, especially in the middle of his creative process. He could go for days without food, much to the chagrin of his wives.

Onaedo let her mind drift back to Dualo while she waited for her father to stop work. She wondered what he would think of her situation. What would happen if she mustered the courage to tell him about Dualo? She pulled herself back sharply. It would be as unprecedented as it was inconceivable.

"Better take the food to my room," Eneda said. "I will eat it there when I have time later. Thank your mother for me."

"I will," she replied. The moment of confession was gone. She couldn't have done it anyway.

# CHAPTER

# 4

Over the weeks, Onaedo found ways to meet with Dualo. She remained optimistic despite the financial uncertainties. Just being with him made her mind numb with pleasure. When she was alone at night and thought about him, she squeezed her legs together until a warm pleasant feeling engulfed her whole body. She became impatient and it was like a stream that carried her in its current.

She had to be careful because Ugodi was suspicious. She had caught her mother watching her speculatively a few times and she began to master the art of covering her tracks.

A couple of times a month she accompanied Ugodi to the women's meeting. It was organized by the Ezeigwe's head wife, the Iyom Ezeigwe for the different women's group. Onaedo usually had no interest in any of the issues the older women seemed so passionate about and only went along because her mother insisted.

However, of late she had ceased to complain about it and had shown an eagerness to attend that she knew had aroused Ugodi's suspicions even more. Of course, her mother had no way of knowing that Onaedo's newfound enthusiasm for mundane women's affairs—such as setting the price of market commodities, allocating stalls, and cleaning the market—had more to do with the fact that Dualo was a permanent fixture at the *obi eze* than any interest in the affairs of women. The Ezeigwe had commissioned Dualo's uncle to do a job for him and so Dualo and the rest of the other workers were there daily. She was careful not to be seen talking to him too often and had to be content to just breathe the same air that he did. It was a very unsatisfactory state of affairs, but she had to make do.

ন্তন

The drought predicted by some clairvoyants had not materialized in Abonani and there was a sense of optimism in the air. For Onaedo however the nights had become darker and lovers' meetings had ceased, at least until the moon filled out again.

She was restless now that there was little to do. Her age-grade was planning to go to the neighboring town of Ibari to learn a new dance that people said was a popular raging fire of a dance, but that would not happen for another month. Most evenings, if she was not helping clean her father's *obi* or his workshop, she was with Ugodi, listening to her tell stories to the young children of the compound, mostly the grandchildren of her father's other wives.

Her mother was a master storyteller and could elevate the most mundane of stories into masterpieces of humorous misadventures and morality tales. Ugodi's impressive retinue of stories was as vivid as it was endless. As she grew older, Onaedo began to take them less literally and, instead, looked beyond the obvious to the cautionary tales of avoidance of ethical pitfalls that they really were. She hoped to be able to tell them to her own children someday as adeptly as Ugodi.

Onaedo had heard the particular tortoise tale that Ugodi had just finished telling, many times before. She often wondered why Tortoise always got caught in the end—he seemed more a dim-witted fumbler than the smart strategist that everybody seemed to think he was.

"I haven't told this in a long time," Ugodi said rearranging her granddaughter asleep on her lap. Onaedo had brought the baby over from Udemezue's house earlier in the day. "Has anyone heard the one about the king who had a beautiful daughter, too choosy about whom to marry?"

Most of the children said they had not, and the ones who had heard it before said they hadn't. Onaedo sat and leaned against the wall, closing her eyes. She would pretend not to listen. She knew the story and was irritated that her mother was telling it now. She knew that Ugodi was indirectly speaking to her. Her mother was transparently annoying sometimes, she thought.

"I have a story to tell." Ugodi began, in the time-tested, dependable style of all storytellers.

"Please tell us," the children responded in concert.

"A long, long time ago," Ugodi began, "at the very beginning of time when the ancient *iroko* tree was but a mere sapling and the palm tree still bore its fruits at the tip of its leaves and there was no separation of land from sky, there reigned a famous king who had one beloved daughter.

"The Princess or *Ada-eze* was a beautiful, young woman, and people from all over *Olu n'Igbo*—the whole Igbo world and beyond—came to behold her beauty. But the young woman had one major fault that caused her father, the *Eze-Igwe* of that country, a lot of concern.

"And I will tell you what it was," Ugodi said pausing for effect. "The young woman found fault with every suitor that came along. Princes, warriors, and rich men were all turned down for different reasons. Until one day . . ." Ugodi paused again. Onaedo sat very still and kept her eyes shut.

". . . one day, a handsome young prince came out of nowhere to seek her out. He told the *Eze-Igwe* that he had heard of his daughter's beauty and had crossed seven seas, seven forests, and seven deserts to marry her.

"He was a likeable man and the *Ada-eze* was immediately smitten by his handsome face; at last she had found somebody who met her exacting standards. She told her father to accept the bride-price and prepare the nuptial feast right away. The *Eze-Igwe* had amassed a large dowry for her, so her husband's people would know that she was a valued daughter and treat her well when they saw all the wealth she brought to the marriage.

"When it was time to go, the *Ada-eze* wept tears of sadness and joy, hugged her father and mother goodbye, and set off for her new home with the groom.

"A few days into their journey, they arrived at a small town, and the prince asked his young wife's permission to return an item that he had borrowed from a friend several days before. The *Ada-eze* indicated that it was not a problem; she would wait for him to return. Everybody understood that debts needed to be repaid and she was happy her husband was a man of integrity who repaid his promptly. If she wondered why such a rich man needed to borrow anything at all, she kept that thought inside her. She was shocked however, when her husband returned without one of his legs. This was unexpected."

Onaedo opened her eyes. Some of the children giggle nervously, while the younger ones stared wide-eyed and wriggled closer to the safety of the middle. The palm-oil lamp began to run low, only flaring brightly when it caught a foolish insect that had come too close to its flame, spitting and hissing angrily as it scorched the poor creature.

Ugodi continued her story. "The *Ada-eze* was too stunned to ask her new husband what had happened to his leg and, as they continued their journey, he proceeded to give back all the parts of his body until they got to the last stop.

"This time he returned his head to his debtor and turned into a snake—a gigantic python." At this point, Ugodi threw her arms wide apart to illustrate the enormousness of the snake while most of the children squealed excitedly and moved even closer together.

"Somebody should please tell me the moral of this story," Ugodi asked when the excitement died down.

"If you are too choosy, you may end up marrying a snake," volunteered one of the children, "Just like Onaedo," she added as an afterthought.

Too late, the girl realized her mistake when her sister nudged her to keep quiet. Onaedo leaned toward her and rapped her on the head with one knuckle.

"You have a big mouth for a little girl," Onaedo hissed, glaring at her in the dim light. "Don't you know that I'm old enough to be your mother?"

"Onaedo, please leave the child alone," Ugodi said, scolding Onaedo sharply. "She's only repeating what she heard others say."

"Wait till we get home," threatened the little girl's older sister who had tried but failed to keep her sister quiet. "I'll tell our mother what you said. She'll slap you till okra seeds fall out of your eyes."

"I said everybody should leave her alone, including you," Ugodi said. "Didn't you see Onaedo rebuke her already? I don't want to hear another word of this."

The child who had made the gaffe was more embarrassed than hurt and started to cry. She adored Onaedo and it was clear that she had not meant to offend. Onaedo relented and motioned for her to come and sit on her lap.

"But *Nne,* did *Ada-eze* kill the python?" one of the younger children piped up, addressing Ugodi.

Everybody laughed, relieved to change the subject.

"Can you tell us a story about the white man and the Delta City?" another child asked.

"I have never crossed the Great River," Ugodi replied, absently turning the baby on her lap. "So I can't tell you much about the white man who they say lives there."

"What about the story that they come in giant coffins that float in the sea?" the child persisted. "They say the coffin is full of cowry money."

"You have to ask Udemezue for those stories," Ugodi said, smiling indulgently at him. "He goes to the Great River and he knows about that. I don't go anywhere and can only talk about what I know. But I have another story to tell. Have you heard the one about the cunning tortoise and his greedy in-laws?"

"Please tell us," they all chorused with excitement and Ugodi smiled as she began her next story.

ന്ദ

Onaedo had not seen or heard from Dualo for a while and there had been no opportunities to meet. It was early morning and her mother was still asleep when she quietly crept out so as not to wake her.

The air was cold and heavy with dew and the sky had begun to lighten from the sun that was not yet visible. She went around to the back of the house to get her water pot.

"Are you ready?" Adanma called out from over the wall.

"Yes. Wait for me, I'll be right there."

Onaedo heard whispered conversations and low-keyed laughter. She closed the gate quietly so the goats would not escape and run riot in the homestead farming plots and moved quickly to join her waiting girlfriends. They were ready for their early morning trip to the stream.

Onaedo had been thinking about Dualo and had already devised a plan to contact him that would once again involve Adanma. They would go with a girl they knew was friendly with one of Dualo's sisters and that would provide a good excuse to visit his home.

The group chatted happily as they strolled. The path widened as it joined the main road. It was lined on both sides by shrubs, tipped with bursts of brightly colored flowers, still gray in the dawn. Their heavy scent impregnated the morning dew. There were very few people at this time of the morning but an orange-headed lizard already chased his mate on the open path before the sun rose.

An indistinct and shadowy figure appeared in the misty distance and the girls fell silent until it was in full view. It was a middle-aged woman, her hair in a bushy, tangled mess with a wooden spoon in one hand. For the past few months they'd grown used to meeting her at this same spot on the road and stood silently to one side until she passed.

"That's Eboka's widow again," Onaedo whispered when the woman was out of earshot. "We should at least say *ndo* when she goes past us, to let her know how sorry we are that her husband died."

"She won't say anything to you because she's not supposed to speak to anybody outside her family until her one-year period of mourning is over," Adanma said. "She's not even supposed to be outside her compound, but they sometimes allow them to come out as long as it's early enough so that not many people will see them."

"I don't like that custom," said one of the girls. "They've made her look like she's mad, the way they let her hair grow into a forest like that and carrying around that spoon. And it's not as if Eboka was not expected to die. He was old and sick for a long time."

"If she doesn't do it they will say she didn't love her husband, or worse, that she killed him. If you ask me, I don't see anything wrong with it. How else are you going to show that you loved him?"

"You don't have a choice anyway. Unless of course you die before your husband and that's a whole different matter."

"And they will always accuse you of having a hand in his death, no matter how old and decrepit he was," another girl added.

"Being a woman is not easy, especially being a married woman," Onaedo said.

"If it was easy, it would not be worth it," Adanma added somewhat philosophically, causing Onaedo to look askance at her.

"Wait!" a breathless voice shouted a short distance behind them. "Why are you leaving without me?"

It was Nonye, and as they stopped to wait for her to catch up, Onaedo gave an inward sigh. She really wasn't in the mood for Nonye's usual tittle-tattle. Most times, she was an entertaining diversion with her colorful exaggerations and melodramatic embellishments but, today, Onaedo wanted to hurry and put her plan into action.

"As if we would leave without you," Adanma said sarcastically as they waited. Onaedo gave her a warning look. She knew that there was no love lost between the two girls.

"Well, I didn't hear you call me," Nonye rejoined, breathing heavily from running. She was a heavyset girl with a pretty face. "If my mother hadn't told me that she saw all of you pass the house, you would have left without me."

"But we did call out to you, didn't we?" Adanma asked, looking around as if daring anybody to contradict her.

Onaedo knew that they had done no such thing but she understood Adanma's antipathy toward Nonye. It was because she saw her as a rival for Udemezue's affections. Nonye, in her usual tactless way, had told Onaedo to Adanma's hearing that she, Nonye, was in love with Udemezue and hoped to marry him someday soon. Onaedo knew that the comment had infuriated Adanma and, although she said nothing at the time, Adanma had conspired at every opportunity since that day to separate Nonye from their group.

Nonye stood slightly apart from the rest, her empty water pot in one hand and her raffia head-pad in the other. She looked a little uncertain, as if unsure of her reception by the others. She had complained to Onaedo that she suspected Adanma was trying to poison the minds of the other girls towards her and did not know why. "Don't worry about Adanma," Onaedo had reassured her. "She can be like that sometimes."

Now Onaedo reached out and pulled her by the forearm. "Come on. We'll be late if we don't hurry."

In fact, Onaedo was getting tired of the feuding between Adanma and Nonye. She knew that each girl was vying for her undivided loyalty and attention and at any other time she would have been flattered. Today she had other things on her mind.

Nonye seemed relieved that she was now welcome back into the fold and Onaedo saw her studiously trying to ignore the dirty looks Adanma gave her. Instead, she launched into her usual chatter.

"Did you all hear what happened to Ego?" she asked breathlessly.

"Which Ego?" a few voices asked.

"How many Egos do you know?" Nonye replied.

"At least three," countered Adanma. "Just tell the story and stop wasting our time."

Nonye ignored Adanma's rudeness. "Anyway, the Ego I'm talking about is our friend the Ego who is Oguine's daughter. She's now married to an old man from another town and she's Fifth Wife," she added, looking around expectantly for their reaction. It was not slow in coming.

"Fifth Wife!" All the girls exclaimed in unison.

"Did I have water in my mouth when I said it?" said Nonye. She looked happy at the impact of her news. "You heard me clearly— Fifth Wife."

"If you ask me, that is too old," Onaedo said. "A fifth wife is for old maids who are desperate to marry and will jump on any old man who pays them the slightest attention. Ego is rather young to settle for that. She should be somebody's first or second wife."

"Well, you don't know the full story," continued Nonye, wanting to catch the thread of her story again before it unraveled in the debate.

"There is more?" asked Onaedo curiously.

"Well don't say you heard it from me . . ." Nonye started, only to be interrupted again by Adanma.

"So who are we going to say we heard it from then? Me?" Her voice was dripping with sarcasm.

Onaedo knew Adanma was irritated that Nonye had been accepted back so readily. Nonye continued her story, ignoring Adanma completely. "The way I heard it, she went and got pregnant, and this was the best arrangement her family could make to avoid disgrace."

This time, the exclamations from everybody were of genuine shock. Onaedo looked at Adanma who seemed to have momentarily forgotten her pretense of disinterest. This was major gossip. Becoming pregnant outside of a marriage was indeed a catastrophe for any young woman. If she were lucky enough to find a husband to marry her before it became common knowledge, then the matter died a natural death. It could be either the real father or any man that wanted her and the choices were usually not many.

"In that case, she's lucky that she found somebody who agreed to marry her at all," somebody commented. Now they knew why they hadn't seen the girl in recent weeks.

"What about the real father?"

"She claims she doesn't know," Nonye replied.

"*What?* Everybody exclaimed together. "You mean that she did it with more than one person?"

"Well, when you see her you can ask her," Nonye added triumphantly. She had done her job well.

"Some girls are just crazy," somebody said.

"Yes, but you also know that Ego's father does not have a son from any of his three wives," another girl added. "This pregnancy could be the answer to his lineage problems. I'm surprised that he's marrying her off before he even knows whether it's a boy."

This was definitely a new facet of the problem, and everybody discussed it excitedly. Onaedo was silent as she walked beside Adanma, only half listening to the conversation around her. A slight wave of uneasiness coursed through as she made a comparison with her own situation. But she hadn't done anything that reckless.

She was distracted by her thoughts and only caught the last bit of the next gossip that Nonye was sharing.

". . . and so my brother left with Dualo for the Delta City," Nonye said. "My mother is not happy because she wants my brother to get married and start a family now."

"Nonye, I wasn't paying attention," Onaedo asked with a forced casualness that belied the very deep sense of foreboding that gripped her when she heard Dualo's name. "What were you saying about your brother and Dualo?"

"I was saying that Dualo's uncle took my brother and Dualo to the Delta king's palace and my mother has been unhappy since. Even though she knows it's for his own good . . ."

"Do you mean Dualo of Umeadi's family?" Onaedo interrupted.

"That's the one." Nonye said, looking at her curiously.

"Ooh, I'm sure your mother is really worried," Onaedo said. "The Delta City is far and they may not be back for a long time." Her voice sounded falsely jovial, even to her own ears and Nonye continued with more devastating news.

"My mother says that they won't be back for at least a year or maybe even two."

"Is that what your brother told her?" Onaedo asked.

"Yes."

"When did they leave?"

"Let me see," Nonye said trying to count of the days on her fingers, "About five days ago."

"You are always full of stories, you foolish girl,' Adanma hissed furiously at Nonye. The other girl seemed stung by this unprovoked verbal attack. With deliberate care, she placed the raffia head pad on the side of the path and placed the empty pot on top of it before turning to Adanma.

"Adanma I'm tired of your nonsense. If you have something to say, say it now," she said angrily. She stood in front of Adanma with both hands balanced on her hips as she blocked her path.

Onaedo quickly moved in between them. "Please stop. You're two grown women behaving like children." The others joined in coaxing them into a truce before they continued their walk to the stream.

Onaedo felt numb the rest of the way. Why did Dualo not tell her he was leaving town? She sat by the bank and felt the icy cold water wash over her feet. Adanma sat beside her. "Don't worry about him. He didn't have the money to marry anyway."

Onaedo said nothing as she watched tiny fish swim up to the banks to nibble at the floating vegetation. A bird swooped down periodically to sip the water before it impaled a fish and flew away as the fish squirmed in the air.

She struggled to hold back her tears. There would be time for that later.

"That Dualo is a fool to leave you like that, without even sending a message," Adanma whispered to her.

"I'm going to bathe," Onaedo said abruptly, getting up and walking into the cool water. She bent to pick a smooth green stone that rolled back and forth on the stream bed. She had collected these colored stones from the stream for years—blue ones that were the color of the sky, yellow ones that reflected the color of the sun or the moon on special nights; there were the common black ones and a couple that were red. This was her first green one, almost like the color of her eyes. She placed it carefully on the riverbank beside her water vessel and took off her waistcloth before entering the water.

She didn't want to talk to anybody, not even Adanma. She washed her mother's clothes before washing her body with the black soap. She rubbed hard but the slippery foam could not wash her of despair. If it was true that Dualo had left town without contacting her, then she wanted nothing more to do with him.

"Onaedo, are you ready to go now?" Adanma asked.

Onaedo wiped the water and the tears from her face as she climbed out of the water. "I'm ready."

Adanma said nothing more. They collected the water at its source from the rocks and started for home.

ෆ

The fever started as a slow burn in Onaedo's head on the way home from the stream and was full blown by the time she arrived. Ugodi took one look at her, drawn and shivering, before rushing to relieve her of the water vessel on her head.

"This child will kill me someday," she lamented in alarm. "Why did you go to the stream if you knew that your body was not right? Did I tell you that I was dying of thirst and that I cannot do without this little water you fetched today? You look like someone who has met an evil spirit and came off the worse for it."

Onaedo surrendered to the ministrations of her mother. She was glad that her fever had come at an opportune time. Her *iso ezi* also started at the same time, which meant that she would be secluded for at least one market week, anyway. Four days. Today was Nkwo; there was still Eke, Oye, and Afor to go. Nobody would see her sorrow and she could grieve in private.

∞

She lay on her mother's mat and tried not to think but her mind went back to her first meeting with Dualo. Strangely, it had been at the *obi eze* at one of Ugodi's meetings. Out of boredom, she had wandered off, meandering in between the rows of little, square whitewashed houses the Ezeigwe had built for his many wives.

She had seen him then and watched him engrossed in his work, meticulously decorating a stool. If he knew she was there, he gave no sign that he had.

"I want to see what you are doing," she finally said, sitting beside him. He later told her that she was a water goddess and he had fallen in love with her right away although he had tried to hide his feelings.

A few weeks later, when she returned, he told her stories of the amazing place called the Delta City. He described wide streets, the grand palaces of the King, and a Queen Mother who even had her own court and a whole regiment of soldiers. These stories were not new, but to Onaedo they seemed more adventurous coming from Dualo.

He described the first time that he'd seen a white man. "Not to speak to of course," he added hastily smiling impishly at her, "but they bought our goods, especially ivory. That's when I learned how to make ivory ornaments, spoons, combs, and horns for them. There is an endless supply of goods the white man traded in the city. I have never seen so many different colors in cloth—red, green, blue, and black. They sold little pots made of glass to very rich men. If I had money I would have bought a mirror for you."

Onaedo nudged him playfully. "But you did not know me then."

"That is true," Dualo admitted. "I tasted their wine too. There is one in particular, as clear as water but bites the tongue with the sting of a scorpion. It can make a man drunk for days, after just a few sips."

Onaedo had tasted some of the 'fiery water' years ago when Udemezue bought some for Eneda from the Great River market. He still had the bottle and took a few sips every now and again. Onaedo had never tired of Dualo's stories and thought he would be around to tell them to her for a long time.

And now he was gone, just like that, without a word.

She turned and felt the sweat pour from her as the fever broke. She cried herself softly to sleep.

CHAPTER

O guebie was back at the Delta Kingdom after days of travel from Abonani. He was satisfied to learn that the wood-worker had arrived ahead of him and had brought all his workers, including his nephew Dualo, with him. Oguebie had arranged for Ideheno to introduce Dualo's uncle to the courtier in charge of renovating the king's palace and he had assured them that there was enough work to keep the woodworker and his assistants occu-pied for years, if they wanted.

That done, Oguebie faced the important business that had made him return to the Delta Kingdom. The city was a busy des-tination of European merchants, mostly Portuguese, who bought leather, ivory, red peppers, and coral beads and in turn sold glass bottles, mirrors, tobacco, and spirits to the locals.

All commerce went through the palace, so conducting private business like the kind that Oguebie and Ideheno planned could be dangerous. Both men decided to meet with the two Portuguese at the isolated church before going further south to the coast. Down there, secret embarkation points fed dozens of waterways that flowed to the ocean. Some Portuguese caravels that arrived at the coast were small enough to navigate the narrower waterways for contraband.

The little timber church was empty when Oguebie and Ideheno pushed open the door. It had once been handsome and ebony black but now had developed large cracks in its grain. It whined on its wooden hinge as they entered. The altar was a wooden table at the front of the room. There were only three stools in the room as most of the congregants brought their own to mass.

Oguebie approached the large cross that stood on the make-shift altar.

"The white man is strange," he said poking it with his walking stick. "They worship a God who has a Son but no wife. But the Son has a mother who is not the wife of the Father." He laughed at his own convoluted logic and picked up a small wooden statue of a woman that was carrying what looked like an infant or something similar in one arm.

"We have to find a way to win the white man over so he can give us more of what we want," he said examining the object before carefully replacing it on the table. "We can start by accepting their religion, even if it is like a leper to us," he said, pausing to look around the ramshackle church. "Look at this place; the walls are almost falling down. Why don't we promise to build them a bigger house and even a school? That way they may give us more guns."

Ideheno shrugged but said nothing. Oguebie looked at him. He had the same feeling of unease that he'd had about Ideheno the last time. He was sure that his friend was withholding something. He would bide his time. "After our last conversation I acquired the goods that the white man wants," he said, sitting next to Ideheno. "I bought all the ivory and peppers that I could find. Those Abonani traders were confused. I'm sure they're cursing me now for spiking up the price of everything and upsetting their trade," he said laughing.

Ideheno looked away without smiling. "Those things are good but that is not what Alvarez and his friend are looking for."

"What are you talking about?" Oguebie asked. "What do they want?"

"Workers."

"Workers?" Oguebie was beginning to sound like a half-wit. "What kind of workers?"

"The kind that can work on farms; the white man's farm," Ideheno replied.

Oguebie stared at him and then burst out laughing. "Where are we going to find people whom we can convince to leave their own farms and follow the white man to work on his? You should have thought about all this before you started making promises to these men that you know we cannot keep."

"They want us to take them by force," Ideheno continued in a matter-of-fact voice, as though he had argued many times about this same issue and was now tired of it.

"That wine that the Portuguese sold you must be very potent because it has entered your head and scattered it," Oguebie said, now annoyed.

However, before Ideheno could reply, the two white men arrived. With Alvarez, the older man, was the same younger man whom Oguebie knew as Pasquale.

Immediately upon entering the building, Alvarez knelt briefly at the altar, touched his forehead and chest and muttered something under his breath before he rose and approached them. He was swarthy and rough looking, like someone who farmed all day under the hot, blistering sun. His black hair was thinning at the top and his dark eyes were small and set too closely together above his big nose. He spoke brusquely with an impatient voice. The younger Pasquale looked more ordinary and seemed more likeable than the older man. But as far as Oguebie was concerned, the white men could not be trusted and one had to be careful when dealing with them. He had had bad experiences before doing business with some of them back in the city.

Alvarez went straight to the business at hand. "How many young men can you find for me before my ship sails?" His eyes darted from Oguebie and back to Ideheno.

Oguebie did not like Alvarez's attitude. He barked and seemed as though he didn't want to hear the reply. Since his knowledge of

Portuguese was still quite rudimentary, he waited for Ideheno to translate.

"Tell him that we'll do our best to give him any number of workers that he wants," Oguebie replied.

*"Algum número?* Any number?" Alvarez asked, raising a quizzical eyebrow.

Oguebie nodded in confirmation. He understood *that* without translation. He still had no idea how to convince large numbers of people to farm for a stranger, but he had been thinking. There was no doubt that only a few people would come willingly. Why would they leave their land, farm and families to work for a stranger? He had to think of a way to achieve their objective but he knew it was going to be hard. Wasn't it said that great riches were always found deep among thorns? He consoled himself. Nothing worthwhile was ever easy. He would find a way.

After their exchange, the two visitors seemed pleased. Everyone shook hands and dispersed.

ﮩﮩ

Pasquale Casimiro de Lima had arrived in the Delta City weeks before with his partner Alvarez Guerreiro. After the meeting with Ideheno and Oguebie, they returned to the city. Alvarez went on to the palace to meet the King's trade representative, while Pasquale made his way to the row of houses where the white traders lived while in the city on business.

He pushed open the wooden door of one of them and entered. It was bare and lonely inside. A wooden table and three chairs were pushed haphazardly against one wall and the one wooden window was half-open. Mat-covered mud ledges jutted out from the walls. They were used as seats during the day and beds at night.

"Can I get you food, Senhor?" It was their black servant. She had seen him come in and had approached from the yard where she'd been stoking a fire.

Pasquale waved her away. She was a great cook, but he was tired of the local food and homesick for food from home; he would give anything for a piece of *chourico* sausage, wine marinated beef *alcatra,* or some cured ham washed down with vinho verde. No point thinking about all that now. Since he would be alone for a while, he decided to write in his journal. Alvarez's trip to the palace tonight was part of their ploy to keep the palace in the dark about their other activities on the coast.

But he did not trust Alvarez. He was sure that he had lied to him throughout this trip. Pasquale had come for gold in Africa and Alvarez had pushed him into trading for slaves.

At first, Alvarez had told him that there was gold in El Mina which was further west along the coast. When they arrived, however, Pasquale discovered that the gold mines had been closed for at least a month due to a labor shortage. Slave labor. And then to add to his woes, he had caught the dreaded *mal'aria* which he had barely survived.

"So where is the gold?" he'd demanded of Alvarez when he had recovered his strength.

"The only gold is the slaves," Alvarez had replied flippantly.

Pasquale had been furious. "You should have told me that we were going to trade in slaves. I don't approve of this trade. You should have told me the truth; we're supposed to be partners," he added.

"If I had told you, what would you have done?" Alvarez asked. Pasquale heard his disdain. "You're still young and idealistic and you don't understand—"

"I'm not a child," Pasquale interrupted with heat. "I've put a lot of my money in this venture and I demand your respect."

"You'll have a profitable return on your investment, my friend," Alvarez said, still patronizing and unperturbed. "You have to trust me. Slave trading is a business like any other. The only difference is we're transporting workers instead of goods. You saw the trade in Lisbon and I didn't hear you raise any objections then."

It was true, Pasquale thought. He *was* ambivalent about the issue. He often walked past the Casa dos Escravos, the big slave exchange on the Lisbon waterfront. Black slaves were bought and sold daily there and none of it had bothered him then. How could he claim moral indignation now?

Moreover, he really needed the money. Pasquale thought about the print shop he wanted and the books he could publish. It would be worthwhile to sell a few slaves to acquire all that. So he'd decided not to argue anymore. He didn't like Alvarez any better than before, but recognized in him an astute business man who would help him earn money.

That was a month ago. They had drifted eastwards down the coast until they arrived at the Delta City. This was Pasquale's first voyage to this part of the world, and it would be his last if he had any say in the matter. After this, he would stick to the European ports around the Mediterranean Sea. The only reason that he had part-nered with Alvarez, whom he barely knew, was because he had been unable to find another ship in Lisbon that had room for him.

When he had almost given up hope of finding a ship, some-body told him to contact Alvarez. He had heard that he was an experienced businessman. It wasn't until later that he learned that Alvarez was also known for a lack of scruples and a foul temper. By then it was too late. Pasquale had wondered why Alvarez, for all his skills, was not a more successful merchant seaman, until he learned that the man was a hard drinker and gambler who thought little of gambling the proceeds of a shipload of merchandise on a wager. He spent wildly on drinking and the prostitutes of Lisbon and other seaports of the world.

The two-hundred-ton caravel, the *Santa Magdalena,* which had brought them from Lisbon, had been a rundown ship with rotten deck planks and ragged sails until Alvarez had skillfully restored it. If Alvarez knew one thing, it was ships. It had been converted into a three-mast vessel that sailed like the wind and was suited for any coastline, no matter how treacherous.

But the *Santa Magdalena* was now anchored off a small coastal settlement in Forcados. And it was empty. Just like Pasquale's bank account in the Medici Bank in Lisbon was empty. He had invested everything in this trip.

ര$\infty$ര

Pasquale pondered his early life as he did often. It had not involved the sea at all, although he came from a family with seafaring traditions. His father had been a sailor but died quite early at sea, leaving him an only child and his mother a young widow. His mother saw the sea as a family curse and swore that Pasquale would have nothing to do with ships or sailing. When Pasquale argued that the Portuguese were leading the world in sea exploration and changing the world, she retorted, "The world can change without you. If you love it so much then you can be a cartographer and make maps for sailors. It's an honorable profession and the reason I paid for your education. You can become a teacher or a doctor, or even a priest like your friend Joao, but not a sailor."

Pasquale didn't want to go into the priesthood like his best friend Joao, but the only work he could find were menial jobs. He took them to support his mother and his elderly, sick grandfather who also lived with them.

It was his grandfather who told him the family legends. "We weren't always poor," he told him, with eyes dreamy with age and memory. "We owned land but gambled it all away. Our ancestors were soldiers and noblemen from the time of the Second Crusades and the founding of Portugal. They fought in the Battle of Ceuta, served the crown and sailed the world with the early explorers. "We made fortunes trading in spices, pearls, and precious stones, and we built castles, but we lost it all through our gambling. Now we're poor again," the old man said, shaking his head.

Pasquale worked at different jobs—dockhand, butcher's assistant, apprentice to a merchant, an apothecary's assistant, and his best job, an apprentice to a print shop owner. Apart from the sea, books were his love but he was determined to make a fortune somehow. Sadly, no opportunities came along.

He started to learn the art of book printing because he thought that if he couldn't travel, he could at least become a master printer. The Guttenberg printing press, a German invention, had revolutionized printing everywhere. Mass produced book manufacturing became profitable in Portugal as it did in the rest of Europe. Popular novels like the *Travels of Sir John Mandeville, Descriptions of Africa* by Giovanni Leo Africanus became readily available and increased the desire for travel.

Pasquale's fortune changed unexpectedly several months after his grandfather passed. He was cleaning out the old man's room and discovered a stash of gems, pearls, emeralds, rubies, and gold coins underneath his ancient oak bed. There was also a letter stating that he had willed all of it to Pasquale.

"Why did we live in poverty when he had all this money?" his mother complained.

"I think that he wanted me to be old enough to spend it wisely," Pasquale replied, elated at his change of fortune.

"I hope you will," his mother had replied. "But I know the first thing you'll do. You'll buy a passage on a ship to some distant and dangerous land."

She was right. But Pasquale did better than just buy a passage. His inheritance was substantial but quite modest compared to what other, more established businessmen put towards an investment. He soon realized that most ships were fully booked and that the only caravel with room and opportunity for speculation was the *Santa Magdalena* under the command of Alvarez and it was sailing to Africa for gold.

At the time, the *Santa Magdalena* had been an old and poorly refurbished caravel of doubtful seaworthiness. He thought it too risky to put money on such a dilapidated vessel. However, Pasquale was desperate for a high yielding investment and so the *Santa*

*Magdalena,* despite its rundown state, seemed the answer to his prayers, especially when Alvarez refurbished it.

Alvarez had also agreed to take him as the ship's scribe, a diarist to document events during the ship's voyage, although Alvarez didn't see the need for a scribe. He remained skeptical, although Pasquale told him that all the important explorers had one. In the end, he had acquiesced and told Pasquale to suit himself; it was his money after all.

Pasquale was overjoyed. He was now both the ship's chronicler and a major investor in the *Santa Magdalena*; he was also combining his two dreams into one—sea travel and writing. He was now a gentleman sailor, a fidalgo by lineage and in time would be rich enough to do what he pleased. Soon he would open his own print shop.

# CHAPTER

# 6

U demezue was preparing for the Great River market. It would take him a few weeks to gather everything that he needed. The room was small and was already packed with half-full baskets. His *obi* was smaller than his father's, and he did not have an attached workshop.

"Is anybody home?" Onaedo called from outside.

"I'm home. Come in," he said gesturing for her to enter. She stood next to him and looked around. "I see that you're getting ready for your trip," Onaedo said, eyeing the baskets of kola-nuts, the pile of animal skins and the few ivory tusks.

Udemezue was glad she had come. When he had seen her a few days ago at their mother's house, he'd looked at her face and knew that something was wrong but Onaedo had brushed aside his concerns by saying she was sick with *iba*. Udemezue knew that what ailed her was more than just fever.

"I thought I heard your voice." It was Udemezue's wife Odera coming in from the yard. "Here, take the baby. She wants to greet you." She gave Onaedo the baby who seemed excited to see her aunt and went back to the backyard to continue the food preparation.

"What's wrong?" Udemezue asked when they were alone again.

"Nothing," Onaedo said.

Udemezue sighed. "You can tell me. I promise not to be angry."
She told him about Dualo. Udemezue listened quietly.

"I don't know why he left without even telling me," she said, her
eyes brimming with tears. She wiped them with the back of one hand,
while bouncing the baby with the other. "All this time I've tried to
hide my feelings, so please don't tell Ugodi. You know how she is."

"Don't worry, I won't. But listen to me, Onaedo, there are a
lot of young men who would marry you, and they're ready now. You
must forget this Dualo fellow and find somebody else."

Odera returned from the yard. She looked from Onaedo to
Udemezue. "What's going on?"

"It's none of your business. I was just discussing family matters
with my sister," Udemezue said.

"And I'm not family? You can't tell me why Onaedo has a river
flowing down her face?"

"Who said I was crying?" Onaedo countered.

Odera looked at her, shook her head, and rolled her eyes. "Let
it be like you said then. I won't ask again. Anyway, I came to tell
you that the food will be late. I turned my back for a moment and
the whole pot of soup burnt just like that," she said snapping her
fingers.

Udemezue and Onaedo exchanged a quick glance, trying hard
not to laugh. Odera was a devoted wife but cooking was not one of
her strong attributes.

"We'll all go hungry then," Udemezue said, catching
Onaedo's eye and shaking his head. He didn't want her to tell
his wife that he had already eaten at their mother's. He would let
Odera fret for a while.

When Odera left to salvage what she could of the rest of the
meal, they looked at each other and laughed. At the back of his mind,
Udemezue was relieved that Onaedo had not done something foolish, like get pregnant.

∞

"Eneda, are you up already?" Udemezue greeted his father as he crossed the threshold of his father's *obi* the next day.

"Yes. Are you here to help me?" the old man asked. He was piling charcoal into the kiln with the help of one of his apprentices. Udemezue thought that Eneda was getting too old to be doing such physical work but his father did not want to hear anything like that.

Eneda sat and turned the coals in the kiln with an absentminded rhythm. The embers glowed a mesmerizing orange beneath piles of gray ash. Udemezue sat quietly in one corner; his father hated unnecessary small talk while he worked.

He picked up a flywhisk handle his father had made. It was easy to see the hours of meticulous work that Eneda poured into his craft in the lifelike metal fly he'd designed to perch at the base. The carved birds and metal leaves almost seemed to flutter if one looked at it in a certain way. Udemezue was sure that they would sell well when he took them to the Great River. Eneda usually gave him some for the market, although most of his work was done on commission and he had very few to spare. Udemezue watched him go back to a corner of the room pick up a block of beeswax. He had already shaped it into a narrow-necked vase and proceeded to carve designs on it. This was the first step in a process that would eventually end in a bronze vessel.

"What do you think, Udemezue?" Eneda asked, handing it to him after a while. Udemezue examined it as one might evaluate a precious article. It was a cold and heavy piece of pale wax, but from its depths emerged details of the vessel it would become. It would have encircling metal ropes and realistic knots that would decorate its curved, smooth body

"*Omaka*. Its beautiful," Udemezue said, giving it back.

Eneda raised it for a final examination, looking for hidden flaws. He frowned, took a small pointed knife, and swiftly scratched details of a small lizard around its narrow neck. He held it up again and this time nodded in satisfaction before pulling forward a container of soft clay. He hummed as his long fingers worked the clay over the hardened wax until it was completely coated. Then he put it aside to dry. He walked back to the kiln where one of his apprentices was working the bellows.

"Take those dry pots here," he instructed. "Udemezue, help me put these in the fire to cook." Together, they put the clay-coated wax objects in the fire.

After they loaded the kiln, he sat with Udemezue and they watched the wax melt inside each clay object as the outer clay hardened.

Later, one of the boys brought a giant, metal spoon with the molten metal, a mixture of copper and tin. Eneda poured the liquid metal into each empty clay mold, swirled it around and left it to cool. He would break the outer clay later to reveal the metal object he'd created.

He gave Udemezue a cup to admire before adding it to a growing pile of pots, bowls, cups, spear tips, fly whisks, and knife handles.

Udemezue had not realized the passage of time. He looked outside. The sun was already at the point it in the sky when shadows grew short before elongating again. Working with Eneda always made him lose track of time.

"Are you sure that you haven't changed your mind about working for me?" Eneda asked, as if reading his mind.

Udemezue smiled and said nothing. He had this conversation with his father all the time.

Eneda shook his head. "Do you want to take any of these to the market with you?"

Udemezue pointed out a decorative bowl, a scabbard, and a fly-whisk. "What are these markings?" he asked, running a hand over the belly of a vase that was covered with pictograms.

"Oh, that's *nsibidi* writing," Eneda said, taking the vase from his son and turning it around.

"What is it?"

"Secret writing. I learned to write as a young boy when I lived with my maternal grandfather among the riverine Ibibio people."

"Oh yes, I remember. You promised to teach me to read it but you never did."

"That's because you are never here and you have to belong to a secret cult there first," his father replied. "Only the members can learn it."

"So, does this say anything?" Udemezue asked, turning the vase over again.

"Of course it says something," Eneda replied. He took the vessel from him and held it to his face. His eyes narrowed in concentration. "It says right here that Udemezue's trip to the Great River market will be very successful."

Udemezue looked at him in surprise until he caught the twinkle in the old man's eye. They continued their work in silence after that.

∞∞

Udemezue lay awake in bed that night, as sleep eluded him. He thought of the choice he'd made years ago to not be a blacksmith like his father. His two older half-brothers were quite well off as blacksmiths, although neither had their father's exceptional talent. They had learned the trade from Eneda and set up their own workshops, independently, in the town. Maybe he should have done the same thing.

"What did you say?" Odera asked from across the room where she sat on a mat with the baby. She still shared the room with him because her house was not ready. He would finish it as soon as he returned from this trip.

"I didn't realize I was thinking aloud," he replied. "Sleep well."

In the distance, the messenger's drum could be heard faint at first, then growing louder as the he approached. He found a firm voice for the important message.

"He's late today," Odera commented in the darkness as they waited for the message.

They could hear his words clearly now. He announced meetings for various groups.

They waited for the crier to complete his message in the manner that every Abonani man, woman, and child knew by heart.

It started by warning the Ezeigwe that an Abonani king did not have more powers than the people he ruled.

*"All who have ears listen to this;*
*This is the warning of the people to the king,*
*Let the Ezeigwe not forget that he rules only by the*
*    agreement of the people.*
*He must seek the will of the people.*
*If he does not, disaster will come to him.*

*Who tells a deaf man that the market is in stampede?*
*Abonani people endure kings only under duress*
*Igbo enwe eze—the Igbo do not want kings.*
*So be careful, Ezeigwe Abonani."*

This strange message, somewhat hostile to the king, was an ancient nightly ritual that puzzled strangers to Abonani. Why have kings at all, Udemezue had heard strangers ask people from Abonani, if you are going to have this nightly ritual of warning them of their impending demise?

"The fathers of the clans and towns make these warnings to prevent the abuse of power. The Ezeigwe's power comes from the people and can be revoked at any time," Eneda told him a long time ago.

The messenger was gone and, as he slept, Udemezue dreamed a strange dream that Onaedo, although a woman, had become a black-smith like their father.

CHAPTER

# 7

"Did I tell you the story of how my uncle married my first wife for me after my father died?" Eneda asked Onaedo one evening. They had just finished eating in silence. "That was long time ago; before I married your mother."

Onaedo laughed and pretended that she hadn't heard the story before because she wanted him to tell it again. The story was something of a family joke and a source of amusement to everybody. Everybody, that is, except First Wife, Eneda's oldest wife, who did not find it funny. In fact, anybody who she heard tell it, was sure to be hit with whatever was handy, a stick, a broom, or a whip.

Eneda chuckled. "I was still a young man when my uncle decided to marry a wife for me. I was a busy blacksmith then, just starting out and trying to perfect my craft. He brought her to me during my busy time and I forgot that she was around. After spending a whole month and barely seeing me, she threatened to leave and return to her father. She was tired of cooking and cleaning for a husband that paid her no attention, and she was tired of sleeping alone at night."

Onaedo knew the rest of the story. Eneda's old uncle, upon learning of the situation, had at once summoned a family meeting with the *umunna*, the male kindred, to bring Eneda to his senses.

Eneda had told them that he was too busy and could not interrupt his work for a meeting in his house to which he had invited no one.

"That's exactly what I said to them," Eneda said, laughing. It was obvious that the story still amused him even after so many years. Onaedo joined in his laughter but looked around a little uncertainly; she hoped First Wife was not anywhere near. "You know what they said to me?" Eneda asked.

"No. What did they say?"

"'You are not the only blacksmith that we have seen in Abonani. When we observe a senile neighbor eat chicken shit, we do not look away and say that this is not our concern, because any sickness he gets contaminates everybody else. People who observe your behavior will think that we have *agwu* or madness in our family, and that is our concern and the reason we are here.'" Eneda paused to take a sip of water. "Anyway they gave me an earful and, after that, I had to promise to become a better husband."

Hearing the story again today, under her current circumstances, Onaedo didn't think it was so funny after all. If she married Dualo and he ignored her like that, she would be furious. She stopped. Dualo was gone. Why still think about him?

"I was foolish then," Eneda added. "She has been a good wife. But back then she could have been the most beautiful woman in *Olu n'Igbo* and I would have chosen my work over her. I think that is what annoys her to this day when she hears this story."

There was a noise outside. Onaedo stepped out of the *obi*. It was only her mother's lineage nanny goat foraging for food with her three kids. One of the female kids would become hers when she married and started her own pedigree. She went back inside and returned to her seat.

"Come, I want you to help me with something," Eneda said, leading the way. "The *Ofala* festival is soon and you can help me put things together." When they were in the backroom, he reached towards a ledge and took down his skin bag before he sat spread-eagle on the floor beside his wooden bed.

Onaedo sat on a low stool across from him as he began to assemble all he would need for the yearly ceremonies of thanksgiving and the Ezeigwe's coming out that was attended by every Abonani man, woman, and child. Eneda was the Ezeigwe's chief adviser, the custodian of the clan's collective memory and chronicler of its history. His charge was to leave clues on his metalwork to tell their story that would survive the passage of time. As blacksmith, his role was very important in the life of the clan. He was the maker of her war weapons and peaceful instruments of survival, including machetes, hoes, and *mbazu* or yam diggers. He also designed the ceremonial paraphernalia used for all important rituals.

He told Onaedo that, many years ago, Abonani had approached him to become the chief priest and hence the spiritual leader of the clan, a position that was second only to that of the Ezeigwe, but Eneda had politely declined.

"I didn't want anything that would stand in the way of my work," he had confided in her. "Of course, I did not say it like that. Instead, I told them that my spirit did not receive that kind of responsibility. They didn't like my decision but they accepted it."

Onaedo knew many people didn't understand her father's passion for his work. Some even thought he had a little *agwu*, the quirkiness that made him sometimes act peculiarly. It was part of his legend and eccentricity and all in keeping with his formidable talent.

Onaedo helped him count each object—two large ostrich feathers, nine cowry shells strung in a strand of elephant hair, one round chalk for painting his body, four smooth, black, shiny stones representing the four market days of the week, the skull of a baboon, along with its teeth and thigh bones, and a small knife with a decorated metal handle.

He carefully placed them in a semi-circle and counted them again. Just like everybody else, he was going to make the biggest sacrifice of the year in the coming weeks, maybe even a goat this time, Onaedo thought.

After he was satisfied that things were in order, he packed the bag and hauled himself up from the floor by grabbing the edge of the wooden bed, nearly losing his balance.

"One day, I'm going to fall out of this thing and break a bone. My back feels like there's something loose in it."

"Do you want help?" Onaedo asked, reaching out to steady him.

He waved her hand away. "It's old age; it creeps up on you slowly like a bad custom." He looked at his wooden bed ruefully. "You know, I paid a local carpenter a fortune to make this bed because I heard it was the fashion someplace to sleep high above the ground. Now I'm beginning to miss my mat on the floor."

Onaedo laughed, stood, and picked up the small clay container with the palm oil-soaked *uli*. The wick gave off a smoky flame. It was almost halfway burned down and she reminded herself to pick more of the *uli* fronds from the special palm tree that grew just outside the compound. It was her marker tree, where her umbilical cord was buried and indicated to all and sundry that this was her ancestral home.

"Sit again," Eneda said. "I want to talk to you." He turned until he was facing her. "Tell me why you don't want to marry all the fine young men that have come to ask for you?"

Onaedo was taken aback. Her father usually paid little attention to her business. This was Ugodi's territory. Did he know about Dualo? She hoped not because that would be disastrous. It was one thing to lie to her mother but lying to her father was a different matter.

Her heart pounded and her mouth was dry. She looked up and saw him watching her and immediately dropped her gaze to the ground. They both waited in the ensuing silence.

"Did I not ask you a question?" Eneda asked again after a while.

"I'm waiting to find somebody that will cherish me," Onaedo finally answered in a low voice, "the way that you have loved my mother."

Her father nodded, listening intently, before he spoke. "To find the same thing I have with your mother will be difficult," he said slowly. "I married two wives before I found her. That is not to say that I do not love my other wives," he added quickly. "I do. But your mother is special. I try not to show any favoritism because I want a peaceful household. But you're a woman and you should not place your eyes on unreachable things or you will never be satisfied or happy. Choose somebody that is respectable and treats you well and the love will come later."

Onaedo nodded and, after a little while, rose and left with the smoking lamp and the empty soup bowl. When she looked back into the room, she could not see him in the darkness.

ᘛᘚ

The *Ofala* arrived with the cold air of the harmattan winds that blew all the way from the far northern lands. This was the time the Ezeigwe reaffirmed the tenets of his office and rededicated himself to his sacred duty to serve the people who gathered at the *obi eze* to watch him do it. The day before the actual ceremony, Onaedo helped her father with his own final preparations.

"The people of Abonani came from nowhere," Eneda said. Onaedo was the only one in the room and she sat to listen to the story of their arrival to the land they now called Abonani.

"Abonani appeared in a manner comparable to how yams appeared to feed man on earth—mysteriously and spontaneously. It sprung from the bowels of the earth in the dawn of time when the world that was so young it was still such a strange place for humans; back then, the ancient and ageless *iroko* tree was still a mere sapling and the giant agama lizard still had a voice and did not just nod his head to every question." He paused as he continued meticulously carving patterns on a block of wax.

"But there is another story. A long time ago, there was a kingdom to the north—a beautiful territory straddling both thick forests and grasslands. The earth was so fertile that yam vines grew into trees and the tubers dug from the earth stood like giants.

"One day, marauders with heads wrapped in dark cloth and riding on horses attacked them. They fought back but eventually they had to abandon their open lands and retreat into the security of the thick forests.

"As the attacks continued, nine men and their families came together and decided to leave. They believed the ruling king was less interested in protecting his people than in supporting his opulent lifestyle.

"They vowed not to have a king again. They wanted to found a new town that they would call Abo-ite-nani or Eboteghete or Abonani for short—all of which meant The Nine Villages said in three different ways.

"So our ancestors began their trek through forests so thick that they grew back right in front of their eyes, even as they cut a path through them. They met hordes of elephants and lions that gave them safe passage. They travelled for many months until they arrived at the Great River.

"Their leader was a man called Somadina—I Will Not Be Alone. He once killed an errant elephant with his bare hands and is immortalized as the primary founder of Abonani, though his *obi* vanished years later. This was because his many wives all produced daughters and his lineage died out. But his legend is undying till today and he does not need sons to tell his story.

"When they arrived at the Great River, they realized that they were not water people and did not have the expertise to tame such a grandiose river. They decided to retreat until they picked this spot and built our town.

"The new society was different from the one they had left. They had no king or *eze* and were ruled by elders and titled men whose words, when spoken, stood firm on the ground."

Onaedo asked automatically as she was expected to. "So why do we have a king today?"

Eneda paused and frowned as he gazed intently at the wax form in his hand without looking at her directly. "It's another long story that will be told another day."

Onaedo smiled and said nothing more. This was their routine.

ကက

*Ofala* day arrived with its traditional fanfare. Onaedo was ready early, even though she had stayed up late into the night polishing her mother's ceremonial ivory ankle braces.

The Ezeigwe's compound was full and some had to stay beyond the perimeter wall. Expectation hung in the air with the waiting. The palace or *obi-eze* was not as grand as the palace of the Delta king, but the Abonani people did not care; they had helped build it and were happy with it.

Onaedo and her friends were already ensconced at an advantageous spot.

"Where is Adanma?" someone asked

"She'll be here later. Has anybody seen Nonye?" Onaedo asked, looking around.

"She's standing over there," somebody else said pointing towards a crowded area of the square.

"Who's she talking to?"

"I don't know. I've never seen him before." The young man was unfamiliar to Onaedo also, but he seemed to know a lot of locals judging from the way he laughed and joked with the people standing around him.

She looked around for Adanma and instinctively sought out Udemezue towards the back of the crowd. He was also surrounded by friends. He was back from his trip and was already planning another one. Trading at the Great River market had been very profitable this time around.

She closed her eyes and felt the warmth of the morning sun. The crowd swelled. She suddenly felt Dualo's presence everywhere like he still worked here. She opened her eyes and the moment passed.

Ugodi sat in the front row with the few women that held titles in Abonani. They were dressed alike in heavy white cotton wrappa and ivory ankle braces or *odu*. They had earned the privilege to sit alongside the men.

The Ezeigwe emerged from his *obi* followed by Abonani's Chief Priest and then the rest of the elders including Eneda. They all sat down and Chief Priest began the ceremony.

The Ezeigwe wore a headband of multi-colored beads that hung over his face; his eyes peeked from between its strands. His thick, dark-red cloth looked warm. He was a flamboyant man and Onaedo recalled that his choice of apparel had generated controversy a few years ago when he decided to jettison the traditional white cotton drape for what others considered unsuitable colors—green one year, blue the next and red today. Eneda and a few others had supported him and forced the affronted traditionalists to accept it, which they had grudgingly done. The truth was that there was no clear rule about what kind of attire an Ezeigwe could wear.

Onaedo did not see Oguebie among the titled men. In fact, she hadn't seen him since their encounter in the forest months ago. She had finally learned about his role in Dualo's sudden trip to the Delta City. It was Nonye again who had apprised her of the details. Dualo's uncle had followed the lure of lucrative work south with Oguebie. Who could blame him? But Onaedo had not felt any better; Dualo should still have found a way to let her know that he was leaving.

She tried to pay attention to the story unfolding. "Many centuries after the Abonani people settled here," the storyteller started, "we were tested with a drought and a famine. Fires destroyed our farms and locusts ate what remained. Hunger arrived with its mat and was prepared to stay.

"Our ancestors consulted medicine men and deities all over *Olu n'Igbo* but overlooked the great deity *Igwe-ka-Ani*. The people did not know it had come with them from the old country. It was secretly housed in a cave outside the new settlement.

"Its existence was shrouded in secrecy; *Igwe-ka-Ani* was the symbol of kingship in the old kingdom and Abonani had said that they did not want any kings in their new society.

"They were angry that somebody had brought the symbol of oppression to the new country. Nobody today knew whether

Somadina knew of this intrigue but he was long gone and nobody could ask him. But by now they were desperate and decided to give the deity renewed status."

Onaedo became lost in her daydreaming again. She knew the rest of the story. *Igwe-ka-Ani* advised the Abonani people to send a volunteer to the land of the ancestors, a place they said was inside the Caves-With-Endless-Tunnels located just outside the town. Umelo was the name of the young man. Barely five days after he left, heavy rains returned to fertilize the earth. Abonani had been saved, but the price that they paid was to follow the deity's directions in appointing a new king.

"Our people did not want an *eze*," the storyteller had raised his voice in what ages ago must have symbolized the nidus of passionate dissent. "Eventually, a compromise was reached. Abonani would agree to accept a king but with limitations. He would have no power of life and death over anyone, whether freeborn or slave. He would rule by consensus, and the priest of *Igwe-ka-Ani* would perform every installation of a new Ezeigwe. So we remind the Ezeigwe every night of his contract with Abonani." He stopped and his eyes swept the crowd. "I have finished my job as the re-teller of our people's story."

ဢ

"What took you so long?" Onaedo asked Adanma who had appeared by her side.

"You know me; I was getting ready," Adanma answered.

"You look beautiful," Onaedo said, looking her up and down. She had a new wrappa and two new combs in her hair.

"Thank you, but there is a man that has been looking at you all morning," Adanma replied, gesturing with an unobtrusive movement of her chin. Onaedo looked without appearing to do so. It was the young man that she'd seen earlier with Nonye. He stared intently at her and she looked away quickly but not before she hastily took a measure of him. He was about her height, dark-skinned and slender in a well-proportioned, masculine way. He looked overconfident, and he had actually smiled at her familiarly when their eyes had briefly locked.

"Who is he?" she whispered out of the corner of her mouth.

"I don't know, but I can find out for you," Adanma replied in an equally low tone.

"Don't bother. I'm not really interested right now."

"Why not? Is it because of Dualo?"

"No, it's not because of Dualo. I'm just tired of men in general."

"That is crazy talk, Onaedo. Anyway, I'm going to find out who he is. You can say no if he comes to talk to you."

"You can't just approach a group of young men and start asking questions," Onaedo whispered urgently, pressing a restraining hand on Adanma's elbow. "Everybody will think you're too forward."

"Let them think what they want," Adanma said shrugging her off. "But don't worry, I'll be discreet."

"I've already told you, I'm not interested," Onaedo hissed.

"We'll see, when the time comes," replied Adanma. She moved away cutting through the crowd.

Onaedo sighed in exasperation. She tried not to look in his direction again but felt his eyes on her.

∞

Later that evening, Onaedo helped her mother undress. She lubricated Ugodi's feet with shea butter and slipped off the ivory cylinders. She thought of a story she heard as a child about a woman in antiquity who had been so proud of her achievements represented by the bestowing on her of ivory anklets that she opted to wear them permanently in idle discomfort till death. Onaedo doubted the veracity of that story but thought that such discomfort done in the name of beauty was stupid. However, she knew that she dared not express such heresy aloud for fear of raising her mother's ire. Ugodi and the handful of female *ozo* titleholders had fought hard for generations to be an alternative authority in the life of the clan; if they had to wear anklets to stay there, it was a small price to pay.

Ugodi leaned over to rub her chaffed ankles.

"Is anybody home?" It was Aku at the gate.

"Come in. We're home," Ugodi called back.

"Did they tell you I've been here twice already?" Aku said, looking at Ugodi's raw legs. "Beauty has its own burdens. Your legs look painful."

Onaedo offered Aku her stool but she waved it away and instead sat on the mat near her sister.

"I admire those things you wear around your ankle, my sister, but I don't think I can ever wear them, not with the pain I have in my joints. My feet hurt enough as it is. Anyway, I don't have the kind of money you do." She turned to Onaedo, "Please, my daughter, bring me some drinking water. My throat is dry."

Aku paused for the first time in her long speech. Onaedo marveled at how her aunt could weave together so many ideas in one sentence without drawing breath.

"Is your throat dry from talking all day?" Ugodi asked, teasing. Onaedo was used to the women making fun of each other and fighting like two territorial cocks when they disagreed. Even their husbands and children knew when to stay out of the way.

"I see that you're just coming back from *Ofala*," Aku said. She fingered the cloth that Ugodi had folded neatly on a stool for Onaedo to put away. "How did it go?"

"It went well, as usual," Ugodi replied. "Where were you? It's not like you to miss something like this."

Aku drank the cold water, wiped her mouth, and asked Onaedo for more. "I didn't go this time because I'm tired of going every year. I decided to rest at home this time. Moreover, we're preparing for our new wife next week. I had to collect all the things that her people have asked for."

"Like what?" Ugodi asked.

Aku gave a long sigh. "Let me tell you now, make sure none of your children marry from Iredu village. Their elders have made a business out of taking advantage of men that come to marry their girls. If she's pretty at all, they place the bride-price so high that one must almost go into debt to be able to afford her."

"Is that so?" Ugodi exclaimed. "It's good you told me because one of my husband's sons is planning to take a wife from there."

"Aah, tell him to run away as fast as his legs can carry him unless he has a lot of money, because they will chew a hole in his money bag to get at it. I told them that their men folk will drive away potential suitors if marriage to their daughters ends up bankrupting a man. *Tufia*!" she exclaimed, snapping her fingers in disgust. "I have never seen a thing like that. The women aren't happy about it, but women are not involved in setting the bride-price. But I still think they know what to do if they want change."

"So why did you people go to marry a wife from there anyway? You could have gone anywhere else."

"You have to ask my husband that. He saw this young woman and decided he now has to have another wife," Aku said. "So I'm just helping him so my enemies will not say I'm not happy. In fact, I am thrilled for him."

"So that husband of yours is not tired of wives. How many is he going to acquire?" Ugodi asked half joking.

That was a sour point for her aunt. Onaedo knew that Aku's husband was notorious for his penchant for ever-younger wives. She had often wondered what any young woman would see in him. He was short and not particularly good looking and always had a dour manner, but her aunt didn't seem to mind and was in fact quite devoted to him.

Predictably, Aku's response was heated. "Is it now against the law to marry wives that you can afford?" she retorted, clearly irritated with her sister. "Do you not see with your eyes how young and rested I look? While he's occupied with his young wife who will soon tire him out, I can indulge in things that are important to me. In any case, I haven't complained to you, have I?"

Onaedo realized that the sisters were on dangerous ground, especially if Ugodi responded in similar fashion.

It was time to intervene. "I picked you some *udala*," she said, coming forward to offer to her aunt the small golden pear shaped fruits. "I found them myself this morning. The last rain of the season fell on them last night, so they're sweet."

Aku looked like she was going to refuse at first, but reluctantly took the peace offering but not before she turned to glare at Ugodi again as she addressed Onaedo. "Thank you, my daughter. If not for you, I would leave now. I didn't come here to be insulted by my own flesh and blood."

She squeezed on one of the fruits until its waxy, smooth, golden skin split open revealing the fleshy interior. She examined it closely for worms before taking a bite. She grimaced. "This one slaps at the cheek," she said commenting on its tartness.

"Be patient, the sweetness comes later," Onaedo said, also offering her mother a fruit.

Ugodi pushed her hand away impatiently. She tightened her lips as if to stifle the rejoinder to Aku's tirade.

Onaedo was relieved when Ugodi changed the subject.

"Udemezue's wife is pregnant again."

"Ooh?" Aku replied, looking more interested in the fruit she was scrutinizing than in Ugodi's concern for her daughter-in-law.

Onaedo sighed. Clearly, the current feud between her mother and aunt was not over yet.

"I need your help to prevent what happened the last time," Ugodi said evenly.

"She'll be fine," Aku replied. She piled the black, bean-shaped *udala* seeds on the mat beside her. The children would dry them later and use them as counters.

"How do you know she'll be fine?" Ugodi asked. "Did you see something?"

Onaedo looked at her aunt and wondered how she'd respond. Everybody knew that Aku possessed what was known as The Sight. She could on rare occasions See into the future. To Onaedo, this was a frightening ability. She remembered, as a child, her dread of Aku soon after she learned of her gift. She had heard it first from other children and asked her mother about it. From then she observed that Aku never seemed to foresee happy events, but only omens that were bad and frightening. It was as if in her aunt's eerie world of mysticism, positive happenings were not worthy of prediction.

Onaedo tried to measure her aunt's response, but Aku was looking at her mother with rising irritation. That was another thing she disliked, discussions about The Sight. To Onaedo, she had always acted like the reluctant recipient of an unwelcome gift. Unlike some others who had even less of a gift, Aku had always refused to build a lucrative business around it. "You would have been rich by now," Ugodi often nagged her. "People would pay to hear what you have to say." To which Aku would reply that there were things more important than riches.

Now she re-arranged the *udala* seeds into a circular pattern on the mat, taking her time before she replied. "I've told you before that I have no control over what I see," she replied. "Moreover, what I see is not always what I want to know; I cannot tell you what is going to happen to Odera this time, but as a midwife, I know that this pregnancy is different. It is going to go well. I don't think she'll do the crazy things she did the last time."

Ugodi seemed unconvinced. "I still want to make sure. I'm thinking of my son Udemezue, who bore the brunt of the whole thing the last time."

Onaedo understood why her mother was so worried. It had taken many weeks of sequestering Odera in the house of the local *dibia* for the medicine man to control her illness. Her baby had had to go to a wet nurse because, it was thought, Odera's breast-milk had been poisoned by her mental illness. Thankfully, it had resolved as suddenly as it had started but not before they had spent a lot of money in search of a cure.

"Well, if you have money to waste on a needless sacrifice I won't stop you," Aku said, sounding unhelpful. "Just name the day and I'll wake up early and go with you."

Ugodi looked frustrated with her sister. It seemed like Aku was in a contrary mood today. Onaedo looked at her aunt, still busy counting the shiny seeds. She looked as well-groomed as usual. Her reddish-brown hair was cut low in a meandering pattern on her scalp. This was most likely in readiness for her husband's upcoming marriage ceremony.

Ugodi told her that, as children, she had doubted that Aku really possessed The Sight and wondered if she made outrageous claims for attention. "But when I stopped doubting was after the incident with our grandfather," Ugodi had told her. Onaedo remembered that story well; the one that recounted what happened to their grandfather in his workshop one early morning. "He was a mask-carver and not a hunter," Ugodi had said, "so he rarely went to the forest. One morning, he was surprised by an albino tiger. It gored him right in front of his workshop just as the market was gathering. Nobody had seen a tiger in these parts for generations, and certainly never an albino one that had only been described in legends. A week before the incident, Aku had described our grandfather's death in full detail to me and my mother. My mother was shocked and warned her not to mention it to anybody else. So when she heard what happened that day she said she almost passed hot urine down her legs; was her daughter Aku now a sorceress? We kept it a secret for as long as we could but, with time, other things happened and we couldn't hide Aku's unusual gift; one cannot cover a pregnancy with one's hands.

"People heard of her abilities and came to revere her for them. But she keeps most of what she knows to herself and most people have forgotten that she even has The Sight," Ugodi added regretfully. "She never wanted to make money from it. Another thing that surprises me is that nobody else in our family ever had that gift, before or after Aku, even though they say that such things run in families."

Ugodi had told her this story a long time ago and, afterwards, Onaedo had examined her own memory and dreams for a sign that she might have inherited The Sight. She was relieved when it seemed she had not.

"Did you discuss the issue of the women's attire at the last women's meeting?" Aku asked, changing the subject. "Onaedo, you were there too."

"Yes I was there, but I wasn't paying attention," Onaedo said.

"I don't know why I take you to all these meetings," Ugodi said, scolding her daughter. "You never listen to what's said."

"Leave the poor girl alone. She didn't say that she never listens; she just didn't listen this time."

Onaedo silently thanked Aku as her mother explained what had transpired at the meeting.

"The women decided that the men could not tell us what to wear. We'll buy foreign cloth if we like. The local weavers have not complained. They know they cannot keep up with demand. I asked one of them almost a year ago to weave something special for me for the ceremony today but when I went to collect it a few days ago, it wasn't ready. Thread was everywhere on the floor but no cloth. Can you believe that? I had to wear my old cloth that Udemezue bought for me years ago."

"I know that particular weaver; she's become quite lazy," Aku said. "But I wonder what was behind that nonsense in the first place. Why did our men think they should now dictate our fashion? We don't dress for them."

"No, we dress to make other women jealous," Ugodi said laughing.

Aku joined in the laughter, their earlier quarrel forgotten. Just then, Adanma's younger brother came in with a message for Onaedo. She wanted Onaedo to come to her house when she was finished with her chores.

# 8

U demezue entered Eneda's *obi* to tell him that he was going back to the Great River market. His father had had guests before Udemezue arrived and Onaedo was collecting the flat-bottomed gourds that were lying around. Some were still half-full of palm-wine and she poured them together to take to the women in the yard later. The sweet smell of the wine made her thirsty but she knew better than to drink around her father.

"The feast is over. Why were you so late?" Eneda asked, reclining on the mud ledge that ran around the walls of the *obi*.

"I was collecting the goods that I'd ordered to take with me to the market. Everybody is rushing to stockpile merchandise."

Onaedo took her favorite vantage point as Udemezue explained to Eneda the reason why he was going back so soon to the Great River market. Her father looked tired and sleepy.

"We had such a successful market the last time. So we decided not to wait. We'll return right away."

"Oh?" Eneda said yawning. "You complained of a bad market for almost a year. What's changed?"

"I don't know why things changed," Udemezue replied. He poured some wine into a large cow-horn that served as a drinking cup. "But for the first time, some white merchants are coming across the river from the Delta City to buy goods directly from us, bypassing the middle-man altogether. That means better prices for our merchandise. Although I cannot tell you what has led to this change, we are not going to say no to it. We made so much profit the last time that I already have almost half the money I need for my title."

"So they're back again," Eneda said, stroking his chin slowly. "I heard that too."

Both Udemezue and Onaedo looked at Eneda in surprise.

"What did you hear?" Udemezue asked.

"I heard what you just told me," Eneda replied, "that the white man is now crossing the Great River to our side." His fixed his gaze on his son as if searching for something unfathomable. Onaedo looked at the wall above his head where a pair of geckos gobbled insects with long sticky tongues.

"Where did you hear this?" Udemezue asked.

"I hear things," Eneda replied. "I may sit here all day, but I know things that happen in all *Olu n'Igbo*." He shifted on his stool as he adjusted his loincloth. "What did I tell you when you first went to the Great River market?" He asked his son but continued without waiting for an answer. "A traveled man is a rich man. His wealth is measured in knowledge and experience. Our people have always been too isolated; we look with suspicion at new things and other people's customs, forgetting that that is how progress comes to a people. I see that you're surprised. Perhaps you think that because I'm an upholder of tradition I should be threatened by progress, but you are wrong. I'm not asking for important things to change. I just want us to be ready for it when it comes. That means we should know our adversaries before they know us.

"And that's why I didn't prevent you from trading, even though I would have preferred that you followed me and became a black-smith; you have the most talent. But my two older sons who are also blacksmiths have done well with it and that makes me happy too. When I saw that traveling was in your blood, I left you alone. All I ask is that you keep a clear eye and an open ear and run when they tell you to run."

"Are you trying to tell me something?" Udemezue asked. Onaedo slapped an insect on her leg.

Eneda smiled enigmatically. "What can I tell you? I've never seen a white man myself, but I hear that they come from their country in boats as big as mountains; everybody knows that. Usually they are content to trade with us through others, and stay back at the Delta City. We all know that too. What we don't know is why he has now suddenly decided to cross the Great River to come over to our side. I want you to benefit from the profit you are making, my son; a good trader must show something for his labor, but I also want you to look beyond the profit."

The room fell silent. All three seemed to hug their thoughts closely. Onaedo's mind wandered. She thought about the young man at the *Ofala*. Adanma had told her his name was Amechi and that he was interested in her. He sounded intriguing. Adanma thought so too.

"I've been meaning to ask you this for years," Udemezue said to their father. "Do you think that it was a good thing for our people to embrace the kingship again?" Onaedo's eyes flew open. This was interesting.

"I've wondered about that too," Eneda replied. "But one should not question a decision the clan made in ancient times to ensure their survival. The times were different then. Maybe we should not have made it hereditary, although the present Ezeigwe is not a bad man, but . . ." he paused looking at Onaedo and she understood that his next words were never to leave his *obi*. ". . . the thing that worries me about him is how he handles his half-brother, Oguebie. He's much too permissive. That man, Oguebie is ready to plunge this clan into something that will engulf all of us and the worry it gives me eats food from my stomach every day. I hear that he has gone back to the Delta City. No one seems to know what business he does over there. All we hear are rumors."

"What is the real story behind Oguebie's anger?" Udemezue asked.

"He is the Ezeigwe's half-brother. Because they nursed from the same breast, people sometimes forget that they are not from the same mother. They were born at the same time to two different wives. The strange thing is that to this day nobody is certain who is the older of the two, Oguebie or the Ezeigwe. They arrived on the same morning. One was born at home and the other while his mother was on the road. They brought the news of the two births to their father at the same time and he had to choose which child he would call the firstborn. Oguebie never accepted the fact that he was chosen to be the second son. His mother died shortly after he was born and that added to his resentment. He felt that nobody spoke for him. It didn't matter to him that the surviving wife took care of both sons; Oguebie would not let it go. He's held a grudge since."

"But that's not the fault of Abonani. It's a family matter with their late father."

"You're right but a lot depended on that choice. That selection decided who the next Ezeigwe would be. Years ago, when their father died, Oguebie raised the issue again with the Abonani ruling council, *ndi-ichie* and *ndi ozo* even bringing witnesses who testified that his mother gave birth earlier on that day. The clan deliberated, but ruled in favor of the present Ezeigwe. Everybody felt by then that Oguebie was a bad seed, always involved in something unsavory. Nobody wants such a man as the Ezeigwe. Now he's angry at everybody."

"I never knew all these details." Udemezue said. Onaedo smiled; she'd heard this story from her father years ago.

"It is not fitting for me as the chief adviser to the Ezeigwe to criticize him, so what I'm saying cannot leave this *obi*," Eneda said, "but as I said, he protects Oguebie unnecessarily from the consequences of his actions at the expense of the clan, and that is a sign of weakness. The love between the two brothers is one sided because Oguebie thinks only of himself."

"He is also as slippery as a snake from what I've heard," Udemezue added. "It's difficult to hang anything on him."

"The man is a tough meat that defies chewing, but one day this huge basket of deceit he has woven over the years will turn over and trap him underneath." Eneda gave another longer yawn. "We'd better go to bed. I have a busy day tomorrow. When you arrive at the market, remember to buy me that white man's book we talked about."

Udemezue smiled. This had been a long-standing joke between them ever since Udemezue told him years ago that he saw a book for sale at the Great River market and had been tempted to buy it.

"The only problem, father, is that you cannot read."

"I told you, I studied *nsibidi* and I have been told there is no difference between the two. If you get me a book, I will study it too."

"The white man's book is different. They teach it in special schools at the Delta City and you would have to go there to study it."

"I can study it right here," Eneda replied. "How difficult can it be? Anyway when will you leave?"

"At first light."

"Then may Ani, the goddess of the land, guide you in your going and coming. That's all. Be careful."

"Let day break," Udemezue replied and got up. Onaedo also bid her father good night and left.

# CHAPTER

# 9

"So are you going to marry Amechi or not?" Adanma asked Onaedo. They were alone in Adanma's house de-husking corn-cobs and putting them into a basket for her mother.

"I don't know," Onaedo replied. She threw a bare cob into a pile and began to remove the silken tassels on another.

Amechi had courted her insistently since the *Ofala*. He had sent her a piece of cloth to show he was serious.

"He's been sending you many messages," Adanma continued. "You had better make up your mind soon before another girl takes him."

"He's not my property," Onaedo replied a little testily. "Anybody that wants him can have him."

Adanma sighed in exasperation. "I know that you still think of Dualo. Did he make medicine for you so that you will have eyes only for him? Look, Amechi is young and handsome and has many fine qualities. His father is quite well-to-do and he is his mother's only son."

"Marrying an only son is not an easy undertaking."

Adanma grudgingly agreed. "You're right. Their mothers and sisters are difficult to please and place all their hopes of lineage survival on you. But I think he'll be different."

"How do you know that? You barely know him. He's lived in Ogidi with his mother's people since he was a little boy. This is the first time that anyone has seen him in Abonani. Who knows what his character is like? Why did he leave for another town in the first place?"

"His mother feared for him, as an only son. She felt that he would be safer with her own people, away from the other wives."

"I will think about it, I promise," Onaedo said, pausing in her task for a moment. "I'm still not sure."

"Don't think about it too long. On another matter, when is Udemezue coming back?"

"They only just left. It'll be a few weeks yet. I see that you still have eyes for him," Onaedo said, teasing.

"No, no I was just asking." Adanma suddenly looked bashful. "I gave him money to buy something for me, that's why I'm asking."

"You gave him money?" Onaedo laughed in disbelief. "What money do you have?"

"You don't know everything that I have." Adanma was defensive.

"If you say so," Onaedo said and shook her head in amusement.

ॐ

Udemezue was at the trading post on the banks of the Great River. It was busy, as usual, with traders coming from all over *Olu n'Igbo* to do business. His party had arrived three days earlier and already the trading had been a commercial success for the Abonani group. He sat near his stall in the humidity, fanning himself with a small mat of reeds, enjoying the sounds of the market.

His stall was strategically located in the front row. From it, he could see the river a short distance away. There were numerous boats on the white sands of the waterfront that belonged to fishermen who were already doing a brisk business selling the morning catch. Others boats were filled with goods that the delta-dwelling people paddled to market. The river was a vast expanse of water. Its far bank was a blurry grey line on the horizon, where clusters of villages marked the beginning of the Delta Kingdom.

The market smelled of raw fish and cooking food. Some of the locals from nearby villages opened their stalls to sell cooked food to the traders for immediate consumption and sold them smoked fish for the journey home. The market was predominantly a man's enterprise, except for the women food-sellers and petty traders who sold small quantities of *ogili*, kola-nut, and black soap.

Udemezue stood, stretched and sat again. The market was a bit slow today. One of his regular customers stopped by to purchase animal skins and kola-nuts. They exchanged pleasantries. "How are home people?" he asked.

"They're all doing well, just hungry," Udemezue replied.

"Hunger is not a problem; it is ill health we fear. If we are in good health then all is well."

Udemezue laughed and replied that there was indeed a lot for which to be thankful. Most of the merchants had known each other over many years of doing commerce; they knew details of births, marriages, deaths, good fortunes, and bad news. On non-market days, the stalls were empty and deserted except for the fishermen.

"They're here!" somebody called from a few sheds away.

There was a slight commotion and Udemezue stood up to take a better look at a small crowd of people that was moving in his direction. Word spread that the two white men were in the market again.

As Udemezue debated whether to go over for a closer look, he noticed that the crowd was moving towards his stall. At the head of the procession were the same two white men from weeks ago. They were dressed alike in elaborately embroidered material from head to toe, with covered feet; one was older than the other. They sweated profusely in clothing not suited for the humidity.

Udemezue thought, as he had when he saw them weeks before, that they were more red or brown than white, unless their bodies under all that suffocating clothing was white.

He was so engrossed in his observations that it took him a while to realize that the older white man had actually stopped in front of his stall. He looked with interest at Udemezue's merchandise while talking to a black man who was their interpreter.

Udemezue heard some of the other traders discussing the men's clothing. One was a man who sold white, woven cotton next to Udemezue. He asked the interpreter if he thought that the two men might want to buy cooler material from him. The interpreter replied coldly that white men did not wear native attire.

"How do you know what the white man wants when you haven't even asked him?" the cloth trader replied. The interpreter ignored further comments and told Udemezue that the men wanted to buy the animal skins and a couple of baskets of red pepper. They negotiated a price, and the interpreter, whose name was Idoma, gestured for their porters to take away the goods. Udemezue received his payment in manila bars and bags of cowry shells. The sale was going well.

As they were leaving, Udemezue saw the younger white man had a book tucked under his arm. He asked through Idoma if he could see it and waited while Idoma translated; even if he could not buy it, he could tell Eneda he saw another one.

The crowd expectantly watched the transaction. The older man scowled at the interpreter who did not look too happy himself. It seemed that the book owner, the younger white man, was the only one that seemed pleased that Udemezue had shown an interest. He approached Udemezue and handed the book to him.

Udemezue turned it in his hands and people crowded around him like flies around fruit.

"Nobody else should touch it," Idoma warned, gesturing for everybody to stand back. Udemezue ran his finger over the thick book. It was wrapped in a piece of woven cloth in a very clever manner. He opened it. There were pictures of people and houses and lines and lines of squiggles. His father was right. It looked similar to *nsibidi*.

He closed the book and gave it back. He was about to tell Idoma to thank his master for allowing him to look at the book but the words caught in his mouth. For a brief moment, he had the strange, uncanny feeling that he had seen the young white man before. It made no sense; he had never met any white people before these two men. Suddenly the image of Eneda was juxtaposed alongside the man standing before him confusing him even further. They shared similar features, especially their eye color. The image was unsettling and Udemezue took a deep breath to return to reality. He wanted to make sure that he was awake and not imagining standing there on the bank of the Great River.

"Will he agree to sell the book to me?" Udemezue heard himself ask Idoma. The interpreter looked at him incredulously. Udemezue wondered if perhaps he had inadvertently asked to sleep with the white man's wife.

"Are you crazy?" the interpreter scolded. "You interior Igbo traders and your presumptions; who do you think you are to ask for a white man's book? You're lucky that he even let you touch it. Now you want to buy it? What kind of money do you think you have and what else do you want to buy from him? Maybe his clothes too?"

"His clothes are too warm for me," Udemezue said in jest, but Idoma wasn't amused.

The younger white man interrupted them and appeared to ask Idoma a question as he gestured towards Udemezue. Idoma reluctantly translated

"He wants to know what you want to do with it," Idoma said to him.

"Tell him it's for my father. He asked me for one."

"Can your father read?" Idoma asked, again translating the man's question.

Udemezue shrugged. "He can read *nsibidi*."

The white man looked puzzled. Idoma shrugged. Udemezue suspected that Idoma didn't know anything about *nsibidi* either and seemed reluctant to prolong the exchange by asking. After conferring with Idoma the man gave the book to him. He thrust the book into Udemezue's hand.

Udemezue returned it to the translator. "Tell the white man
that I examined the book already and I do not wish to buy it anymore."

By now Udemezue regretted his request for the book and the
controversy that had been created, especially since he didn't think
that he had enough money for it. Idoma seemed quite annoyed and
Udemezue didn't want to be on the wrong side of a market interpreter on whose goodwill his business depended. They were the
lifeline between the Abonani traders and the non-Igbo-speaking
merchants from across the river.

"The white man says that you can keep the book," Idoma said.
"And he does not want anything for it." The interpreter looked
at Udemezue as if he had just pulled a trick that he somehow had
missed.

Udemezue was astonished. "Are you sure that he wants me to
keep it? Why would the white man give me such a valuable gift?"

"You tell me." Idoma looked even more displeased.

By now, the two white men were embroiled in their own heated
argument. It seemed that the older man didn't approve of the transaction but the younger one stood his ground. He spoke rapidly to
Idoma who appeared apprehensive and confused by the disagreement between the two men. Finally, he turned again to Udemezue.
He regarded him balefully, clearly blaming him for the quarrel
between his two masters.

"I don't know why you want a book that you can't even read,"
he muttered under his breath. "Now the man is quarrelling with his
brother. Anyway, he says it's a gift for your father." He lowered his
voice even further, so that only Udemezue heard. "I hope you know
that I was instrumental in this act of generosity. I told him that your
father is a very important king, a blacksmith in your country and
so would value this gift. I will return later for my own payment."

Udemezue knew that Idoma had told the white man no such
thing. He looked down at the book to hide his contempt for the
interpreter. The crowd watched the exchange in silence and when

it was clear that Udemezue had what he wanted, some congratu-lated him on his good business sense. His companions from Abonani were pleased that one of them had acquired something this impor-tant. This was an important document and somebody would have to learn to read and interpret it just like they did in the schools in the Delta City. Udemezue hurried into his shed and grabbed one of his father's bronze vases from underneath the table.

"Tell your master that this is my father's handiwork," he said handing it to Idoma. "My father would be honored if he took it with him back to his country."

"Don't forget my payment," Idoma warned again as he carefully placed the vase in a basket resting on the head of a porter.

Udemezue nodded. He was too thrilled to resent Idoma's exploitation. He would present him with a flywhisk handle later. He had made a profit already this trip and he could afford to be gener-ous, even to an obnoxious fortune-seeker like Idoma.

∾∾

The appearance of the two white men continued to generate excitement at the trading camp even after they left. Over the next two days, both men returned to purchase more goods but they didn't buy anything more from Udemezue.

On the third day, the older man returned, accompanied only by the interpreter. He stopped at Udemezue's shed where now only a few goods remained. They were sparsely laid out as he packed for his journey home to Abonani.

The crowd that trailed them was smaller today. The novelty was wearing off. He stopped at Udemezue's shed but showed little inter-est in the goods.

Udemezue studied him closely. He was different from his younger brother who was more approachable. This one had pierc-ing, red-rimmed eyes beneath brows as thick as two hairy insects. His mouth seemed like it never smiled. Udemezue wondered idly if he had a wife and daughters that made him laugh sometimes.

The man launched into an exchange with Idoma whose discomfiture increased as his eyes darted from Udemezue to the white man and back. Finally, he approached and requested that Udemezue step away from the sparse crowd that had gathered for a private conversation with him. Udemezue was surprised but followed.

"My master, his name is Alvarez; he wants to know if you will sell him some of your slaves," Idoma asked, showing the unease of one who did not know quite how to go about an unusual errand.

Udemezue was taken aback. He wondered if he had heard correctly. But Idoma's discomfiture, the way in which he smiled foolishly at nothing at all, with eyes that darted like two mice seeking escape from a tight corner, told Udemezue that he had not been mistaken.

"He wants to know if those men sitting by your stall are for sale," Idoma said again, pointing to Udemezue's porters, busily preparing for the journey home.

Udemezue looked at his porters. They were Abonani men, young men just starting out in the trade, apprentices that accompanied the older, more established traders like Udemezue. Their job was to help carry the goods and perform minor tasks, to lay out the sheds and do some low-level bargaining with customers, until they had learned enough to start their own businesses.

Udemezue turned to Idoma and quietly told him in Igbo that he was not interested. "I'm not going to hold this request against you because I know that you are only the messenger," he added. "I'm an Abonani man and it would be an abomination for me to sell my kith and kin. Please tell your master that these men are my father's servants and apprentices and they are here to help me. I intend to go back to Abonani with all of them."

"He will be angry if you do not try to meet him halfway. Maybe . . ." Idoma started to say before Udemezue interrupted him, this time with anger.

"Look, Idoma, I have no quarrel with you. Please give my message to the white man in the way that I gave it to you. My answer is the same," And with that he turned and went into his shed.

He saw Idoma return to his master to relay his message. The man stared at him coldly before he turned around and strutted off.

Later, as Udemezue packed one final time, he wondered if Eneda had been right to caution him before he set out on this trip; the white man's presence may have not, after all, been the profitable venture he had so naively presumed.

CHAPTER

# 10

Pasquale had decided not to go back to the market across the river with Alvarez. Today he was glad for a little solitude and would even be happier when they set sail with the meager cargo they had acquired.

They had left the Delta City days ago and now he stood in a temporary settlement further south. He tried hard not to listen to the noises coming from the large thatched building where they held some of the prisoners they had captured. There weren't that many left. They had ferried most of them out to the *Santa Magdalena* that was anchored in one of the natural waterways that ran to the ocean.

They didn't have permission from the Delta palace to conduct trade and so all their business was clandestine. He hoped that Ideheno and Oguebie were trustworthy. The danger was that they could be betrayed at any moment and by avoiding the established trading channels they risked the wrath of the palace and the coastal traders, if discovered. But Alvarez was the ultimate risk taker, a man who enjoyed living dangerously.

Pasquale climbed a ladder to a wooden platform before entering the main room of one of the houses. The sleeping-quarters were built on stilts to keep them dry during the flooding season. He always worried about the precariousness of the structure. It only required a strong wind to tear the structure apart like a bundle of straw and blow them all into the river. But the structures were sturdier than they seemed because that never happened. The worst that he had experienced were insects that sometimes fell from the rafters, startling him while he was writing.

He looked around the bare room. There were two sleeping mats, one for him and the other for Alvarez. They were far from luxurious. The other buildings housed the rest of the crew of the *Santa Magdalena*. They would sail west in a day or two to the castle in El Mina. They would sell the slaves there and collect their certificates of sale from the factor in El Mina. When they reached Lisbon, they would exchange the certificates for cash, and he knew that he would have enough to buy the printing shop.

For now, he had to survive this hell-hole. He unbuttoned his tunic and threw it across the floor of the dimly lit room; he heard its soft thud. He stood at the door and watched the water ripple, as a light breeze skimmed the surface of the slow-flowing river. He felt cooled already. Down below, he watched their native servants as they prepared the meals and commodities for the voyage ahead. He thought of their trip of the past few days. It had been profitable, not as lucrative as he would have wished, but rewarding enough. He was also pleased with the merchandise that they bought from the market. He thought about the man at the market to whom he had given the book a few days ago. That had been a strange encounter. He'd had a weird feeling looking at the man and was pleased that he had given him the book, although he didn't know why. He doubted very much that the man's father could read the *Missale Romanum* written in Latin, but he hoped he would at least be pleased with the gift.

He tried to remember what he had done with the metal vase he had received in exchange. He found it underneath his tunic and held it up. It was all executed in metal with metal ropes and knots; the best that he'd seen anywhere. He wished that he'd bought a few more. Nevertheless, he thought, this one would make a good conversation piece when he got home.

He went back to the door to survey his surroundings. The smell of smoke from the cooking stations down below mingled with the freshness of the forest vegetation. The river had beautiful white sands at its banks. It spread into an enormous delta with myriad waterways before emptying into the ocean. The camp clearing was bordered by palms and giant mangroves and canopies of vines that swung above like giant hammocks.

A flutist in the camp below played a soulful tune on a hollow reed instrument. The rest just went about the business of the camp. The day was still bright, but when the sun journeyed behind the ring of trees, darkness would descend quickly. He liked it when they played their music. It made the night less frightening.

A noisy group of red-tailed monkeys gathered on a tree. One descended to steal from the camp. It took a piece of coal before it was shooed away, protesting loudly as it rejoined its mates. Farther upstream, a family of dwarf hippopotami rolled about in the mud.

Pasquale had heard many stories from his old grandfather about this land. He'd read books too, but nothing he had seen so far was as strange as the accounts of those travelogues that he had pored over at home. There were no three-eyed humans with multiple ears and noses as the natives had been portrayed in drawings. He had seen nothing of that at all. In fact, aside from the different attire and language, they seemed no different from any of the other black people he had seen in Lisbon and they were like any man, any Italian, French man or Florentine merchant. He would be accurate with his own accounts, he decided, even if it went against the dogma of others. He wanted to be taken seriously in the future as a scholar.

His grandfather had told him that one of their forebears had even lived among these people for a few years. Pasquale now wished that he had paid closer attention to the old man's stories. He tried hard to recall one in particular about a young woman with whom that ancestor had fallen in love. She had been the daughter of an important man and there had even been talk of a child that they'd had together. That was all he could remember now. It was so long ago and his grandfather's tales had always been very long on drama and short on facts.

He sighed and looked over at the long building on the side. He usually avoided even looking at it. He knew what was inside. It was guarded at both ends by half a dozen armed men from the crew of the *Santa Magdalena*. That was the *barracoon*, the structure that held the prisoners, captives, slaves, or whatever else they chose to call them. They were all here against their will. None had volunteered to come, so they were held prisoner instead.

Alvarez came into the camp. He had been to see his woman in one of the villages. His relationship with the village headman had settled into an uneasy truce when Alvarez promised not to attack the village if they let him conduct his business uninterrupted. The woman had agreed to marry him to please her father but refused to follow him to his country, which Alvarez told Pasquale suited him well.

Alvarez climbed the ladder, removed his tunic and entered the room. "We should set sail for Sao Tome tomorrow after we load," he said.

"Sao Tome?" Pasquale asked, confused. They were supposed to go to El Mina.

"I decided that we should take the shipment of slaves there. You've heard about Sao Tome, yes?" Alvarez asked. It sounded like he would be amazed if Pasquale had.

Pasquale was annoyed that Alvarez treated him like a child. After all, it was he, Pasquale, who was financing most of this trip.

"Of course I've heard of Sao Tome," Pasquale replied shortly. "As a matter of fact, I have a friend in Sao Tome; a priest, Padre Joao. He's a childhood friend of mine who went there a few years ago. Why aren't we going back to El Mina?"

"Going to Sao Tome is a better plan. It's less than a week away," Alvarez said. "We can sell the slaves there and take the sugar from there back to Antwerp. It is better than going to El Mina. If you prefer, we can go to Brazil," Alvarez added, as if that were a real option. "But that voyage is much longer and dangerous. It's more profitable to do business with the plantation owners in Sao Tome and then carry the sugar home from there."

Pasquale nodded. Their whole plan now sounded unnecessarily complicated. This was another reason not to like Alvarez, this unpredictability. Pasquale now knew first hand also that Alvarez was a violent and dangerous man. A few days ago, he had shot and killed one of the natives in front of everybody on account of a minor dispute. He claimed that the man had stolen alcohol from him, but a short while later Pasquale had found the empty bottle under a pile of clothing. Alvarez had consumed the wine himself but had been too drunk to remember. The incident had created tensions with the local population; he feared a mutiny soon. It was then that Pasquale had promised himself to sever their partnership as soon as the trip was over. He would find another ship with a sane captain.

But Pasquale had to admit that going to Sao Tome was a good idea. It was near the Guinea Coast where they were now. Sao Tome was a colonial island outpost of the Portuguese Crown with vast sugar plantations. Padre Joao, his friend, was an Augustine monk whom he remembered had been sent there from Lisbon by the Bishop. Pasquale had lost touch with him since then and wasn't even sure he was still alive. Sao Tome was said to be rife with swamp fever, *mal'aria*, and other diseases that frequently wreaked havoc on white colonists. He hoped that Padre Joao was still alive. If he was, Pasquale would make every effort to find him; it couldn't be that difficult on an island and it would be comforting to see an old friend again.

CHAPTER

# II

Onaedo was in her mother's house the day the delegation from Amechi's people came, asking for consent to start the enquiries into a marriage contract. She had taken time to study the visitors when her mother sent her to serve them kola-nuts and that also gave them an opportunity to scrutinize her to see if she measured up.

Afterwards, she hid outside her father's *obi* to listen. The visiting group included Amechi's father, a short energetic-looking man who led his *umunna*, his male kindred. After the preliminaries, he talked at length in metaphorical terms about the ripe fruit that they had seen in Eneda's compound and didn't give the intermediary an opportunity to speak. Onaedo later told Adanma in jest that she began to think that she was a real fruit.

But everything had gone well and when Eneda had asked her whether she wanted to marry Amechi she had said yes.

"Then you will return the empty gourd of wine to him and his kindred to show that you accept his proposal."

Onaedo agreed. She liked Amechi although not in the same breathlessly smitten, exciting way that she had Dualo. She remembered her conversation with Eneda a while ago when he had advised her to aim for what was reachable. The truth was that she could have done worse. Amechi was not a bad match.

ᖊᖊ

Onaedo felt the hard floor through the mat and opened her eyes. She tried to force the sleep back into her eyes but it was no good. She heard voices outside and soon the women, the wives of the *umunna* and the *umuada* who were her own female kindred would invade the room, looking for the new bride-to-be.

Her mother was already awake and had left to continue the preparations she had started weeks ago. Once Onaedo had agreed to Amechi's proposal, everything had proceeded with speed. Ugodi and Aku made frantic preparations, and as usual disagreed on almost everything.

From where she lay she could see her accumulated dowry—iron pots, nests of baskets, wooden spoons, a metal one that Eneda had made especially for her. There were bales of cloth and two dwarf stools. She reached for her colored stone collection piled under the bed. There were about twenty now. She separated them, one from the other. She would take half of them with her and leave the rest.

She felt under the mat that covered her mother's bed until her fingers closed around a lumpy rag. Inside was a gold necklace, balls of gold with tiny spikes bound with a copper wire. It was a very rare and expensive piece of jewelry that Ugodi had saved years to buy. She put it back.

"I'm glad you are awake." Her aunt stood with her mother at the door. "Where is your dowry?"

"There," Onaedo said and pointed to the baskets.

"Is this it? Two baskets?" Aku asked. She looked into another corner in an exaggerated manner, searching for more.

"What do you mean? Is this not enough?" Ugodi asked indignantly. "How many pots and mortars does one young woman need to establish a home? This is more than I had when I came here as a new bride."

"Please don't make me laugh," Aku said. She held up her hand and started counting off each finger. "I'm looking around and I see only one mortar and one pestle. Isn't she going to need a big pot at some point?"

Aku unknotted the edge of her wrappa. "*Biko*, before you disgrace us further, take this and send for more baskets and mats," she said, giving her sister the money. "I have more manila bars at home, in case you need more."

Onaedo wasn't sure whether Aku was joking.

"Put your money back." Ugodi brushed her hand away. "I don't know why you provoke me or why I listen to you. You don't bite your words before they come out of your mouth. This is a good dowry; you just want to find fault where there is none. Did you see the gold necklace?"

Onaedo brought it out once more from its hiding place. Aku examined it and gave her grudging praise. "This is good," she said, giving it back. "But I still say that she needs more pots."

Some of the women outside pushed their way noisily into the room.

"Good, we were waiting for you to wake up so we could examine your dowry," said the leader of the group, a distant cousin of Onaedo's by the name of Nneoma. She pounced on the items with the enthusiasm of a collector that had just seen an elusive item. She examined each in critical detail before passing it along the small line of women standing behind her. They began to ululate loudly in praise of Ugodi and the good job she had done raising a beautiful daughter.

"Ugodi this is a dowry fit for a princess," somebody said.

"I have something of my own to add," said Aku, and from the top of her cloth, pulled a string of blood-red coral beads, which she gave to Onaedo. Each stone was smooth and glassy and in its depths were flecks of black and brown. Onaedo held up the necklace for the others to admire. She hugged her aunt tightly.

"This must have cost a fortune," Nneoma said, squinting into it before giving it to the woman beside her.

After examining the treasures to their satisfaction, the women drifted outside to resume their chores.

"Ugodi, are the *umuada* also cooking today? I thought that this was the function of Eneda's wives and the wives of the *umunna*?"

"That's what I thought too, until Nneoma arrived yesterday with a group of the *umuada* and insisted that I set up a cooking station for them. I did it, of course. One doesn't argue with the lineage daughters of the family. Moreover, the most senior of the *umuada* is not here. She traveled almost a month ago. If she were here, this wouldn't have happened."

"I don't envy you. There are many strong-willed women in this family. Let's see what's going on."

෨෪

Onaedo greeted the women who were cooking. The yard was scattered with cooking stations with each group cooking something different.

"Eh! Ugodi, so those men let you take this much meat?" said one of the women.

Ugodi laughed. "They didn't have a choice after I threatened to take the cow's testicles and eat them myself."

"Eh? You threatened to eat the testicles? I would have loved to see their faces when you said that."

"They just gave me what I wanted." A thick cloud of smoke rose from one of the tripods; it made their eyes water. Some of the women burst into song when they saw Onaedo coming.

"Come here and greet us," they said, and hugged her as though she were a long-lost relative and not someone who they saw daily.

"That's why I talk good about you, Onaedo," one woman said. She was Eneda's cousin and had travelled from Ogidi, a town half a day's journey away. "See how you came out to greet us? The other day, we went to cook for one of my friend's daughter's wine-carrying ceremony. Do you know, this girl never said a word of thanks to anybody, even those of us that spent the whole night cooking and cleaning? I almost left in disgust."

"Young women of today are not raised right," another woman interjected. "They have no home training; that's the problem."

"Not all of them."

"We'll miss you when you're gone, Onaedo," said another woman as she plucked *ugu* leaves from a stalk.

"You had better rest as much as you can because when you go to your husband's people, they'll expect you to wake early and do all the housework," advised Nneoma.

"Never mind that. You're Eneda's daughter, and no one will treat you like a person of no consequence," another said. She spoke as she plucked leaves and threw them into a container of cold water.

"What has that got to do with anything? Once she's somebody's wife, she'll leave her father's *obi* behind. No matter how wealthy her father; she'll be her in-laws' servant."

"Ah, Nneoma sometimes you talk like someone whose head is not correct. When did marriage become slavery? Because your husband's people treated you badly, does not mean that we have to listen to your nonsense. Next time wash your eyes with water so you can see clearly and marry the right husband," the first woman said.

"*Tufia*! I will not marry another man ever again," Nneoma exclaimed. "I refuse to be a slave again to anybody."

"It is enough now, Nneoma! Don't spoil Onaedo's big day with this kind of bad talk," the first woman scolded. "If you had children, maybe you wouldn't have been in such a hurry to leave your husband."

There was silence after that comment; most people who heard it did not approve. Onaedo stole a furtive glance at Nneoma to measure her reaction and saw the glimmer of tears in her eyes. Everybody knew that Nneoma was barren and that it was the main reason that her husband had sent her away. The women were furious at the one who had made the comment.

"You shouldn't have said that. It's not Nneoma's fault that she doesn't have a child. It's what her *chi* decreed for her."

"Don't mind her," another woman added joining in to scold the woman who had made the offensive speech. "We all know about her bad mouth. That's why she had to go all the way to Ogidi where she is not known, to find a husband; no Abonani man would have married her with her lack of tact."

Onaedo knew that a large angry storm was brewing as each of the women now took sides in the developing argument. She left to avoid being drawn into it.

CHAPTER

# 12

Onaedo oiled her body in preparation for the red, black, and white dyes her friends would apply on her skin. She hadn't wanted the many tiny diamond-shaped permanent *ichi* tattoos put on her face but had allowed the woman to tattoo her stomach instead, just below her navel.

She looked into Ugodi's mirror that hung on the wall. She had loved the mirror from the first day that Udemezue brought it home, but her mother disliked it, convinced that a malevolent spirit lived in the glass and had refused to look at it. Aku told her that it was nonsense and asked her to give it to Onaedo if she didn't want it. She did and it was now a part of Onaedo's dowry.

Onaedo was always startled to see her face so clearly the way others saw it, especially her eyes that looked so much like her father's. She stood closer and tried to measure her feelings by the expression on her face. Maybe she looked happy; she missed Dualo but hid her sadness well from the casual observer. She sighed and stroked the metal amulet round her neck with its strange, blood-colored stone. Her hair was unruly and still damp from washing it the night before. She would sit in the sun later to dry it and Adanma and Nonye would plait it in a circular crown of braids; they said that it was the latest fashion. She could feel it uncomfortable on her head already. She decided that after the wedding, like her aunt and mother, she would wear her hair short. She looked around for the decorative hair combs that Udemezue had bought for her a few weeks before. She remembered that they were in a basket under her mother's bed. She reached into the basket. Beside it on the floor was the book that Udemezue had bought for Eneda, half-hidden between her mother's ivory ankle braces. She picked it up and sat on the bed to examine it. As she turned pages, she became fascinated again, by the strange-looking people inside. Both the men and women were dressed in strange clothes that covered the body including sometimes, the head. Weeks ago, when he had returned from the Great River market, Udemezue had presented Eneda with the book. Everyone had flocked to Eneda's *obi* to see it, and one or two made a show of trying to read it. A few had seen books before but nobody owned one. Eneda began to grow weary of the crowds that interrupted his daily work and so he gave the book to Ugodi. She was often away from the compound and the people would stop coming if she wasn't there to show it to them.

But Udemezue was another matter. His demeanor puzzled Onaedo; it had been very odd since he'd returned from his last trip to the Great River. He seemed troubled and contemplative. He had had long nightly discussions with Eneda to which she was not privy because she was now spending more time being sequestered with the women who'd been educating her on how to be a successful married woman. Ugodi and Aku had left no stone unturned in their efforts and she was glad it was over. Despite the demands on her time, Onaedo had sought out Udemezue a few days ago. It was then that he told her about his experience with the two white men—the one who wanted to buy his companions and was angry when he could not and the other who had given him the book.

"I thought I was looking at Eneda," Udemezue said to her. "It gives me chills even now to think of it now. If he were darker, I would have said that he was Eneda's younger brother."

"A renegade ancestor reincarnated as a white man?" Onaedo had asked.

"A renegade ancestor? Only you would say a funny thing like that," Udemezue had said laughing. "You are like an old woman sometimes."

Onaedo wondered again about Udemezue's encounter as she put the book back in its place.

ཉཉ

Aku came back to check on her. "Where are all your friends? They should be helping you prepare."

"They'll be here soon. I've already started," Onaedo replied. She'd drawn red patterns on her arms and belly and was adding black paint.

"Give that to me, I'll help you," Aku said. She dipped a feather in the black clay. "I don't think that you've grown eyes behind your head yet."

Aku drew multiple patterns. She stood back to admire her work. "*Imaka*. You look beautiful," she declared. "You can sit now," she said stacking the paint bowls. "You remind me so much of our mother today."

She paused suddenly and with a strange expression, regarded Onaedo.

"What's wrong?" Onaedo asked.

"Nothing, but please sit. I think I just saw something."

Onaedo was suddenly uneasy. She had never been the subject of any of Aku's divinations and didn't want to start now.

Aku seemed to be in a trance. She touched her arm, at first lightly, then with a pressure that made Onaedo wince in pain. "Is your heart still with another man?" she asked.

Onaedo stared at her. Aku seemed different, more intense, with eyes like dark ponds and a strange smile. Onaedo wondered if her aunt was a witch and shrank from her.

"What did you see?" she asked fearfully.

"I see another man. Is there somebody else?"

"That was a long time ago; he no longer matters," Onaedo said.

She pulled away from Aku and would not meet her eyes. She knew that Aku had suspected her relationship with Dualo all along, though she'd not spoken to her about it. Why was she acting so strangely about it now?

"Give me your hand for a moment," Aku said and took her hand, more gently this time. Her voice softened and she sounded like the old Aku again.

"I didn't mean to alarm you," she said. Aku sounded as though she was speaking to herself. She frowned several times and shook her head very slowly. Onaedo loved Aku but her aunt scared her when she talked like this. She focused her thoughts on something else to wish away bad omens, and turned to watch a fly on the floor as it washed its wings with its hind legs.

After a long silence, Aku turned to look at Onaedo. It seemed as though a spell had been broken. "Sometimes the things I see frighten me, too."

Onaedo nodded. She really wanted to get up and leave but knew she couldn't.

"When I was a young woman," Aku began, "I set my sights on marrying your father who was one of the most eligible young men then. I was introduced to him first but once he saw your mother, who was tall, dark, and beautiful, he didn't have eyes for me or anyone else."

Onaedo stared at her aunt in amazement. She had never heard that Aku and her mother had been love rivals.

"Don't look so surprised," Aku said smiling. "I was angry but not for long; that's why I'm telling you that disappointment is written, especially for women. A woman's life is rooted in overcoming sorrow, so you have to wear the garment that is cut out of the cloth of patience. To continue my own story, I married soon after and when I remember the incident with your mother, I laugh at my own foolishness."

"I never knew any of this."

Aku laughed. "How would you know? The story is older than you." She leaned forward and lifted the amulet with her finger. It dangled on its string around Onaedo's neck. "This is strong medicine. Eneda had a *dibia* make it to save your life when you were a baby. You were so sick that we all feared you would die. Take care of it," she said, and let it drop. She hesitated before carefully choosing her next words.

"I have seen something else, my daughter, something that I cannot interpret. Who knows? Perhaps it isn't to do with you."

"What did you see?" Onaedo asked.

"I saw water."

"Water?" Onaedo was puzzled.

Aku shrugged. "I don't know what it means but I saw a large river or maybe a sea. It was so large that I couldn't see the land on the other side. And then I saw a giant coffin on it."

"A coffin?" Onaedo asked with alarm. A coffin was never a good sign.

Aku paused. Something had just occurred to her. "Perhaps it wasn't a coffin at all; maybe it was a wooden box. But it was large."

"It must signify something bad."

"Maybe it's not about you this time," Aku said slowly. "The more I think of it, the more I'm convinced it concerns Udemezue who goes to the Great River. He's always near water there."

Onaedo frowned. "I hope it's not something bad for him. You must warn him." She couldn't bear it if anything happened to her brother.

"Don't worry. I'll tell him to be vigilant," Aku said.

"I think I hear Adanma coming. She'll want to help me prepare," Onaedo said. She took her combs in her hand.

"Make sure they style your hair right. Tell them not to make the plaits too tight," Aku said. She stoked Onaedo's head. Her hand felt heavy, Onadeo thought, like something dead. It raised the hair on her arms and she recoiled, but Aku smiled reassuringly. "I'm off to help your mother with the cooking," she said, and without saying anything more, she left.

ಬಬ

As Aku walked away, her unease returned. She had tried to reassure Onaedo but her mind was in some turmoil. A coffin was always bad, especially one as large as the one that she'd seen. She made a decision. Tomorrow, she would go to the *chi* shrine of their mother and ask for protection for Onaedo. She wouldn't worry Ugodi, about it; she wasn't even sure what it meant.

CHAPTER

# 13

O naedo was almost ready, but Amechi and his people were late. The start of ceremony would be delayed further because the bride-price still had to be settled.

Onaedo sat in her mother's room with her friends. She wore a new, green and black waistcloth. The string of coral beads that Aku gave her hung round her neck. Her breasts, belly and back were covered in patterns drawn in red *uli* and black lines and white dots.

"Isn't her hair ready yet?" asked one of her two older half-sisters. She'd arrived the night before and had travelled for days from her husband's home. Adanma rolled her eyes and continued braiding Onaedo's hair; it was an intricate design. Everybody had already complained that it was taking too long.

Outside the room, Onaedo saw Ugodi and Aku. Ugodi's cloth was new and solid blue, while Aku wore a piece in blue and white stripes. Her mother looked towards the gate each time somebody came in.

"*Ngwa*, go to the main road and see if they're coming," she instructed one of the children.

He returned to report that the guests were nowhere in sight.

"Are you sure? Go back and look again." The child ran to look and returned to confirm what he already knew. The guests were late.

Inside the room, Onaedo sighed. If Ugodi stopped worrying maybe everyone would relax.

"The women in the back are upset because the food might go bad," Ugodi was saying to Aku. "What's keeping those people? I don't want to serve re-warmed food."

Aku nodded in agreement. "And they have to negotiate the bride-price before anybody eats. Did I not warn you about those people?"

Ugodi looked at her a little surprised. "You did? When? If I recall, you were full of praise for everybody from Amechi's village, even his aunt that you said owed you money."

"Well, I'm saying something else now," Aku replied, without the slightest trace of irony as she folded her arms across her chest.

Onaedo came out and showed them her finished hair.

"Come, let me rearrange your cloth," Aku said, and adjusted Onaedo's waist cloth. She smoothed the stack of beads between her waist and her navel. "Now you look beautiful, my child," she said.

"What were you telling Ugodi about Amechi's village?" Onaedo asked.

"I was telling your mother that they may be good people but they're notorious for being tardy. They're never early to anything. I saw that myself just the other day when I attended one of their weddings. I tell you that by the time they'd delayed all the proceedings and the poor bride arrived home, it was so dark that the groom couldn't tell the difference between his bride and the old matchmaker who had accompanied her home." Ugodi and Onaedo burst out laughing.

"Laugh all you want," Aku said, suppressing her own amusement, "I just hope that they arrive before dark so Onaedo doesn't suffer a similar fate."

"*Tufia!*" Ugodi teased. "Not my own daughter. If they don't come soon, I'll tell the young men to start serving the food so the people already here can start eating."

"Is that so?" Aku asked sarcastically. "And after eating all the food for the wedding, will you marry your daughter as well?"

"What do you want me to say?" Ugodi replied. "Look at Ejiofor sitting there. He looks as if hunger will knock him down at any minute," said Ugodi. She nodded her head in the direction of an old man waving the early heat away from his face with a broad fan. He sat with the rest of Eneda's *umunna* and looked up anxiously each time the gate swung open. Then he would glance hungrily towards the backyard as if hoping the food would appear, despite the absence of the guests. Onaedo saw him do it a few times.

"If he's hungry, it would serve him right for not eating in his house before coming out," Aku said.

"His only wife left him, so he has no one to cook for him."

"Really? Why did she leave?" Aku asked. Onaedo wanted to know too.

"Why are you asking me? How will I know?" Ugodi had the look that said she had something to say but wanted them to tease it from her.

"I think you know," Aku said. "She's the second woman to leave him in two years. If you ask me, I think he's impotent. That's why the women leave," she declared with certainty.

"You didn't hear that from my mouth," Ugodi said, laughing.

Just then, the gate was nudged open. "Oh, I see our in-laws have arrived," Aku said as a large group came through. "And it seems that they've brought quite a crowd. They've come with their women and children too."

"That's good. I don't know why in this village we restrict women from going with the men to bring home the bride. We should all attend, if you ask me," Ugodi said. She regarded the newcomers looking pleased.

"They won't ask you, because they want to eat all the food themselves when they get there," Aku replied. She silently counted the people as they arrived. "Well I hope you cooked enough for this crowd," she said when the last person passed through the gate, an old woman guided in by a young boy. "From what I know of them, not only are they habitually late but they eat like ravenous locusts.

Within a short time, all your food will be gone," she said. Ugodi shook her head in exasperation and left and Aku exchanged an amused look with Onaedo.

❧

The two families began the bride-price negotiations when Ugodi brought the bowl filled with broomsticks. She left immediately and the men began.

In silence, the bowl was passed between the two families. Broomsticks were added and taken away each time until an agreement was reached for the final bride-price correlating to the number of sticks left. It was the sign that the women had awaited and they brought out the food.

"I hope that they got a good price for you," Adanma whispered to Onaedo.

Onaedo shrugged. "They never tell us, but I'll ask Udemezue; maybe he'll tell me."

Amechi's family, she later learned, had paid two bags of cowries and five manila bars for her—the highest amount paid for any bride in Abonani for as far back as anybody could remember.

❧

Amechi sat between his father and his best friend. Onaedo watched them. When he wasn't whispering something to his friend, Onaedo thought that he looked bored. He was a slender man with well-proportioned, orderly features. One could confidently call him handsome. His red and white cotton loincloth had a matching piece stylishly hooked around his neck in the latest fashion. His complexion was neither fair nor dark but an in-between color. Adanma kept up a running commentary on Amechi's every gesture until Onaedo asked her to stop.

"Adanma, I have eyes and have already agreed to marry him; you don't have to convince me anymore."

"I don't want it to be said that I didn't do my part," Adanma replied.

"You had better go out to greet them now," Aku said, when she and Ugodi returned. "Otherwise, they will think that we're giving them a hunchback for a wife, or wonder why we are hiding her." Everybody laughed, rose, and followed Onaedo to make her round of greetings.

Onaedo watched Amechi surreptitiously. His eyes lit when she appeared. She took the wine from her father and sipped from the bronze cup that he'd made especially for her. She carried it shyly past the sitting men until she came to Amechi. She hesitated before handing him the cup. He drained it amidst loud cheers of encouragement from his friends; there was no doubt whom she had chosen.

# 14

A sizeable crowd waited at Amechi's mother's house. It was the couple's first stop before finally arriving at their own place. They would live temporarily in an accommodation that had belonged to Amechi's grandfather. It had been his *obi* when he was alive. They would live there until Amechi built his own compound on the land his *umunna* allocated him as soon as he had indicated to them he was taking a wife.

"Why don't we have a house yet?" Onaedo had asked a few weeks earlier, when she arrived for first official one-week visit to her future in-laws. The plot had not even been cleared then. Amechi had smiled his charming smile and given an answer she couldn't even remember now. She looked around the crowded room of his mother's house and suddenly felt tired. She wished that she could lie down.

"Our new wife is beautiful," someone said, for what seemed like the hundredth time. They fingered her hair, her clothes, her jewelry, and everywhere else that they could.

An old lady with only two front teeth rubbed Onaedo's stomach approvingly. "She will give us many sons," she said gleefully, her cackle ending in a spluttering cough. She joked about how Amechi should get to work right away to start making sons.

"And daughters too," somebody added.

"Yes, daughters are also important," the old women repeated and laughed. It seemed to say that sons were preferable first; daughters could come later.

Amechi sat next to Onaedo; he also looked tired but nodded in agreement. He whispered to Onaedo that he couldn't wait to have her all to himself. She giggled nervously, unsure what to say.

It was almost midnight when the old lady clapped her hands for silence and started her welcoming speech. She was the head of the lineage daughters of Amechi's family, and they would give their verdict on the events of the day. It was unanimous. Everybody present agreed that the blacksmith's daughter was a most welcome addition to the family.

ᘔ

Onaedo awoke with the confusion of an unfamiliar place before she recalled the events of the night before. Her head felt like one of those gullies that heavy rains cut into the earth after a storm. She had drunk too much palm-wine last night. So had Amechi. All her memories were blurry and not very pleasant.

The early-morning cold seeped in from underneath the door. Amechi snored rhythmically. His weight pressed lightly against her side and his warm breath caressed the side of her face. She pushed at him gently to pull her leg out from beneath him; without waking, he tried to grab her. Nothing had happened last night or maybe she had been too tired or too tipsy to remember anything.

She picked up a broom left outside the door and went to look for Adanma and her other friends. They had come with her last night and were in the next building.

"Is it morning already?" Adanma protested. She covered her head with her sleep cloth as Onaedo tugged at it.

"Yes, wake up all of you," Onaedo whispered urgently. "We have to sweep the yard to show that we're not lazy women."

"I don't care what they think, I'm not the one he married," Adanma replied.

"The sun is not even out yet," another voice complained from underneath another cloth few feet away. It was Nonye. Adanma had forgiven her when she'd lost interest in Udemezue. "How are we supposed to see what we are doing in this darkness?"

"The sun will be up soon," Onaedo replied. "I'll pour cold water on all of you if you don't get up now."

"Don't you try that," Adanma said. "I'm awake now."

She sat up, stretched, yawned and folded her cloth. "My whole body is sore; I'm not used to sleeping on this kind of mat. I hope you appreciate all I'm doing for you."

"Thank you, here are the brooms, let us go." Onaedo handed one to each girl. "Hurry." This was her first task and she wanted to create a good impression.

Outside in the yard, she stood for a moment and with dismay saw the size of the task. The compound was bigger than she remembered, much larger than her father's. The row of red and white-washed mud houses seemed to stretch forever; the temporary house Onaedo shared with Amechi was just one of them. She took a deep breath. There was still a lingering smell of stale food and palm-wine from last night.

"I don't care what these people think," Adanma whispered and shivered in the morning air. "This compound is too big."

"Please lower your voice. I'm sure they don't expect us to do it all."

"I'm going to start at that end," Adanma said, pointing to one corner. "You start near the gate and the others can spread out in between."

They had worked for a while before the compound began to stir as everyone prepared for a busy day. Onaedo shooed away two brown and white hunting dogs that wandered the compound sniffing into corners and startling a mother hen and her brood of fluffy new chicks. Some children, bleary eyed from sleep, gathered round to watch the novelty of strangers doing their morning chores.

"As if they've never seen somebody sweeping a yard," Adanma muttered under her breath. Onaedo giggled.

One woman greeted Onaedo, calling her 'my new wife'. Another stoked a fire, blowing vigorously into it, and Onaedo went to help as was expected of her. She scooped water from a giant round-bellied earthenware pot and placed it carefully on the growing fire for the woman.

"Don't work so hard. It's too early in the morning," some of the other women called out.

"Leave them alone. That's how they show what good wives they'll be."

Amechi's mother emerged from her room. She was a darker, stouter version of her son.

"Oh, you are up already," she said with feigned surprise as though she hadn't expected Onaedo and her friends to be awake before her. "You can stop sweeping now. The place looks clean enough," she declared, releasing them from further duties. She gave Onaedo a forced smile.

To Onaedo, Amechi's mother was an enigma. She had never shown a great deal of enthusiasm for her son's marriage or even towards her new daughter-in-law. Onaedo had not paid her much attention even during the short time that she'd stayed with her. She would have liked their relationship to have been warmer, but concluded that Amechi's mother was a timid woman who liked to keep to herself. Maybe later she would try to win her confidence.

"I thought that this nonsense would never end," Adanma whispered loudly to Onaedo when they were out of earshot. "I think the whole thing is really stupid. I hope they're not expecting you to do this every day."

"Ssh! You're going to put me in trouble. You know that I'm expected to only take care of my own yard."

"I hope so, for your sake," Adanma said, as they put the brooms away. "Anyway, we're leaving now so you can pretend to cry, like you are going to miss us," she added her eyes twinkling.

"But I am going to miss you all," Onaedo said sniveling. "Please greet my mother for me."

"Don't talk nonsense. This place is not *ani muo*. You're so near that I'm sure if you call over these walls loudly enough, Ugodi might even hear you."

"Don't exaggerate," Onaedo said as they put the brooms in the corner.

"It is near," Nonye added. "If I come here to fetch fire, it will still be burning by the time I get home."

"Alright, I agree," Onaedo conceded. "But promise to come and visit soon."

"After you're settled, we will."

They all took turns hugging her goodbye.

# 15

O guebie was helping to load prisoners into the small boats that Alvarez and Pasquale had provided. This was the second time in a year that he was doing business with the two men. This time they'd managed to procure more people. He saw the outline of the white man's ship out in the distance. It was partially obscured by fog that had descended with the mingling of the warm and cold morning air.

Oguebie tried hard not to look at the group of captives sitting on the muddy earth in front of them. They were shackled securely to one another with metal cuffs with barely enough room to move. For the first time, he allowed himself to feel shame. He wondered if the price he paid was too high; trading in slaves to overpower his brother and rule Abonani. His sense of injustice had ruled him for years, when someone had pulled him aside and whispered in secret that he had arrived first in the world and was the rightful first son. The thought that his birthright had been stolen had become a bitter and festering sore within him and when the people of Abonani had rejected his claim to his father's seat and given it instead to his half-brother, he felt that the whole clan had plotted to wrong him.

But he had been patient and now his time had come; he was ready. He would take over by force and bring progress to Abonani; he would bring more success than they'd ever imagined. He would have a regiment of warriors just as they had in the Delta Kingdom. *My time has come*, he thought again. But of late there was doubt, a lack of conviction which had come about because he knew that if he were honest, he would have to acknowledge that Abonani might not lend itself to the kind of dictatorship that he planned. They didn't even have a real king because it wasn't their way to obey without question. "But it will have to be done," he said aloud.

"What did you say?" Ideheno asked, as he approached.

Oguebie pulled himself together. "I'm saying that we have to hurry and move these people to the ship. I hope there are enough boats to take them all at once."

He watched Alvarez and Pasquale as they counted the prisoners. They were mostly men, but there were a few women and a handful of children.

"Do we need to bring children too?" he asked Ideheno. "What kind of work can they do on the white man's farm?"

Ideheno shrugged, "I don't know. Ask Alvarez. He says that they make good servants for wealthy people in their country." he said.

As if on cue, Oguebie saw Alvarez pick his way through the prisoners, followed closely by Pasquale.

"How many are they by your own tally?" Alvarez asked when he reached the two men. He wiped his puffy red face with a cloth.

"Forty," Ideheno replied in Portuguese.

Alvarez nodded. He said something to Pasquale that Oguebie didn't understand, but two of the porters left and returned from a hut with four guns. Ideheno took them and thanked the men.

Oguebie pulled Ideheno aside. "Is this all he's giving us for all we're giving them?"

Ideheno placed the guns in a long basket. "This is all he has now but he's promised us more. Don't worry, this is only the beginning."

"But he's given us only four guns, Ideheno. It's not enough." Oguebie was annoyed. How had Ideheno made such a bad agreement?

"Just have patience." Ideheno said again. "Our work is done here for now and we should return to the city. I want to show you the land that I promised to give you."

Oguebie nodded and let the matter drop, but he made a mental note to be more closely involved next time, to strike a better bargain.

ल्ल

The *Santa Magdalena* was on its way by the time Oguebie and Ideheno arrived back at the city. Oguebie was relieved it was over; he'd lived in fear of discovery by somebody from the palace. They hid their stockpile in Ideheno's home and sat to eat an early snack that one of Ideheno's wives had prepared.

"We'll eat a meal later," Ideheno told him. "I've arranged an appointment today at the palace to meet one of the king's ambassadors just returned from Lisbon."

"Oh?"

"He has a lot of interesting stories to tell about the white man's country. But before we go, I want to show you your land so that you can make plans to build on it," Ideheno said.

Later, as they walked down the streets, Oguebie marveled once more at the development throughout the city. People strolled down the wide roads that transected it and rows of houses lined the street on both sides in a way that he had not seen anywhere else. Although he did not like the way that so many people lived so close together, Oguebie realized that there were advantages to living in a city like this. It would provide anonymity from his fellow Abonani townsmen. He had not seen the woodcarver and his apprentices for a while, but Ideheno had made good on his promise to keep them in the city with lucrative contracts.

Ideheno showed him the places of interest. He did this proudly every time Oguebie was in town, repeatedly taking him to places they'd visited before.

"Can you see how real those eagles look?" Ideheno asked him now. "It is as if they are about to take flight." He pointed to the turrets of the palace upon which were mounted large, metal birds with wings spread wide. Oguebie made the right noises, although he had to admit that this time he was still as impressed as the first time Ideheno had shown them to him. He was sure that he could commission Eneda, the blacksmith, to produce something like this for him in Abonani when the time came.

Men dug a moat as they approached the outer gates. Oguebie was impressed by the different structures that each Delta king had added to improve the ancient city.

"These trenches keep the city safe from invaders," Ideheno explained. "My brother sees enemies everywhere. That is why we have to be careful with all our plans," he added.

They turned back towards the part of town that housed the artisans—ivory carvers, blacksmiths, builders, and sculptors—hundreds of whom the king employed daily to work on dozens of projects in and around the palace.

"Here it is," said Ideheno, pointing to a bushy patch of land, overgrown with tangled weeds and wild grass. Oguebie thanked him but wished privately that he could have been given a place within the palace walls, but those were reserved for members of the king's family and his courtiers. The land area was quite large and he didn't want to sound ungrateful.

During the short walk back to Ideheno's quarters at the palace, Oguebie listened to his friend's new ideas.

"There is another ship arriving tomorrow," he told Oguebie. "They also want workers for the white man's farm across the sea. If we do it right this time, we can make a large profit and acquire, not just guns, but other goods that we can also trade."

"Where are we going to find the large numbers of people they want?"

"We have to go further inland," Ideheno replied. "Maybe even as far as the Igbo lands and the places that you are familiar with," he added.

Oguebie looked at him with concern; this was not the plan to which he'd agreed. What Ideheno was suggesting was too close to home; he could be recognized. Moreover, the few Abonani people here might take stories back home and that would mean that he would have to act before he was ready. He wouldn't let that happen. This was the time to enact his *other* plan.

"I know a place where we can find people," he said. "There are two towns I know of that have barely tolerated each other for years. If we can instigate trouble between them, we can arm one side and ask them to help us capture their enemies. That way we'll have all the people we want. But we need more guns for the plan to work."

"Alright," Ideheno replied. "The man that we're meeting tonight will help us with this business and also in understanding the ways of the white man."

Oguebie didn't really care about understanding the white man; all he wanted from him was more guns, more goods, and the time when he could return to Abonani as a prosperous and powerful man.

❧❧

It was still light when they returned to the palace. They entered a long corridor with large pillars that supported the roof. The passages were really galleries designed specifically to showcase the palace art, hundreds of embossed metal plaques and inlaid mirrors on pillars that stretched from roof to floor.

"This is my grandfather," Ideheno said, pointing to the figure of a king carved in ebony and mounted on a horse. "He was a great warrior king and began the modernization of the kingdom before the Portuguese arrived."

Ideheno told him that successive kings had constructed a maze of apartments and rooms arranged around dozens of separate courtyards.

"How many people live here?"

"Too many to count," he said with pride. Oguebie wondered why Ideheno thought he could do better than the present king. This place was already well established as far as structures were concerned. There wasn't a lot more to add he thought, but said nothing.

The man they were to meet wasn't at home, so they returned to Ideheno's house. Oguebie had been in the palace and knew that most of the living quarters were similar in style to Ideheno's. Each had a small square yard around which were built rows of rooms, and each room opened onto the yard.

Ideheno brought two chairs so that he and Oguebie could sit in his courtyard and enjoy the rest of the evening.

"We have to make plans for the future," Ideheno said to Oguebie, but Oguebie wasn't paying attention. He listened with half an ear as he watched Ideheno's youngest wife in her room across the yard. She was weaving cotton threads into a broad piece of cloth on a wooden loom. From where he sat, Oguebie saw the white and blue stripes snake their way to the floor. Through the weaver's guild to which she belonged, she made quite a good living trading with the Portuguese and other hinterland merchants. He wanted a wife like that; a woman that knew her way around the place. Suddenly she looked up. She caught Oguebie's eye and smiled knowingly at him before looking away. Oguebie looked sideways to make sure that his friend hadn't seen. It wouldn't do for Ideheno to suspect that Oguebie was sleeping with his wife.

"Mother wants to know if you want to eat now," said a young girl that approached. It was one of Ideheno's younger daughters. Oguebie looked into the room again but it was empty. The girl's mother had most likely gone to prepare the meal.

"Tell her that we are ready," Ideheno replied. A short time later, the girl returned with her mother. They crossed the cobbled yard with two bowls of soup, made of mashed *cocoyam* and *ewedu* with green vegetables that smelled of hot pepper. The men drew a table between them and ate as the woman continued her chores; this time she didn't look at Oguebie.

# CHAPTER

# 16

Onaedo's married life wasn't as free of problems as she'd expected. She and Amechi didn't move into their new compound because their house wasn't completed. Yet Amechi was unable to organize his friends and brothers to finish the project and, in fact, became so irritated each time Onaedo raised the issue that she stopped asking altogether.

Then Amechi grew angry with her for what he considered her betrayal. He returned one night after a day of drinking and started shouting at her.

"You've been with another man before I married you. Did you think that I wouldn't know?"

She was surprised at his verbal attack and all she could do was beg him to keep his voice down. There was no use waking everyone; she was sure that he'd regret it by morning. But he'd ignored her pleas, and in the dim light of their temporary quarters, his eyes blazed like a madman.

"I heard about you and Dualo. It isn't a secret in Abonani."

She'd been too astonished to reply; she hadn't given Dualo a thought in months. It was after that incident that she began to notice Amechi's excessive drinking and knew that it was not normal. He would sometimes start in the morning when honest men were at work and drink steadily throughout the day.

"A man who begins the day with *nkwu* is not going to amount to anything useful," she remembered Eneda saying many times about other people. Now her husband was one of them. She tried to hide her concerns from her mother. She didn't want Ugodi to know that she'd discovered in a short time that her husband was not only lazy but also prone to fits of temper. The alcohol made him unable to perform as a husband. His attempts were patchy, at best, although sometimes when he was in a good mood and sober he made an effort to achieve some satisfaction for both of them. But that was infrequent, and more often his anger exploded like dry *harmattan* tinder at the slightest provocation, its flames searing and destructive to anything in its path. She remembered the story of the *Ada-eze* and the snake, and wondered if that was her fate. Had she married a charming suitor only for him to transform into a snake on their way home as he gave back his disguise and revealed his true self?

Amechi began to wake up late in the day and when he did leave the house, he went to the square instead of the farm. There he sat around and chatted idly with the masquerade carvers doing their daily business. When Onaedo complained, he accused her of incessant nagging.

"If you don't like being married anymore you can go home," he sneered. "And I won't even ask for a refund of the bride-price." That last jibe was supposed to hurt since it was an insult when a husband refused to take back the bride-price. It meant that he wanted to rid himself so desperately of a bad wife that he didn't mind forfeiting the bride-price that he'd paid.

Amechi's mother was of no help and pretended that she did not understand what was going on when Onaedo complained to her. "Go back to your husband and be patient," she counseled Onaedo coldly. She didn't understand why Onaedo bothered her with trivial matters. "Nobody said that marriage was easy."

Onaedo found out later that she had spoiled her son by giving him most of the money that she made from her pottery business; that kind of indulgence only encouraged his laziness.

"From what I have heard, his mother's family back in Ogidi is afflicted by *agwu,* which is a kind of madness," Adanma told her one day. She was the only one whom Onaedo had told of her marital troubles.

"I don't know what to think anymore," Onaedo replied sadly. "All I know is that I'm stuck here."

"To think I encouraged you to marry him."

"You thought you were doing it for the best. I haven't told anybody else yet, but I think I'm pregnant."

Adanma stared at her, barely able to contain her excitement. "Are you sure?"

"I think so," Onaedo replied. "My body feels the way they say it should feel when one is pregnant."

"This is very good news. Everything is going to get better now."

Onaedo looked at her doubtfully.

ငာၽ

Busy times in Abonani came and went and came around again. Onaedo threw her energies into farm work until she began to tire easily and couldn't rise early anymore.

She got up at midmorning and was thankful that Amechi was already gone. She was going to join the other women who had also delayed their departure to feed young ones or catch the late market.

Her mother-in-law walked in with her habitual unhappy demeanor, which seemed to sour even more whenever she set her eyes on Onaedo. However, today she looked at Onaedo with less hostility and was, in fact, almost friendly. Onaedo noticed that she had become friendlier as her pregnancy had progressed. Onaedo hoped that it was a son that she carried, for everyone's sake.

"I don't like the way the baby is lying today," Amechi's mother commented. She poked Onaedo's pregnant belly. It stretched tight and smooth like the skin of a drum. "Too low, if you ask me, like it is in a hurry to come out. You're not ready yet. By my counting, the baby should not be here for another two months." She looked at Onaedo as though she'd done something wrong.

Onaedo felt the baby kick as if in protest at being prodded so early in the day. Her pregnancy had generated a truce between her and Amechi's mother, just as Adanma had suggested it would. She had recently confided in her mother and aunt about her troubles with Amechi. Aku had been very angry. She had wanted to have some words with Amechi's mother but Onaedo had begged her not to.

Her relationship with her husband had also improved; in fact, he seemed to be excited at the prospect of fatherhood, and seemed to have cut down on his drinking.

"I think you should stay home today and farm the plot behind the house instead," Amechi's mother continued. "If the baby wants to come early, at least you won't be caught on the road. I'll leave one of the young ones to stay while I'm away at the farm. At the first sign that the baby is coming, send for your mother and her sister Aku."

"I'll stay home today," Onaedo agreed. She was becoming more tired with each passing day. She would rest at home this once.

She cleaned her house and her mother-in-law's too. The yard was quiet and empty except for the children too young to go to the farm or market. They played under the charge of an older child. Onaedo watched them for a while, remembering her own childhood games not so long ago. Back then, she couldn't wait to grow up so she could go to the farm with the others. Now she was older, married, and would soon be a mother. Her failing marriage saddened her; she hoped that the arrival of their baby might make things better.

She sometimes wondered what a life with Dualo might have been. But such thoughts were not frequent. He was gone and had not returned to Abonani in over a year and that was just as well. She hoped that she wouldn't have time to think of anything else when her baby arrived.

As morning rolled into early afternoon, she settled down for a nap. But sleep was a long time in coming and, when it did, it was roiled by unsettling dreams. She was chased by snakes and dwarf hunters, and every monster of her primal fears. She saw herself arrive breathless at the banks of the Great River and plunged in it to escape her pursuers. One grabbed her tightly by the waist.

So tight, in fact, that she woke with a start. She looked out into the yard where the sun was already high in the sky. Heat rose from the ground in a haze. She was thankful for the cool mud walls that kept out most of it. Suddenly, she felt an odd wet sensation between her legs, and rose. A pool of water had collected beneath her. She again felt the unyielding grip encircling her waist, almost pulling her down; this time, there were no little dwarf men chasing or grasping at her because she was awake.

"Please somebody call Ugodi and Aku right now!" she called out. One of the older children quickly came to investigate. He saw her and ran to fetch help.

# CHAPTER

# 17

The two women fussed over Onaedo all day. Aku wiped the sweat from her face and Ugodi placed warm rags on her lower back.

"You can cry if you want. It's good for you," Aku said. Onaedo barely had enough energy to nod, she was that exhausted. She had been in labor all night, and it was already well into the next day. She was angry too because she'd not expected this much pain. Nobody had warned her as they'd extolled the joys of motherhood. She wasn't sure if she'd ever do this again.

"Do you want to push now?" It was Aku again. Onaedo was too tired and didn't answer.

Aku shook her head in exasperation. "Ugodi, please come and talk to her. I don't know why she won't do anything she's told. Maybe the *agwu* has come already and taken her mind."

"*Chukwu ekwena*! God forbid! There will be no *agwu* here. I saw enough of that with Odera. My child, please, do what she tells you."

Ugodi cajoled Onaedo while Aku brought the birth para-phernalia from her basket. She had a roll of new cloth provided by Amechi; she would wrap the child in it after its delivery onto a banana leaf, its first contact with Ani the earth goddess. Near it, she placed a sharp knife and a small bowl of drying-corn paste for the umbilical stump.

Aku organized everything with precision. She was an experienced and reputable midwife and had rarely lost a mother. In her many years of practice, it was also uncommon for a baby under her care to be damaged or die. There were stories of babies slipping through the fingers of an incompetent birth attendant, breaking a limb or falling on its head, but with her aunt, Onaedo knew that she needn't worry.

As the waves of pain hit her, Onaedo relinquished her hold on the present and moved toward and away from her pain. She heard Ugodi say something but could not hear her clearly. Then she heard Amechi's mother push against the door.

"Is my grandchild here yet?" she asked. "I knew that this baby would be eager to come out. I said it yesterday before I left for the farm."

"Oh, you're back," Aku said. Onaedo noted a disapproving note in her voice. "You can't come in now; she's not ready for visitors."

"This is my house, Aku, in case you've forgotten." From the birthing mat, Onaedo saw them as if in an upside down world, two women engaged in a battle for control, facing off at the door. Ever since Onaedo had told her mother and Aku of her problems with Amechi's mother, Aku especially had not hidden her hostility towards the woman. She pointedly ignored her in public and was barely civil to her when they spoke.

Amechi's mother, for her part, had nothing good to say to Onaedo about Aku either.

"Your mother's sister has madness in her head," she told Onaedo more than once. "Let them call it divination or fortune telling, but I know something's not right with that woman." Onaedo wisely did not repeat any of it to Aku.

"It's not time for you to come in," Aku said, pushing the other woman back gently. "The baby is not here yet, but I want you to fetch more *arigbe*. I didn't bring enough leaves with me, and make sure that somebody has sent for your son. He should be around in the compound in case we need him to fetch something important that only a man can provide."

"What is it that only a man can provide?" Amechi's mother asked with annoyance.

"I don't know yet. Just tell Amechi to be here," Aku said. She tried to shut the door.

"I'll go myself and find whatever you want. It's my grandchild we're talking about," Amechi's mother said. She wedged herself in the doorframe.

"I'll call you when we have the umbilical cord. Then you can show us the child's tree and we'll bury it."

"It will be buried beneath the *ukwa* tree. I chose it a long time ago."

"Then find something to do," Aku snapped. "I'll call when I'm ready."

If she weren't in so much pain, Onaedo would have advised Amechi's mother to leave, because Aku was not going to let her in. Everybody in Abonani knew that Aku, unlike other midwives, never allowed anyone into her birthing rooms. It had been the talk of Abonani for years, and those that supported her practice said that she was right in not wanting distractions from bringing a child into the world. Others thought that she was high-handed and territorial. In the end, there was nothing anybody could do. If Aku didn't want people around her, then that was the way it would be.

"She's gone," Aku said as she closed the door. She had won.

ುಲ

Aku looked at Ugodi and knew that there was a problem. The birth was taking too long. It was true that Onaedo was very young and had not yet finished growing but Aku's first mothers were often this young. She tried not to let Ugodi see her anxiety.

"The baby is coming out," she heard Ugodi announce. She looked down with relief as more of the baby's head appeared.

"My daughter, you have to push hard now," she instructed Onaedo before turning to her sister. "Ugodi, come here. Help me. Make sure the baby makes contact with Ani before you pick her up. The earth goddess must touch her first."

Ugodi spread more banana leaves on the ground and knelt at Aku's side to catch the baby. It came.

She laid it quietly on the leaves without making a sound. It was a girl. Aku saw her puffy face and tiny lips curled in a pucker. Her cord was wound round her neck like a pale snake; Aku quickly cut it in the middle. It came loose and a healthier color came to the baby. She drew a breath and let out a faint cry. It grew stronger when Aku picked her up.

"It's a girl," Aku said. She gave the infant to her sister and turned to Onaedo.

"Can I see her?" Onaedo asked, reaching out. She looked tired; her lips were dry.

"Wait a little," Aku said. She gave her a sip of cold water from a clay bowl. "You still have a little work to do and then I promise I'll give you your baby." Onaedo nodded wearily, fell back on the mat and closed her eyes.

Aku gave Onaedo's belly another worried look. It shouldn't have been still so big.

"Is anything wrong?" Ugodi whispered "You look like you just chewed some bitter *onugbu* leaf."

"I don't know yet," Aku replied, her thundering heart belying her calm exterior. She hoped that her fears wouldn't be realized. Not with Onaedo, of all people . . .

But it happened when Onaedo pushed again. Another baby came slithering out onto the mat in a bloody mess. It was a boy this time. Aku stared at the second baby, as he lay motionless on the mat. The transparent membrane that enclosed him showed the ghastly blue-black color of his skin. But for that, he looked perfect and beautiful in every other way.

Ugodi drew near for a better look and turned to Aku, her shock clear. She was the first to find her voice, low and urgent. She whispered with, "*Chukukwu ekwena*! God forbid! Aku this is an abomination. *Twins?* What will we do?"

"Keep your voice down!" Aku hissed furiously. She looked back at Onaedo drifting in and out of exhausted sleep. She was oblivious to the unfolding drama. Aku's mind searched for a plan.

Twins. It was what had troubled her earlier about this birth. Her experienced eye had told her what her heart had refused to believe, because Onaedo was her own. Maybe this was why she'd seen the bad omen on Onaedo's wedding day. The coffin or box was this. A death. A baby's death.

She turned to Ugodi. "Don't attract attention. There are people outside who will come in when they hear the baby. We must stop them. You must stop them while I take care of Onaedo and the babies."

"Are you crazy? There is no way to take care of this. *Ejima?* Twins have always been an abomination from the beginning of time. It is against Ani. What will we do?"

The baby boy did not move. The other baby wriggled in Ugodi's arms, drawing attention from her brother who lay quiet on the mat. Fear had replaced the earlier joy.

"And you are now the priest of Ani?" Aku hissed angrily at her sister. "You know what Ani wants, do you, now? Who said *ejima* was an abomination? Tell me. Who said that?"

Ugodi looked at her in shocked silence. The baby girl whimpered again in her arms; she hugged her close.

"What is it?" Onaedo asked. She tried to raise herself on one elbow, but fell back weakly. "Why are you both whispering? Where is my baby?"

Aku pressed her hand on Onaedo's shoulder. "Just lie down and rest, my daughter. We have important things to do before your baby will be ready for you to hold. You've done well and you're strong, and your baby is fine."

Onaedo nodded. "I'm so tired," she said and dozed again.

"What are we going to do with twins?" Ugodi whispered to her sister.

Aku regarded her sternly. "I'm telling you, hold yourself together. Now you know why I don't like anybody with me when I catch babies; other people bring confusion."

Ugodi looked at her, perplexed. "I don't understand why this doesn't frighten you. You know how the clan regards this. The babies must be taken to the forest and left there. The mother must be purified for lowering us all to the level of animals with many babies."

Aku glared at her. "Just listen to yourself. Onaedo, your own daughter, has lowered us to animals?"

"I'm only saying what . . ."

Aku interrupted her. "Just keep quiet."

"What do we do now?"

Aku said nothing. She surveyed the mess of blood, birth cords and afterbirths.

"Has this happened to you before?" Ugodi asked again.

"Will you keep quiet? You think that this is the first time that I've seen this? Clean the baby I gave you. There's the warm water, over there."

Ugodi's hands trembled as she did as she was told. Aku looked at her; her panic was for good reason. Aku knew that *ejima*, twins, or any multiple birth was taboo in Abonani and most of *Olu n'Igbo*. The so-called unnatural phenomenon of multiple births was acceptable for animals but not humans. But who had decreed that? That was the question she had asked quietly, many times, over many years. She had never found a satisfactory answer. But now was not the time for questions. She had to move fast.

She gathered the birth products and wrapped them in a wilted banana leaf. Now only the boy was left. She paused and turned to Ugodi who was watching her.

"Look, we all know a twin birth is an abomination." She talked slowly as if imparting the wisdom of the universe to her sister. "It's the law of the land, decreed in ancient times, and we have to obey. But nobody knows where the custom came from. Who was it that decreed that one child was better than two or three if one had them all at once? Who in their right mind made that law?"

Ugodi looked at her but said nothing.

Aku continued. "I did not set out to be disobedient to Ani. My eyes were opened on the day I was called to deliver a baby and discovered that I had *ejima* in my hands; just like today, the first girl was born alive and the other was dead. I was alone with the mother and so I hid the dead one in my basket. Even the new mother did not know what I did. It was just by chance that I happened to be alone in the room. I saved one child that day instead of losing two. From that day onward, I've insisted on being alone to deliver babies."

"What did you do next?" Ugodi asked. She looked as sick and ashy gray as the dead baby on the mat.

"I will tell you later. First help me tidy up."

"Am I awake or should I pinch myself to wake up?" Ugodi said softly. She sounded brittle, but calm. The gravity of the situation had sunk in. "What do we do now?"

"Word of this must not get out," Aku said. She glanced at the still infant on the mat. "He's so handsome. He has his mother's good looks."

"Should we rub his feet to see if we can make him cry?" Ugodi said. She extended an arm to touch the tiny lifeless body.

"Leave him alone," Aku said sharply, pulling Ugodi's arm away. "He's gone. Leave things as they are. His *chi* did not agree that he would be the one to survive. We must let him go." She paused and said more gently, "That's how it's meant to be. Everybody has his or her own *chi* that determines destiny. His own has said he should not live."

She looked over at Onaedo who seemed to be in an exhausted sleep. They could talk for a moment before somebody came in.

"That first time it happened, I took the dead one and threw it away, deep into the Dead Forest. You know I often go there to look for rare herbs, so I know it well. Right away, I was afraid of what I'd done but it was too late to undo it. I lived in fear for days. I could not sleep or eat as I waited for the gods to take revenge. I was sure that I'd be discovered and that the whole of Abonani would be punished for what I had done. I waited for one market week—*Nkwo, Eke, Oye, Afor*—a second week also came and passed, then a third, and a fourth, and still nothing happened. Then a whole year passed. That was when I started to question." She stopped and watched her sister, gauging her reaction.

Ugodi shivered and the new baby became quiet. "This story gives me chills."

"Yes, it also sent chills in my head but I asked myself what kind of god would decree that a woman would carry a pregnancy for nine months, go through the double pain of labor for twins and then throw the children away? Eh?" Aku could feel the anger she felt about this gather inside her. "Where does that happen? What god is this that is so hostile to women? What was the reason behind it? I asked the priest of Ani this question a long time ago. I said to him, Ani is a female deity; they even show her sometimes with a baby in her arms; why would she want women to suffer like this? He did not have a clear answer for me and I did not ask again, because I didn't want to raise his suspicions. After all, what does a mere woman know of such things?

"It seemed to me," Aku continued, "that if the world was upside down and it was men that underwent childbirth, this law would not exist. They would never have allowed it; somebody would have challenged it a long time ago. As women, we have no control over important events in our lives. They let us take titles but our voices are silenced when important things are discussed. Moreover, we are our own worst enemies because we never question that which would harm us."

"We cannot do much," Ugodi said. "The laws of the land keep everything in place. If not for them, people would do as they pleased and there wouldn't be order."

"That's what they tell us. My question, which I dare not ask aloud, is *Who decided that ejima was a bad thing?*"

Ugodi sat heavily on a stool. She cradled the sleeping newborn child in her arms. She looked dazed. Aku stopped talking for a minute, worried, but Ugodi asked her to continue. "I have to hear everything."

"There was a legend of an Abonani woman," Aku continued. "After years of infertility and a miraculous pregnancy, she decided to follow her twins to the forest when they threw them way; she was obeying a mother's heart. She was never seen again, and it is said she took her children and left for a distant, unknown land, a faraway place where twins are revered, even worshipped. Sometimes I wonder how come these people with *ejima* that live amongst them are not all dead. How are their gods so different from ours that they accept their *ejima* while our own gods want us to kill ours? This is what gave me the strength to continue doing what I do. I said to myself that I would save the babies I could. Fortunately I've not had to do this often."

The last was a lie. She'd done it more times than she'd admit to her sister. She didn't want to scare her more than she was already. She didn't tell Ugodi that over the years, she'd been required to do more and more to maintain secrecy. More than she could put into words.

Aku looked at her bloody hands and went to the corner to wash them. She had one more task to complete. She looked at Ugodi. She still looked lost and Aku felt some sympathy for her. It was a lot to digest in one day. She knew that Ugodi would not understand the reasons for her actions so far from the norm. Aku wasn't even sure that she understood her own reasons, but inside her burned the zeal of a crusader. She had fought a silent, unsung war for years and nothing would stop her now. Her victory was in seeing those children as adults without anybody knowing any better.

"What happens if both children are alive?" Ugodi asked. "How do you choose which one to save?"

"It doesn't happen often," Aku replied. She busied herself collecting her things. She had lied again; she'd said enough for one day. Ugodi was strong but Aku wondered if it was wise to have unburdened herself to her sister. Ugodi was a traditionalist; her husband was a man of importance in upholding the traditions of the clan. On the other hand, this was her daughter. Aku knew that this would disturb Ugodi but that she would overcome it for her daughter's sake. Moreover, Aku was relieved to share the secret that had weighed on her for so long and her sister was the only living being that she could possibly have told.

"Can I see my baby now?" Onaedo's question startled the two women. Aku had almost forgotten her.

Onaedo tried to pull herself up again "Why are you both whispering?"

Aku looked at Ugodi and placed a finger across her lips as a warning. "Please give her the baby."

ကာ

Aku worked swiftly. She separated the two afterbirths. Nobody would know there were two.

The boy's lips moved suddenly as she wrapped his head. She stopped. She wondered if it was her imagination. His little blue lips opened again but he was silent, with eyes glued shut. His chest didn't rise and fall with life. For a brief, irrational moment, like Ugodi, she debated within herself whether to try ushering him back to life. Then she stopped; there was no point. He was half of another, an unwelcome duplication. She would let him return to *ani muo*, to join the departed ancestors, back to those that had sent him here in error. She hoped that he would go quietly; otherwise, she would have no choice but take matters into her own hands. He could not be allowed to live and jeopardize his sister.

But he seemed to know what was at stake, because he did not create further problems and did not draw another breath. She tidied everything up quickly and, holding him briefly to her chest in silent prayer, she wished him a safe journey before laying him gently in the basket and covering him with banana leaves. She hurriedly removed the rest of the evidence before somebody came into the room.

This was dangerous work. If word ever got out, she would be as good as dead. She shivered whenever she remembered the many times she had almost been found out.

"What are you going to do with it?" Ugodi's voice broke into her thoughts. She gestured towards the basket. "That baby."

"Don't concern yourself with it," Aku replied. "Take care of Onaedo and the baby girl and I will see about appeasing whatever gods need to be pacified."

"How do you get away with this?" Aku saw new respect in her sister's eyes despite her earlier fears.

"I'm still here, am I not? You are my mother's child, and so I will tell you the truth. I'm not inexperienced. Have you not wondered why I'm the only midwife who never appears to have a twin birth to report? Nobody has noticed, and so I have gone about my work undetected. I'm like the palm-wine tapper who never reveals all that he sees when he's up there. I've seen strange things that would blind the unprepared eye.

"Many years ago I visited a strong medicine man in another town to make me the strongest protection possible for this dangerous work. He told me to go home. When I asked why, he said that whatever I was doing was right and that I need not fear. I was surprised, since I hadn't told him my line of work but, from that day on, my heart became stronger."

"But if a second twin is born alive what do you do? How can you hide something like that?" Ugodi asked again.

Aku held her sister's gaze in a steady stare. "My sister, are you sure that you want me to answer that question?"

"Yes, I want to know."

"I wrap them tightly until they stop breathing," Aku whispered, bending close to her ear. "I stop them from crying. The most difficult one was when there were more than two and it became dangerous to take away two and leave one. That was the only time I ever revealed the birth and they took all three. After that episode, I swore to find a way to save at least one. I take the bodies and bury them right away in the Dead Forest. Can you keep all this to yourself?"

"Yes," Ugodi answered. She looked ill.

"Even from Eneda?" Aku persisted.

"You're my sister, the only other child of my mother. We came from the same womb. You're closer to me than any husband could be. I'll never reveal what you've told me today." Tears filled Ugodi's eyes and ran down her cheeks.

"Why are you crying?" Aku said. "Dry your eyes unless you want people to start to wonder what's wrong. It will be all right."

"Look at my new daughter," Onaedo called out from the mat. "Whom would you say she looks like the most?" Onaedo's joy was like a dash of cold water bringing Aku and Ugodi abruptly back into the present. Onaedo held up her baby daughter and the two women looked at each other.

"We should prepare for visitors," Aku said.

CHAPTER

# 18

Oguebie looked around his new house. It had turned out better than he'd envisioned. The style of the house was different from that which he was used to, more modern, he thought. He didn't have an *obi* like he did at Abonani. The main house was built in a U-shape with rows of rooms on either side of his living quarters that were in the middle.

He sat on a wooden lounge-chair in his main room and snuffed tobacco. He had moved most of his family here as soon as the house was complete. Regretfully, he had to terminate his liaison with Ideheno's wife when he moved out of his friend's house. He missed her midnight visits to his room; she'd come while her husband slept. He longed for her thighs that wrapped around him as he thrust into her, and tried to keep quiet their illicit pleasure. He sighed again.

"Come here," he called out to a small girl crossing the yard with a pitcher of water on her head. "Where is your mother and where is the food that I asked for a long time ago?"

"I don't know," the girl answered sullenly. Why was she always in a bad mood? Oguebie wondered, debating whether to scold her or just let her go. Just like her mother. Only two of his wives had agreed to leave Abonani with him and the girl's mother was one of them; the others had stayed behind, which was just as well since he still needed to have his eyes and ears back there. Moreover, it was time to marry a local woman, to establish a foothold in his adopted city.

"Go and find out where she is," he shouted at the girl who rolled her eyes rudely and left to look for her mother.

Oguebie sighed. He felt lost and dislocated here in the Delta City. He was a foreigner; his acceptance in court was only the result of his relationship with Ideheno. That was how he had to play it for now. He had been back to Abonani only once in the past year, and luckily, there had been no indication that they knew what he'd been doing. He and Ideheno had been very clever in hiding their dealings with the Portuguese and capturing slaves. They'd started another business with the Portuguese as a way to hide their activities. It was a legitimate trade that dealt in commodities in exchange for velvet, silk, and alcohol. But it was a slow business and the bargaining was tiresome; sometimes it took days and weeks to complete. That type of unhurried trading was no longer compatible with his temperament and his new craving for instant wealth.

From time to time, he and Ideheno traveled away from the city on slave raids with any Portuguese merchants that were in the country on business. Alvarez and Pasquale had returned twice and had brought more guns and other ware for sale. This wasn't really fulfilling for Oguebie and hadn't been the kind of major trading that he'd envisioned. Altogether, the whole enterprise was spiraling into disappointment, but he was nothing if not resourceful. If there was a way to increase his business he would find it, even if it meant taking more risks. He got up and gathered his cloth about him. He had a meeting with Ideheno at the palace.

"I'm leaving," he called out to nobody in particular. He wasn't really hungry anyway; his youngest wife had already fed him a snack of palm-nut soup with fried peppered snails.

The crowd was thinning outside. People hurried home after a day of hard work. There was a new project, a massive extension of the wall that surrounded the city that would be miles longer than it was now.

He strolled leisurely and contemplated his future once more. His mood lifted as he looked around. He still had a lot to learn and life wasn't so bad. Much work remained, and he had to find another plan.

ॐ

Pasquale had been back in Lisbon for a year and there had been no more voyages. He looked around his print shop and tried to feel contentment with his success. His dream had been realized beyond his expectations; the printing press was very profitable.

Orders for his books poured in at an exhilarating rate and he had to struggle to maintain his inventory so as not to disappoint his customers. It was as if all of Lisbon was undergoing a Renaissance of reading and writing. He even thought of purchasing a second press. *But there would be nowhere to put it in here,* he thought, looking at the gigantic wooden contraption that occupied the room already. It was a Gutenberg Press and he owned one now. Nobody would have thought two years ago that he could have afforded something like this. Even his mother had been impressed when she visited the shop.

Pasquale ran a finger over the types—alphabets carved on wooden blocks that spelled words and sentences and whole stories when laid flat within a wooden frame. The lettered blocks were coated with black ink, and pages of books were created when blank sheets were pressed over them to produce prints.

He went into the back storeroom to inspect his dwindling supply of paper. The paper shortage plagued every bookmaker in Lisbon; to address the problem, he had invested in a local paper mill. He had loaned the paper manufacturer money to purchase vats, water mills, and a storehouse. They purchased cotton rags from Italian merchants before breaking them down into pulp, the raw material for paper. It was a laborious process and made books more expensive than they needed to be but it had made him rich. He had been able to afford the manufacture of books because of his very lucrative trade in slaves from Africa.

Despite deep misgivings, he had made two very profitable journeys back to the Guinea Coast and Sao Tome with Alvarez to buy and sell more slaves before finally withdrawing his money from the *Santa Magdalena*.

Pasquale stood in the middle of his shop, looking at the shelves crammed with books at various stages of manufacture. His senior apprentice was Rafael, a thin, pale, curly-haired youth of about fifteen years. He was engrossed in setting a new page. The junior assistant was a black boy of seven or eight. He waited patiently with a small ink pail, ready to paint the letters before pressing.

"I think that you've missed a letter here," the child said pointing out the offending word to Rafael.

Pasquale looked over Rafael's shoulder. "Gregorio is right, let me help," he said, rearranging the letters. He turned to the child smiling. "That's very good Gregorio. Soon, you'll own your own shop."

Gregorio looked at the floor and said nothing. Pasquale felt ashamed of himself. The boy was a slave, a clever one, but a slave and would never own a print shop.

"Bring the ink here," he told him.

Both boys began to paint the letters and press blank sheets over them. They replenished the ink frequently as the wet pages rolled out.

Pasquale always felt guilty around Gregorio. The boy had recounted to Pasquale how he'd been returning from an errand with his mother when they were captured. They were loaded on the same ship but, during one of the stops, he'd been separated from her. Pasquale guessed that his mother had been taken off the ship at El Mina and perhaps sent to the New World—Brazil, Chile, or someplace like that. He remembered that he had felt sorry for the crying child and had insisted to Alvarez that they bring him to Lisbon and not sell him in Sao Tome.

Pasquale had renamed him Gregorio and for the first few months, the boy had cried incessantly. He was so homesick that

Pasquale had briefly considered returning to look for his people—a very impractical thought, he later admitted. The boy's mother was gone, probably to another part of the world or perhaps even dead. Under the care of Pasquale's mother and his fiancée Sofia, Gregorio had overcome the worst of his melancholia. But it worried Pasquale that the boy seldom smiled or played with other children although he watched them in the streets with a sad, longing look.

Despite that, Gregorio learned quickly. He became fluent in Portuguese in a very short time. Under Sofia's tutelage, he'd learned to read. The boy must be a genius, Pasquale thought, and had even considered making him the primary apprentice. He thought better of it in light of Gregorio's young age and because the older Rafael would have been resentful of such an arrangement.

Pasquale watched Gregorio study each type meticulously, silently mouthing each word as Rafael laid them out. He looked smart in the faded jacket and old grey breeches that had once been Pasquale's. He knew that Sofia tutored him in secret and was responsible for the speed with which the boy had learned to read and write.

Pasquale smiled as he usually did when he thought about Sofia. He was in love for the first time in his life, to a clandestine scholar in a place where it was not usual for women who were not nuns to pursue so much knowledge. But Pasquale did not mind. He cherished and encouraged his future wife's studies, tacitly encouraging all her intellectual pursuits. He loved her even more when she told him that she was the happiest young woman in Lisbon when she thought of marrying a man that owned so many books.

He wiped his hands on a rag. "We should lock up for the day," he said. They had pegged the wet pages to dry on the lines that ran back and forth across the length of the shop. There was enough material for at least a dozen books, and a dozen books in a day was a very generous income. Yes, business was good and life in general, even better. He had no reason to complain, yet . . .

"Time to go," he said to both boys. "Tidy up and lock the shop. I have business I need to attend to this evening."

They prepared for the next morning; Rafael bid them good-night and left.

"Hurry on home," Pasquale said to Gregorio outside the shop. "Tell Mama that I have business in town and will be home late."

"Yes, Senhor," the boy replied and turned for home while Pasquale walked to the harbor.

ﮨﮨ

Pasquale knew it was the call of the sea that drew him again. Just like before.

He looked up and saw that he was already at the waterfront. He saw the *Santa Magdalena* and knew that Alvarez was nearby. He'd come to the bookshop yesterday to ask if Pasquale was interested in investing in a slave shipment again. Pasquale had said no, his shop was doing well and he didn't need the money. He'd boasted to Alvarez of his financial successes and informed him that he'd moved his mother to a bigger house in a newer, cleaner part of town.

But Alvarez had looked at him and shrugged as if he were looking through a veneer of respectability and seeing something of which Pasquale was unaware. "I just thought you might be interested, my friend," he had said, as if he'd not heard Pasquale. "The profits now are a lot more than they were. Slaves are worth more than gold and they're in demand at the mines of El Mina and the plantations of the Madeira, Sao Tome, and Brazil. Another thing that might interest you is cotton; you need that for paper." Alvarez had said, "You can buy cloth cheaper from the Delta City than from the Italians. But if you say that you've made enough money . . ." he let the rest hang unsaid in the air. He looked around the print shop with a haughty air that annoyed Pasquale.

". . . then I won't bother you any further," Alvarez said. "You know where to find me if you change your mind," he added, and left.

Now Pasquale had come looking. He stopped in front of the tavern where he knew he would find Alvarez. The smell of wine and spicy food told him that the night's business had begun. He entered the dark room to find his old business partner and knew he was ready for a new adventure.

CHAPTER

# 19

O naedo counted the days in her head; it was now almost eight market weeks since the birth of her daughter. The baby was due for naming. That was why Udoka, Amechi's oldest living female relative, was visiting this morning.

"How are you and the baby?" she asked. She leaned on her walking stick and regarded Onaedo with rheumy eyes. She wiped them with the back of her hand and didn't try to take the baby, for which Onaedo was relieved; from the way her old hands shook, she was bound to drop the child. Udoka was given the task of finding a suitable name for Onaedo and Amechi's new daughter. She had treated her task with the gravity it deserved by consulting far and wide, within the family and outside it. She'd taken note of all the important events in the family and the community at the time of the birth.

"I have consulted with two *dibias* to find out who has reincarnated in this child and they both said the same thing," the old woman said. She leaned on her stick for balance as she took her stool from the young boy who carried it for her wherever she went. She placed it on the floor carefully before she sat down.

"Who is it?" Onaedo asked apprehensively. She hoped it was no one quarrelsome.

"They both said that she's Eneda's oldest sister. She was married to a man from another town and died under suspicious circumstances. Her body was returned to Abonani for burial on her father's land as tradition demands," she said. She leaned forward and her voice lowered into a hoarse whisper. "Anyway, that is who has come back in your daughter."

"Is she back for revenge? Is my daughter going to be alright?" Onaedo asked. She was unprepared for the news.

Udoka looked at her and laughed. "Don't worry about your daughter. She's starting her own life, a new life. I've chosen a few names for her and will send them to your father and Amechi's father; I will advise them of my findings and they can each make the final choice on names," she said. She began to eat a breakfast of roast yam and sliced locust beans soaked in palm oil. Onaedo also presented her with a white hen as a gift for her exertions.

The next day Adanma came to visit. "Unoma? That is what you are going to call her?" Adanma exclaimed when Onaedo told her about her choice. They sat in the yard in front of Onaedo and Amechi's temporary building. Their new compound still wasn't ready, but it was near completion. Or so she hoped.

"Unoma means a Good House, a Peaceful House" Adanma said. "What's good about this place? Your husband's done nothing but mistreat you since you came here."

Onaedo shrugged. "It's not up to me. That will be her name because Amechi's father has chosen it. My name for her is Ogugua, which Eneda also chose. Ogugua—The One Who Consoles."

"I can't say I like that name any better. Why such a big name for such a small child?"

"There's nothing wrong with Ogugua. As the name suggests, she's The One Who Consoles Me. Remember, my father is still in mourning for the death of First Wife; that's why he chose it. It has many meanings for him."

"I still think that you could have found a better name," Adanma said. "Every time you hear her name, you'll think of death."

"Are names not supposed to mean something? Isn't that why we go into such trouble to find a suitable one?" Onaedo asked. She really wasn't in the mood for this argument about names.

Adanma snorted, unconvinced as she played with the baby. Onaedo watched. Adanma had kept her promise to visit often and their friendship had remained strong. She seemed to glow with happiness and contentment.

"I see that Udemezue is treating you well. When is your baby coming?" Onaedo asked.

"Oh? Am I showing already?" Adanma asked, patting her rounding belly.

"Ugodi told me. Anyway, I'm very happy that you are married to my brother. You're my friend and now my sister-in-law too."

"You've always been my sister, Onaedo, although we are not of the same mother."

"That's true. So how is Odera treating you as second wife?" Onaedo asked. She missed hearing the family gossip.

"I've had no problems with her," Adanma replied. "She was resentful at first but after a while, when she saw that I was not interested in usurping her place, she left me alone. I'm lucky, your family has been very welcoming to me, unlike Amechi's mother who is a witch," said Adanma. She gave back the baby.

"Ssh! Please keep your voice down," Onaedo whispered looking around. "Why do you say that?"

"Everybody in Abonani knows," Adanma retorted, "Anyway I was joking. She's not a real witch, just a wicked woman."

"You're right about that. I don't have the mouth to tell anybody what I'm going through here," Onaedo said warming up. "She treats me like a slave, let me not lie to you. When Ugodi was here for *omugwo*, the period after the birth when I should be resting, I spent the whole time trying to make peace between them. Because we don't have our own compound, they were in each other's way and Ugodi complained aloud that Amechi should have built me my own kitchen. Both women are headstrong and neither would give in to the other. So when First Wife died, I was relieved. I begged my mother to go home to my father and help with the funeral because I did not have the strength for the fighting between her and Amechi's mother anymore."

"But your mother was right; you should have your own kitchen and not be inside one cooking pot with your mother-in-law. So now that Ugodi returned home to your father, what will you do? Amechi's mother is crazy. Can she help you take care of a newborn baby?"

"The baby is older and I have a helper now. When she left, Ugodi sent my little cousin Ogechi to help me and she's still here. Let's talk about something more pleasant," Onaedo said. Just then, a voice called from over the wall. They both looked towards the gate as it opened to let Aku through. She had a small gourd in one hand and greeted the young women before turning to Onaedo.

"Have all your wounds not healed yet?"

"I'm better," Onaedo replied, happy to see her aunt. After her mother's departure, Aku had volunteered to visit her frequently to help with different rituals like bathing the baby, taking care of her umbilical stump and making sure Onaedo was breastfeeding properly, eating and sleeping well.

"Here, drink this palm wine," Aku said. "It will make your milk flow better." She put the gourd on the floor beside Onaedo and took the baby from her.

"I don't want to get drunk this early in the day," Onaedo joked as she took a sip.

"Keep it away from that husband of yours," Aku replied.

"I should leave now." Adanma got up and offered her stool to Aku. "My husband will want his food soon, but I'll be back soon to visit."

"I'll escort you to the gate," Onaedo said following behind.

ന്റ

"It's said that the *harmattan* season is a tough time to give birth," Aku said later. "Its drying wind makes everything painful. I can see how slowly you are moving."

"The pain is bearable now that my wounds have had time to heal," Onaedo said and sat down again beside her.

Aku adjusted her position on the stool and rested the baby face down on her outstretched legs. She scooped warm water from a big clay bowl onto the baby who protested loudly. Onaedo dipped a finger into the warm water, and stirred it absently. A thin layer of ash blown in from the fireplace settled on its surface. She'd been debating whether to talk to Aku about her dreams. She was used to vivid dreams, especially since her pregnancy, but they were more intrusive, of late, leaving her tired and wondering about things in the morning.

"I'm having a lot of dreams."

"What kind of dreams?" asked Aku, massaging the baby gently with a lump of shea butter.

"In my dreams I see two children—a boy and a girl. When I try to hold their hands the boy pulls away and runs. I try to call him back, but he ignores me and keeps running." She looked worried and chewed her lips nervously. This particular dream awoke something that remained elusive.

"Does the boy you describe look happy or sad?" Aku asked, rubbing the baby's limbs each in turn.

Onaedo thought for a moment. "I don't know, but I've noticed he's the exact image of my daughter, and I sometimes can't even tell them apart. I wake up when he jumps into the river and swims away."

"Listen to me, my daughter." Aku stopped rubbing the baby. "I don't interpret dreams but I think that he's probably your next child telling you that you will be pregnant again and it will be a son the next time."

Onaedo frowned. For a moment she felt that Aku was keeping something from her. Maybe she'd had a Sighting and didn't want to alarm her.

"My mother's sister, did anything happen the day that my daughter was born? Something worries me and confuses me. I cannot clearly remember what happened that day . . ."

Aku shook her head, cutting her off. "Nothing happened. Your daughter is healthy and well." She stood with the baby whose skin was now shiny with oil. "It's getting cold. Let's go indoors," Aku said, leading the way.

CHAPTER

# 20

The relationship between Onaedo and Amechi deteriorated again after the birth of their daughter. Months after the birth, Amechi fell back into his old ways, which meant he did nothing all day and picked a quarrel with Onaedo at the slightest provocation. Then he drank even more.

Onaedo had made a new friend. Her name was Ndidi. She was one of the young wives married to a half-brother of Amechi's. Onaedo found her a sympathetic confidante.

"I see it in his eyes sometimes. I think he would like to beat me," Onaedo said to her one day. She'd vented her feelings for months. "I won't give him a reason, but if he does, I will fight back."

They sat in front of their house, the old one that they still lived in because Amechi had not bothered to complete their new house yet. She plucked a chicken as Ndidi broke open kola-nut pods and cleaned the nuts inside. Ndidi nodded and said nothing.

"Did you hear what I said?" Onaedo asked. She wanted Ndidi to tell her something funny, as she often did. The older girl amused her with an endless stock of humorous stories and droll wisdom on life's issues. She had a sense of mischief that appealed to Onaedo.

"Do you want me to tell you that you can't fight a man, especially your husband?" Ndidi replied, laughing. "If a man comes after you, run as fast as you can. Didn't your mother ever teach you that a woman doesn't fight with a man unless she wants to be hurt? I always knew that you were a little crazy."

Onaedo laughed. "You can leave my mother out of it but I meant what I just said."

"That doesn't mean that you should be so foolish as to fight your husband."

"You're right," Onaedo said. She pulled hard on the feathers of the hen. The chicken had developed wryneck, twisting its neck into sinuous curves. Amechi's mother had asked her to kill and cook it right away before it died from whatever was ailing it. She prodded the dead bird and submerged it in the hot water to help loosen its feathers.

Ndidi carefully piled the clean kola-nuts on a wooden platter.

"We still don't have our own compound after all this time and he's not even ashamed," Onaedo said. A cloud of steam rose from the hot water and she paused to wipe her brow. She placed the half-plucked hen on a pile of leaves to prevent the skin from peeling off if left in the hot water for too long. "His mother still orders me about like a servant and not a full grown woman in her own house. She's a wicked woman."

"Ssh, don't let her hear you, but you are right. Before you married Amechi, we used to wonder what kind of woman he was going to marry that would tolerate him and his mother. She's a foolish woman who spoiled her son and made him useless. She sent him to her people in Ogidi to help make him industrious but they didn't do better in raising him."

Onaedo hissed in disgust. "Now they think that they'll take it out on me, Eneda's daughter, but they don't know who I am. I am tougher than dry meat; the kind that fills the mouth. I wish I hadn't married him. There was another man that I loved. He would have been much better for me."

"You shouldn't say such things where people can hear you," Ndidi said looking around uneasily.

"I have nothing to hide. I've already sworn at the family shrine that this baby is Amechi's child just like every pregnant woman must do with their first child."

"I wouldn't know anything about that," Ndidi said. She had no children, even though she had been married for over three years. Despite that, she maintained a very optimistic attitude to life; Onaedo thought her name suited her perfectly because Ndidi meant Patience.

"Ooh."

"Don't worry. Here, eat some kola-nut," Ndidi said, shrugging away Onaedo's unspoken apology. She gave her half of a kola-nut.

"Can women break a kola nut?" Onaedo smiled as she wiped her hand on her waistcloth. She ate it and took a sip of water from a clay bowl. She didn't like the tartness of kola-nuts very much but liked their sweet after-taste, made even better with cold water.

"Let them come and catch me," Ndidi said in a conspiratorial low tone and they burst out laughing.

Onaedo laid the chicken on a cutting stone and went to retrieve a knife from the rafter of the cooking house she still shared with Amechi's mother. She returned to sit beside Ndidi.

She'd made up her mind that she was going to leave Amechi. That was the only logical thing to do. She was fed up. Even Amechi's father had not been much help. Words had failed the normally verbose man in the face of his son's lackadaisical attitude. All he could offer Onaedo, after he had upbraided his son to no avail, was to counsel patience. It would all pass he said, Amechi was going through a bad patch. But the words of her father-in-law were spoken with little conviction. I'm not to blame, was the unspoken message she heard; after all, I raised other sons who are all successful.

The problem with leaving was that she didn't want to admit failure; she couldn't bear to disappoint her family. She knew that marriage was like hot soup—Eat it slowly and it will cool down eventually. That was advice she'd heard Eneda give others in the past.

"You're lucky," Onaedo said to Ndidi after a while. "Your husband is quite devoted to you. Everybody sees it."

"That's true. We are going to marry another wife so that we can try to have a child." The way Ndidi said 'we' made Onaedo envious. Here was a husband and wife that considered marrying another wife a joint effort.

"Ogechi, bring the baby here," Onaedo called to a young girl of about nine or ten who had appeared from the backyard with the baby on her back. Every so often, she stopped to hoist the baby into a comfortable position.

"Shouldn't that child be walking by now?" Ndidi said smiling at Ogugua as the toddler tried to slide off the older girl's back. "Onaedo, you'll make your daughter a cripple if you don't let Ogechi put her on the ground once in a while."

Ogugua smiled shyly at both her mother and Ndidi. She had a solitary black bead strung around her chubby waist and rushed unsteadily across the short distance to her mother as soon as her feet touched the ground. She beamed a self-congratulatory smile when she reached the safety of Onaedo's knee.

"You see, she can walk when she wants to," Onaedo said, smiling indulgently as she stroked her daughter's tightly curled hair. The child searched for her mother's breast, found the nipple, and begun to suck enthusiastically.

Ndidi reached over, patting Ogugua fondly on the head. "Eh, Onaedo don't tell me that this old woman is still sucking on your breast."

"I haven't been able to stop her."

"Rub *onugbu* leaves on your breast. That is how the others do it. The bitterness will make her stop."

"I did that and she just sucked the bitterness and spat it out," Onaedo replied "But the reason I have not stopped her is because I don't want another baby yet."

"Eh?"

"They say if you continue to give your baby your breast then you can delay the coming of the next baby."

"Now I know something is wrong with you. Whoever heard of preventing the births of children that your *chi* has given you? But the dog said that those of us with buttocks don't know how to sit on them," Ndidi said, frowning and shaking her head.

"Didn't you hear what I have been saying about Amechi?"

"I heard you, but that's not a reason to chase children away."

Onaedo remained quiet because she knew that she'd upset the childless Ndidi again with this talk of not wanting any more children. One didn't extol the virtues of sight to a blind man. She regretted the turn the conversation had taken.

She dried her hands and motioned to Ogechi. "Finish cutting the hen and let us cook dinner." She stood with Ogugua still attached to her breast and balanced her firmly on one hip. She bade Ndidi goodnight.

Ndidi replied without looking up as she walked away.

ငွာ

As their married life continued to deteriorate, Amechi became more unreasonable in his treatment of Onaedo. He would demand that she leave everything she was doing and attend to his every whim. Onaedo knew now that something was seriously wrong with her husband. He definitely needed the services of a *dibia* she concluded, but nobody approached a medicine man for a problem with mental illness. It was a taboo that was as strong as any other, and Onaedo knew that she had a serious problem on her hands.

She was sweeping the yard and heard him stir inside their house, the temporary one they still lived in. She looked up to see him come from the room. He had just awoken from a nap and it was late in the afternoon already. Looking at him now with his puffy face and thickening waistline, the pouch that had come from too much drinking and too little work, she wondered why she had ever found him handsome.

Amechi rubbed his eyes and yawned before he saw her. His face tightened and she braced for trouble.

"I'm hungry," he called out rudely. "Leave that thing you are doing and prepare my food."

She sighed in exasperation. She wanted to remind him he had eaten just before his nap and that it was still a couple of hours before the evening meal. She decided not to aggravate him or the situation. *Maybe he'll leave me alone if I do what he wants,* she muttered under her breath. She bit the retort that hovered at the tip of her tongue.

She got him the food and placed the bowl on the floor at his side before she went outside to complete her task.

"I see you want to poison me," Amechi bellowed a few minutes later, coming out of the room with the bowl in one hand. He glared balefully at her. "You're using salt to cover the taste."

"The food is fine," Onaedo said, laying the broom on the ground again and taking the bowl from him. "Let me taste it in your presence to show you it's not poisoned."

"You are just a bad woman," Amechi replied, clearly looking for further accusations to throw at her.

She looked at him contemptuously. She thought he was ridiculous, standing there like a quarrelsome woman with the wooden bowl in one hand still half-full of the okra soup and gathering his loincloth with the other. It was clear that he had no legitimate complaint.

"I took care to prepare that soup, I even . . ." Onaedo started to say, but trailed off when Amechi interrupted.

"Why don't you keep your mouth shut?" he shouted following after her. "I'm your husband and you should give me more respect." His voice rose with his temper. His eyes were bloodshot and the stale odor of his breath from a morning of drinking filled the air.

She bent to continue her task. If she ignored him, he would calm down as usual; this had been the pattern of late.

What if my daughter has inherited this *agwu*? She thought. She poured a handful of dust on some chicken droppings to dry it before she swept it away. Why had nobody revealed this significant family flaw during the enquiry stage before the marriage? Now it seemed too late for her to do anything about it.

She tried unsuccessfully to block Amechi's voice from her mind as he continued to taunt her. "Woman, you were desperate until I married you and now it's a different story. I can't say anything to you without being attacked."

"Who is desperate?" Onaedo retorted, unable to stick to her resolve of not answering back. "I had a lot of suitors to choose from before you came along. I don't know why I was crazy enough to marry you."

"Just keep quiet and sweep the yard, foolish woman," Amechi said, sounding triumphant. Onaedo knew he was happy that he had gotten a reaction from her. "Look," he said pointing, "there are goat pellets everywhere. Is this how you sweep a yard?"

Onaedo threw all caution to the wind and stood, hand on hip. "Look who's talking. The laziest man in *Olu n'Igbo*," she jeered. "When was the last time you did any work?"

It was then that her face exploded in a shower of flashing lights. She had never been hit so hard. Putting her hand to her burning cheek, she glared in rage at Amechi. *No more of this*, she thought and taking Amechi between the legs she heaved with all her strength. He landed on the ground, dust rising around him, his eyes wide in surprise. Onaedo jumped on him, pinned him on the ground with her weight and pummeled his face with both hands.

"You wicked, bad woman!" screamed Amechi's mother who had suddenly appeared at the doorway of her house. She rushed towards them. "Get off him! Leave him alone! I say leave him alone!" Her shrill cries rent the air.

Onaedo's head jerked hard as the older woman grabbed her hair and tried to swing her away from her prostrate son.

"I knew you were trouble the first day you set foot in this compound." She turned an accusatory eye on Onaedo, panting hard. "You and your arrogance will destroy this family. You're a foolish girl. My son should never have married you. It was my husband's idea and I should never have agreed."

Onaedo knew that she was outnumbered when the other wives and children gathered. Thankfully, they did not join the attack, although they did nothing to help her. She had to make a move. It was now, or never.

She extricated herself from her husband and quickly ran into the house. She rushed to a narrow ledge that ran along the wall just below the thatched roof of their room. She found what she was looking for, the small package that held her jewelry, her dowry and most valuable possession. She weighed it in her hand to make sure it was intact. It wouldn't have surprised her if her husband had found it somehow and sold it for palm-wine. Luckily, he hadn't. She ran outside again and went behind the house.

"Quick! Quick! Get Ogugua and follow me," she called to Ogechi who was playing with the toddler. Ogechi gathered the baby, and thrust her towards Onaedo. They ran out through the gate.

The clouds in the distance were heavily overcast with the promise of rain. Onaedo felt the air cool as they ran. A faint, low rumble of thunder signaled a deluge in some distant place. They continued to run, not sure of who followed. Onaedo had stopped briefly to tie Ogugua more firmly to her back.

"Can we slow down now?" Ogechi wheezed noisily. She bent to catch her breath.

"Yes, I think that we're safe now," Onaedo said. They slowed their pace and continued in the direction of Eneda's house, putting distance between them and the confusion of the compound behind them.

CHAPTER

# 21

U demezue finished his breakfast and walked the short distance from his compound to his father's. He wondered why Eneda wanted to see him so early and so urgently.

He met Onaedo at the front gate. She had a small basket under one arm. It had been almost three months since she'd left Amechi's house and returned home. Udemezue had felt a surge of anger the day he'd heard what Amechi had done. In fact, he had organized a handful of his friends to find Amechi to give him the beating of his life, but Eneda had got wind of their plan and stopped him.

"Suppose you commit *ochu* defending your sister? Murder is a worse crime than beating your wife. Leave the *umunna* of both families to take care of it. His father has already approached me through an emissary to apologize. They want to know if Onaedo wishes to come back so they can start the process of formally asking for her return. "Moreover," Eneda added laughing, "Onaedo disgraced him by throwing him on the ground. What kind of a man is beaten by a woman?"

Udemezue had seen the humor in it too but he knew underneath it all Eneda was worried. His mother's house was too cramped for Onaedo and her child and Eneda told him that he must think the unthinkable; if Onaedo did not reconcile with Amechi or remarry soon he would have to build her a little place of her own.

"The *umunna* is not going to like it," Eneda had said. "They'll ask me where in *Olu n'Igbo* that a woman is given family land? But what choice do I have? Where is the provision in our custom for a once-married daughter to return home with her child and not to go back to her husband? Do they expect me to throw her away? Surely, there must be a place for her. She belongs with the family."

Udemezue had asked Onaedo privately what she wanted to do and she had said she wanted to give it more thought. Udemezue suspected that she had no desire to return to her husband. He couldn't say that he blamed her; the man was a lazy good-for-nothing who, to crown it all, had allowed himself to be beaten by a woman.

"Where are you going so early?" Udemezue asked and hugged her.

"I'm meeting Aku at the Dead Forest. She's going to show me some new plants today."

"Yes, I heard that you're becoming quite good as a healer and a catcher of babies. Aku must be teaching you well."

Onaedo nodded. "I still have a lot to learn. By the way, how are Adanma and the new baby?"

"They're doing well. I was wise to marry her; she's a good wife."

"Talking of wives, how is Odera getting on with her? It seems that they've put aside their differences."

Udemezue smiled at her. "I married two good women and so I do not have a woman-problem. What about you, are you ever going back to Amechi?"

She looked away, avoiding his gaze. "I don't know."

He started to say something and changed his mind. *She will decide at her own time*, he thought.

"Go well and be careful," he said as she walked away.

ౚ

"The Ezeigwe said that it was important, so I sent for you to go with me." Eneda said to him. He slung his bag over one shoulder and took his walking stick in his hand.

Udemezue wondered why it was necessary for him to accompany his father to the Ezeigwe's palace. Eneda usually went to see the Ezeigwe by himself and didn't need or request anyone's company. However, of late, more and more his father had requested his presence in his workshop as Udemezue's trading missions to the Great River had become fewer. With more stories of kidnappings, it seemed too dangerous to travel. Now Udemezue stayed home and did more hunting and farm work. He suspected that his father still hoped he would become a blacksmith.

The Ezeigwe's *obi* was deserted. "Where is everybody?" Eneda said irritably. Udemezue knew that his father was annoyed because he rarely left his workshop in the morning, his most creative time of the day. It was exasperating to find that the Ezeigwe was not in the *obi eze*. But the Ezeigwe had said it was a matter of life and death and so they waited patiently for him after learning he was at his mandatory morning prayers in the innermost chamber of the *obi eze* where he consulted daily with the departed ancestors.

Udemezue looked around the reception room of the *obi eze*. Unlike his father who came here often to consult with the Ezeigwe, he had been inside only on very rare occasions. Its white-washed walls and line drawings of stylized animals and hunting parties gave it a sense of energy and activity. The carved wooden plates and ivory tusks that hung on the walls made the room seem important. In the slanting morning sunlight, the room seemed alive so that even the lion skin, draped over the ceremonial chair, seemed to blink now and then. Udemezue smelled the vague hint of *utaba* that hung in the air and wished he had brought his own tobacco pouch.

Snuffing *utaba* bought from the Delta City had become a fashionable pastime in Abonani for the men and women who could afford it. The *utaba* leaves came from the Portuguese merchants. There was a brisk business in Abonani pulverizing it into a pleasant-smelling, but pungent powder. Udemezue had considered going into the *utaba* trade but the powder always made him sneeze so violently and incessantly that he suspected that he wasn't suited for that particular occupation.

"I'm greeting Eneda, the greatest blacksmith in *Olu n'Igbo*." Both Eneda and Udemezue turned to see who it was. The young man seemed to have appeared from nowhere.

"Thank you my son, how are your people?" Eneda replied automatically. Udemezue didn't recognize the man and, from the expression on his father's face, neither did he. The man was probably younger than he was, Udemezue thought, otherwise they would have been in the same age grade and he would have known him. He was dark-skinned, and well-built with a blue and white stripped cloth that was wrapped around him with the rest thrown casually over one shoulder that spelled casual elegance and prosperity.

"My people are doing well," the young man replied. "I was away for a while but I found them in good health when I got back. My mother is getting old but she's still strong." He flashed a dazzling smile that lit his face in an engaging way.

"My son, old age is catching up with the best of us," Eneda finally admitted. "Please remind me again who you are."

The man seemed only too happy to introduce himself. "I'm Dualo, son of Umeadi."

"Eh? Which Umeadi?" Eneda asked, still not sure who he was. But Udemezue knew right away. This was the young man Onaedo had been in love with and grieved for when he left Abonani two years before. So, he was back.

"I've been away at the Delta with my uncle," Dualo said, and explained to Eneda in careful detail who he was.

Eneda nodded. "Of course. I know your father's brother, a very hardworking man. Now I know who you are. Your father Umeadi was a fine man who died early. I didn't know that he had a son who is now a grown man. So you went to the Delta City? How was it there? How were our people that live there?"

"Things are becoming bad," Dualo replied. "The white men with whom we used to trade are now encouraging our people to fight one another and capture slaves for them."

"So things *are* getting bad. We hear things here, too." Eneda said.

"It's been so for a while and is becoming worse," Dualo replied. He looked at Udemezue who had not said a word to him. "They are raiding the countryside with the help of a few greedy merchants. It's become too dangerous for us foreign artisans, and so we decided to hurry home where we know the land and can fight them. All the white man wants now are slaves to take to their farms in faraway lands; they're not interested in any other trade."

"This story is disturbing. Did you see our kinsman, Oguebie?" Eneda asked. "We heard that he was out there with you."

Dualo looked around furtively and moved closer to Eneda. "To tell you the truth we didn't see much of him because he doesn't associate with us at the Delta City. From what we heard, he hunts slaves for the white man. They say that he joined with another ne'er-do-well relation of the king there and that they do business together."

Eneda shook his head. "It is shameful for an Abonani man to be involved in something like this. Slavery for criminals who commit immoral acts against the clan is one thing, but it is something else to steal and sell innocent men, women, and children who have done nothing wrong. The world is surely going mad when people can attack towns with which they had no quarrel and kidnap their citizens for sale."

Dualo nodded. He looked at Udemezue again and mustered up some courage. "Can I ask you something in private?"

"Me?" Udemezue was surprised.

"Yes. Can we go outside?" Dualo requested, gently insistent.

Intrigued, Udemezue followed him outside.

"I know that you don't know me," Dualo said when they were in the front yard. "And please forgive me for being presumptuous, but I can't help myself from asking about Onaedo your sister. How is she? I hear that she married Amechi Ofoka."

"How do you know Onaedo?" Udemezue asked, pretending he didn't know who Dualo was. He didn't want to give him an easy time.

"I wanted to marry her a long time ago but I had no money then," Dualo replied. There was a faraway look in his eyes.

Udemezue was surprised by his frankness. He shrugged. "She's married to somebody else now."

"I know. She has a daughter, too, I heard. Somebody told me when I came home two weeks ago."

"She left him and has returned home," Udemezue said, relenting.

Udemezue saw the barely suppressed joy that leapt into the other man's eye. "I heard that too but wanted to confirm it when I saw you. Since I came back, I heard rumors that Onaedo had left her husband but there was also talk that they might reconcile. When I saw you I said to myself, *Let me talk to her brother, man to man and hear it from her own people.* I think my *chi* has ordained this for me. First he sent me away to make money and become my own man, and then the wife that was ordained for me is available again."

Udemezue would not be so easily won over. "You know this is not how things are done," he said. "If you want to marry my sister you must follow custom and formally approach the family."

"Of course," Dualo added hastily, still barely able to hide his happiness. "I was only hoping to learn if I still have a chance. I'll send my people right away to knock on your door."

"If she agrees."

"If she agrees," Dualo echoed.

When they rejoined his father, Udemezue could not help but think how fortunate it was for everybody that Dualo had come back to town and was obviously still enamored of Onaedo. And he had done financially well. Udemezue regretted the fact that, for many decades, the middlemen had prevented him and other Abonani traders from crossing to the other side of Great River to trade directly. Artisans like Dualo were not restricted from crossing and, if appearances were to be believed, he had done extremely well. In any case, he wished Dualo well in his newfound prosperity and hoped Onaedo would agree to take him back. He loved his sister dearly but would like to see her leave home especially if she was going to be happy in a good man's house.

ഌ

Udemezue came back to the *obi eze* to find his father and the Ezeigwe in deep conversation. The Ezeigwe apologized for making them wait.

"Two men from Ibura came to see me yesterday," the Ezeigwe said to Eneda without beating about the bush. "They were sent by their town's ruling council and what they told me has taken all the food from my stomach. I did not sleep last night."

Eneda and Udemezue exchanged a glance. Ibura was a neighboring town whose founders had arrived many generations after Abonani. Their relationship was one of uneasy rivalry but there had been no major issues between the two places for at least five generations.

"The Ibura people sent me word yesterday, that there have been some hostile incursions into their land and some of their people were kidnapped," the Ezeigwe continued.

"That's terrible," Eneda exclaimed, whistling and snapping his fingers at the same time. "But what has that got to do with you or our people?"

"They suspect us. It appears that one of our people is involved," the Ezeigwe said.

"Then tell them that it's not so," Eneda said. "We've intermarried and traded for generations with them and would certainly not be involved in such a thing."

"I might as well tell you that Oguebie, my own half-brother is the one implicated. They're not sure it was him, but a man resembling him was seen.

"Oguebie? Why am I not surprised?" Eneda commented looking dismayed. "But are they sure? We know Oguebie has done bad things in the past, but I didn't think he was this bad. To commit this kind of infraction against a neighbor is quite farfetched."

"That's why I called you; I need advice. If he's guilty then his behavior is definitely growing worse. Not content with stealing one of my wives, Oguebie, my brother, who sucked the same breast as me, now wants to plunge the clan into war with its neighbor," the Ezeigwe said.

Udemezue had listened quietly as the two elders spoke. Now, he coughed uncomfortably and exchanged a knowing look with his father. Everyone in Abonani knew the story of how Oguebie had enticed the Ezeigwe's youngest and most beautiful wife and took her with him to the Delta City. It had been a great scandal and the talk of Abonani for weeks. Everybody had sided with the Ezeigwe and when the errant pair had returned briefly to Abonani, Oguebie had been made to pay a significant fine and had undergone a stringent land-purification rite.

As if regretting that he'd raised the subject, the Ezeigwe sought to minimize his embarrassment. "She was a useless woman anyway, always causing trouble amongst my other wives. She was beautiful but had an empty head. A pretty face in itself cannot satisfy a man, so I said good riddance when she left. I didn't even ask her father to repay the bride-price." It was obvious to Eneda and Udemezue that the memory of the incident still rankled.

"This is a serious matter with which we will deal immediately," Eneda said steering the discussion back to Oguebie's most recent egregiousness. "The other elders have to be informed of what is going on."

"Well that's what I wanted to discuss with you. I want you to keep this between us for a while. We need to discover if this is true and find ways to appease the Ibura people if Oguebie was involved." The Ezeigwe looked unhappy.

*At times like this, being a ruler must be difficult,* Udemezue thought, but what was going on with these two brothers? He remembered the story that Eneda had told of them not long ago. He exchanged another look with his father.

Eneda shifted to the edge of the chair before he spoke to give his words more emphasis. He seemed a little annoyed. "I'm sure that you know that we can't keep this thing a secret for very long. Even as we speak, I'm sure that the rumormongers are talking. I hope you know what you're asking. It's never a good idea to keep important things from the clan. It comes back in a bad way."

Eneda stood and gestured to Udemezue to follow suit before he turned back to speak to the Ezeigwe. "Keep me informed. I'm sure we can find a way out of this predicament. It jeopardizes the peace that we've enjoyed with our brothers in Ibura for generations. I'm going back to work."

On the way home, Eneda walked briskly, and Udemezue had to keep up a fast pace. He knew that his father was very disturbed by what had just occurred.

 introduction

Onaedo walked quickly to catch up with Aku at the outskirts of the Dead Forest. As they proceeded deeper among the trees, the morning crackled with the song of birds as they called out to one another. The branches and leaves shivered as they took turns taking off and landing. Small animals ran across the path stopping briefly to look at them with curiosity before disappearing in the undergrowth.

"Isn't this the root that you said one could boil to rub on the skin to cure yaws?" Onaedo asked. She held the plant she had just uprooted. It had tiny rounded green leaves and succulent dirt laden white roots.

"Yes, that's the one," Aku replied barely glancing at it.

Onaedo frowned. What was wrong with Aku today? She had been distant all morning, as though she had something on her mind.

Onaedo took a deep breath as she looked around. They were now in the middle of trees that towered endlessly above them, their leaves dripping water from days-old rain showers. The sun above was obscured by the thick foliage, but it managed to penetrate in scattered intervals, in form of light shafts that lifted the gloom and gave the place a verdant, mysterious, otherworldly glow. Her heart filled with the spiritual connection that she felt each time she came here with Aku.

She loved this part the most, the chore of collecting rare plants, berries, and flowers that Aku taught her to use as remedies for headaches, swollen eyes, fevers, yellowness of the eye, and watery stools that cramped the belly. She was a fast learner and Aku said that she had a natural gift.

She was so engrossed in her thoughts that she almost ran into Aku who had stopped in front of her to scrape an odd-looking spongy, green growth from the trunk of a giant tree. She detached it carefully and placed it in her basket before turning to Onaedo.

"I have something to tell you." She looked so somber that Onaedo became alarmed. "It's something that happened the day your daughter Ogugua was born," Aku said, holding Onaedo's eye in a steady gaze.

Onaedo's heart stood still. She knew that her suspicions about that day were not just a figment of her imagination. Something had happened, she didn't know what, but she was about to find out.

"You had twins that day—a boy and a girl," Aku continued. "The boy died and I took him away and buried him over here," she said, pointing to a spot on the ground next to the path. Onaedo followed her pointing finger to a mound of earth, flattened by rains until it was now almost flush with the surrounding soil. A son? A son that, until a moment ago, she hadn't known she'd had was lying underneath that dirt? Her son?

She turned back to Aku in fear and shock. "*Twins? Ejima?* Why didn't you tell me?"

"And what exactly would you have done? Tell me, my daughter, eh? What would you have done?" She sounded sad, but she had that peculiar look in her eyes again; shafts of sunlight cast a reddish glow on her skin and hair giving her an ethereal quality.

"He was my son," Onaedo said. "I should have been told. Did my mother know?"

"Your mother is a traditionalist. The only reason that she went along with what I did that day, was because you are her daughter; otherwise, she believes that the law of the land should not be questioned," Aku moved closer and touched Onaedo's face. "She thinks that because men give women a little power, confer titles on them, and put giant elephant tusks on their ankles, that they don't have to ask questions. Why do we kill a child that was born on the same day as its brother or sister? Why do we, as women, tolerate the custom? Why is it not a cause for celebration to have two children at once? They cannot answer that question."

"So you have done this before? Let twins live?" Onaedo asked. Everything was becoming more surreal.

Aku raised one finger. "One twin." She sounded matter of fact as though they were discussing the price of cocoyam in the market; she spoke of profound deeds in words of everyday conversation. This was her way of dealing with such a weighty issue.

"That is why I'm teaching you all I know. I want you to take over my work when I'm gone, whenever the ancestors call for me to join them. This is the work that must continue, no matter what."

"I can't do it," Onaedo said with emotion. "I can't kill like that. It's wrong, and I will be found out."

There was a sharp sting as Aku slapped her face. "Don't talk nonsense. It's the right thing to do. Don't you see that you have to sacrifice one to save the other? Do you regret that you have Ogugua now? Would it have been better to let both of them go? You know they would have both been seized and left in the forest. "Right here," she said, throwing her hands out wide, "They would have said to you that only animals have more than one baby at a time, that it is an abomination. You would have been empty-handed, with no baby to show for all your labor. That is wrong and that's why you have to do what needs to be done. You will be careful. I'll show you how."

"I'm not strong like you."

"You will be. Stop crying now." Aku wiped her tears with the edge of her cloth. "I did it for your daughter. I swear to you, I didn't kill your son. He was dead already. Everything turns out all right in the end, I promise you, but you must keep this to yourself."

Onaedo nodded and looked around again in the buzzing forest. Life continued despite their human drama. Her dead son, buried under a small mound of earth, had already broken free by now, and through the roots of the plants that grew from him, had become part of the Dead Forest that was not dead at all.

# CHAPTER

# 22

When Onaedo heard that he'd returned, she would have nothing to do with Dualo. Though tempered by time, her heart still ached. But for weeks he refused to give up. He bombarded her with messages through emissaries, with pleas and gifts. Finally, she relented. He was joyful.

"My heart was heavy the whole time I was away," he said to her at their first meeting. "I thought about you every day and hoped that I would earn enough money to come back for you. I didn't even know that you were already married until I got home. Then I heard what happened."

"You're lucky that the man I married was a useless man or you would have lost me forever," Onaedo said half scolding. She was surprised at how quickly she had forgiven him and how natural things felt again. With Dualo's return, she felt as though she had held her breath all this time in anticipation and only now could breath normally.

"I have a strong *chi* that does not sleep and helped pull you out of that bad marriage. You married the wrong husband," Dualo replied.

"Yes, because the right one left me without a choice," she said, punching him on the chest playfully. They were in Ugodi's house and her mother entered and left several times, trying to eavesdrop on their conversation.

"But we'll do it the right way, now that we have a second chance," Dualo said. "I was clever this time that we were in the Delta City and did a lot of business on the side. My uncle was not even aware of it until I approached him to pay off my debt."

"I'm sure he was not very pleased."

"You should have seen his surprise, but he had no choice. I own myself now," he said, taking both her hands. "All I need is a wife. If you will agree."

"Let me think about it," Onaedo said, smiling across at him. She knew her answer would be yes.

Onaedo was the happiest she had been for a long time as they made plans for their future together. When Dualo's people approached Eneda and the *umunna,* they were all happy that Onaedo had found another husband and somewhat relieved that a difficult decision had been averted. She would move into a new husband's house and so avoid the thorny decision about what to do with her, so they reserved their disapproval regarding the speed with which she had left her first husband and agreed to take the second bride-price. In any case, there would be the added bonus of a second wedding feast—a rare situation.

The first bride-price was remitted back to Amechi's family with the agreement that Ogugua would be returned to her father's people when she was old enough for marriage.

For Onaedo, there was no more need for secrecy with her relationship with Dualo, especially since her marriage to Amechi was officially over. They were free to meet openly, although a few people still complained about the impropriety of it all.

The final marriage ceremony and the carrying of palm-wine between the two families, would take place in a week. Dualo had already built a house for his new wife, right next to his. "But you will not have time to be in it," he said jokingly, "because you will be in my *obi* all the time."

Onaedo laughed happily. She was visiting him this time and they had just finished a late lunch of yam pottage she had cooked. The wooden bowl was washed and turned upside down to dry on the ledge. There was a storm brewing, uncharacteristic for the time of the year. Thunder reverberated after each lightening streak raced across the sky in a bright zigzag.

"You had better go before the rain starts," Dualo said, looking at the blue-black clouds from the doorway. He turned back to her. "Unless you want to sleep here in my house and go home in the morning."

"And give more fire to the gossip mongers?" Onaedo said. She joined him at the door to observe the gathering storm.

"They're already talking anyway. This wouldn't make much difference. I can arrange for you to stay in my mother's house."

"I'd like to stay but my daughter will miss me if I'm not home tonight."

"Then next time bring her with you."

Onaedo laughed, picking up the bowl. "How will it look bringing my young daughter to meet my lover?"

"If I don't mind I don't think it's anybody else's business," Dualo said, pulling her close. They stood like that for a long moment before she pulled away. "Come and see me off."

"Listen to me, Onaedo," Dualo said, gently taking her hand, "I do not have water in my mouth so you can hear me clearly; I will never leave you again the way I did before. You are my heart and everything that I have is yours from now on."

"I know that you won't leave me again, but I have to go now," she said, smiling at him and withdrawing her hand. "If I run, I can be home before the rain."

"Wait, I'm coming with you," Dualo called after her.

"Don't worry, I can find my way home. Once I'm past the square, I'm home," Onaedo replied. The winds carried away her voice.

"I'm coming anyway," Dualo shouted over the wind.

She felt the invigorating cold wind bathe her with light moisture as Dualo's arms propelled her forward. They were like little children again, laughing as they raced to beat the downpour. The roiling skies grew darker. Branches thrashed and leaves rubbed against each other as the first drops hit the earth and released the smell of wet dust.

They ran past a handful of farm people hurrying home in the opposite direction and the road grew empty again. Dualo ran behind her as they crossed the square. It was empty, framed on all sides by tall trees before the path resumed. She smiled as she remembered the secrecy with which they planned their meetings in the past.

"Try and catch me!" she shouted over the wind and increased her speed.

Then she heard a noise. It seemed to come from behind her. She turned to call out to Dualo and saw he was surrounded by a group of strangers. She stopped and watched the scene as if she were far away, rather than just a few steps. She debated quickly whether to go back to him or to run to the nearest village for help. Then they hit him. He fell to the ground and she ran back to help.

"Dualo! Dualo! *Ogini?* What is happening?" Too late from the corner of her eye, she noticed that another man had crept from the surrounding woods. She took a breath to scream, felt the blow to her head, and fell to the ground. Darkness claimed her.

# 23

P asquale felt sick. They'd travelled inland for days and didn't have much to show for it. The forest was much thicker here than anywhere he'd seen before, and he wondered if they'd been wise to follow Oguebie this far inland. The dark skies of a moment ago had cleared suddenly after a brief downpour and everything was dry again as evening approached.

Oguebie was arguing with Alvarez and Ideheno about a young woman who was lying on the ground, something about the fact that she was the daughter of somebody important. He could barely follow Oguebie's broken Portuguese but Alvarez put his foot down.

"We're taking everybody and we're leaving now," Alvarez said to Oguebie. He told their escorts to tie the other prisoners. "I can't pay you until we get back to camp."

The captives made a small group of five—four women and a young boy of about ten. Each was bound at the wrists with thick ropes. The women whimpered miserably, while the boy openly cried. He reminded Pasquale uncomfortably of Gregorio. Was he weeping for his mother too? One of the women whispered some-thing to the boy, placing a dirt-stained and bleeding arm around his shoulder. His tears ceased as he nodded several times. The woman's children were probably wondering why she was so late getting home, Pasquale thought. Did they know they would never see her again? He pulled himself together. This wasn't the time for these kinds of thoughts. There was work to be done and more money to be made.

Alvarez gave him a gourd of water and Pasquale swished it round his mouth. He swallowed to ease his parched throat and gave it back. There would be a lot to write about later, he thought, more new trees, more strange creatures, more crimes committed. But was this really a crime?

Pasquale wondered whether the journey into the hinterland was taking its toll on his sanity. Maybe the *mal'aria* that had afflicted him back in El Mina in the early days had returned. He felt the skin behind his neck. There was no evidence of the burning heat that came with the sickness.

But he was beginning to see things too. The woman on the ground seemed familiar. He was sure that he'd never seen her before but, suddenly, from behind her face, he saw the vision of one even more familiar. He saw his cousin Juana who had ran away from home more than ten years before. It couldn't be her, so why did he think it was? *The fever is back,* he thought in panic, *and I'm seeing visions.*

He wiped his neck again and stole another glance at the young woman. There was a trickle of blood from her nostril that formed a clot on her cheek. He felt sick. Next time he would stay back at camp and let others do this dirty work. It was better not to see any of this.

ოთ

Oguebie heard his name called. His heart jumped. He turned and saw that Onaedo was awake.

"Oguebie what are you doing?" Onaedo whispered. "Why am I tied like this? Where is Dualo?"

"Shut up, woman!" shouted one of the other strangers. He struck her across the lips.

Oguebie saw the dark lump of blood on the corner of her lower lip. "Don't touch her again, you fool," he said to the man that had struck her.

"Oguebie what have I done to you that you should do this to me?" Onaedo continued. The man who had told her to shut up before, ignored her this time. "Tell them to let me go."

Oguebie was in a dilemma. He had wanted them to leave her behind when she was unconscious, that way he could not be identified. But now she was awake. Oguebie was also ashamed. He knew at this moment that he'd crossed a line from which he couldn't return. He was a titled man, and an *ozo* title-holder didn't involve himself in an abomination like this. He might as well collect his family and go into exile because the punishment, if he was discovered, would be worse. There might be murder involved, he thought, and looked at Dualo. He had not stirred since falling onto the wet earth.

Onaedo had seen him so she could not be sent back. He moved away from her line of vision as Alvarez ordered her to be tied.

Pasquale pulled Oguebie aside. "Do you know the girl?" he asked through an interpreter.

"I know her," Oguebie answered in his mangled Portuguese. Pasquale looked at him steadily. "Untie her. Let her go."

"He can't do that," said Alvarez. He had come up unnoticed behind Pasquale. "We need the sale on every one of these *escravos*. Don't forget that this is a business."

Pasquale argued for a few minutes, pointing out that they had more prisoners than they could manage for the journey back to the canoes. "The woman is hurt and might die on the way. Just leave her here for her people to find her."

Oguebie held his breath; this was last thing that he wanted now. Alvarez poked Onaedo roughly. She moaned and tried to sit up.

"I think she can survive the journey," he said, straightening. "She's healthy and will bring a good price in Sao Tome. One of the *fazendeiros* might even want her as a house servant there. The plantation owners value young women." He smiled slyly.

Pasquale grew angrier. Oguebie did not understand the private joke that had amused Alvarez, but he was relieved that he had stepped in; it would have been disastrous for him if Onaedo returned to Abonani.

ಬಡ

Onaedo knew for certain that she had reached *ani-muo* because, if this was not the land of the departed ancestors, she did not know where she was. Oguebie or somebody who looked like him tied the men and women. She desperately searched for Dualo. What had happened to him? Had he crossed over with her or was he still in the land of the living? She thought she saw Adanma but couldn't be sure. What could Adanma possibly be doing here? She had a baby at home. Was she this woman who looked like her lying on the muddy ground and whimpering as if she was in mortal pain?

Then she saw Dualo. He lay silent, still, unmoving where he had fallen. A deep fear gripped her. She was injured but she was alive. There was a dull ache at the back of head and she tasted the saltiness of her blood. She yearned to go back to sleep so that they would leave her alone but they pulled her roughly to her feet. Then they tied her with something. She tried to scream, and they showed her the gun. She had seen that before. It killed things instantly. She shut her mouth and followed them.

CHAPTER

# 24

U demezue was one of the first people to arrive at the Ezeigwe's compound but, in a short time, everybody else was there too. He was impatient because darkness was poking its head into the sky and the sooner they started the better.

He did not want to give words to the despair that he felt on learning that Onaedo and Adanma were among the missing. What had he done wrong? What sacrifices had he not made that his *chi* would treat him so shabbily? There were about eight people missing from Abonani on first count, maybe more, maybe less, as rumors flew and people checked on their families.

People came to the *obi eze* without being summoned. Many of the older men sat silently, contemplating, trying to understand a world suddenly gone awry. The younger ones debated angrily. How were they going to counter the problem that had now arrived at the doorstep of Abonani?

"This offence cannot be tolerated," someone said.

"We will show those Ibura people."

"They must think we are weak women that they can come in here and take our people at will!" another shouted.

"Are we sure that the people that did this were from Ibura?" someone asked. It would be just as outrageous to falsely accuse their neighbors of the despicable crime, as it would be for the Ibura people to have committed it in the first place.

But only few people wanted to weigh the evidence. There had been witnesses; somebody's in-law or sister's son had seen it. Even Oguebie, who had come back to town briefly from the Delta City was out on an errand earlier and said he had witnessed the whole thing. He had been lucky to escape, he'd said and he thought he recognized one or two individuals from Ibura. Udemezue looked around for him now. *I want to hear the words from his mouth,* he thought. But Oguebie was gone.

The gathering mob wanted revenge. Some of the men were armed with machetes and one or two waved matchlock guns—the kind that sometimes exploded when fired and blew off one's hand.

The Ezeigwe arrived and there was silence. He counseled restraint. "We will not fall headlong into this like foolish people. We will ask questions first."

Somebody shouted that there was no time to waste with questions. "We should sharpen our knives and head out to Ibura now."

"Eneda and the others who lost somebody want us to do something now," somebody else said and the rest cheered.

"Let us walk the cautious path the Ezeigwe suggested," another person suggested.

An agreement was reached. Udemezue observed Eneda who sat next to the Ezeigwe. His sorrow was palpable. Enough time had been wasted. He beckoned to the group he had put together at very short notice. They were twenty strong. They left the square. It was first to Ibura on a fact-finding mission and then to the chase to find those who were taken.

ໝ

Aku spent a restless night, waiting for morning before going to see her sister. She had been out of town when the incident occurred but she'd heard that Udemezue and others had left to look for Onaedo and Adanma.

The night had become fearful and like everybody else in Abonani, she had to wait till morning to leave her home. The town crier forfeited his rounds when it was rumored that the kidnappers were still nearby. It was eerily silent save for a few dogs that howled at the moon which was only a thin slice in the sky.

When dawn finally arrived, Aku was exhausted from lack of sleep. As she walked over to her sister's house, she noted that the path to the stream and the markets were all deserted. She wondered again about her Sight of nearly two years ago. She wasn't sure now whether the coffin she saw was for the dead baby boy or for Onaedo. Everything was mixed up and confused. For now she had to see Ugodi—later, she would straighten things out in her mind.

She pushed open Ugodi's gate. "Is it true? My mother's daughter, is what I hear true? I came as soon as I could."

Ugodi was sitting on a dwarf stool in front of her house. She began to sob when she saw Aku.

"I'm glad that you're here," another of Eneda's wives said to Aku. "We've taken turns sitting with her all night. We're afraid of what she might do. She just cries and won't talk to anybody."

"Where is Onaedo's daughter?"

"She's playing with the other children over there," she said, pointing towards a small group of children.

"What about Adanma's baby? Is he alright?"

"He's with Odera. Udemezue left yesterday. To search for them."

"So I heard," Aku said sitting down beside Ugodi. She wiped her own tears and set about the business of taking care of her sister.

CHAPTER

# 25

For Onaedo and her fellow prisoners, the journey progressed quickly. They were not allowed to slow their pace for any reason. To do so risked punishment that was swift and severe. The two white men who led the group and their foot soldiers looked fierce as they wielded their guns.

Onaedo concluded that she was still alive and that Adanma was real and not an illusion. She had talked to her to make sure but Adanma hadn't said much. She appeared to have lost her very self.

The situation was dire, like none she had ever been in before, awake or in her many vivid dreams. She'd been thrust into a world that looked familiar on the surface—the *ukwa* tree that they passed at old Nnemuka's farm still had its recognizable crooked branch that looked like an old woman's leg—but was strange on other levels. The roads, the earth, and the trees were strangely removed from her sphere of influence. In this world that she travelled, she was invisible and untouchable. The situation repeated vividly many times as they travelled on familiar yet strange roads. She silently named and renamed things—trees, shrubs, animals— as she clung desperately to reality. Bush hogs, shy antelopes, stray dogs—they all stopped long enough to look before bounding away in panic.

Then the intrusive, loud report of a gunshot brought Onaedo rudely back into the present. She was tugged and pulled violently to the ground when the people to whom she was tied, fell down in fear. She didn't know why their captors ran forward, cursing and firing shots in the air. Then she saw why. A group of women in the distance with their male escorts had scattered into the nearby bushes. They must have rounded a bend and seeing Onaedo's group they had panicked, leaving behind broken earthenware, scattered kola-nuts, oil-bean wraps, coco-yams and precious livestock that littered the path as they fled into the surroundings. When the commotion was over Onaedo rose and helped Adanma clean the mud from her body. It was the first time they were near enough to really speak. "How did they get you?" Onaedo whispered.

"I was on my way to my mother's house," Adanma replied. She had a shallow cut above one brow. Her eyes were red-rimmed and tears welled. "Did you see Oguebie earlier? Can you believe what he did to us?"

"Yes, I saw him," Onaedo replied

Adanma wiped her face with the back of one hand. "But he's gone. There's nobody who will help us now. Nobody knows us here." A look of incredible sadness came into her eyes that brought Onaedo to tears. She was thinking the same thing.

"I know you're thinking of your new baby," she said, touching Adanma on the forehead. "Don't worry; they will come for us soon. Abonani men are fearless. These people will be no match for them, even with their friends and their guns."

"Onaedo, think; how many guns do we have in Abonani? Not more than two or three. These people have over ten or more."

"Shut your mouth, both of you," an armed man yelled at them, waving his gun threateningly. The younger white man reprimanded him and he dropped his gun to his side.

છછ

They avoided populated areas and walked in silence except for the leaves shuffling underfoot and the twigs that cracked and broke beneath them. They had stopped to eat—pieces of cold boiled cocoyams dipped in palm oil for which they had no appetite.

"I think Dualo is dead," Onaedo whispered again when they had another opportunity to talk.

Adanma nodded in silent agreement. They were sitting on bare ground in a clearing and she slapped some black ants from her legs.

"They are coming to free us," Onaedo said in a fierce whisper, more false bravado to hide her anxiety than something she believed was true.

"Who's coming for us?" Adanma asked.

Onaedo looked at her with irritation. "Haven't you heard anything I said? Udemezue and all the other men in Abonani are coming for us."

Adanma shook her head doubtfully. "Do you see how people run away when they see us?"

"I'm not going to follow you and be miserable," Onaedo said decisively, annoyed that Adanma had no hope. "When they get here, they'll know what to do."

Onaedo had fought hard when they tried to tie her. During the struggle, the men had hit her and left her with a deep laceration on her back. She felt its burning pain as it began to fester. As she chewed on the piece of cold cocoyam she thought of escape. Her back wound still hurt and she drew her shoulder back to relieve the throbbing. She had plucked familiar leaves from the side bushes and Adanma had rubbed them in when they stopped to rest. Then it was time to resume the trek.

The fabled Great River appeared before them on the third afternoon. Although it was the first time she had seen it, Onaedo recognized it right away but she didn't see its silvery beauty or its teeming market. All she saw were empty stalls that were like prisons and the heart numbing knowledge that she was far from home.

Onaedo was frightened here. She had never seen so much water in her life. She stayed close to Adanma. The smell of sweat and fear was everywhere.

A group of fishermen stood by their boats at the river's edge a short distance away. From where she was, Onaedo sensed their apprehension but their captors did not attack them. In fact, they approached them and bought a large quantity of fish from them and then stocked their own boats at the water's edge.

They separated and regrouped the captives. Onaedo maneuvered herself to still stay close to Adanma. Onaedo was worried about her. She looked empty. Earlier, her breasts had become engorged and painful but Onaedo had had no cloth with which to bind them for her to ease the pain. "My baby must be hungry," she said to Onaedo and was ready to cry again. Shortly afterwards, she had begun to moan, a low and insistent sound and when the men hit her to shut her up, she barely flinched. Eventually they just ignored her.

"What will happen to my baby?" she asked Onaedo again.

"Don't cry. Udemezue will not stand by and let them take us away. They are already looking for us; I know this in my heart."

Onaedo wasn't sure that she still believed this herself. She fought the terror and grief that overwhelmed her. Thinking of her daughter made her want to cry too.

Adanma looked at her listlessly and nodded absently when Onaedo said they would be rescued. Onaedo was more concerned about the silence that had replaced her moans.

The crossing was precarious and the passengers were badly frightened. When they put ashore on the other side, they saw three long sheds with guarded doors and a group of houses balanced strangely on stilts.

The prisoners were separated and put in the sheds. Onaedo and Adanma remained together but it was the last time that she saw the others from Abonani. The new people with whom they shared their shed were strangers; some didn't even speak Igbo and they were a mixed group of men, women, and children.

It was dark and gloomy inside the building, despite the sunshine outside. The only door was closed at all times. Onaedo looked around the long, thatch-covered frame and saw no escape. At least not yet. It was strangely restful and it gave her time to think. *Where are Udemezue and the rest? How would they cross the Great River to find us? Have they assembled enough guns to rescue us from this place?*

A man came with more food. As he closed the door, there was a sudden commotion outside. Onaedo looked at Adanma and saw a flicker of hope. Onaedo strained to hear what was happening. Maybe Udemezue and the other Abonani men were already here.

The door opened abruptly and everybody looked up. Half a dozen more captives were pushed into the room and the door quickly shut.

"Don't worry, they'll be here soon," Onaedo said to Adanma. Adanma didn't answer.

# CHAPTER
# 26

U demezue and his party walked for days before they finally arrived at the market. The diversion to Ibura had caused some delay but it hadn't taken them long to discover that their neighbors knew nothing about what happened at Abonani.

"We have people missing from our town too," they told Udemezue and his group when they met with their elders. They reprimanded the men for believing that they'd been involved in the atrocity. "We're going to send some of our people with you to see if we can find our own people too."

Udemezue learned along the way that the raiders and their victims had gone towards the Great River. Their lack of weapons worried him—there were two dozen men in his party and only three guns between them. The rest had only machetes and sticks.

"Don't worry," Udemezue's friend Emenike reassured him. "We'll find a way to deal with the situation. Let's find them first." Udemezue nodded. His friend Emenike, the indefatigable optimist, was a great comfort. Udemezue reminded himself of his parents' agony, and knew that they couldn't afford to fail.

Now they were here. He approached his crumbling stall. The market was silent. Empty sheds were like dark, empty mouths that had nothing to say. Everything felt lonely and forlorn. Most of the traders had kept away for fear of the kidnappings. He wondered if they would ever return.

They approached the fishermen from the morning fish market, who were now packing up for the day.

"We've seen many groups crossing in boats," the boat-men replied in response to their enquiries, "We don't know who they are and we keep away for fear of attack."

The head fisherman was a small, wiry fellow with a mouth as wide as one of the glassy-eyed fish lying at the bottom of his boat. Udemezue disliked him without knowing why.

"We'll pay you if you take us across," Udemezue said. He withdrew three manila bars from his shoulder bag. He'd come prepared.

"That is a lot of money," the man replied. There was a gleam in his eye. "Who did you say was missing?"

"My wife and sister and many others," Udemezue replied.

"It will have to be in the morning," the man replied, but he took the bars and put them inside a sack in his boat.

"Why can't we go now?" asked Emenike. "Tomorrow might be too late."

"There is an army of men on the other side. You have to plan your landing well so they won't see you. The white man and his people have many guns and what you have will not match him," the man replied looking pointedly at their meager arsenal. "Wait until just before sunrise. It's still dark then."

Udemezue agreed. The fishermen sold them some fish and they prepared their camp for the night.

After the meal, Udemezue walked near the water. Emenike walked at his side. "This was once a great market," he said to his friend. "Look at it now. A terrible thing is happening here and we're unable to stop it."

"Do you think we can trust those men?" Emenike asked.

"You mean the fishermen? What can we do? We have no boats and even if we had, we are not water people."

They walked beside the brooding river that reflected the darkening sky of the approaching night. The water looked secretive, a silent witness to something. They stopped briefly and Udemezue dipped his toe. He watched the fleshy whiskers of a fish as it undulated in the jet stream before it darted away. He looked to the opposite bank that appeared as a dark blanket in the distance. *We'll be there tomorrow*, he thought. *A few men will wait here, just in case.*

He watched the river again. He'd always taken it for granted; it was part of the backdrop. Now he tried to think of the stories of the river that Ugodi had told him about this river that she had never seen.

"Emenike, do you believe that there is a river goddess?"

"I think so. But Abonani does not worship her. She's not one of ours," his friend replied.

"But does she exist?"

Emenike shrugged. "I don't know. Maybe she does for the people that believe in her. I suppose that she's like every other goddess, if she performs feats for her people they will worship her and obey her rules."

"Did you ever hear the story of the woman with the only child who came to her for help?"

"Yes, my mother told me that story."

"I will pray to her tonight, if it will help," Udemezue said quietly.

"How do you know how she likes to be worshipped?" Emenike asked. "You cannot wake up one morning and start praying to a strange god."

"I'll pray to this stone here," Udemezue said, and nudged a yellow and red stone with his toe, "if it will help me bring back my wife and sister."

"Suit yourself. But don't be disappointed if she ignores you," Emenike replied. "I'd like to hear that story again, though. I heard it last as a child."

"I may have forgotten some details, but it's about a childless woman who pleaded with the goddess for a child. 'Even if it's just for a short while,' she said, 'I would like the pleasure of holding a child of my own.' The goddess agreed but told her that she would be back in the future to take back the child. The woman agreed, and shortly afterwards, she gave birth to a daughter. The baby had both a crippled arm and a crippled leg but the mother was over-joyed nonetheless. For years, the goddess did not return for the girl and the bargain seemed forgotten.

"One day the child, now a young woman, fell sick and died. Her distraught mother realized that the goddess had called in her debt, but she was determined to get her daughter back. She spent days and nights on the riverbank pleading with the goddess to return her daughter. Finally, the goddess, worn down by the mother's persistence, gave her a most beautiful girl in exchange for her lost daughter. 'Go home with this child, woman, and leave me in peace.' But the woman refused to leave. 'I only want my own daughter. I don't care that she is a cripple,' she begged. Finally, the goddess returned the daughter, but now she was physically perfect. 'You are a good woman. Take your daughter and go. Your love for your daughter, perfect or not, makes you deserving. I will bless you with many more children.' And so she was."

"But she must have been too old to have more children," Emenike said somberly.

Udemezue looked at him and shrugged. He usually appreci-ated Emenike's sense of humor but laughter had long fled from him. "It's only you Emenike, who will see the inconsequential side issue and ignore the main reason for the story. Anyway, I will plead with her to help me get back my wife and my sister."

They were silent for a while as Udemezue now recalled that it was his grandmother who had told him this story, not Ugodi. His grandmother had died a year before Onaedo was born but every-body recognized her when she was reincarnated in Onaedo.

It was dark when they returned to their camp. They lay beside the dying fire, but sleep was elusive for Udemezue. His sleeping cloth was thin and protected him from neither the cold nor the hard ground. His thought often of his young son who now did not have a mother. How was he going to raise him without Adanma? Sleep, when it finally came, was as fitful and restless as the mind that had invited it in.

He woke with a start a few hours later. He sat up and looked around. He rubbed his eyes, unsure of what had woken him. The sun was already beginning to paint the sky orange in the distance. Emenike and some of the other men began to stir around the dying fires.

"What is it?" Emenike asked him.

"I don't know. I'm uneasy," Udemezue said. All was strangely quiet. Something was missing. The he realized what it was. The boatmen were gone. He rushed to the water's edge and saw them like tiny specks, as they pulled further away into the distance. Without them, there would be no river crossing.

"I knew it. Those cowards," Emenike muttered in disgust. "They are too frightened to do the right thing."

CHAPTER

# 27

The day after their arrival at the camp, Onaedo and the other prisoners were led outside in groups and told to sit on the dusty ground under a tree.

*It looks like an oha tree,* she thought, *but its leaves are different, too broad . . .*

Her attention turned to a man who was laying out some tools a few yards away. Her attention was riveted; he was a blacksmith. She knew that right away. One of the white men dropped a mass of metalwork in front of him and he busily laid out the ware. There were odd-shaped metallic rings with claws and teeth, chains, and metal cuffs. Onaedo observed him with some curiosity, fighting a wave of nostalgia for her father and home. She imagined Eneda working late into the night making his beautiful and useful things. Not like the hideous wares this man now displayed. *Where did these ugly things come from?* she wondered.

More of the white people had arrived in a fleet of dugouts. They tied them to stakes and the boats bobbed up and down in the flowing river, as they half-rested on the sandy bank.

A man came towards them. "Go there," he said and pointed to the blacksmith. A group of the male prisoners hopped over. Onaedo watched the blacksmith put the menacing contraptions around each man's ankle and then anchored each man to the next. When he had finished, none of them could move without the tacit consent of the group.

It was now her turn. Onaedo looked at Adanma, but she would not meet her eyes. Onaedo was silent as the man's rough hands closed the cold metal around her ankle. She tried to imagine it was her *nja* coils and that she was preparing for a dance rehearsal but such thoughts, fertile with hope could not survive in this arid place.

The blacksmith was sinewy with white-peppered hair that made him appear older than he probably was. As Onaedo looked at him a sudden thought occurred to her. What was there to lose? Blacksmiths had a strong brotherhood and travelled far and wide. She bent forward. "Have you ever heard of Eneda from Abonani?" She whispered.

The old man recoiled. He looked carefully at Onaedo. "Of course I know Eneda. Who doesn't? He's one of the greatest blacksmiths that ever lived." He looked puzzled. "How do you know him?"

Onaedo was excited. She hadn't even known the man spoke Igbo. "I'm his daughter."

"What are you doing here?" the man whispered glancing around to make sure that they weren't overheard.

"These people have kidnapped us from Abonani," she said. "Do you know where they're taking us?"

He looked at her with compassion. "Yes, I can see your father now in your eyes. Those strange eyes. He's renowned in our trade. Some people are born with the gift and some people acquire it through hard work. Your father had both. How did you come here?"

Onaedo licked her dry lips. She would give anything for a drink but she had a story to tell this old man who had heard of her father. She searched for her jailers. Nobody paid her attention. She turned to the man again and clutched his arm urgently. "Do you know these people? Can you beg them to let us go?"

He drew back and looked at her for a while. He sighed, shook his head, and picked up an anvil. He began to bind the shackles together.

"I knew your father because our mothers were from the same place, although we were not related by blood," he said under his breath. "Later, when he went back to Abonani, I heard stories of his great talent. I was in the trade too but we never met again. I've heard he never leaves Abonani."

He stopped talking abruptly. One of the armed men had come close with his gun raised. He spoke sharply to the blacksmith who quickly returned to his task. He neither looked at nor spoke to Onaedo again.

After the last link was hammered, the blacksmith gathered his tools and went to the white men. One gave him bronze manilas. He dropped them into a cloth bag that was slung across one shoulder before he walked away. He didn't look back.

ಬಚಿ

Later that night, the man appeared to Onaedo. She was one of the prisoners taken outside to sleep because it was too hot inside the shack. There was no thought of escape now, because they were anchored firmly to one another. Their white guards were some distance away, arguing good-naturedly. They ate roasted bush hogs and drank palm-wine bought from local women. Their raucous laughter disturbed the quiet night.

That was when Onaedo saw the blacksmith slip in. "Listen carefully," he whispered. Onaedo wasn't sure whether she was awake or asleep. "I left your *iga* loose so that you could slip it off and run," he said, reaching into his bag. "Here are a few cowries in case you need to buy something on your way home. I'll wait for you in the forest if you can get away," he said, pointing to the trees. "Keep your eyes open, choose a good time and then run. I'll help you get home if you can find me."

Onaedo then noticed that her clamp was loose. It was wide enough for her to slip off her ankles. It was the same for Adanma sitting next to her. Some of the prisoners overheard the conversation and begged the man to set them free too.

"I can only help a few of you or they'll find out and kill me."
Their voices grew louder and Onaedo saw a guard look in their
direction. The blacksmith sensed danger and fled into the night.

ৡৡ

Onaedo was worried about Adanma.

"Are you not asleep yet?" she asked each time she awoke and saw
Adanma awake and looking into the darkness.

Onaedo hoped that she would be able to attempt the escape. She
had become so pessimistic. "Listen, Onaedo, I'm tired," she said.
"We'll never get home. I don't want to struggle anymore."

"Ssh, keep quiet," Onaedo said. "I've told you that talking like
that will only bring us bad luck." She was afraid too.

As morning approached, the darkness gave way to a brighten-
ing sky and they were assembled on the riverbank. Onaedo held up
her hand before her eyes; it was barely visible.

"Into the boats," their captors shouted, running and pushing
them into the dugouts again. She was confused. She hadn't known
that they were going back into the water.

Onaedo lost her balance a few times as she climbed into the boat.
The unsteady canoes and endless expanse of pitch-black waters were
unnerving. Some of the prisoners protested and tried to hang back,
while others cried and cursed as they were pushed into the boats.
Their guards became angry and whipped and beat them to maintain
order. It was soon clear to Onaedo that an uprising was not likely and
opportunities for escape were going to be limited.

As the canoes pushed off, Onaedo was glad that Adanma was sitting next to her despite her listless stupor. The two men paddling the
canoe had their backs to them. At the other end, another man stood
and looked toward the horizon as if searching the skies for a sign.

When the boat moved into mid-river, Onaedo reached down
and loosened both their shackles. It was now or never. If her *chi*
was awake then their escape would go smoothly. She hoped that
the blacksmith had waited, but if not they would find their way

home on their own. She encircled Adanma's upper arm and pulled her close.

"*Ngwa*." She whispered. "Get ready," Adanma nodded. It was the first time in a long while that she'd shown signs of life. The other prisoners watched silently as they both slipped over the side of the dugout with barely a splash. None of the guards seemed to notice. The water wasn't too cold, Onaedo thought as she cut a smooth path through it. Daylight had quickly spread across the sky and it was much easier to see. Suddenly, she heard a commotion, muffled by the weight of the water on her ears. She feared they'd been seen. She saw Adanma a few feet ahead. She was swimming strongly, her arms moving firmly and rhythmically. Onaedo followed her, glad that her spirit appeared to fight back at last. The shouts grew closer. Adanma was still in front of her. The plan was to swim away and come ashore farther upstream; they would make a run for it as soon as their feet touched dry land.

She lifted her head to take a breath of air and to see which way Adanma was going; she had lost her momentarily so Onaedo stopped to tread water. She looked around telling herself not to panic. Adanma was most likely still in front of her. She had to keep going. The shouting from the canoe sounded nearer but she dared not look back now; she might lose her resolve if she did. She ducked under the surface and pulled at the cross currents to propel herself forward.

*Adanma must have moved even faster*, she thought, *I have to catch up with her*. She was about to lift her head again to try to locate Adanma when something under the water caught her attention. She looked at it in horror. It was a body. It was Adanma. She was only a few feet away but looked strangely distant. Her arms were raised above her head, floating from side-to-side in a death dance. Then she began to sink.

Onaedo wanted to shout out to her, to tell her to stop being foolish and swim faster, that they would be caught and taken away in the white man's giant tomb waiting somewhere out at sea if they didn't swim away faster, that Udemezue and their new son were waiting; but no words came. It was too late. Adanma didn't care anymore, didn't want to struggle. In fact, this was the most peaceful that she'd seemed in days.

Onaedo was mesmerized. Then she began to run out of breath. She needed to surface, needed air but she couldn't leave Adanma. She tried again to wave at her but Adanma was calm in her stillness. With her eyes open, Onaedo thought she saw a flicker of life, but then Adanma vanished into the dark depths below. At the same time something gripped Onaedo by the legs. She sailed through the air and landed. Hard. She lay still. She was not going to open her eyes.

# 28

The girl was secured for days on the ship deck. She was one of a few that were kept above deck. The rest, numbering just over a hundred, were down in the hold. After her attempt to escape from the canoe, they'd guarded her closely but not before she had received a whipping for her attempt. Pasquale had intervened and put a stop to it. He was tired of all the brutality.

"Give her food, clean her wounds, and leave her alone," he said. "She's more valuable to us if she's healthy."

"She sets a bad example to the others by resisting and running," Alvarez argued. "If she's punished, the others will learn."

"How often has that worked in the past? They still try to escape or commit suicide even if they see others punished," Pasquale shouted back at Alvarez.

"Alright, alright. Maybe you want her for yourself?" Alvarez laughed, as he held up his hands. "You can have her."

Pasquale scowled at him, turned on his heel, and walked across the deck, his shoes crunching on the salty deck. He brought the girl fresh water from a cask. "Drink this," he said in Portuguese, and held a cup to her lips. She looked at him questioningly at first before she understood the command. She drank without taking the cup in her hands.

Something around her neck caught his eye. It looked like a cross with a miniature ruby in the middle. The design was familiar but he couldn't immediately place it. He wondered vaguely whether she was a Christian. *Had the Church come so far inland?* He reached for the pendant but she shrank back. He dropped his hand quickly. He looked up to see Alvarez watching him, a knowing smile on his lips.

"Give her something to eat," Pasquale instructed one of the men, then made his way down to his little cabin, thinking about the girl. Meeting with her was the second time he'd had a strange encounter with a native. The first was the man at the market.

With a flash of insight he realized why the pendant was familiar. His hand went to his neck. It was bare.

"*Como estúpido de mim*! How stupid I am!" He exclaimed. "That's my pendant." Indeed, it did look just like the one he owned. Its unique design was identical in fact to his. It was the work of Edmondo, a local jeweler whose family workshop they had patronized in Lisbon for generations. How had it fallen into her possession? Had somebody from his old neighborhood given it to her? It wouldn't be far-fetched; many of his countrymen had lived along these coasts; men who had come to trade and stayed. It was also possible that the design wasn't unique to Edmondo and that another jeweler had made it for others. He unlocked the cabin and squeezed sideways into the tiny space. He sat down on the bunk and pulled a dark mahogany box from underneath the bed. He rummaged quickly through half a dozen gold coins, a carved ivory quill, a gold encased watch, a handful of gold nuggets, and a deck of playing cards, until he found what he was looking for—a small silver cross pendant at the bottom of the box that was identical to the one the girl wore.

He held it up in the dimness of the cabin and examined its red stone. Then he slid it over his head and around his neck. The whole thing was confusing and he was tired of the games his mind was playing with him this whole trip.

He was homesick. He closed his eyes to look behind his eyelids. Sofia appeared; he could smell her hair and feel the softness of her neck and thighs. He opened his eyes to clear the erotic thoughts.

The ship listed slightly portside. The weather was unsettled; they were sailing into a squall. He hoped that it wouldn't become a big storm. The voyage to Sao Tome was not supposed to be difficult. He wanted to be done with it. He took the quill in his hand, dipped it into his inkpot and started to write.

ॐ

The sailors' shouts heralded the approach to land. Onaedo had been sent down to the hold with the others. By now, her captors had probably concluded that there was no escape for her and they did not need to watch her so closely. They were right. She'd seen the sea and saw that it was endless, no land in sight in any direction. She had concluded that this must be the seven seas of Ugodi's fables; the same one that the intrepid traveler crossed to get to *ani-muo*, the land of the ancestors. All the water had joined together to form one gigantic water.

In the belly of the ship, they heard the noise of celebration with a mixture of alarm and fear. There was relief when news came down that their ordeal might be ending. But to Onaedo, this meant that she was so far from home that she might be lost forever. She didn't know how anybody could ever find her again.

From a narrow crack in the wood above, light filtered in, relieving the almost-total blackness. The sound of running feet above was like a drumbeat in her ears. The putrid stench around her had been overwhelming for days. A terrible disease had swept through their crowded compartment a few days ago leaving destruction in its wake. Everything smelled of feces and death.

Onaedo moved; her foot touched something wet and slimy. It had come from a woman lying close to her. She'd been as still as a fallen tree trunk all night and Onaedo knew she was dead. They would come for her as they had come daily for the others. Her lifeless body would be thrown overboard and, with a splash, she would sink to the fishes. Onaedo prayed that the disease would not take her next.

The clamp around her ankle bit deeply into her flesh. She longed to stand, she wanted to walk. Through the crack, she saw a small sliver of sky above. She lay back on the damp wood and closed her eyes. Tears of despair rolled down her cheeks.

# 29

Pasquale came out early to watch the approach to Sao Tome. Its silhouette of volcanic rocks made him think of craggy fingers jutting into the dawn sky. It grew more defined as the ship made landfall. The sun grew warmer and the sea air more humid.

Alvarez stood beside him, breathing noisily. "It's a wonderful day when we reach land. I have to tell you, my friend, this journey has been my worse. Do you know how many we lost to this stomach flux?"

"How many?" Pasquale asked. He could guess. He had seen the dead bodies they had thrown overboard. A watery, bloody stool had climbed on board the *Santa Magdalena* with the last batch of captives they had acquired. It was every slaver's nightmare because of the speed with which it spread and overtook a ship. Death had arrived swiftly and without warning to crewmen and prisoners alike and in a few short days, the deaths had been counted in dozens.

Pasquale had had to stop Alvarez on a few occasions from throwing over the ones that were sick but still living. He claimed that it was to safeguard the rest of the prisoners and the crew but Pasquale had argued for segregating the sick. Some might still be salvageable. He had been right and a good number had survived.

"We lost thirty," Alvarez said sounding gloomy. "A lot of money."

*And it would have been more if I had listened to you and thrown the others overboard,* Pasquale thought. But he was also as upset at the financial loss they were going to incur. Upset, but not surprised at the intensity of the malady. The severity of the disease could only be imagined from the smell coming from below deck. They were lucky that any had survived.

"We'll take a big loss," Alvarez said, and spat into the sea.

Pasquale watched a dead body, gray-green and bloated, bob in the water not far from the ship. Another few corpses floated a short distance away, and a circle of seagulls squawked noisily above them. Soon they'd have something to eat. When the bodies were tiny dots in the horizon, still he could smell the putrid flesh. Or maybe it was the salty smell of the sea.

He was glad that this part of the journey was ending. He would meet up with Padre Joao on the island, and they would relax and catch up on news. He returned to his cabin for his map of the island.

ﬞﾡ

Pasquale squinted at the map of Sao Tome. Since their last visit, he had added a few features that the original map had omitted. He measured it carefully with a ruler. It was ten leagues long and four across at its widest part. He had read somewhere that the island had been created by a volcano. It was now a fertile land, good for growing sugarcane.

He traced a finger along the western coast on the map where clear streams rushed down the craggy pillars before splashing into the sea. They were heading to the east where the island bays offered good shelter.

"It is beautiful weather to land," Alvarez said joining him from the captain's cabin. Pasquale looked at his partner's dirty tunic, straggly, overgrown black hair and beard and knew he didn't look any better. It would be a luxury to put ashore and have a hot bath and a shave.

"God help us, who have we here?" Alvarez muttered under his breath. Pasquale followed his gaze to two small boats that approached from the shore. It appeared that each held three or more men.

"*Pirata!* Pirates!" Alvarez exclaimed. "Go below. Get the guns." The crew made their way to the munitions store while Alvarez and Pasquale watched the boats approach from the bow. Their concern was well founded; pirates often put to port at Sao Tome. They were armed and ruthless, and would loot and kill.

All this was part of the unruly reputation of Sao Tome from its early years. Most of its inhabitants were law-abiding colonials—traders, farmers, and noble men, but among them were also the *degradados*—criminals sent to serve out their terms in the colonies. Recently, a ship sailing under the standard of the Portuguese crown had been hijacked, all its cargo had been stolen, and the island's governor had been out-manned and out-gunned by the pirates. On the island itself sometimes the politics could be deadly. Even the Church was not exempt.

"*Boa vinda a Sao Tome*! Welcome to Sao Tome," the men in the boat called to the *Santa Magdalena*. One waved a white flag as they drew close to show that they had no ill intent. Pasquale recognized one of the men. He was Diego da Silva, a local *fazendiero* that owned one of the biggest sugar plantations, or *fazendas* on the island. He and Alvarez had been friends for some years. The men on the *Santa Magdalena* breathed a sigh of relief.

Alvarez called to his friend as the small boats came alongside the ship. He directed the crew to let down the rope ladder for Diego. Diego da Silva owned the Fazenda Sao Marcello, a large sugar plantation with its attached *casa grande* or great house and slave quarters—*senzala*. He had emigrated from Portugal many years ago and was now one of Sao Tome's most successful landowners.

He leaped onto the deck and beamed at both men. "My great friend Alvarez, I've waited a long time for a ship to come." His face was moist with perspiration and he dabbed it periodically with a white cotton cloth. His skin was sun-darkened and his curly, red hair was cut short.

"Welcome abroad," Alvarez replied. "This is a better welcome than we had the last time."

"We took care of that problem," Diego said. He smiled and steadied himself against the swaying deck. He turned to Pasquale. "Welcome again to our island," he said gripping his hand.

Pasquale liked Diego, unlike Alvarez's other friends on the island that talked too loudly and drank too much. He was very entertaining and Pasquale had found his gregariousness refreshing. From him Pasquale learned that Sao Tome was discovered when two Portuguese explorers, Joao de Santarem and Pedro Escobar, first set foot on it on St. Thomas' day of 1470 AD and named it after the saint. The island became a trading post and a staging point for trade between India and Europe. It was fast turning into a slave depot, and people were captured in increasing numbers from all along the African mainland kingdoms and sold for profit. The slaves were crucial to the production of the islands most valuable commodity: Sugar.

Sugar that now sweetened the jaded palate of Europe. It had become an addiction and Sao Tome was poised to provide the quantities that were needed. Pasquale had never understood that craving himself but there was money to be made. The sugar economy drove the island's prosperity, and the profits from it proved an irresistible attraction for fortune hunters. People like Diego arrived from Portugal to make fortunes here. But there were dangers too. The *mal'aria* was bad, and attacks from escaped slaves that returned to wage war against their former masters were frequent. Despite these problems, Diego told him he had never regretted settling in Sao Tome.

༄༅

Pasquale had a hot bath and a change of clothes in Diego's house, which was a sprawling colonial home. Its pillars and arches was a bold imitation of the style of Venetian palaces that Diego told him he remembered from his youth, travelling through Venice, Florence, and Rome. It seemed like he had wanted to add a second floor but had changed his mind half-way, giving the homestead a half-finished look. Despite its design flaws, Pasquale found the Casa Sao Marcello quite comfortable. It was opulent by island standards. Unfortunately, Diego's wife had died some years before and there was no lady of the house. The three men sat on the veranda.

"How is the old country?" Diego asked. He gave Pasquale and Alvarez each a goblet that he filled with port.

"Same as usual," Alvarez replied.

"Then I'm glad I'm here and not there," Diego laughed. Pasquale smiled. He had occasionally thought he might bring Sofia to Sao Tome with him, maybe for good, and buy his own sugar farm. He had no doubt that Sofia would make a good colonial wife, but he had to think about his print shop and his mother. She would never survive here.

His mind turned to the slave shipment. He hoped that they would get a good price for the ones that had survived. The crew had moved them to the *barracoons* on the seafront. He had counted them carefully as they came off the *Santa Magdalena*. Sixty-seven in all. There would be an auction in a day or two. They would need Diego for that. His familiarity with the island meant that he could find buyers quickly. He had already indicated that he wanted to buy a few for his own use.

From the courtyard, a group of black women appeared with plates of food of fried fish, sweet roast pork, and *feijoada,* a stew made of meat and beans. They placed the tureens of *calulu,* fish, and vegetables beside trays of papaya and mangoes. Some had wraps over their waists covering the buttocks and upper thighs and another cloth that covered their breasts.

A thin, older, black woman who ran the household was the only one dressed in a long, gray, formal gown. She watched over the others like a hawk. The other women were younger, and a few of them smiled boldly at the guests. Pasquale wondered which of them was currently sleeping with Diego. He usually made no secret of his mistresses; when the nighttime entertaining was done with, his choice would be obvious to his guests.

This was Pasquale's third visit to Sao Tome, and he found the lifestyle quite different from what he was used to. It was a more permissive society compared to back home. Women were in short supply here and the colonials were encouraged by the Crown to cohabitate with the blacks to maintain a viable population—a situation that was fraught with contradictions.

Pasquale looked at the parade of females and wondered, as he had before, where Diego found the energy for all his dalliances.

"I have a local woman who has made me a strong potion for my manhood," Diego had boasted to him once and Pasquale had wondered if it were true.

Diego was telling them now that his sister would soon be coming from Lisbon to help run his household. "She's older, a widow and will help me take care of the children."

He had at least eight children, two from his late wife and the others from his various mistresses. Pasquale wondered how an older, more conservative woman would find the unconventional ways of the island. On a previous trip, Diego had talked incessantly about being enamored of the daughter of one of the *fazendieros*. Her name was Renata and Pasquale had met her once and thought she was one of the most beautiful women he'd ever seen. She and Diego had been lovers for years and had two sons. Pasquale had not heard her mentioned for some time and wondered what had become of her but didn't ask. He could not keep up with Diego's women.

The children came into courtyard to play and were a few steps down from the veranda.

"Antonio!" Diego called out. The oldest boy, a young man really, stopped the game and brought the children to greet the guests.

"You remember Antonio and Roberto, my sons of my wife Helena?"

"Antonio has become a man since the last time I was here," Pasquale said, shaking the young man's hand. Antonio smiled. He was long limbed and his white tunic and cotton breeches fit him well.

His sun-browned skin gave him a vigorous glow, and his teeth and green eyes flashed attractively when he smiled.

He loitered briefly to ask Pasquale about Portugal before he led his siblings away.

༺༻

Onaedo was in another building, another prison, she thought. She lifted the bowl of thin fish soup she shared with the others and took a sip. The woman across from her was looking on with mild hostility.

She said something incomprehensible and stretched a bony arm toward Onaedo. She wanted the bowl. Little fights had already broken out sporadically when somebody took more than their share or was slow to pass the bowl.

Onaedo ignored the woman and took another long sip of the hot, peppery broth before relinquishing the bowl. At least it wasn't cold and tasteless. She sympathized with the woman who had been impatient for her turn. It was the best thing they had eaten in a long time. The taste was strangely familiar; like the *nsala* soup that warmed a woman's insides after childbirth; similar to that which Ugodi and Aku cooked for her every day for a month after her daughter was born.

She lay back on the mat. She was still hungry and hoped that sleep would come. She was relieved to be away from the rocking ship onto firm ground but her spirit was still sick with what she'd endured and the uncertainty of what was to come.

This place was like a long, giant chicken coop. It had only one door and was heavily guarded. Small, round openings at the top of the high walls, let in some air and relieved the darkness.

The men were separated from the women and were at either end of the room. A newborn she'd helped deliver in the dark hold of the ship suckled at her mother's dry breast. She wouldn't survive unless her mother ate better food to help make enough milk, Onaedo thought.

Onaedo turned a few times trying to get comfortable. What was this strange new land? She'd heard that they were here to work on the white man's farm. What were they going to plant? How long were they going to keep them here? Were they going to let them go home between the planting season and the harvest when there was nothing to do? What if she wanted to go home right away? She knew that Eneda would pay any sum of money to have her back home, but who would send word to him?

Questions without answers and nobody to ask. Even the black people that brought the food didn't have much information. They glided in and out like silent ghosts delivering water, food, and medicine and spoke in a different and strange tongue.

She would give anything to pray to the gods she knew like Ani or Idemilli or even in her grandmother's humble *chi* shrine. But she had nothing for prayers: no kola-nuts, no white feathers and no white clay. Nothing.

A thought occurred to her that gave her some comfort. Their jailers had removed their shackles before herding them into this building. Perhaps they would let them have some freedom. She would work hard and maybe they'd let her go home. She closed her eyes to the fading light that came through the small holes in the wall.

 infinity

In the *casa grande* Diego set up the card table after dinner. He brought more wine and announced that other guests would be joining them for the rest of the night's entertainment.

"I'll go and look for Padre Joao at the chapel," Pasquale said.

"I see that you're still not a gambling man," Diego said as he laid out the primo pieces on the table.

"I have no luck," Pasquale replied. He strapped his sword around his waist and prepared to leave.

"Send my greetings to the padre," Diego said, filling Alvarez's goblet. "The padre is one of the few honest men in Sao Tome," Diego said. Pasquale agreed. Alvarez barely noticed when Pasquale left; he was too busy ogling the serving women.

He went to his room to fetch the books that he'd brought for the padre; three volumes of the popular novel *Amadis of Gaul*, that he had printed in his shop. He stuffed them into a bag along with a bottle of quality red Dao wine.

He was eager to see his childhood friend again. They'd rekindled their friendship after his last couple of visits. Pasquale could bare his soul to the padre without fear.

He went into the twilight and his mind turned to his friend. The priest had told him he opposed the trade in slaves, but had been unable to explain to Pasquale's satisfaction why the Church participated in it. The trade had its evils, thought Pasquale, but there were advantages. It was lucrative business. He thought about Gregorio and the young woman on the ship. He tried not to think about them but they stuck in his mind.

He stopped briefly to get his bearings as he reached the heart of the new city. It had spread out like a stain on the landscape since his last trip. A new courthouse was next to the jailhouse and new eating-houses had sprung up to add to the numerous taverns. And that was not counting the brothels.

He had patronized one the last time he was on the island and afterwards had been wracked by so much guilt that he'd sworn never to be unfaithful again—not that he was not still tempted. He turned away towards the direction of the small church as he stroked the cold steel of his sword.

∾

The dirt path leading to Padre Joao's small church widened into a courtyard. It was really a chapel, but everybody called it a church. It was a simple, square building with a small cross mounted on the roof. The yellow light from within was faintly visible through the cracks around the door and windows.

The door creaked open with his second knock and opened wide when Padre Joao recognized him. His tired face lit up and he pulled Pasquale in, hugging him enthusiastically.

"Bless me, Padre," Pasquale said bowing slightly.

"Don't stand on such ceremony, my brother," Padre Joao replied, kissing his friend on the forehead. When the priest smiled, the fatigue and deep facial lines faded and his bearded face looked almost Christ-like. His shabby black robe was gathered at the waist by a black leather strip. It had two worn patches at his knee and then dropped to his ankles.

The priest led the way. "Come, give me news of the old neighborhood," he said sitting down on a front pew and patting the space next to him.

"Things haven't changed a lot," Pasquale said giving him the bag of gifts.

"I see that your publishing business is profitable," Padre Joao said when he saw the books. "Thank you."

Pasquale looked around the room. A couple of benches had been added to the back row, but otherwise it was unchanged from his last visit. The altar consisted of a table with a crucifix. A wooden door to the side led to sleeping quarters and a sacristy where the padre robed before mass.

"I wasn't expecting you to return so soon," Padre Joao said, rearranging his heavy robe. He looked thinner. His dark hair was longer too. His eyes were brown and compassionate. "I thought that you wanted to give up this trade."

"I have to make a living," Pasquale said. The conversation was made him uncomfortable.

The padre changed the subject. "I need new priests here. Just in the past year, two priests have died."

"Have you thought of coming home?" Pasquale asked. "Back to Lisbon?"

"Why?"

"It's not much of a life here. No libraries, so few books, no colleagues, no brother monks . . ." Pasquale's voice trailed off. He shrugged.

Padre Joao smiled and shook his head. "No. One can commune with God even here, my brother. God chose me to come here; it was not of my own will. He will tell me where to go next. In any case, my work here isn't done. I'm at war with the *fazendeiros*. They treat the slaves poorly and don't like what I say about it because I speak against their livelihood. But I speak out against nothing, I speak *for* human dignity."

"I thought that things were getting better," Pasquale said. The padre nodded. "Better, I agree, but not ideal."

"The only ideal is paradise, Padre," Pasquale replied.

"It seems that you've become a student of theology," he said. He rose and took two pewter cups from the inner room. When he returned, he opened the wine bottle and poured a little into each cup before giving one to Pasquale.

"When my printing business becomes more profitable I'll give up the slave trade."

The priest nodded. If he was skeptical, he did not show it. "I'll be leaving for the Congo in a month."

"I heard from Diego that there's trouble brewing with the natives there," Pasquale said.

"Their king is a famous Christian known to be a friend of the king of Portugal. He even sent his son as an ambassador to the Portuguese court as a goodwill gesture. How do we repay him? By sending him thieves and brigands who steal his people and foment wars."

Pasquale shifted uncomfortably. He remembered Oguebie and his friend and the havoc they had helped wreak around the Delta. "So what are you going to do when you get there?"

The priest shrugged and sipped his wine. "I don't know yet. There are other Christians there. I will find them. Maybe we can stop these atrocities."

"Isn't that the price of doing business? If we don't trade in slaves, we'll be defeated again by the Spaniards, the French, the Dutch, or even the godless English, heavens forbid."

Padre Joao continued to speak. "I suppose you may be right, there."

"And we do God's work with the money from slaves. That's how we've spread God's word to the heathens."

"I agree that we cannot run the church or orphanages without the money but I know in my heart that what we're doing is wrong," said Padre Joao

They were silent for a while, each man deep in thought.

"I have a request, Padre," Pasquale said after a while.

"What is it?"

"There's a slave girl I brought from the Delta City in the Guinea coast. I think that she'll be useful to you here."

The priest looked at him with some curiosity.

"No, it's nothing like that," Pasquale added hastily. "I have no designs on her. But there's something strange about this girl. I cannot tell you what it is, except that she has a familiar look and reminds me of certain people. Do you remember Juana, my cousin, who ran away from home when you and I were boys?"

The padre laughed. "How can I forget? Don't you remember? We were both in love with her."

"Oh yes, young love," said Pasquale.

"What happened to her?" the padre asked.

Pasquale shrugged. "Nobody knows. She left with a sailor and nobody has heard from her since. She may even be dead for all we know."

"Juana was always a wild one."

"This girl from the bush looks so much like her. She could be her sister. She had the same look about her."

"But she's black?"

"Yes, but still, the similarities are striking."

"Now that *is* strange," the priest said, placing his empty cup on the bench.

"I feel that I should help her in any way that I can."

"What do you want from me?" the priest asked.

"I want you to purchase her and use her in the church or the orphanage. Make her a Christian and teach her to read and to write. If she learns well, she can teach others."

The priest sighed. "You ask a lot, my brother. This church has no money and we've not purchased any new slaves for almost a year."

"Don't worry, I'll provide you with the money."

"In that case, it will be arranged," the priest replied. "I'll bring her here. She can live with the nuns. She'll learn a lot that way."

"Thank you, Padre," Pasquale said. He bent to kiss the priest's rough hands as he prepared to leave. "Good night."

# CHAPTER

# 30

O naedo felt the band of panic across her chest like a too-tight cloth. This was happening a lot to her now. She often forgot where she was each time she woke up. Then she would remember and a suffocating darkness would engulf her. From where she lay, she could make out the dark silhouettes of the others. She struggled to think thoughts that might lift her spirits but they didn't come readily.

The door opened suddenly and let in the bright sunlight. A heavyset white man entered, followed by two others. A murmur of apprehension swept through the room. Onaedo recognized the first man. She had seen him yesterday when they had brought the captives from the belly of the diseased ship. The man had taken some time to look at them as they were shoved into the shed. She suspected that he was an important man here, because of the way others greeted him.

Now she watched him stop in the middle of the room. He looked toward the male prisoners. He pointed to one of them and the man's two companions grabbed the young man and took him outside. The process was repeated with another captive before the man turned to the women. Onaedo looked down quickly to avoid all eye contact. She didn't want to leave the security of the long house.

Suddenly, hands under her armpits lifted her and took her outside. She tried to resist as she floated in the air, but there was little time to react before she was pushed towards a wooden cart attached to two animals. She fell painfully onto the wooden floor while the animals looked on, bored, swishing their bushy tails and shuffling their feet. She sat up and tried to escape from the cart but then thought the better of it. There were many people standing around, and none looked helpful. The two men who were also taken from the shed sat silently, watching. She decided to do the same.

The white man walked to the cart and turned her round. He touched the almost healed scars on her back. His rough hands were oddly soothing. He turned her around and looked at her. She saw a brief look of surprise before he spoke to her. Realizing that she hadn't understood, he turned and spoke to one of his servants. The slightly built black youth with tiny facial scarifications turned to Onaedo and said something that she didn't follow either and so she looked at him and said nothing. The master seemed annoyed and spoke sharply to the young man, before mounting his animal. She later learned that it was a horse. She had heard about them but had never seen one. The man with hair the color of palm-oil rode in front while his servants drove the cart with Onaedo and the others behind him.

తిని

*I hope she's not a stubborn one,* Diego thought, as his horse led the way. The scars were from the lash and indicated that she might be obstinate, a fighter or a runner. He had only seen the scars when the girl was outside when it was too late to exchange her for another prisoner. The last thing he wanted was to waste more time here and risk Alvarez appearing. Not that it mattered, because a bet was a bet and he had won fair and square last night. But with Alvarez, it was better not to take chances.

Last night, Diego had played with Alvarez and the others when, in a drunken and reckless gesture, the ship captain had wagered three slaves from the shipload that they had brought to the island. The other *fazendeiros* who had joined in the festivities, thought it was the height of foolishness to gamble with such a valuable commodity, but this was Sao Tome and Alvarez was an inveterate gambler. Nobody was going to stop a fool from parting ways with his slaves if he so chose. They had all joined in and placed wagers.

"If you lose, I'll sell them at auction tomorrow," Diego had said. "If I lose, I'll pay you the value of all three."

Alvarez had readily agreed. Diego's strategy had been to ply his guest with enough vinho verde and port to befuddle his judgment. But Alvarez had proved shrewder. His love for drink hadn't dulled his mind as much as Diego had hoped and the game had continued for quite a long time with both men drawing even.

Diego was aware of Pasquale's return late in the night but the young man had gone straight to bed without looking in. Diego was glad for this because the last time that they'd gambled, Pasquale had raised an objection. Alvarez was too drunk, Pasquale had said, and it was wrong to take advantage of an inebriated man.

But last night, thankfully, there was no Pasquale and the card game had continued into the early hours of the morning. Finally, Diego had won. He'd gone to bed elated, but not before giving Alvarez more wine and the most comfortable room in his home. Diego had then waited for first light to collect his booty from the *barracoon*.

They arrived at Casa Sao Marcello, and he instructed the servants to take the new arrivals to the slave quarter known as the *senzala*. This was where the two hundred or so slaves that worked his sugar plantation lived with their families.

He was pleased with his day's work, Diego told himself, as he made his way back to the main house.

∽∾

Pasquale was having a bad start to the day. He could barely control his anger as he banged loudly and repeatedly on the door. Finally, he heard somebody stir inside.

*How did this happen?* He thought as he gave the door one last kick.

"Who is it at this time of the morning?" said an annoyed voice from inside.

"Come out immediately," Pasquale said. He hoped that there was a good explanation for what he'd discovered when he went down to the slave enclosure down by the beach.

"What is it? Why are you awake so early?" Alvarez said. He stood by the open door still dressed in his clothes from the day before. He rubbed his eyes and yawned. His breath stank of stale alcohol.

Pasquale waved a hand across his face in disgust. "What happened to the girl?"

"What girl?" Alvarez asked, looking genuinely perplexed.

"The slave girl from the ship," Pasquale replied.

"I don't know what you're talking about. All the slaves are in the *barracoons.* They were there yesterday." His words were slurred and he rubbed his head, as though in pain. Pasquale looked past him to see one of the women from the night before on the bed. She sat up with an anxious look and covered her breasts with a piece of cloth.

"The girl is missing. I arranged her purchase with Padre Joao but she's gone. The guards said you gave Diego permission to take her."

Alvarez looked surprised before realization dawned. "I remember the wager last night but I didn't expect Diego to collect on the debt so soon," he said and shrugged nonchalantly. "He is within his rights to collect on his win, and since I own more than half of the cargo on the *Santa Magdalena*, I can wager any part of my share of slaves to pay my debt. You've no right to object."

"Not the girl. I wanted her for the church," Pasquale said. "It was my penance."

"What penance?" Alvarez asked.

"It is a matter for me and the Creator."

"You never told me that you had special plans for the girl. If you had, I wouldn't have allowed Diego to take her," Alvarez said.

He was growing annoyed. "Listen, I'll make amends. You can have three more slaves above your rightful share. That'll make things right"

"That won't do. We have to get the girl back right away," Pasquale said, his voice rising.

"We can't. She belongs to Diego now and my head is pounding with that rotten wine he served last night," said Alvarez. He yawned, scratched his stomach, and turned back into the bedroom.

Pasquale stared at his back in disgust. He was tempted to jump him and wrestle him to the ground, but knew that it would accomplish nothing.

*I have to look for Diego,* he thought gloomily. Pasquale hoped that he could convince Diego to sell the girl back to him.

# CHAPTER

# 31

It had been almost a month since Onaedo arrived at the plantation. Her dreams had started again. She saw her mother frequently but she never remembered what Ugodi was doing. Aku talked to her about their work, and her daughter usually held her hand. She was worried about her father because he worked in dead silence and never uttered a word of welcome or reprimand. Most times he did not even look at her.

Dualo was rarely featured. She tried hard, even when she was awake, to feel the comfort of his touch or to invoke his laugh but he was strangely unreachable. *He's dead,* she said to herself.

Tonight Ugodi was waiting.

"When are you coming home?" she asked impatiently. "We don't have all day." She stood empty handed by the *uli* tree that was Onaedo's lineage tree, the one where her after-birth was buried and showed that she belonged to Eneda's household.

"I need more water," Onaedo replied. The village stream had magically appeared between them and she bent to scoop up the water.

"You must come now. Udemezue will bring the rest," Ugodi said, and tapped her foot impatiently.

Onaedo was relieved that her mother had come for her. They had to be home soon because it was time to give Eneda his meal. She took it to him and then offered to help him with the knife he was making. He looked up and smiled. You're a girl, he said, this is not a job for a woman. Onaedo smiled back; she agreed. She never wanted to be a blacksmith even though Eneda had told her that she had more talent than anybody he knew. Now it was time to go, because Ugodi had returned for her. She touched her on the shoulder and told her to get up. This surprised Onaedo because she hadn't known that she was lying down. She smelled the familiar coconut oil and felt her mother's rough, warm hands on her bare shoulders.

She looked up at the dark-skinned woman leaning over her. It was not Ugodi, because her mother didn't have a gap in her front teeth when she smiled. This woman was younger and her hair was long and held in two fat plaits on either side of her kindly face.

"So, you are awake," the woman said in Igbo. Now Onaedo knew her. Her name was Maria. She was a fellow Igbo woman she had met at the *senzala* on the first day she arrived. What was Maria doing in Abonani?

"You have to wake up," Maria said. "I need your help."

Onaedo rubbed her eyes. She was awake and she was not in Abonani. She was in the *cabana*, the square hut that belonged to Maria, her husband Agostinho, and their three sons—just one of the dozens that made up the senzala. Maria had been excited to see her when she learned that Onaedo could speak her language.

"Come and stay with us, she invited Onaedo. "That house where you're staying is too crowded. People are packed together like yams in a barn."

Onaedo thanked her and moved in with her only possession—a mat that Senhor Diego had provided to every slave. Married slaves lived as family units in a *cabana*. Agostinho had cleverly partitioned theirs so that there were two sleeping rooms. Onaedo shared one with Maria's three sons.

"I have not seen any Igbo person here for a long time," Maria told her the first night she moved in. They had chatted till morning, reminiscing about memories they never shared.

"You cannot imagine how happy I am to see you," Maria said more than once.

Onaedo felt lucky too, especially when Maria told her that she had heard of Abonani. But she'd never been there and didn't know anybody that Onaedo knew. She came from a small town called Nnokwa that Onaedo had never heard of either. "I was brought here seven years ago," she told Onaedo in Igbo. "Luckily for me, I met Agostinho who had come a year before. I married him shortly afterwards. When you are here, you learn that life waits for nothing."

Onaedo agreed. She had learned quickly that it was better to agree to everything here. Later, she would figure things out. She had to do a few important things first, like learning to speak Portuguese. Maria's children volunteered to tutor her in the evenings, after she finished her work in the sugarcane fields. She soon learned, however, that the *senzala* version of Portuguese was very different from that in the *casa grande*.

"I thought I was back home before you woke me," Onaedo said, folding her mat.

Maria looked at her with sympathy. "I think you are a seer like your mother's sister," Maria said.

"I hope not," Onaedo said. The last thing she needed now was to be burdened with a cursed gift. She'd told Maria about Aku and the rest of her family, and surprised herself at how much she'd revealed about herself in so short a time. In captivity, there were no strangers.

"Onaedo, the women who are cooking tonight want you to get the vegetables from the garden before we leave for the farm."

Onaedo took a small basket outside. The *senzala* was simply a square with rows of *cabanas* and long sheds on all sides. Two giant trees at one end provided shade when the sun was high in the sky. Activity in the *senzala* started early most mornings as people prepared to leave for the sugar fields.

She walked through the narrow space between the buildings to get to the small plot behind. Each family tended its own small garden of vegetables and spices. There was nothing beyond the garden plots but dense forest. To the side, some distance away Casa Sao Marcello stood in stately solitude. In hushed whispers she'd been told that Senhor Diego lived there in splendor. She also learned that one might spend one's whole life in the *senzala* and never see the inside of the house.

She surveyed the planted rows from which the green okra shrubs sprouted with their bright yellow flowers. The silky tassels of the corn were beginning to dry, and red and yellow hot peppers made colorful splashes in between dark green leaves. She filled her basket, as she walked to a cluster of banana trees. Some of the ripe ones had been half-eaten by bats. She'd never seen bats before but they were numerous in her new home and were a rich and tasty source of smoked meat. It was the only meat readily available to the *senzala*.

She had to hurry. She always took too long in the garden. "You are going to be late," one of the women said as she took the basket from her. Her pregnant belly stood in sharp contrast with her thin arms and legs. The women who were about to give birth were permitted to stay home. With the help of those too old or sick to go to the fields, they helped prepare the communal food. Onaedo washed her face and hurried off with Maria and the others.

ന്ദ

Onaedo had settled into plantation life quicker than even she realized but the determination to leave and find her way home never left her.

She reasoned that if she worked harder, maybe she would be permitted to leave.

"You have to work faster," the overseer bellowed. His name was Marco, the thorn in everyone's side. "Our quotas were down last month because of you lazy people," he said. His whip twitched, hungry to zip across a bare back.

There were many overseers, mostly white men that Onaedo learned were almost as poor as the slaves, but Marco was a particularly spiteful breed and took delight in tormenting the workers. He was a slight, leathery-skinned man with a big voice. To Onaedo, he had the eyes of a bird; they blinked incessantly. Onaedo thought he liked to pick on her but it could have been her overwrought way of thinking since she'd arrived. For now, he seemed to lose interest and wandered away to harass somebody else.

Onaedo aligned herself with the others in her group and began to cut the thick stalks of cane with a machete. When it snapped, it crashed down, its leaves waving as it fell.

"You want to kill yourself? You cut it so it falls away from you," one of the men called to her from across the next row. "And you cut from the bottom. You'd better not let him see you waste the cane like that." Onaedo nodded.

This farm was the biggest she had ever seen. Even the communal land that Abonani people had leased for generations from the people of the fertile Oze valley was not this vast, and that land could feed the whole of *Olu n'Igbo*. The boundary of this farmland was so big it had two streams running through it. And it all belonged to Senhor Diego and not to the people who farmed it daily.

"Why does one man want to own so much land?" she asked Maria and Agostinho. "How can he possibly cultivate all of it, even if all his kinsmen helped him?"

"He cannot. That's why they bring us here and make us do it for him," Agostinho replied bitterly. That was the first time she knew of sugarcane, the tall thick grass with the sweet liquid inside that had turned the white man into an addict for its sweet taste.

"They put it in everything they eat," Agostinho told her, "and they sell it for a great price back in their country."

"It's too sweet," Onaedo said. "It cannot be good to eat so much of it."

"You can tell that to them but I don't think they'll listen," Agostinho responded with a dry laugh.

But there were some marvels. To Onaedo, the sugar mill was one of them. As they walked from the *senzala* to the fields each day, they passed by the giant wheels that worked the sugar press. Eneda

would have been interested in that had he seen it. He may even have
built one. Falling water turned the wheels, with help sometimes from
horses or male slaves, their bodies strained to their very limits with
the heaving and pushing.

Sugarcane cultivation was backbreaking work. Onaedo hated it.
Her hands cracked open and wept blood from handling the rough
cane and wielding the machete. She breathed in the cane dust and
listened to the night coughs of the others. She missed farming season
in Abonani with its camaraderie, food-sharing, and jokes as friends
and families worked together.

The rationed clothing was meager and did nothing to hide her
nakedness or that of the others. Her body had become a focus of
attention. It was embarrassing.

"I know how you feel," Maria said. She gave her an extra piece
of cloth and told her that she'd been hoarding it for a while. "You can
have this one; I have others."

"Thank you," Onaedo said, adding it to her barely-covered
breasts. Maria was worried about her. She regarded her briefly and
then sighed. She turned her attention to one of her sons, sitting in
front of the cabana after eating an early evening meal.

Maria lifted the boy and put an ear against his lips. "I don't
know what's wrong, Onaedo. I've never seen him like this."

Onaedo examined him; he didn't seem particularly sick, but
Onaedo knew that Maria fussed over her children like a mother
hen and lived in mortal fear of losing them. Since arriving in Sao
Tome, Onaedo harbored no real desire to start a healing practice.
She had left all that back in Abonani and told Maria emphatically
that she wanted it to stay there. But delivering the baby on the ship
had served to highlight her abilities. So the people of the *senzala*
had found a path to her door, actually to Maria and Agostinho's
door, telling her that they trusted her more than the white man's
hospital or even Isolda, the other medicine woman in the *senzala*.
Onaedo had encountered Isolda, a big woman who spent most
nights pacing the *senzala* and talking to herself in her native Fante.

She lived with one of the old women a few *cabanas* down from Maria and Agostinho and was so crazy that people feared her more than they feared their illness.

Onaedo reached towards Maria's boy. He was as hot as the glowing embers of the dying fire. His hair was entwined in long *dada* locks that fell just short of his shoulders.

"I don't think the fever is that bad," Onaedo said standing. "Wait here. I'll go for some herbs for him."

She walked past the vegetable farm towards the mantle of encircling trees. She had discovered a clearing in the middle of the tree grove by chance, chasing a bush rodent one day. It was then that she'd stumbled upon the natural garden with familiar plants and herbs. The plants here were so luxuriant it seemed like it had been grown for a tribe of giants. She hoped to build a shrine here to perform simple rites in honor of all her ancestors. She plucked the leaves she needed and took them back to the front yard to boil them.

"It's too bitter," the boy protested when they gave it to him later.

"I'll make it sweeter," Onaedo said, mixing in some molasses.

When the *iba* left his body, taking the heat with it, he fell asleep between the two women.

ᘏᘏ

"Tell me how you came here, Maria," Onaedo asked on another night.

"You want to hear it again?"

"Yes." Onaedo replied. It was nighttime and the giant trees stood darkly around the camp. The moon was nearly full. They sat together at their favorite place in front of the *cabana*. The old woman that lived with Isolda the medicine woman was starting a story and most of the children had gathered around her underneath the giant tree. Onaedo had been tempted to join them but had decided against it. Reminders of Abonani would bring her to tears.

Agostinho came in and sat a little apart from them. He usually said very little and tonight was no exception; his wife more than made up for his innate reserve and, moreover, he spoke a strange Igbo dialect that Onaedo didn't understand.

The fire burning in the stone tripod hearth was dying. Kernel-less corncobs were piled beside to be used later as fuel.

"My story isn't different from many others," Maria said. "There was a war with our neighbors, and we lost. Then our problems started. In a blink, the peace we had nurtured for many generations disappeared in a war that had no reason. When it was over, we tallied the losses and we were asked to compensate our rivals for all the people that they'd lost, even though they had started the fight and had killed more of us with the guns that they'd acquired from the white man. That's how strange and upside down everything had become in our world. The rules of warfare were manipulated and we couldn't protest this injustice. The people with the guns, it seemed, won the argument."

Agostinho grunted in agreement from his corner.

"I was a widow at that time," Maria continued. "And since I had borne no children with my late husband, it was an easy choice when I was asked to go to the neighboring town as part of the appeasement. To tell you the truth, I didn't mind too much at the time because I wanted a change anyway and I was going to be married to a new husband when I arrived. Little did we know that the real plan was to give us to slave merchants. Or that the war was a deception created by the slave traders just to capture slaves. Now, I would like to think that if my people had known about this they would have resisted, but I realize that it would have been pointless. They had no guns and, therefore, no power. So, my sister, that's how I was taken by the white people and brought here."

She stopped. Onaedo saw her tears. They shone in the light of the dying fire. Her husband must have seen too because he chided her gently. "Have I not told you not to tell this story anymore if it upsets you so much?"

"I still want to tell it because it helps," Maria said, wiping her eyes. "Onaedo should know that she isn't alone in what happened to her. I see sadness every day in her eyes." Her voice was soft, as it always was when she spoke to her husband. Onaedo envied their closeness. It reminded her of what life would have been with Dualo. From across the yard came the noise of raucous voices. People were drinking palm-wine and fermented sugar cane alcohol. They did it to drown their sorrows.

"Agostinho asked Senhor Diego for permission to marry me as soon as I was baptized. And then my children came. Isn't it a strange turn of fortune that, after years of living as a free but barren woman, I've now been blessed with children but I'm a slave? I know that it's not what you want to hear now, but you'll forget Dualo, your mother and father, and even your child, and start a new life."

"I don't think that will happen for me," Onaedo said. How did one start a new life as a slave? How could she forget the child that had sucked on her nipples? That would be impossible to forget. Maybe one day she'd see the practical truth of Maria's advice, but that day had not yet come.

"I'm going to try to return to my home," Onaedo said after a long pause. "I don't know how, but I'm going to try. I will not die here. My soul will be lost here if it cannot find its way back home to my ancestors."

"We've heard that there are people on the other side of the island who are our people," Agostinho said. "It's said that one day they plan to seize the white man's ship and sail it back home. If we can find them, we can go home."

Maria shook her head. "That's foolish talk. Don't you know how dangerous it is to run? If they capture you, they'll cut off your head."

"I'm only trying to help," Agostinho said. "We should encourage people like her to leave before she becomes tied to this land like we are. Now we don't know how to leave. We stay here planting and harvesting a useless crop that's not even food."

Maria said nothing. A pregnant moon cast a strange stillness in the *senzala*. Onaedo wondered if it was the same moon that she had gazed at in Abonani. Could it tell her the way home if she could talk to it? It was now serene in the other *cabanas*. The children came in when the old storyteller ran out of things to say.

"The tranquility sometimes was not what it seemed," Maria said. "That is when they come for the women," she whispered to Onaedo.

Her heart felt cold and heavy with anxiety. She had heard about this, seen it with her own eyes. It was mostly the overseers that came. They took the women, Maria had said, and didn't return them till the morning and sometimes not even for days. They like the young ones like you; that's why you should marry soon."

"A husband cannot protect her here," Agostinho said. "Those men are *degradado*, criminals in their own country."

"Can Senhor Diego not stop them?" Onaedo asked

"The Senhor? He has too many concubines and mistresses himself, so how can he stop anybody else? His women are all types— white, mulatto, and black. Their children stay in the *casa grande*, but when he tires of the women he sends them away. But the children stay and the nuns from the orphanage teach them how to read and write." She shook her head. "He's as bad as the rest of his countrymen."

Maria leaned forward to examine the pendant around Onaedo's neck. Onaedo had hid it away before but had started wearing it again. "Where did you get this?"

"It came from my father."

"The white man's priest gives these to people who worship his God. Was your father one of them?"

Onaedo shook her head. "Not my father, but my ancestor to whom it belonged."

"That explains it."

"But she stopped after a while because the Abonani people wanted no part of her strange god."

"The world in which we live is strangely connected," Maria said, as they prepared for sleep.

## WEST AFRICA

## 16th CENTURY

CHAPTER

# 32

U demezue had seen with his own eyes the changes that had come to Abonani and the whole countryside after the disappearances. He felt like a failure for not bringing Onaedo and Adanma home. Tragedy was played out daily in his mother's slowing steps and graying hair and also in his father's growing silence and exhausting work hours.

He remembered the day that they reached the Great River to find that the fishermen had left them behind. The head fisherman had left their manila bars on the beach. Udemezue and his group had had to wait a full day for another group who agreed to take them across. On the other side, nobody they asked had seen Onaedo's group.

"There are so many people here. We cannot tell one from another," was the constant response.

Udemezue was directed to a blacksmith, but he also denied seeing the group. The man had sounded defensive and Udemezue had wondered why. Then he had learned that he made shackles for the white man. Udemezue wanted to go back to beat him up, to curse him, to tell him that in Abonani his homestead would be destroyed for such an abomination against his fellow men.

"Let him be," Emenike said. "We've lost. They're gone. Let's go home."

So they had swallowed their disappointment and returned to Abonani without their loved ones.

When he arrived home, Udemezue took his infant son to Adanma's mother. Onaedo's daughter stayed with Ugodi. He no longer went to the Great River market. Instead he aided Eneda at his workshop and put more energy into his farming.

*Maybe it is written in the lines of my palm that I was meant to be a blacksmith*, he thought as he left his house one morning to take his turn in guarding the town. Trenches had been dug around all the villages in Abonani and wooden lookout towers had been erected around the perimeter of the town.

Udemezue stopped at his mother's to eat and to make sure she was all right before attending to the business of the day. He had to do this more often, as Ugodi fell deeper into grief at the loss of Onaedo.

"Udemezue, my son, you won't believe what happened last night," Ugodi said when Udemezue walked through the door. She had started to complain a lot and seemed frightened when Udemezue was not around.

"My prize goat, the one I inherited from my mother's lineage, fell into one of those ditches they have dug everywhere and broke her neck. She had babies only a few weeks ago. I'm supposed to pass it on. When they brought her to me this morning I wept. That goat has given me at least ten goats over the years and now she's gone."

"I'm sorry about your goat," Udemezue replied. "Next time I go to the Afor market at Ogidi, I'll buy you another one."

Udemezue knew they were talking about more than goats; Onaedo was the unmentioned and the unspoken.

"Since we are talking about Ogidi," Ugodi said, "I'm going there with Aku to see a man they say knows things." She motioned for Ogugua to come sit on her lap. Udemezue avoided looking at the girl; he saw Onaedo's face in her. It was too painful.

"Everybody says this man is good at finding missing people," Ugodi said. Deep lines of worry creased her brow. Her search for

Onaedo in the house of every *dibia* had become a source of disquiet in the family, especially since it became clear that none of the medicine men were able to deliver on their unrealistic promises. They took money from the desperate and gave disappointment in return.

"I'm leaving," he said, rising.

"Go well," his mother replied. "We'll leave as soon as Aku arrives." She listlessly stroked Ogugua's hair. Udemezue said nothing more as he took his bag and left.

જી

"Are you ready?" It was Aku. She had agreed to see the latest *dibia* with Ugodi just as she'd agreed to go to the others before.

"Come greet me, my little daughter," Aku said, gesturing to Ogugua. Ogugua approached and sat on the ground beside her. She began to play with the brightly-colored stones that had belonged to Onaedo. Aku remembered how Onaedo had collected and stored them meticulously on the ledge in her mother's hut.

She watched Ugodi and thought about how life had changed in a few short months. Ugodi's world had collapsed when Udemezue had failed to return with Onaedo. "We'll look for her. We'll find her," Ugodi had said with conviction. When the days passed without news, she had struggled to hide her disappointment. "If I lose hope, she will die."

Aku sighed. She had her own private worries. Her work had suffered. She had hoped by now to have relinquished minor duties to Onaedo.

"Have you found a new helper yet?" Ugodi asked. There was a question behind the question.

"No. I've not started looking," Aku replied.

"Why not?"

"Why are you asking me now? I thought we were going to see the *dibia* in Ogidi?" Aku asked shortly.

"I want to know if you've seen anything since she left. Anything?"

"No. If I had, I would have told you."

Ugodi turned away. "I'm ready now. Let's go. Did you remember to arrange for the escort?"

"I decided against it," Aku said.

"Why?" Ugodi asked.

"It will draw unwanted attention. We're two old women, not the type of people they take. If we take our walking sticks and bend over like old women, nobody will look at us twice."

"I hope you're right. Let's go."

ᔕᔑ

The sun was near its zenith when they stopped to rest. "Ogidi isn't far from here, if I remember correctly," Aku said, while they rested in the shade of an abandoned shed.

"I hope this *dibia* is a good one," Aku said. "The last one was a charlatan. He took all our money and gave us nothing."

"We have to do all that we can, Aku," Ugodi replied with a low voice "We must bring her home."

"You know, I called her my daughter too, though you brought her into this world. I'm trying not to lose hope either. But I don't think that they know what they're doing."

"We have to try," Ugodi said, again, and resumed walking. Aku sighed, rose, and followed.

In Ogidi, they were led straight away to the priest by a young girl of about ten years whom they had asked for directions. According to their young companion, there were many who came to consult him. "He is the greatest dibia in *Olu n'Igbo*. He found my mother's missing goat." Both women looked at each other and smiled. The girl pointed to the *obi* where the priest lived. They gave her a piece of boiled yam from the basket to thank her.

His *obi* was also his divination house and he was alone. It was dark and gloomy inside, and one had to look hard to see his misshapen face. It hung like a thick, brown rag on one side of his head. It was grotesque, yet drew the eyes, so that it was difficult to look away. Aku thought the malformation gave him an aura of authenticity.

His voice, when it emerged from within the depths of the curtain of skin, was almost feminine—soothing and mesmerizing. He asked questions and listened solemnly to their petition. Ugodi finished speaking.

"Grieving mother," he said, "I will tell you all that I know."

Aku tried in vain to find the eyes buried in the folds of skin yet didn't want to seem ill mannered. The medicine man continued. Aku suspected that he must have grown accustomed to curious stares long ago. "You've travelled a long road. You're both known beyond your thresholds for the strength of your hand, and so your petition will be looked upon favorably.

"First, we will start the *a-juju*, the initial enquiry. Then we will appease the benevolent spirits with good sacrifices. I will need you to provide a white fowl, four yams, and four eggs. Then we have to distract the malevolent ones; the spirits that cause harm. We give them the bad sacrifice. That is not difficult to find—the animal entrails, rotten eggs, dead lizards. When we throw that to them they will stay out of our way.

"Then Ani, the land goddess, and Idemilli, the water deity, will return your daughter to you."

"We'll do all that you ask," Ugodi replied. "I must have my daughter." Aku heard the excitement in her sister's voice. She hoped it would not be in vain.

"A mother's love is more potent than any medicine or charm," the *dibia* said. "It has no equal in the whole of creation. I've felt your daughter's presence today and her *chi* is strong."

The excess skin on his face swung back and forth as he stoked the fires to burn even hotter. "It's cold outside," he said, noticing as if for the first time how profusely his visitors were sweating. "The spirits never want the hearth to grow cold."

Ugodi looked at Aku. They nodded politely.

"What about the other one, Adanma my daughter-in-law, did you get a message from her too?" Ugodi asked.

The *dibia* frowned. "The message from her is not very clear at the moment. I'll need more time and more offerings," he said, and listed the things they'd have to provide. "This is a difficult task, even for me."

Aku coughed loudly. The man looked at her sternly. "Woman, I hope that you're not challenging the spirits."

Aku said she was not. The *dibia* looked at her steadily. "I know of you, Aku. The spirits support the work that you do for women but you must be careful that pride does not overtake you."

Aku felt a chill. What did he mean? Her mind went to the twins. Did he know about them? She felt Ugodi's eyes on her but wouldn't look. She stared into the fire as if she had discovered something interesting in it. The *dibia* closed his eyes and muttered under his breath for what seemed an eternity. Then he opened his eyes and told them to go home. "Come back in one week. By then my consulta-tions will be complete."

When they emerged, the day was still bright. Aku's uneasiness had grown during the visit and she was confused. She felt that she'd been accused of something. In her sister's face, she found nothing but faint optimism.

∾

"Do you think that he knows what he is talking about?" Ugodi asked, as soon as they were out on the road again.

Aku shrugged. "He seems to know something. We'll wait and see."

They walked in silence for a while, each woman deep in her own musings. They reached the broad road that went all the way back to Abonani.

Ugodi paused and turned to her sister. "For the first time I have real faith."

Aku looked at her. "I hope that—" she stopped in mid sentence and nudged her sister violently. Ugodi looked back. There was a long line of men and women coming in their direction. They were tied to each other. Leading the group were half a dozen men; they carried guns. Aku did a quick calculation and realized that they would not get very far if they decided to run.

"Bend over your stick and pretend to be ill," she whispered urgently.

The group was now only a few feet away. Aku looked away in fear, but not before she saw the white man with them—strange-looking and wearing stranger clothes. She closed her eyes and her steps faltered as she leaned into her walking stick. She could smell the fear in the air as the group drew closer and could almost feel one of the armed men grab her shoulder. Then they were gone. Like an evil wind, they had blown past.

Aku breathed a sigh of relief. She looked at Ugodi. The shock on Ugodi's face reflected her own. A depressing silence followed.

"Why are you stopping?" Ugodi asked. Aku had paused in mid-stride, her head raised like an animal scenting the air.

"I have something to tell you that cannot wait," she said, turning to Ugodi. A strange feeling had come over her. "My mother's child, you have to listen to me because I have something important to say to you. I have gone with you to the whole of *Olu n'Igbo*, from the beginning to the end, and if today you ask me to put my head in the fire, I will gladly do it for you. But I have to tell you that I don't believe that any of these people we have seen so far, know where to find Onaedo. We are no nearer to finding her than the day they took her."

"That's not what you just said."

"I was wrong," Aku said, holding Ugodi's gaze.

Ugodi took a deep breath. "Are you suggesting that we give up?"

"You know that's not what I'm saying."

"Then what are you saying?" Ugodi replied. She was almost shouting. "I had only two children and now I have one, like One Eye that owes Blindness a debt of vision. What if it comes to collect?"

"I will tell you what I mean," Aku replied calmly. "I was merely pointing out that there are dubious people, who—"

"You are the Seer, Aku," Ugodi sneered. Aku stood before her sister's bitter anger. She was not surprised. She had been expecting this. "Why have you not seen for me?" Ugodi continued. "Eh? I have been waiting for you to tell me where to find my daughter. So answer me now. Where is Onaedo?"

"She's gone," Aku said. "They took her into the water."

"Into the water? What water? What are you talking about now?" Ugodi asked.

"I'll explain it to you. Come, let's sit down for a moment. I'm tired of standing," Aku said.

Ugodi followed her to a small clearing where a tree trunk shaped like a long bodied man rested on one elbow. Black ants scuttled away when Aku swiped at the torso before she sat down. Reluctantly, Ugodi sat down beside her.

"A coffin was floating on water; that is what I saw on the day she was married," Aku said, looking at the road that they had just left.

"You saw this and never told me?" Ugodi was incredulous.

"I didn't know what it meant," Aku replied. "But I know now that she is gone. Especially after seeing those people today."

She looked at Ugodi.

"You had better not hide anything else from me," Ugodi said, her eyes flashing in anger. "You keep too many secrets. Is my daughter now dead?"

"That one I cannot say, because I don't know," Aku replied. She continued to look at the road. A group of women with heavy baskets walked by, chatting noisily. They were accompanied by men with guns, a couple with machetes and some with sticks. They greeted the two women and told them not to tarry too long.

"Don't worry. We are just resting; we will soon be on our way," Aku reassured them.

When they were alone again, Aku looked at Ugodi and saw the hard set of her face.

"I don't believe you; I don't believe Onaedo is dead."

"Look at me." Aku spoke sternly. Ugodi turned until their eyes met. "The time has come to start thinking about what to do now. Onaedo and Adanma need a decent burial to ease their way into the after-life. It's necessary to give them a place with the ancestors so that they can come back in reincarnation."

"*Tufia!* God forbid." Ugodi shouted and leapt to her feet. "I will not bury my own child. Whoever heard of such a thing? Who is going to keep my *chi* shrine when I'm gone? How will she come back to me when I'm too old to have any more children?"

"She'll return through somebody else in the family. You know it will happen that way."

"I don't want to hear any more of this," Ugodi said and retied the new cloth she had put on to see the *dibia* who she had hoped would help bring back her daughter; it was to show the *dibia* that she was a woman of means and would pay whatever it took to get her daughter back. She tied it across her chest, firmly—like her decision.

"I will not bury Onaedo. It's an abomination to die before the people that brought you into the world. Onaedo will not do that to me."

"People don't die on purpose to punish the living," Aku said.

Ugodi silenced her sister with a raised hand. "She'll never receive a burial while I'm still alive. That's all there is to it. I'll look for her till the day I die. When that day comes, they can do what they like because I won't be here. But you should have told me what you saw long ago so I could have taken steps to prevent this."

"Nothing could have stopped what happened."

"How do you know? You think you know everything; it's just like what you do with the twins. How do you know that you're right about *that*, and that Ani goddess isn't angry with you and has taken revenge?"

Aku looked away. She couldn't bear the accusation in her sister's eyes or the distrust that sprouted like a poisonous plant between them. She had hoped that this day would not come, but it had.

She stood and picked up the small basket with their uneaten food.

"You can believe what you like, Ugodi. Let's go." They walked the rest of the way home in silence.

CHAPTER

# 33

O naedo made her way to the Casa Sao Marcello. Since the first
day that she'd been unceremoniously removed from the slave
barracks almost a year ago, Onaedo had rarely seen Senhor Diego,
but she knew the big white man was the owner of everything and
everybody in the *senzala*. There were also the overseers, the men he
employed that supervised the daily activities of the sugar fields. They
managed the mills and the presses and came to the *senzala* on occasion to announce a new rule or to take women away.

In the past year, stories Onaedo heard about Senhor Diego
painted a complex picture of a tough, exacting master, but one who
could be fair to his workers. Now, as she stood on his threshold, she
tried to put all the parts together. They were all captives here and her
task was to find a way home. She would try to reach him, to tell him
that her father would be willing to pay whatever it took to get her
back. With her improved Portuguese, she was sure she could make
herself understood.

She was still deciding this when the summons came last night
for her to come to the *casa grande*. She was surprised because she had
not solicited for it but she saw it as a good omen for her plans. The
following morning, she walked along the wide path, passing between
trees that provided shade all the way to the front clearing of the

main house. She was met at the main gate by Senhor Diego's house-keeper, an elderly black woman by the name of Violante. She was more feared in the *senzala* than even Senhor Diego; it was said that she was as mean as a mad dog. Nobody knew where she originally came from but she had been at the *fazenda* longer than anybody else. She held sway over Senhor Diego's household after his wife died and ruled it with an iron fist.

Onaedo now stood before her. She was thin and bony. Her scrawny neck was stuck like a coconut on top of her narrow shoulders. Her skin was the dark ash-gray of cold charcoal. What struck Onaedo most was the incongruity between the splendor of her gown and the gaunt frame of Violante herself. The garment was carefully sewn, its dark green was like a luxuriant forest, and it looked as soft as Violante's face was hard. The neck and sleeves were edged in black lace and, around her neck, was a curious necklace of dried beans strung together with a twine.

Onaedo looked at Violante's weathered face and Violante regarded her with cool hostility. One of her eyes was dead and white; she was blind in that eye. Her tight, unsmiling mouth reminded Onaedo of mean-spirited Ezinkwo, who owned the stall next to her mother at Eke Abonani market. Did everybody have a double somewhere?

"What are you staring at?" Violante asked in a querulous voice, speaking in Portuguese.

"Nothing," Onaedo replied hastily. She couldn't look away from the good eye.

"Come inside," Violante barked.

"Yes, Senhora," Onaedo said demurely and quickly stepped inside to avoid the closing door.

"Walk carefully and don't break anything," Violante said over her shoulder as she led the way. Onaedo understood Portuguese well enough to understand important commands.

The hall was dark and gloomy and seemed to have nothing that was remotely breakable. Onaedo was surprised at how bare the place was compared to the stories she had heard in the *senzala* about the opulence of the *casa grande*.

She hurried along and tried to focus on the older woman's tightly wound headscarf. Wisps of gray hair escaped at the nape of her neck. Onaedo felt the air on her bare belly with each swish of Violante's gown. Compared to her, she was almost naked in her old, two-piece waist and breast wrap.

She had no time to look inside any of the open doors that lined the corridor. The smell of cooking food wafted into the hallway. It reminded her of how hungry she was.

Violante stopped in front of an open door that appeared at the end of the corridor. She stepped aside and motioned for Onaedo to go through. The room she entered was large, with a table that dominated the room. It was pushed underneath a large window that looked into a paved courtyard. Several paintings of men and women hung on the walls. They drew Onaedo's attention. They seemed so alive that she could almost see their faces move as they smiled or frowned, with eyes that seemed to follow her around the room. The rest of the wall was covered with pieces of colorful thick cloth in red, yellow, and brown. The larger pieces under her feet felt as soft as the skin of a newborn animal; she could have stood on it all day just to feel its soothing caress.

She was so busy admiring her surroundings she hadn't had time to pay attention to the two men in the room. She recognized both of them right away; Senhor Diego was the one standing near the window. He was a big man with bright red hair, and he turned when the two women entered the room. The other man was thinner with a short brown beard and mustache, and he had on a long drab cloth. Onaedo knew that he was Padre Joao, the priest of the white man's God. He performed marriage ceremonies for the slaves in the *senzala* and baptized the new arrivals. She had undergone a baptism a few weeks ago at which he had officiated. He had taken an interest in her out of the large group of newly arrived slaves and asked through one of Maria's sons what her name meant. Onaedo meant

Golden Jewel, she told him, and the boy had spent some time translating that for him.

He had looked at her, then, as he dipped his hand in some water
in a bowl and drew a wet cross on her forehead. "Your new name is
going to be Aurelia because it means the same thing." She hadn't
been surprised; here, everybody received a new name, it seemed.
It wasn't very different from Abonani where often a person took a
second name to reflect his or her character and achievements. But
they still kept the one they were given at birth. That was what she
wanted to tell the priest but she didn't have the right words. Before
she could find them, he had moved to the next person.

Aurelia. She had turned it around on her tongue and it sounded
strange, not like anything she would have chosen for herself.

Violante started to say something, but Senhor Diego cut her off.
"Tell her that she'll now divide her duties between the field and helping Padre Joao at the chapel," Senhor Diego said without preamble.
Onaedo understood part of what was said before Violante translated
it. He sounded like he was discussing important things with the
priest and wanted to return to it. He had barely looked at Onaedo
as he spoke, but the priest, on the other hand, smiled benevolently.
Onaedo didn't understand why she had been given new duties at the
church but, before she had time to think about it, Violante ushered
her from the room and back into the corridor.

"Roberto! Get back to your lessons, right now," Violante yelled
at a boy of twelve or thirteen years who had dashed out from one
of the rooms in front of them. He had straight black hair and the
brightest green eyes that Onaedo had ever seen. He stopped running
and seemed to debate whether to obey or not. He decided to comply
but he gave the old woman a rude gesture with his middle and forefinger before turning slowly back into the room.

This act of defiance angered Violante and she hustled Onaedo
through the main door and slammed it behind her. Onaedo looked
around at the empty yard, wondering if she had just dreamed the
whole thing. She shook her head and walked back slowly to the *senzala*.

"Where have you been?" It was Marco, the overseer. He stepped from behind some trees, reached out and pulled her towards him.

"What were you doing at the *casa grande*? You're late for your work." He placed a hand on her breast and tugged on her cloth. She held it to prevent it from slipping. Her heart pounded as memories of another night flooded her mind, paralyzing her into inaction.

"Come with me," Marco said authoritatively. He released her and waited for a moment as if daring her to object before he turned around and walked ahead nonchalantly.

Onaedo followed slowly behind, thinking furiously of escape. She had always known this might happen and that someday they would come for her, as they did for the other women in the *senzala*. She wouldn't allow what happened to them to happen to her.

They turned onto another path that led to a group of houses. The overseers lived there. Eight sturdy structures stood next to each other, each with its own small compound, although none as elaborate as the Casa Sao Marcello of Senhor Diego. Each was a basic structure with a low-pitched roof, arched doorway, and overhanging eaves. Small groups of children played in the front yards. Most of the overseers were married with families but a few like Marco, were not.

His house was at the end of the line. It was as unkempt as she imagined it would be. He waited for her to catch up before he crossed the threshold. The front room smelled of something musty, and there were two chairs and a table with dirty plates. Marco turned and pointed towards a door that led to a bedroom.

"Go in there and wait," he said. "I'll be with you soon." His smile wasn't reassuring.

The bedroom was bare except for the bed with a coarse mattress of dry sugarcane leaves. She sat on the edge and waited. He came in and looked at her as if for the first time.

"You are a beautiful young woman," he whispered running a hand down her cheek. "Your eyes are bewitching. I've looked for a wife for a long time, and I think that I've found her." His hands dropped to her lap and he pushed her against the rough mattress.

"Senhor Diego wants me to move into the *casa grande,*" she said suddenly. "That's why I was there today," she added.

Marco stopped. He raised himself on his palms to look at her with heavy lidded eyes. She saw uncertainty in his face before he sat beside her.

"If you're lying, you'll regret it," he said as he slumped back on the bed. He gestured her towards the door with a wave of his hand.

As she left, she saw two empty containers of *casaca,* an alcoholic drink made from fermented sugar. He was already snoring as she hurriedly closed the door behind her. She didn't know what she would say the next time that Marco wanted her.

≈

"My sister, it is a wonderful thing to work in the chapel," Maria later exclaimed when Onaedo recounted her meeting with Senhor Diego and the priest. "Taking care of the church is good work," Maria continued. "You must give thanks to your strong *chi* for this. I know it's that *fetisco* around your neck; there is strong medicine that protects you, even here."

Agostinho agreed. Church work was usually given to slaves that had been at the plantation for years.

Onaedo wondered at her good fortune.

≈

After Padre Joao left, Diego had the study to himself. He splashed some brandy-wine into a goblet of blown Venetian glass and held it up to admire the glass and the golden wine inside it. He had bought the glass from Italian merchants who had stopped at the island on their way to Calcutta. He acquired possessions from merchants that wanted slaves in exchange for goods. He loved the opulence that he had worked hard for—the large mirror on the wall was from a landowner who had come looking for slaves for his plantation in the New World, the Persian rugs from Moorish traders in Lisbon, the silk tapestries and paintings that hung in his office once belonged to a *fazendiero* who sold up and emigrated to Brazil. Diego hadn't been born wealthy but had become a rich man by sheer dint of hard work. It was all in jeopardy now.

He sighed and took a large gulp, which did nothing to mellow his thinking. He was being squeezed by the failing sugar business just like one of his presses that squeezed all the sugar from the canes. The problem was over production; every island owned by the Portuguese Crown from the Madeira to the Azores, was a sugar plantation, and every *fildalgo* with any *reis* to spare aspired to be a plantation owner. Competition in the sugar business had become fierce, so fierce that his yearly export of one hundred tons of sugar cake had bottomed at the sugar exchange in Antwerp and he had sustained a major loss.

He looked around the room gloomily. He blamed the Governor for not standing up to the Crown and the high taxes that were killing the farms. Then there was the diversion of slaves to the dry mines in El Mina that hadn't produced a single gold nugget in years. They should have been allowed to sell their excess slaves in the open market where they would have made a greater profit. The Governor feared treason each time there was a suggestion of revolt. *Well treason or not,* Diego thought, *we'll all be ruined if something doesn't happen soon. We have to protect our livelihood.*

He stood to watch the children playing in the courtyard. Antonio, the oldest at nearly seventeen wasn't in the yard this morning. The youngest girl was just two. He hoped that his sister would arrive soon to oversee his ever-increasing household.

He recalled his discussions of a few hours ago with Padre Joao. He was annoyed with himself for agreeing to share one of his valuable slaves with the Church. He had refused months ago to allow Pasquale to buy her back after the gambling fiasco with Alvarez. Obviously, he had pushed Padre Joao to ask for the girl, a request that Diego couldn't refuse, although he had wanted to.

"Why must it be this woman? Can you not have somebody else?" he asked when Padre Joao had first put forward his request. But the padre had fixed him with his solemn eyes that subtly reminded Diego of the invaluable support that the Church had given him when Senhora Helena, his wife, had died, and the nuns that had tutored the children, prepared their meals, made them garments, and comforted them in the first few months after her death. Diego grudgingly relented because he knew that he owed Padre Joao a great deal. He wasn't a religious man himself—God knew that he'd had his fair share of intemperance with his drinking, gambling, and womanizing—but there were times a man had to make peace with God and Padre Joao had been a good instrument of the Lord's work for the times that Diego had sought redemption through penance.

"God loves a repentant sinner," Padre Joao often said. He didn't condemn Diego, who walked an erratic road to redemption.

Diego steadied himself against the table. The old leg injury throbbed. He thought of his sister Immaculata again. She was a few years older than he was and they had been close as children. That was before she married a rather dour man that Diego had disliked from the start. Now that she was a widow and her daughters were grown, Diego hoped that she would agree to come out to Sao Tome to relieve Violante of some of her responsibilities.

Not that he had anything against Violante. She was a trusted servant and had been a stable and efficient hand in his household for many years, but she was getting on in years. The children had begun to exploit her weaknesses. They were slow to obey her and had even, on occasion, exhibited the kind of unruly behavior that she wouldn't have tolerated when she was younger. Violante would have taken the cane out with Diego's tacit approval. But that was in the past. Violante was aging and getting tired.

"I hope the padre doesn't ask for anything more," he said aloud. He drained his wine glass as he thought about the young woman that he had volunteered for church duty. "If he does, I'll surely refuse him." He felt a little happier after making that pronouncement, although he knew that he'd not refuse Padre Joao anything that he asked for.

ຕະ

It was a week later before Onaedo arrived early on the first day of the job at the chapel. She was anxious and excited at once. She didn't know what she would be expected to do. She knew, however, that this was a lucky turn of events. She even fantasized about asking the padre about helping her go home. She could even ask him for protection from Marco.

She looked inside the small room with its rows of wooden chairs. During morning mass, the wealthy *fazendeiros* with their wives and children sat on the front rows. The overseers and their families sat behind them. The black house servants stood at the very back row and slave children sat on the floor. Onaedo and the rest of the *senzala* stood outside.

Sunday mass was mandatory. As she often strained to hear what was happening inside, she marveled at the foolishness of abandoning one's own gods to pray to the gods of others. If not for the fear of punishment, she wouldn't have come at all, especially during the wet season when the rain poured down and the walk home was in the shivering cold. But she liked the Mother god because her travails had appealed to her. Who better than a mother who had so brutally lost her son would understand her own yearning to return to her daughter?

"It's not like that," Maria had said when Onaedo outlined this theory to her. "Mother Mary is not a god. She is the mother of God."

Onaedo had looked at her doubtfully. "Then she should be. She is a great mother. Like Ani."

Onaedo didn't agree with Maria but she wouldn't argue about it. Onaedo had recruited the Mother Mary to add to her female deities. Agostinho had helped her build a shack in the clearing in the woods; a tiny hut made of palm fronds where she did her supplications and stored the medicines that she used for her healing practice.

She stepped inside the church, hesitant, like a mouse flicking its whiskers in the air to assess danger. She smelled only the lingering incense from morning mass; it was the fragrance that she associated with the saints that could grant prayers.

She heard footsteps and saw Padre Joao come from the inner room. He stood for a while, gazing at her, as if he found her fascinating. She felt caught up in something rapturous just looking back at him; there was something about the priest, the mixture of joy and melancholia that he exuded. She found it enthralling. When she thought back on her experience that day she knew it had played a vital role in her final acceptance of his faith.

Now he walked towards her and welcomed her in Portuguese before pointing to a broom that lay in the corner of the room. He showed her where he wanted her to clean and she immediately set to work. He returned into his inner room, leaving her to sweep, to wipe the altar table, and polish the wall behind it. It was plastered with the smoothest bricks that she had ever seen, which shone in the color of the sky and the sea on a calm day.

Padre Joao returned to a spotless room with a book under his arm. "You are a good and a fast worker," he said, placing the book on the table and waving her towards the wooden form. "I made a promise to a friend. Now is time for you to learn. Come, sit with me."

She sat beside him, hands clasped on her lap. Inside the open book, she saw the same pictures of the same people as in her father's book. They had the same beautiful clothes and long suffering faces.

Padre Joao pointed to the inscriptions he had written on a white leaf he placed inside the book. He mouthed them aloud so she understood what he wanted of her. When she understood, she studied each word carefully, memorizing each one so that she might recognize them next time.

Hours later, Padre Joao closed the book, indicating an end to the session. "It's time to take a rest from reading," he said finally in Portuguese. "Go to the orphanage to help Sister Constancia and we'll continue our lessons later."

She nodded her thanks and tried hard to contain her happiness.

"These lessons are a secret," he mouthed, pinching his lips together with his thumb and forefinger.

Onaedo nodded again; she understood that.

CHAPTER

# 34

Despite her resolve to find her way home as soon as possible, Onaedo was beginning to adjust to life on Fazenda Sao Marcello. Over the course of a year, it had grown familiar to her. Nevertheless, her desire to return to Abonani had not diminished; it had become a fire within her that had become more contained but nevertheless burned just as hot.

Three days a week, as she sweated in the fields, she thought about her daughter. As she chopped and stripped the sugarcanes, she thought of her father in his workshop. And then she felt the presence of her mother and aunt as she prayed to Mother Mary on the days she worked in the church.

Like turning the pages of one of his books, bit by bit, Padre Joao revealed to her the ways of the white man's God. He taught her to read the scripts. And then he told her about Pasquale. She was angry but said nothing. She didn't think that she should thank the man who severed her from everything she knew and cast her adrift to weather the storm of survival in this new land. She couldn't bring herself to be grateful for the sorrows he had given her. So she waited, hoping that she would meet him one day and ask him where his heart was on the day that he paid Oguebie his blood money.

As she toiled under the burning sun in the midst of the sugarcane haze that left dust on everything, she was grateful once again for the days away from the fields working for the priest and the nuns. She began to write and to teach Maria's sons. A few letters at a time—momentous achievements measured in tears.

ର୍ଷ

She'd arrived early at the fields, hoping to avoid being picked on by Marco. He wasn't yet there. She joined the group of women she worked with and they began to cut a swathe down the field. The women bundled the canes and prepared them to be carried to the mill. She placed a thick pad of rolled fiber on her head in readiness for the load to be placed there.

"You have to bend lower," said the woman who was helping her. It was Isolda, the medicine woman. To Onaedo, Isolda had been nothing but helpful and friendly but she was a healer, the only one before Onaedo had arrived and a silent rivalry had developed between them. Onaedo usually avoided her, but this week they had been assigned to the same work detail.

Onaedo knelt down on one knee to take the load but the binding cord broke, the canes slid from her shoulder and clattered to the ground.

"Hurry! Hurry! You two lazy pigs, we don't have all day." It was Marco. Since their encounter, he had not tried to force her again. She was sure Padre Joao, to whom Onaedo had appealed, had warned him off. But Marco had become more vindictive and seized every opportunity to punish her for nothing.

Onaedo and Isolda hastily reorganized the bundles and hurried away from the arc of Marco's lash.

They arrived at the sugarcane press that was housed in a brick building a short distance away. Big metal rollers rotated slowly and gleamed in the sun. The men that pushed its wheels stopped very briefly to greet the women as they arrived and tipped their canes into a growing pile. One of the overseers approached.

"We don't have enough workers here today," he said pointing to Onaedo and Isolda, "we need you to stay behind to feed the presses."

Onaedo was dismayed. Working the press was the second worse job on the plantation, only better than turning the hot caramelized sugar in the boiler room next door; *that* was like the burning heart of hell. Even Eneda's workshop with its hot furnace that was lit all day was never that hot. In the boiler room, iron pots boiled sugar-water into a thick, golden liquid at first pleasant to smell but which soon became sickening in its sweetness.

Nevertheless, it was more dangerous to work the press and feed the canes into it. Onaedo picked up a cane and pushed it into the turning rollers. Its pull tugged on her arm but she held it until the cane was as long as her arm before letting go. The trick was not to let go too soon and risk jamming the machine. That brought the overseer's punishment but one couldn't wait too long either and risk losing an arm.

"That thing is like an animal that will bite off your arm into an ugly stump," Isolda said, picking up two canes and deftly shoving them in. "Did you know that that's how Estevao lost his arm?" Onaedo knew Estevao and the other one-armed men and women in the *senzala* who had tangled with the crushing mill and lost.

"At least he's alive," Isolda added and laughed.

*That woman is crazy. What's so funny about losing an arm?* Onaedo thought, wiping her brow with the back of her hand. She watched the press and the clear, sweet liquid that drained slowly through a spigot into a wooden bucket.

Both women worked harmoniously and although Onaedo knew not to allow herself to be distracted, she allowed her thoughts to wander once again to plans of leaving Sao Tome and returning to Abonani. She realized now that all the plans that she made when she arrived were ill conceived and impractical. She had not even mustered the courage to approach Senhor Diego. Padre Joao now seemed her best hope. She had to think of the best way to present her case to him.

She reached for another cane and was consoled by the thought of working in the chapel with Padre Joao tomorrow.

෴

Diego woke early, as was customary for him, and tried to work on the account ledger for the *fazenda*. After going through the figures several times, he gave up trying. He couldn't balance the account because the money that had come from selling his export didn't cover expenses and taxes. His last consignment of sugar had been at least half a ton short when moisture had entered the storeroom; the sugar cakes had become soggy and infested with weevils and they had to destroy the entire consignment.

Diego stood up abruptly and walked to the window that looked into the sun-washed courtyard. It was splendid in the early morning light. His heart lifted as it always did at this time of the day; his house was one of the few things that still gave him pleasure. The yard was empty of children at this time of day. When the nuns came from the orphanage for the daily lessons, games weren't allowed.

Thoughts of his deceased wife were paramount on his mind today. Helena had been a good wife, raising all his children including her own two. She'd been an angel of a woman, claimed by this land just like the others before. He became despondent again. He couldn't afford to fail, not with his many servants, his concubines, his mistresses, and all his children.

He needed a wife. He had hoped that Renata would accept his proposal. She was tempestuous and passionate and was the mulatto daughter of Senhor Henrique de Azevedo. Her mother was a freed slave and Senhor Henrique was the wealthiest *fazendiero* in Sao Tome. Diego had courted her relentlessly, but Renata had laughed at his proposal of marriage and told him that she valued her freedom more than being his wife. Not even the fact that she had borne him two sons had kept her in his house. With her father's influence, she was a wealthy landowner in her own right and had other lovers. She didn't need a husband, she told him.

He fanned his face with a small reed mat. The day was becoming warmer. He returned to the table and closed the ledger. He'd seen hard times before, and knew he'd survive.

He picked up a letter in spidery script that lay open on the table. It had been delivered late the night before. It was from his sister, Immaculata, telling him that her journey to Sao Tome would be delayed by almost a year. For family reasons, she said, but in between the lines, he heard a subtly veiled tone of grievance. He knew that Immaculata resented the fact that he had come to Sao Tome and left her to care for their elderly parents. When they died, she was left to tie up all the associated family finances while caring for an ill hus-band and raising two daughters. Granted their inheritance had been meager to non-existent, but she had had to manage everything by herself while Diego had left for Sao Tome on an adventure.

When they were children, it was Immaculata who had dreamed of travel to distant lands. Not him. Regrettably, as a woman she was limited. He had tried to assuage his conscience by sending her money, but had known that she hadn't been satisfied. When her hus-band died, he had invited her to come to Sao Tome. It would bring her out of Lisbon, he hoped, and fulfill her lifelong desire. Diego read the letter again.

"*. . . I'll have to put together the dowry for my daughters or arrange for their acceptance into the convent if I cannot find husbands for them . . .*" He sighed and pushed the missive aside without reading any further. He already knew what it said. Immaculata needed money; she wanted husbands for her two daughters and didn't want them to be nuns in an abbey, which was what happened to girls from families with no money for a dowry. Diego had to find the money for her somehow.

He eyed the ledger again. No amount of tweaking was going to change the grim reality of his situation. He reached for his silver-topped cane, acquired from Senhor Henrique in a game of primo, and walked out of the house towards the plantation. A pity he had not been as lucky in getting Senhor Henrique's daughter to marry him.

෨෨

Diego was inspecting the new mill that had been delivered from Oporto in the same ship that had carried Immaculata's letter. It was a major expenditure for his *fazenda* but he would lease it for blocks of time this harvest season. With a bit of luck it would pay for itself soon.

He walked out of the brick building and almost ran into Marco. The overseer was yelling at a group of workers while angrily pointing to an overturned pail. Then he raised his whip against a young woman who had bent down to pick up the container. Diego walked over quickly.

*"Pare-o agora!"* he said, shouting at Marco to stop. The overseer looked surprised but obeyed.

"She's stubborn, that one," he muttered. "She just wasted a whole bucket of sugar." He pointed to the big brown stain soaking into the dry earth.

"It's enough. Let her go," Diego said. The woman picked up the container. He recognized her as the same young woman he had leased to Padre Joao nearly a year ago to help at the church. She's just a girl, he thought, maybe seventeen or eighteen years old, although one could never tell with these people. He hadn't seen her since that meeting, but he recognized the unusual eyes with the penetrating inner light. He had noticed their strangeness the first the day he picked her out of the slave barracks after winning his bet against Alvarez and again when he gave permission for her to work at Padre Joao's church.

Diego had heard rumors that she might be one of the slaves that Padre Joao was teaching to read. The priest's actions were becoming a source of annoyance to some of the island *fazendeiros* who thought that he was breeding insurrection among the slaves. Diego wasn't worried about the priest's actions. He'd already planned to indenture some of his long-time workers and offer them freedom after a certain number of years in his service, in exchange for renting them land that they would cultivate for him. It made financial sense, but he knew it was unpopular with the other *fazendeiros*. They didn't want free blacks on the island. It was a contentious issue between the forward-looking men like Diego and those who wanted to preserve the status quo. Diego was not about to let his entire holdings collapse under the weight of debt. These were difficult times that required innovative ideas. He watched the young woman hurry away with the empty bucket.

He turned to Marco. "Be careful how you treat the workers. We need them healthy to work the land." Marco nodded sullenly and returned to the fields.

ري

Diego thought about the young woman as he walked back to the *casa grande*. An idea was forming. Violante needed help and, from all indications, Immaculata wouldn't be in Sao Tome for at least another year, or possibly more. He would talk to Padre Joao about the young woman. She worked for the church but she still belonged to him. He would have her also start work at the *casa grande* as soon as possible to help Violante.

He congratulated himself on his foresight in leasing her services to the priest instead of selling her outright to the Church. If it was true that Padre Joao was teaching her to read and write then she was even more valuable. The children would respect and obey her more if she could speak and write Portuguese.

CHAPTER

# 35

O naedo was anxious. It was weeks after her encounter with Senhor Diego and Marco. She was worried that Marco may have told him she was a troublemaker. For weeks, she waited for some indication of Senhor Diego's displeasure but, apart from the usual minor skirmishes with Marco, nothing else happened.

It was her day to work for Padre Joao and she was late. Marco had delayed her by making her work longer in the fields to make up for shortfalls. The 'Island Fever' season usually left the mills and fields shorthanded.

By the time she arrived, she had missed her lesson with Padre Joao. She quickly dusted the altar and the wooden statues and then put flowers she had picked around their feet. She wiped the statue of The Divine Mother carefully. She had adopted this important figure of the white man's religion as her own personal redeemer. The way she held her baby in her arm reminded Onaedo of wooden carvings back in Abonani of Ani, the earth goddess. She sometimes also carried a child in her arms, on her knees or even on her back depending on the inspiration or disposition of the executor of her image. She was going to revere this Holy Mother just the same way she had done Ani. She was happy with her resolution of a conflict that had bothered her since she was compelled to adopt the white man's religion and discard her own. This way, her own gods would not be angry with her for abandoning them while she was in this strange land.

She looked around one last time, closed the church door and set off for home. The path went through a series of clearings and small patches of thick vegetation. Forest flowers appeared among rocks and vines entwined on tree trunks. A flutter of stray butterflies settled for the night. The undergrowth rustled; her heart skipped a beat. Memories of dwarf night hunters and eerie night-lights came flooding back.

"Why are you walking alone at this time?" A towering shadow blocked her path. It was a black man, but he was unfamiliar to her. She thought she knew everybody in the *senzala*. But she did not recognize this man.

"Don't you know that it's dangerous to be here alone at this time?" the man that she had never seen before asked again.

"Who are you?"

"I can't tell you who I am." He bent slightly to look closely at her. Onaedo was getting used to the gloom and saw him better. His eyes were dark and deep set. When he smiled, he revealed very white teeth. She could even see a big scar that ran across his forehead like a deep frown.

He turned away abruptly as if sensing danger. "They're looking for us everywhere."

"Are you one of the followers of The Lame One?" she asked, sure he was a fugitive slave. Everyone knew of the Lame One—a legendary escapee who lived on the far side of the island and regularly waged war on the white man.

He looked at her with a frown. "Lower your voice and don't ask any more questions." Then his voice softened. "Listen, I'm here to meet with others of our people. Do you want to come with us?"

Onaedo felt her heart leap in excitement. This opportunity might never come again, her chance to finally escape. There was nothing to lose.

"I don't even know your name. How can I trust you?" she asked.

"Before I tell you my name, tell me what the white man calls you, little sister?"

"Aurelia. But my real name is Onaedo—Gold. Gold Jewel," she replied. She realized they were both speaking in the bastardized Portuguese of the *senzala*. "Padre Joao told me Aurelia also means Gold," she added as an afterthought.

"Onaedo," the man said slowly. "Then you are from the Igbo nation."

"Yes. I'm far away from home. Lost."

He laughed. "You are far from everywhere, little sister. We all are. My fellow warriors come from every nation and they are all very brave men—and women. My name is Nosakhare, but everybody calls me Nathan."

"I want to come with you," Onaedo said. She moved towards him. She wasn't frightened anymore.

"Let's go then," Nathan said. He turned and led the way further into the trees. Onaedo hesitated only briefly before she followed. Nathan walked quickly, silently through the forest that had become eerily quiet. She broke into a quick trot several times, but it was difficult to keep up. She started panting and tears came to her eyes as she tripped over a tangle of vines. She called out for him to wait and bent to free herself. She straightened and looked around her. She was alone.

"Nathan?" she called out. The forest was silent. It caught her voice and swallowed it like a hungry beast. Nathan had simply vanished. *He must have walked on without noticing that I'm no longer behind him*, she thought. *He will be back as soon as he sees I'm no longer with him. He promised to help me get home.*

She quelled the panic that pushed her breath back into her chest as she stumbled blindly, trying to catch up with him. Chaotic thoughts ebbed and flowed in her head. They would seize one of the white man's ships when it sailed into harbor. They would sail to the Delta City and she would find her way home. Nathan had promised her that, but she had to find him first.

She continued to walk in the direction in which she had last seen him before she realized that she was lost. She was about to turn back when she heard the familiar sounds of the *senzala*.

"Do you know anybody by the name of Nosakhare or Nathan?" She asked Maria later that evening.

"Where did you hear that name?" Maria stared at her in surprise. They were at their favorite spot sitting in front of the house.

"I met him in the woods."

"Are you sure that was his name?" Maria asked

"That's what he said."

"You must have been mistaken," Maria said shaking her head in disbelief. "Did you notice anything about him?"

Onaedo thought for a while. "Nothing aside from the deep scar here," she said running a finger across her forehead.

Maria seemed perplexed. "Then you have seen a dead person, Onaedo," she said in a whisper. "Nathan was hung on that tree many years ago." She pointed to the giant acacia where people usually congregated. The children loved to play underneath its shade and the old woman narrated her tales sitting on a giant hump on its root. For an instant, Onaedo saw Nathan hanging from a branch with his eyes closed and tortured lips that mouthed *'Irmã Pequena'*—Little Sister. She stared until he was gone again.

"What is it? You look like you just went to *ani muo* and back," Maria said looking at her.

"Nothing," Onaedo replied.

Maria looked at her quizzically before continuing her story. "Nathan was wild and headstrong. One day he decided to run away with a group of men. Senhor Diego had gone to Portugal that year and left Marco in charge. They were caught before they reached the end of the front road. They had been betrayed and were hanged as a lesson to the rest. We were all witnesses to that terrible day. When Senhor Diego returned, he reprimanded Marco but that was where it ended. Nathan's life wasn't worth that much, it seems, but he'll always be a hero to us. So, if you really saw him, it means that you can see people who have passed. You have a gift like I have always said; just like your mother's sister, Aku."

For days afterwards, Onaedo was frightened by what had happened and what it implied. She was afraid of Aku's gift and didn't want any part of it. But Maria seemed to think that it offered possibilities and spread the word through the *senzala* about it.

"Can you to tell me about my husband?" Isolda asked Onaedo a few days later on their way to the sugar cane fields. "I've heard that you have the Sight so you must know. My husband was sick the day I was kidnapped years ago. Tell me what happened to him."

"How would I know a thing like that?" Onaedo asked.

"Don't you See things like they say you can?" Isolda was a well-built woman and Onaedo just reached to her earlobe. She wore a tattered gown that looked like it would fall apart if one looked at it too hard. Stories circulating in the *senzala* had her as a maid to one of the plantation owners' wives, but Isolda's behavior had been so odd and unsettling that her mistress had sold her to Senhor Diego who was only too happy to return her to the fields.

She gazed at Onaedo and smiled. When her face softened she didn't look so fierce. "Has anybody ever told you how beautiful you are? I knew that you had powerful eyes on the first day that I saw you. Why are you not married yet?" Isolda asked. She looked at Onaedo like a rare specimen and then shrugged as if she'd already lost interest in the answer to that question. "I asked you whether you saw my husband."

Onaedo was nonplussed. "I don't know anything about your husband. I don't even know where he—?" She was stopped by Isolda's laughter.

"Don't worry. I wanted him dead anyway because he was such a cruel man. I was collecting more poison for his soup the day I was kidnapped." Onaedo wondered if she had misheard Isolda, after all her Portuguese was not yet fluent. But when Isolda looked at her and laughed Onaedo knew that she hadn't.

"Don't look so surprised, little sister. Have you never heard of a wife poisoning a cruel husband? One day you'll understand. You're

still a child. Come here," Isolda said taking Onaedo's hand and placing it across her ample bosom. "I know that you're not *enganador*.
You are not a fake. You're real. I can see it. You have a strong power
in you but you don't know it yet. Use it wisely."

With that, she dropped Onaedo's hand and wagged a finger
at her. "And if you ever see my husband, don't you tell him where
to find me." She turned and walked away without another word.
Onaedo walked slowly behind, convinced without a doubt that Isolda
was raving mad.

CHAPTER

# 36

The following Sunday after mass, Violante came to the *senzala*. She looked thinner and her scrawny neck seemed like it would collapse under the weight of her turbaned head.

"Pack your things and come with me," she commanded Onaedo.

"I don't have anything to pack," Onaedo replied. "Where are we going?"

Violante shook her head and said nothing as though she couldn't be bothered with answering impertinent questions. She looked at Onaedo with her good eye as if daring her to disobey. Onaedo glanced at Maria and saw her exchange a look with her husband. Agostinho had come from behind the house to join the women when he heard Violante.

"What does Senhor Diego want with her?" Maria asked.

Violante looked at her with withering scorn. "Since when did the master's business become your concern, woman?" She turned once again to Onaedo. "Are you ready or are we going to spend the whole day here?"

"I'm coming," Onaedo said, going into the cabana. She re-emerged shortly with two folded pieces of cloth; they were everything she owned. She heard the buzz of whispers in the *senzala* as everyone watched. She knew the story that was circulating like a bird trapped in a room—Senhor Diego was taking her as his latest concubine.

"In case you want to know," Violante said, looking pointedly at Maria. "All she is going to do is help me take care of the children, so you can carry that gossip to all the others who have nothing better to do."

"I'm ready," Onaedo said. She turned and hugged Maria.

"I swear by the saints, that woman thinks she is a white woman," Maria muttered under her breath. "That is a kind of madness in itself."

"It will be all right," Onaedo replied. As she followed behind Violante, she prayed that she had not heard Maria's comment; the last thing she wanted was to begin on a bad footing with this fearsome woman.

ฌ

Onaedo's introduction into Senhor Diego's household wasn't as traumatic as she'd feared, but Violante was as difficult as she promised to be. She had learned some more about the older woman in the short time that she was at Casa Sao Marcello. Violante had been the personal maid and companion to the Senhor's deceased wife. Senhor Diego trusted her with everything and gave her free reign of his house. Violante ruled with a heavy but deft hand and apparently did not like most of Senhor Diego's mistresses.

"Don't get any ideas about receiving special favors from Senhor," she said to Onaedo during her first week at the *casa grande*. "You're here for the children, that's all. Don't forget it." Onaedo had nodded in agreement although she didn't understand what Violante had meant. She'd barely seen Senhor Diego. He attended meetings most days at the municipality with the other island *fazendeiros*.

Working with the children had proved easier. Antonio, the eldest son had taken to Onaedo right away. She lent him the Latin version of *The Travels of Sir John Mandeville* and the *Odes of Horacius*, books she had borrowed from Padre Joao as her own reading had progressed. She and Antonio had become firm friends.

"How did you learn all these things as a slave?" Antonio asked her one day. He had found Onaedo in his father's study one afternoon looking at a stack of books. Senhor Diego's library was rather sparse and Onaedo learned later that he didn't like to read; he only collected books because it made him look learned to guests and visitors.

Antonio was a tall and lanky seventeen-year-old with curly black hair that fell across his brows. He had the same bright green eyes as his younger brother Roberto and it wasn't difficult to see that they had inherited their looks from their mother. A picture of her, painted when she was a young bride, hung on the wall in a place of pride in the office.

"Where did you learn to read?" he asked again. He looked earnest and as endearing as a puppy.

"Here and there," Onaedo replied evasively. Her lessons with Padre Joao were still secret. Antonio didn't seem to mind her reticence. He was more interested in showing off his own reading skills.

"I'll be leaving for Lisbon in a year to attend the university at Coimbra, to study Medicine," he told her and showed her the books he was studying. Onaedo smiled as she looked through them. When she looked up, she caught him looking at her strangely. She shifted uncomfortably. She had seen that look in grown men before—the look of lust and desire. She knew that she had become the object of Antonio's youthful desires and hoped that he would grow out of it soon. They were about the same age, but in terms of life experience, she was older. She had been married at least once, borne a child, been sold and bought and had travelled far from her world.

Antonio reached out to give her a book and let his fingers linger on hers suggestively. She looked at him sternly. If she didn't stop him, there would surely to be trouble. She was glad he would soon be going away to school in Portugal.

ॐ

Onaedo tentatively started to keep a record of her daily life. She was encouraged in this endeavor by Padre Joao.

"All the great writers did this," Padre Joao said. They were at the church during one of their lessons. He had just given her a ceramic inkpot from Ceylon and sheaves of expensive woven paper. "They recorded things for posterity to ponder."

Onaedo looked doubtfully at her own childish writing. These would never be philosophical treatises but she wanted to record everything.

Later in the nighttime, after she had supervised the children, prepared them for their lessons with the nuns, and made sure they had studied their school-work, she wrote by the moonlight that came into her room through the window. Her precious candle was only a stump now and she was saving the rest for the darker nights. The two young maids that slept on a mat on the floor were already snoring.

There was a faint noise outside her door. She carefully placed the quill on the table beside the inkpot and went to investigate. There was nobody outside, so she returned. She changed into a light, old nightshirt that Violante had lent her. "I don't want anyone looking like a pauper around here," she had said ungraciously, and thrust the garment at her.

Onaedo climbed into the cane bed with its rough mattress. She was half-asleep when she felt a body against her back. She turned and felt soft lips planted firmly on hers as a hand cupped her breasts. Her face was bathed with the smell of the cinnamon cakes she had baked for dinner. She pushed away the hand that was over her breast.

"What are you doing, Antonio?" she whispered sternly.

"*Eu te amo.* I love you," he whispered and pulled her towards him. He pushed his hand in between her legs. She lay still for a moment, thinking what to do next. She didn't want to wake anyone.

Antonio fumbled with her clothes before he found the path he was looking for. When it was over Onaedo told him to go.

ལྷ

For days Antonio followed Onaedo around like a lovesick puppy. He paid very little attention to the nuns' lessons and sought

Onaedo at every opportunity to whisper his longing for her and to tell her how he couldn't wait for nightfall to be with her.

"We must stop," she told him. "Your father will be enraged if he finds out."

Antonio laughed, stared into her eyes, and told her how much he loved her. Onaedo was in a dilemma. She was in a trusted position in Senhor Diego's house and felt that this reckless nightly liaison with Antonio was a betrayal of that trust. But she didn't know how to stop Antonio. He was the heir apparent, and she didn't want to make trouble by complaining.

"I'm not going back to Portugal," he announced to her one day. They were alone in Senhor Diego's office. "I'm going to stay here and marry you. I'll make Papá set you free. Then we'll purchase our own farm and have many children."

Onaedo looked at him aghast. He seemed to have turned into a man in a just few months. He had grown a beard that gave him a solemn look that was not unlike Padre Joao's. But this whole situation was out of control. Before she could say anything they heard footsteps in the corridor and Violante came into the office.

"I've been looking for you," she said to Onaedo. "I need help with supper. The Senhor is expecting important guests tonight."

She stopped and looked at both of them suspiciously but said nothing more.

ন্তঃ

The few times that Onaedo saw Senhor Diego, he didn't say much and just asked about the children's progress. A few times, she noticed how he looked at her strangely, as she went about her tasks. His attention made her self-conscious, but most days she did not see him at all.

Onaedo was tidying the parlor during the children's siesta one day when a striking mulatto woman stopped her. Her smooth skin was the color of lightly tanned leather, and her gown was the most fabulously exquisite Onaedo had ever seen. It was front-laced in brilliant blue, trimmed with black bands of fabric and scooped low enough in front to show a tantalizing view of the top curves of her breasts. Her black curly hair was pulled back in a severe chignon behind her neck that served to emphasize her perfectly balanced face with its slightly wide nose and full lips that were faintly rouged. Her heavily black-fringed gray eyes assessed Onaedo critically.

"So you're the new maid, Aurelia?" she asked in Portuguese as she fluttered her fan, thin gold bracelets clinking faintly on her wrist.

"Yes, Senhora," Onaedo replied.

"Tell me, how are my children doing?" the woman asked, sitting on the edge of a stuffed chair in the parlor.

Onaedo shook her head. She didn't know who the woman was or who her children were.

At that moment, Violante appeared and greeted the visitor effusively before waving Onaedo away. Onaedo later learned that the lady in blue was Renata, the most famous of Diego's mistresses and the mother of two of his children, Dinis and Erico.

She was one of the island's socialites and Onaedo knew of her wealthy father and the grand home she owned in the city. People said she did not want to raise children there but the real reason it seemed she allowed her sons to live at Casa Sao Marcello with their father was because she was too busy to raise them herself.

After that first meeting, Onaedo saw Renata occasionally, but she never addressed her directly again. In fact, she rarely acknowledged Onaedo and, when she did, she made Onaedo feel like a lowly servant. Onaedo, on her part, had learned a long time ago to stay away from Senhor Diego's mistresses.

CHAPTER

# 37

Onaedo's biggest problem remained her relationship with Violante, and it took her a long time to finally find a way to win over the old retainer. With time, it became clear to her that Violante, for all her show of efficiency, was old and tired, so that despite all pretences to the contrary, she was relieved when Onaedo carried more of the burden of caring for the children and running the household.

Onaedo continued to have stolen moments with Antonio while supervising the younger ones. Antonio made sure that all the children showed her absolute obedience. As the year continued, she wondered what direction the love affair would take. She didn't have much longer to wait before it all came to a head.

Senhor Diego came home one day in a state of excitement. He called to Antonio as he strode along the hallway. Onaedo heard him and came from the pantry where she had been taking stock of the household supplies.

"There's good news from Coimbra," Senhor Diego said to his son. "They have a place for you at the university and a ship sails in three days." Antonio was looking over his father's shoulder at Onaedo who had come up behind him. He wore a stricken look that was lost on his father.

"You'll be an educated man, a doctor," he said and clasped Antonio's shoulder. Diego beamed proudly and turned to Onaedo. "He will be famous in all of Europe."

Two nights later, Onaedo was curled in her bed with Antonio after they had made love silently.

"I don't want to go," he whispered into the dark room.

"You must," she replied.

"Will you wait for me?"

"Of course. I'll be here when you return," she replied, and wondered if she would ever see him again.

"I'll come back for you, I promise," he said, kissing her firmly as he ran a hand over her hips.

"My father would say that a man must never make a promise that he knows he cannot keep," Onaedo said.

Antonio was silent for a while. "Your father was a wise man then. You said he was a *ferreiro*?"

"Yes, he was a blacksmith and a very wise man."

"And you were a blacksmith's daughter," he said slowly into the dark room as if the thought was intriguing to him. He turned to her and traced the outline of her face with a finger. "Will you try to run away when I'm gone, to go back home to your people?"

Onaedo was silent. He waited for her response to a question that really had no answer. Soon he fell asleep with his arms still wrapped tightly around her. It was a while before she too slept.

❧

The months after Antonio left found Onaedo walking around with a longing that was almost physical. She poured her feelings into her writing but, afterwards, made sure that she hid it away; the last thing she wanted was for someone to discover documentation of the details of her affair with Antonio. She reached beneath the bed to pull out a small mat into which she had rolled her manuscripts. She heard one of the maids come in and turned to find the girl in a state of agitation.

"What's the matter?" she asked with alarm.

"M-a-e Viola-la-la-n-t-t-t-e wants you." The girl usually stammered badly when she was nervous. She turned and ran back into the yard. Onaedo went after her.

Violante's room was across the courtyard on the opposite wing of the house. It was dark inside, save for a candle that burnt with a low yellow flame.

Onaedo let her eye adjust to the light before she moved towards the old woman. She was curled up in a tight ball on the bed. In between short gasps, she answered Onaedo's questions. She had developed stomach ache over many days but it had become worse tonight and her stool had become as black as cow dung.

"Wait here with her," Onaedo said to the young maid, whose name was Irina. "I'll be back."

She ran back across the yard to one of the rooms and woke one of the young male servants to accompany her to her medicine shed. They went in the direction of the *senzala,* turning into a narrow hidden path that led to the small thatched house in the clearing. She felt around in the dark and found what she wanted stored in a glass container. When they returned to Violante's room, she mixed some of the liquid into one of the old woman's bone china cups. She told her to drink it and settled herself on the floor by her bedside.

"Did you sleep here?" It was Violante. She was sitting on the edge of the bed. Her eyes were still a sickly yellow and her lips were dry and cracked.

"Yes. You were very sick last night," Onaedo said. She sat upright and rubbed her eyes.

"I'm better now. You can go and leave me alone," Violante said. She closed her eyes and fell back on the bed. She was snoring in a few minutes.

Onaedo returned later that day and the old woman accepted without protest the food that Onaedo gave her. By the second day, she was able to sit on a chair in her room and, by the third day, the

yellow color was gone from the white of her eyes—both the good and
the bad eye.

ɷɷ

Weeks later, Onaedo was summoned to Violante's room. The
old woman had become noticeably thinner after her recent illness,
but she had taken command of the house once again. It was late and
she was dressed in a white night shirt.

"Sit here," she said to Onaedo. This was now their routine most
evenings. After the evening meals, Violante would ask her to come
to her room, and Onaedo dropped everything she was doing and
obeyed. Violante would ask that she tell her about her life before
she came to Sao Tome, and Onaedo would tell her about Abonani,
her child, her father, her mother, her marriage to Amechi, and her
love for Dualo. Violante listened quietly. Sometimes she sat on her
chair. Sometimes she lay on her bed with her eyes closed. She never
volunteered anything about herself and never seemed to tire of hearing Onaedo's stories.

"Has anybody told you that you are a beautiful woman?"
Violante said to her one day.

Onaedo looked away, embarrassed. This was the second time
that somebody had told her that. The first was Isolda.

"It is true," Violante said. "I don't know why you didn't marry
Gaspar. I heard that he was quite devoted to you."

Onaedo was surprised she knew that much about the *senzala*.
There had indeed been a Gaspar that had been interested in her, but
he grew tired of her constant melancholia and lost interest.

Ever since her illness, Onaedo found Violante's uncharacteristic
benevolence awkward. She was accustomed to the acerbic Violante,
and unsure of how to deal with this more malleable, softer version.

However, it seemed that Violante had determined that since
Onaedo had been instrumental in saving her life, she was going to
repay her in any way she found fitting. She started by giving Onaedo
an armoire of gowns. She'd hoarded it under her bed for years.

"You can keep all of it," Violante said over Onaedo's protests that it was too much. "They belonged to the Senhor's dead wife and most of them are for a woman younger than me anyway. I have no use for them anymore. When I'm stronger, I'll give you lessons on how to become a good plantation wife."

"Plantation wife?" Onaedo looked at her puzzled.

"I think that you'll make a good wife for the Senhor Diego," Violante said after a long pause.

Onaedo was taken aback.

"Don't tell me that the thought has never occurred to you," Violante said, smiling enigmatically, her bad eye unblinking as she looked at Onaedo. "Haven't you noticed the way the Senhor looks at you?"

"Me?"

"Are you not a woman?" Violante laughed. "Listen, you're beautiful and you're young. You're tall, your breasts are firm and your eyes . . ." she paused to gaze at Onaedo, "your eyes are the most unusual that I've ever seen in a Guinea woman. You should use your womanly powers to get things from men, even white men."

"What about Senhora Renata? I hear the Senhor has loved her for a long time."

"Maybe so, but Renata has other things that occupy her," Violante said.

Onaedo didn't ask her what she meant. But she thought for days about the conversation, and especially about what Violante had said about using her feminine wiles to get things. But since her heart was still with Antonio, the last thing she wanted was to be a focus for Senhor Diego's attentions. Unless . . .

She did begin to notice that Senhor Diego seemed to desire her company more, even as she tried to avoid him. He sent for her more often, and even started conversations. He asked her about her country, was surprised to learn that her father was a renowned blacksmith and told her that he never knew that people from those parts knew much about anything. Then came the night when he was dinning alone and reached for her hands as she poured out water in a cup, throwing her into a panic.

"I want you to come to my bedroom soon," he said to her, and she nodded because she didn't know what else to say; he owned everything and could just as easily have commanded her to come to him. She wondered about Antonio, and how he would feel if he knew his lover was about to become his father's too. She was despondent when she thought of him, wondering if he would ever return to Sao Tome. Deep in her heart, she believed that he would not.

She had received one letter from him six months after he left. He'd paid a young sailor to deliver it to her in secret. Her initial exhilaration had been tempered by what she had guessed he *hadn't* written. Each word had moved him further away from her, and she couldn't help but sense his excitement about his new life. He wrote to her about what he had learned about other European cities in the short time that he'd been at Coimbra. He wrote about the centers of medical excellence he hoped to visit in Paris, London, Venice, and Padua to study with the luminaries of modern medicine.

Never once did he mention that he missed Sao Tome or that he was looking forward to coming back home, although he said he wished she were able, somehow, to be there with him. She intuitively knew that his interests were already elsewhere. It seemed that Antonio was lost to her.

Now Onaedo was anxious about what to do about Senhor Diego. His intentions and desires were clear. Onaedo confided in Violante the details of her past trysts with Antonio.

Violante's mouth grew hard as she listened. "You had no choice, so I can't blame you. But for now, my advice is that you should welcome Senhor Diego. You'll be better off than with a boy who doesn't know his own heart. He's gone and won't come back."

Onaedo was sitting on the older woman's bed. She looked sadly at the floor.

The older woman spoke again, in a softer voice this time. "You'll forget Antonio. He'll become a physician and marry a Portuguese woman from a noble family. But you should start to secure your future here. You should welcome the Senhor's advances, have his children, and work to get your *carta del alforria*."

That was it. A letter of emancipation or *carta del alforria* was what every slave dreamed of. She knew that she should focus her energies on getting it and continue her plans of returning to Abonani.

"Go and make yourself beautiful," Violante said. "Have a bath with the *lavanda* oil I gave you and then go to his room. If he comes, let him do what he wants to do."

Onaedo was vexed. She could tell that Violante hadn't felt the love of a man. It was one thing asking her to forget Antonio but another to ask her to act like a *prostituta,* those women in the brothels in the city whose profession was to sleep with men for money. Before arriving here, she'd never heard of such a thing, of women living like that. However, she knew that Violante was giving her good advice. Her life was here. For now. Before, she could not have imagined sleeping with a man that hadn't formally paid a bride-price for her. But this was a most peculiar world she now lived in and things were different.

Maria said the same. "You should count yourself lucky that the Senhor wants you. You could have ended up with a *degradado* like Marco."

So a few nights later, she stood on a flat stone in a thatched enclosure behind the servant's quarters, bathed, and rubbed her skin with coconut oil infused with lavender leaves. She dried herself and went to Senhor Diego's bedroom.

She had on a crisp, white, cotton lounging shirt that had belonged to Violante. In the dark room, she saw the empty bed. She removed her top cloth and climbed into the bed to wait.

❧❧

Diego climbed the steps and opened the door before he reached it. Violante had stayed up to let him in. He ignored her knowing smile when she took his walking stick and tunic. That woman could be exasperating he thought with annoyance but there was no point letting her know that.

The candlelight was dim when he opened his bedroom door. At first, he could barely make out the shape of the woman on the bed, but he could smell the spiced oil the more musky scent of coconut oil. He sat and removed his shoes. The woman helped him. He reached to feel the lightness of her shirt. He slipped it off and kissed her lips and her breasts as he got into the bed beside her naked body.

ಜಜ

Onaedo felt her heart beat against the hair of his chest. She was nervous. All her memories had faded, and she lived only in the moment. Even thoughts of Dualo did not come. She pushed Antonio away and thought no more. Diego moved over her and settled in between her parted legs. She held on to him and tried hard to forget.

CHAPTER

# 38

"Are you pregnant?"

Onaedo looked at Violante in surprise. "I don't think so. Why do you ask?"

They were mixing sweet pastry on the giant wooden table that took up almost all the space in the kitchen. The brick oven was already heated, and the smell of nutmeg, cloves, and cinnamon in the dough mixture was warm in the air.

Violante shook her head. "I have only one good eye but I see much better than you do."

Onaedo was only half-listening. She was busy adding the days and knew that Violante was right. How had she missed what her body had been telling her for weeks? The morning queasiness, the craving for blandness and hankering for the taste of earth now all made sense.

She touched her belly tentatively and thought about the first time that she'd been pregnant. She was sure that her daughter must have her feet firmly on the ground by now. She wished that the life in her had been from Antonio but, because of the many months that had passed, she knew it could not be so. This was Senhor Diego's child without a doubt.

In truth, Senhor Diego had been kind to her and she had no complaints. She'd hid the secret of her feelings about Antonio and feigned passing interest whenever his father bragged about news of his latest achievements. He was now in Paris, his last letter had said. She had not replied.

"So?"

"You're right, Mae Violante, I am pregnant," Onaedo replied.

"Good. Now we have a new life to think about." Violante was pleased. She told Onaedo that she'd been married once to a slave in El Mina but that he had died before they could have children. She never explained how she came to be in El Mina in the first place or how she had finally ended up in Sao Tome. Despite Violante's natural reticence, however, Onaedo had learned some things about her. She'd been kidnapped many years before, as a child. She'd served a man for many years before she'd been sold again and brought to Sao Tome.

"I cannot even tell you with certainty where I came from," she had confessed to Onaedo one day. She had also forgotten her native tongue. "But I think it was Efik," she said, fingering the dark, red, dry beans strung around her neck. "My mother gave me these beads, calabar beans they are called. Somebody told me once that they are used to identify witches, but I don't know if that's true or how they could be used in that manner. This is all I remember of my mother."

"I know a woman in the *senzala* that speaks Efik. Maybe you should talk to her," Onaedo said.

Violante had shaken her head dismissively. "I know of her but it's better that I don't know. It's been too long. Don't look at me with that pity in your eyes; I know that you think I'm lost, and you may be right. But carrying things from the past isn't always helpful. It only makes you think of things that can never be again. You should make the best of today and tomorrow; forget the past."

Onaedo had looked at her with more compassion. Nothing could ever change her resolve to go back to Abonani. Violante was indeed a lost soul.

෩

Onaedo told Padre Joao the news when she was about six months pregnant. They were sitting in the sacristy of the church, at the only table in the room. In it were bookshelves and two tall cupboards that held everything Padre Joao needed for mass. On the top shelf of one were chalices, a silver paten, and decanters. In the other were altar linen and bottles of red wine.

Padre Joao rubbed his beard thoughtfully. "You know, the Church won't allow me to administer marriage sacraments to you and Senhor Diego. Marriages between slaves and owners aren't permitted."

"I know."

"But I think that we can get around it, if Diego is agreeable," he added.

She shrugged and said nothing. When the time was right, she was going to implore Senhor Diego to set her free. She didn't need to be married to him.

"My friend Pasquale will be coming to Sao Tome in about three months," said Padre Joao.

Onaedo looked at him in surprise. She'd waited a long time for this, for the opportunity to ask Pasquale to do the right thing and take her home. Yes, she had to admit that she was desperate to see him again.

"He sent a letter through the captain of the *Santa Vitoria*," Padre Joao said. He paused and looked at her thoughtfully. "He would be pleased to know that you've become a strong Christian. But I know that you have questions for him."

Onaedo turned away and took a book from the shelf. She was excited just to think about what it might mean for her. In her imagination, she walked into her father's compound with her new child, and saw the joy on Eneda's face. She heard him turn and call out to Ugodi at the top of his voice. "Come and see what I'm seeing. Onaedo is back." Udemezue, on hearing the news would rush to her and lift her feet off the ground in great joy. Then Ugodi would send for Aku . . .

"Aurelia, did I ever tell you that you look like a close cousin of Pasquale's?" Padre Joao said, drawing her back into the present. "Pasquale believes that there's a connection."

"You told me of her once, but I've forgotten," Onaedo replied, and tucked the book under her arm

"She ran away from home and was never seen again. A really wild young woman," Padre Joao said, shaking his head. "Anyway, Pasquale thought you might be related to him. I, myself, found it far-fetched even though I know that many Portuguese have lived among your people. But that was before I saw you. The resemblance *is* striking."

"There's a story that was told to me about an ancestor that had a white man's child, but if the man was related to Senhor Pasquale, I cannot tell. We never knew a name . . ." she said, her voice trailing off in uncertainty. She also remembered Udemezue's encounter with a man that looked like Eneda. These kinds of stories were heard some-times, Onaedo thought. One could not tell how much importance to attach to them.

തയ

Onaedo thought of Pasquale again as she walked home. She would try not to be angry and would ask him nicely to help her and was sure that he would. She felt the cool evening breeze on her pregnant belly as she thought about freedom. Or maybe she should ask Senhor Diego, instead of Pasquale. She slowed and shifted the weight of the book from one arm to the other as a new, less pal-atable thought came to her. Would Senhor Diego fear that if she had her freedom that she'd leave Sao Tome? Would that make him decide against it? She would promise to come back, but she knew that Senhor Diego wouldn't believe her because she didn't believe it herself. If she ever reached home, she would *never* come back here.

She hadn't had too much time to think about Senhor Diego. Her feelings towards him were complicated; she was fond of him, perhaps she even loved him a little, especially since he had given up others and kept her. Even Renata didn't come anymore.

For Onaedo, the big question was whether Senhor Diego cared enough about her to give her freedom. She was still a slave; an exalted one, no question, but still a slave. She wanted her freedom.

She slowed her pace and put a hand on her belly. The baby had been quiet all day. She bent her head. "Don't worry; we will be home very soon, my child," she whispered in Igbo.

CHAPTER

# 39

O naedo stood as she tried to be comfortable. Then she sat on the edge of the bed. She felt the next spasm and grabbed hold of the bedpost. She'd never felt quite comfortable in this room. It had belonged to the late Senhora Helena and was situated next to that of Senhor Diego himself. Senhor Diego had imported the bed at great expense from Lisbon as a present for his then new bride according to Violante. Now it was hers.

She looked around in the dim light from the candle and waited for the next contractions. She had removed the cloth canopies that draped the bed to increase ventilation, but the room still felt hot. She went and sat by the dressing table and looked into the mirror. Her brownish green eyes stared back at her. Her hair was in thin rows of braids that were plastered on her scalp and twisted in a bun behind her neck. She had rounded out a bit with pregnancy but Violante complained that she was still too thin.

The pain was worse the next time, and so she stood up again and went to the adjoining door to wake Senhor Diego.

She touched his shoulder. "I think that the baby is coming," she said.

"Go back to your bed," he said getting up. "I'll send for Violante." In a few minutes, the old woman ran across the courtyard with a lit candelabrum. She placed the light on the dressing table and pushed Onaedo back onto the sheet-covered mattress.

"Lie quietly. Don't scream."

Senhor Diego had returned to his room. Violante turned to the two maids who had followed her.

"Get the hot water, *rapidemente*!" she said to one, "and you," she said, pointing to the other girl, "bring Isolda from the *senzala*."

Onaedo felt the pressure of her baby as it tried to push out. It wouldn't be long. When Isolda arrived, she took charge of the birth. *It will be quick this time,* Onaedo thought, *and this time I'll be awake.*

"*Gêmeos! Meninos gêmeos!*" Violante cried and clapped her hands. *Twins. Twin boys.*

Onaedo was exhausted, stunned, and suddenly gripped by a deep anxiety. Twins. Again. She saw them—Aku and Ugodi—standing across the room, telling her that this time it was going to be alright. They were safe. She looked at them. She would go down to the clearing with them to her prayer hut. Just to be sure.

Senhor Diego came back into the room. "They're beautiful, Senhor," Violante said, and placed a child in his arms.

"Afonso," Senhor Diego said holding him up. He was the bigger of the two with curly, black hair and jet-black eyes that peered out for a moment before they squeezed shut.

"And I'll call this one Alberto," Senhor Diego announced, as Violante placed the second child in his arms. "He looks like my father Alberto already, with the same brown hair and brown eyes."

Onaedo felt the tears in her eyes as she thought of her daughter and the son who hadn't survived.

ରୠ

The other children welcomed the twins and pestered Onaedo to allow them to play with them. They were both even-tempered babies. She had restarted her lessons with Padre Joao when he summoned her urgently one afternoon.

She put the twins down for their siesta and hurried over to the church.

"Come with me," Padre Joao said, as he opened the door. It alarmed her to see him so distraught. His brown robe swept the floor as he moved and she followed him into the sacristy.

"I've just received bad news from Lisbon." He regarded her with red-rimmed eyes that spoke of some sorrow before his lips did. "Pasquale is dead."

Onaedo felt dizzy; her throat went dry. She sat on the chair nearest her. "Dead? How did you hear this, Padre?"

"His wife Sofia wrote me a letter. I received it last night."

"How did he die?" Onaedo asked.

"There was a fight with Alvarez. It was about money." He rubbed a sleeve across his face. "Sofia didn't give more details. She only said that Pasquale was mortally wounded and succumbed to his injuries."

That night, Onaedo lay beside Diego and mourned. It was yet another setback in her plans to leave Sao Tome. She had put her hopes on Pasquale's return and help and now that plan was dead. At this rate, she feared she would never leave, but that she would be trapped where she was for the rest of her life.

She felt Diego's touch and moved closer to him.

CHAPTER

A grim-faced woman stepped off the tiny boat and looked around disapprovingly. She had just disembarked from a ship anchored further out to sea after a long crossing from Europe. She had left the port of Lisbon three months ago.

"So this is Sao Tome," she said to no one in particular, nearly losing her footing on a small rock. The man that was waiting came forward to welcome her.

"I'm so happy to see you got here safely, my dearest sister," Diego said, lending her his arm.

She smiled tightly and hugged him lightly before looking around again. He imagined how things must appear through her eyes, the rocky beach, the seawater that rushed in and nibbled at it before retreating into the ocean, the intimidating circle of dense vegetation a short distance away.

"I don't know what I expected," Immaculata said. "I thought I would see barbarians rushing out of the bushes, wielding spears, dancing and chanting like in all the exhibits we have at home." She took a deep breath and shook her head slightly.

He laughed. "I assure you we that we're a lot more civilized here than you've heard at home. We're pioneers, securing the world for the Portuguese King and converting the heathens to the path of Christ."

He stopped, embarrassed at how awestruck he sounded. When was the last time that he had converted anybody? But he wouldn't apologize for the great work they were doing in building the empire.

The letter from Immaculata had been a surprise. Even more surprising was the fact that she was on her way to Sao Tome. He'd forgotten that he'd even asked her to come after nearly five years of postponement. She had explained in her previous letters why she couldn't come. She had to settle the affairs of her two daughters—one had married a well-to-do merchant, and the other had ended up in a convent as she'd feared; there had not been enough dowry money to find a husband for both. Immaculata had stayed behind to help with her grandchildren but didn't get along with her son-in-law. She had no use for him, and that's when she decided to leave and come to Sao Tome. She had written to confirm the arrangements for her immediate passage to the remote island. Diego was still reeling from her sudden decision.

"Be careful!" she snapped as one of the men dropped her wooden trunk unceremoniously on the sandy beach. She looked around her and took a deep breath.

"It's very warm here," she said as she pulled out a beautifully painted Chinese paper fan from the pleats of her gown and unfolded it. "So this is Sao Tome, the land of renegade and godless colonists," she muttered under her breath. Diego heard it and knew in that instant that things were going to change, and not necessarily for the better.

Immaculata was dressed in a deep, mourning black with a matching cape. Diego wondered why she was still in a widow's apparel years after her husband's death. It wouldn't be unusual back in Portugal to be dressed in this way but was really incongruous here. *She'll learn soon enough in this wet, sweat-drenching heat,* he thought, picking up her small cowhide box.

"You haven't changed much, little brother," Immaculata said, regarding him with a critical eye. "At last, I'm here to take care of you like Mama had always wished."

Diego wanted to say that he was a grown man now and didn't need to be taken care of, but instead he smiled at her. Then he ordered his servants to place her luggage on the cart. He helped her into the seat beside him and turned the horses toward Casa Sao Marcello.

He stole another glance at her. She was older, of course, and her once thick, jet-black hair was now streaked with large wefts of iron gray that were revealed when she pulled back her black cap. *She's still bossy too*, he thought as he watched her order the servants around, and not in the nice protective way he remembered from their childhood. Now, she looked bitter and hard, her lips clipped together like the clams that the children dug up along the shore-line. Her nose was narrower than he remembered, too. Only her eyes remained the same, but even those, her most attractive feature then, had lost their beauty to the harsh set of her face.

"I trust that your trip was comfortable," he volunteered after a long silence.

She looked at him and nodded. He had the feeling that she wanted to say something, but thought the better of it. Perhaps she thought him foolish for asking a question whose answer was obvious. Sea crossings were always lengthy, rough, and especially for women, uncomfortable.

He felt like a tongue-tied boy around her. He sighed and wished that he hadn't invited her. What had he been thinking? His children were taken care of and the household had run seamlessly for years now; he did not need another housekeeper.

ॐ

For weeks after the arrival of Senhora Immaculata, Casa Sao Marcello underwent a drastic change. Onaedo made sure the chil-dren were on their best behavior, especially when the Senhora was around. The twins didn't run around the house and yard, and even the baby Beatriz, still being breastfed, didn't cry when she was hungry but lay quietly in her basket.

Onaedo, although still recovering from a long and difficult pregnancy with Beatriz, made sure that the house ran seamlessly. She organized the meals, arranged flowers in the house, darned fine net *lacis* doilies for the dining table just as Violante had taught her, and kept the children busy with their lessons and always out of the way of Senhora Immaculata.

"There's no pleasing that woman," Onaedo complained bitterly to Maria on the rare occasions that she visited the *senzala;* there never seemed time anymore for old friends. "She criticizes everything I do. Now she's moved me from my room to another part of the house. According to Senhora Immaculata, I'm not fit to take the place of the late Senhora Helena, and no woman should be allowed near her brother unless she's a pure Portuguese woman. I swear she's insane, because she doesn't realize that such a woman does not exist in Sao Tome. Now she's making plans to import a wife for him from Lisbon."

Maria laughed. "With the Island Fever that we have here? She's going to fail. But why does Senhor Diego permit it?"

"Senhor Diego's growing old and tired these days; moreover, I think he's a little frightened of Senhora Immaculata. He remembers her ordering him about as a boy and doesn't want to fight her even now," Onaedo said. "He told me not to worry, that things would return to normal soon enough and just to ignore her."

"What about the twins and Beatriz?"

"They have no standing in her eyes."

"But it's not her decision," Maria said, her eyes flashing. "Don't let her have her way."

"Senhor Diego doesn't support her in that respect. But I'm still useful to her because I tutor the children now that the nuns don't come. She doesn't have the patience to do it herself."

"Then you mustn't let her defeat you. You must fight back."

"I wish I knew how," Onaedo replied and rose to leave.

వ

To Diego, Immaculata had not brought the reprieve that he'd envisaged. In fact, her arrival could be described as a disaster. She had long ago ceased to be the carefree, warm-hearted, older sister of his memories. She was bent on turning his life upside down, and her first order of business, she said many times, was to find him a wife, although he told her that he had all he wanted in Aurelia.

Dinner-time was usually a fight; Immaculata had insisted that Aurelia not sit at table with them.

"Your association with that *escravo* woman is not recognized by the church," she pronounced many times. "She's not welcome at my table."

The children said nothing. Roberto, the oldest since Antonio had left, looked away. Diego knew that Immaculata's disparaging remarks annoyed him. Diego looked at them and felt ashamed. He should stand up to his sister more. Immaculata was a bully. Diego bit down on a piece of bread and took a scoop of his *caldo verde*, savoring the potato. This was a New World import that most people were eating on the island. Along with the shredded cabbage and hot *piri*-flavored sweet-pork, this was a most enjoyable meal. It was a shame that Immaculata spoiled everything. It was Aurelia's cooking that had made Casa Sao Marcello famous among the *casas grande* of Sao Tome.

He wiped his mouth with a cloth. This was not Immaculata's table but, somehow, she ruled it. It was time that he put his foot down. Aurelia was his wife even if the Church didn't recognize her. That's how things were done here and Immaculata would just have to accept it.

He looked at Roberto and made up his mind. "Go and get Aurelia. Tell her join us for dinner."

Roberto smiled. He knew what was required of him and he left. Immaculata's mouth closed like a beak; she looked like a predatory bird as she tried to hide her displeasure.

Diego ignored her. He concentrated on spooning the last bits of cabbage into his mouth. When he finished, he pushed his plate away and sighed with regret. Life had become quite complicated.

CHAPTER

# 41

O naedo was hanging the clean clothes to dry while she watched the twins. A few months ago, they had both turned seven years old on St Thomas' Day on the 21st day of December—the same day as the founding of Sao Tome.

She stopped for a moment and watched them. Their person-alities could not be more different. Alberto was fearless. He was the one that scurried up the highest tree without any thought of danger, much like Onaedo had done as a young girl. He often teased his more wary brother, Afonso, for being overly cautious.

"Be careful, Alberto," Onaedo called, as he poked a hornet's nest. A few of the angry insects were already chasing the other children.

"Be careful, Alberto," Beatriz said, mimicking her.

Onaedo looked at her and frowned. Beatriz was four already and although she tried to copy her brothers, she was content just to be near Onaedo. She looked like Diego but had brown hair instead of his fiery red that came from his northern Portugal Celtic ancestors. Onaedo regarded her daughter; she worried about her, but then, she worried about them all. Their future was anything but certain. She had to find a way for them to leave this place. She'd tried to buy her passage many times but she had no papers to show that she was a free woman. Senhor Diego had consistently refused to set her free. "I don't want you to leave," he said many times and would grow angry if she persisted. Until last week.

Last week he'd finally relented and promised to consider her request. "I'll think about it," he said. Onaedo had to be satisfied with that.

The last item she retrieved from the wooden bucket was a dark red gown, the last present from her mentor Violante. She'd died a year ago. She stood still reliving the morning it happened. One of the kitchen maids had knocked frantically on her door.

"Come quickly! We can't wake Mae Violante!" Onaedo had had a feeling of déjà vu, when she looked at the old retainer on her bed, in her wine red brocade nightdress, stiff and cold with her arms askew, eyes closed in restful repose. She was late this time. Violante had departed. She'd shed many tears, knowing that her closest ally at Casa Sao Marcello was gone. She was the only person that had resisted Senhora Immaculata. Onaedo had felt utterly alone.

Her burial had been simple. Senhor Diego had paid for the requiem mass that Padre Joao said for her. Afterwards, Onaedo, the household servants, and some of the people from the *senzala* took the body to the grave in the woods far away from the cemetery where the white settlers were usually buried.

There, Onaedo had performed for her old friend the burial rites of the Efik people. Violante had relented in her final years. As her body failed her, her memories had returned. Or perhaps it was the void in her heart that she could no longer deny. At any rate, towards the end, Violante had turned inwards and towards the past.

"I grew up around the Anang River," she said to Onaedo one day. "I remember it clearly now. Promise me that when I die you will call upon the saints of the white man's religion and perform mass for me. Afterwards, you will also pray as diligently to Abasi, the great Creator of the whole world and bury me in the custom of my people. One must always be pragmatic. All the answers may not be in one place despite all that they say. So you must look in different places." Onaedo followed Violante's wishes carefully and knew that she would have been pleased.

Onaedo held the red gown to her chest and remembered she'd left something in its pouch. She put her hand inside it and pulled out the brown-bean necklace. Violante had given it to her before she died.

"Keep it safely. It will help you one day," she'd said. She examined it again. It wasn't particularly valuable, not something that she could sell for money; but she slipped it into her own gown.

"Mae, let's go." Beatriz pulled on her gown impatiently. Onaedo had promised to show her how to make a cake by herself.

"I'm coming, be patient," Onaedo said, and reached for the empty pail.

Senhor Diego was having guests tonight and she had to supervise the dinner he had ordered.

❧

Diego was entertaining about half a dozen guests. Most were his friends—other island *fazendeiros*. They had gathered in his parlor to play their usual game of primo and discuss the island news.

". . . so the governor took Gustavo's license and gave it to someone else," one said. "Of course we all know that there is a woman involved in this rivalry."

"Who's the woman?" another man asked. He sipped the wine that Diego had provided.

"Renata," the first man answered. Diego called to the servants to bring more cakes. He pretended he hadn't heard his ex-lover's name. He knew that Renata had been furious when he had taken Aurelia as his common-law wife, despite the fact that she'd refused his marriage proposal many times. He didn't understand why she was so angry this time; she'd never bothered about the others. She'd vowed to humiliate him and this was how she'd do it, by making him jealous. He had heard she had become involved with the new governor.

*I don't really care; she's free to do whatever she wants,* he thought.
He had never really understood women anyway. He felt a familiar
pain at the bottom of his stomach that had nothing to do with what
he had just heard. He massaged his belly but didn't feel anything
amiss, nothing to explain the constant discomfort that had bothered him for months. He was tired all the time, too, and his appetite
had waned. *Something is wrong,* he thought. Even his breeches were
loose around his waist. The nuns' apothecary potions hadn't done
him much good.

"One thing I have to say about Sao Tome," observed another
man, "is that it's never without great excitement for a man."

The man making the comment was Felipe de Toledo, a visiting
*fazendiero* from Brazil. He was the only one that was not local. The
ship that brought him was docked in Sao Tome for a few days on
the way to India. On his return, he would buy slaves from the slave
depot in Sao Tome and take them to his large sugar plantation in
Brazil. By all accounts, it produced better sugar on more land than
the largest *fazenda* in Sao Tome.

"Is there no excitement in Brazil?" one of the other men asked.

"Not so much," replied Felipe. "We have so much to do; the
lands and the *Indios* need to be tamed so that leaves little time for
distractions."

"I don't believe you, Senhor," another said to him, laughing.
"Where there are men, there are always distractions. I hear that the
Indian women are quite striking."

Before Felipe could reply, Diego added that he'd heard that
there was so much land that it would be impossible to settle it for
the next one hundred years. He wanted to move the conversation
away from women in general, and Renata in particular.

"That's true," Felipe replied taking the bait as he refilled his
cup. "Indeed, the land is abundant and the men, few. It's paradise
itself but without workers to cultivate the land, it can also be hell.
The natives, the Tupi Indians, that is, can't withstand the rigors of

plantation life. It's not their way. That's why we need more blacks, more *escravos*, more slaves.

"You've come to the right place, my friend," Diego said. His troubles were forgotten when a deal was at hand. "We've just received a shipment from the Congo and the Guinea coast. You can have as many of them as you want. They're strong men and women; take your pick. And children too."

"Then we have a deal," Felipe replied looking pleased.

"Did you bring the Indian *tabaco*?" Diego asked, pouring his guest more wine.

"Ah, but not for sale, not to you, my friend," smiled Felipe pulling out a big pouch from his belt. "This is a gift for a generous host." He gave it to Diego with a flourish.

The men all took a few leaves of tobacco and rolled them carefully before lighting one end and then they settled down for an evening of cards, brandy-wine, and smoking.

# CHAPTER

# 42

Many months later, Diego realized that his physical problems were serious and he could no longer ignore them. His health had declined steadily for months, and now he was as weak as a hatchling—too feeble to fly the nest.

It was already mid-morning but he felt like spending the whole day in bed. He looked around his room through half-closed eyes at the daylight that streamed in through a window. Everything seemed familiar and strange all at once. It was almost as though he wasn't anchored to the bed. He reached out but felt an empty space instead of the warm womanly softness that he'd expected.

Where was she? He tried to move his legs but they felt wooden, heavy, and leaden. It also frightened him that his mind of late had become porous like a fisherman's net. His thoughts were like fish; some were caught while others wriggled back to the ocean through the holes.

He moved his leg again. There was something that he had to do but he couldn't remember what it was. The pain came. He closed his eyes until it pushed red-hot pokers of pain through his back before he called out.

"Are you in pain again?" It was Immaculata. She leaned over him solicitously. Diego opened his eyes and frowned slightly. What was she doing here? It wasn't her whom he wanted. Now, he remembered what it was he wanted to do, what he had almost forgotten.

"Immaculata." His voice was a whisper but he had to speak. It was important. "In the top drawer of my desk are the documents for Aurelia and the children; the *carta del alforria* that belongs to them. Bring it to me and then go and find her. Tell her to come right away."

"All right," Immaculata said, and smiled at him. "Here, take this for the pain. It will make you feel better," she said, and lifted his head gently to give him the laudanum mixed with port wine. She'd had the foresight three years ago to bring what remained of her husband's supply, she'd told him.

Diego wanted to tell her to wait until he took care of this urgent business, but he couldn't. His body craved the deeply satisfying pleasure and profound peace that only the laudanum could bring. He took a long sip.

"Go on, take some more. The pain will be gone soon," Immaculata said giving him more.

The effect came fast. He felt the lift and the lightness that a bird in flight must feel. As he watched Immaculata leave, he wanted to call her to return; he needed more. But his voice would not come. So he lay back, closed his eyes, and waited for her to return. He thought about Aurelia and all his children. He hoped that they would be safe but couldn't really think clearly. It was so peaceful here . . .

ॐ

Onaedo was in a daze. She knew that Diego was very sick. She secretly gave him her own medicines when Senhora Immaculata wasn't looking. But it was not working and for a while she had not felt his energy when he slept with her. In the last few weeks he lay beside her happy just to feel her body against his. And now he was gone.

It was Padre Joao, naturally, who conducted the funeral service for Senhor Diego. Nobody went to the fields and the church was filled with everybody who was anybody in Sao Tome. The governor and his new bride, Renata, were there and so were many city officials, nuns, neighboring *fazendeiros* and their families.

Senhora Immaculata was in charge of all the funeral arrangements and had grudgingly allowed Onaedo and her three children to sit at the back of the church.

"You weren't officially married, so you cannot be an official mourner," Immaculata had said spitefully. Her smug smile when she looked at her during the requiem mass troubled Onaedo who ignored her as best as she could. With Diego gone, she was at his sister's mercy unless she did something about it. Onaedo looked at Immaculata in her widow's garb. She seemed to be in perpetual mourning. Onaedo was glad that she'd had the foresight to secure her children's future. Senhor Diego had finally fulfilled his promise to give them their freedom.

"So what do we do now?" It was Maria. They were walking home after the service and burial.

"I don't know. There's a lot of talk but I don't have any more news. Senhora Immaculata would die before she told me anything. But we will know soon."

Maria stopped and looked at her steadily. "I hope you asked him for your freedom papers before he died? I don't understand why he did not want to give it to you to keep."

"He showed me where he kept it."

"Good," Maria said. They continued walking. They were going to the meeting that Senhora Immaculata had called for everyone at Fazenda Sao Marcello. Overseers, field hands, tenant farmers, slaves, mothers, fathers, children, young and old were all summoned to the *casa grande*.

During the last months of Senhor Diego's life there had been a minor upheaval at the plantation. Rumors flew around like the nighttime bats. As the sickness had overtaken him, Diego had let things slide. The *fazenda* was said to be sinking under the weight of debt and Senhora Immaculata had taken on ever more responsibility for the plantation. Before he died, people had said that Senhora

Immaculata was planning an auction; she would sell the farm and take the sick Senhor Diego back to Portugal. The consternation this information caused had been palpable everywhere in the *fazenda*.

Ultimately, Senhora Immaculata had not sold the plantation, but as Senhor Diego had grown weaker, she had dosed him with so much medicine that sometimes he was like a stranger to Onaedo. Sometimes Diego had looked at her with the same disinterest with which a bored child might regard a previously desired toy that had fallen out of favor.

Onaedo had always believed that Senhora Immaculata would never sell; she enjoyed running the place with her own brand of cruelty. Moreover, she wanted to hold everything in trust for Antonio and Roberto, the only two of Senhor Diego's children she recognized.

*The rumors would end today*, Onaedo thought. Soon, everybody would know Senhora Immaculata's plan for the *fazenda* and all its workers.

છજી

A small crowd had gathered in front of the *casa grande*. Onaedo stood in the front next to Maria and Agostinho. Senhora Immaculata was on the veranda looking like the Angel of Death must have looked when he appeared to harvest souls. This analogy frequently came to her mind of late whenever she thought of Senhora Immaculata. Onaedo had learned of the fearsome angel from one of the *cristãos novos*, the New Christians, those Jewish children that had been repatriated to the island from Portugal and forcibly converted to Christianity. One of them was a boy of twelve, called Isaiah, that worked in Padre Joao's sacristy. He helped Padre Joao serve mass and tidy the place. One day Onaedo had found him reading a hand-copied passage from the Talmud his father had secretly sewn into his coat. This was forbidden in Sao Tome. The boy told her of the Angel of Death who was made on the first day of creation, with many eyes and cloaked in a mantle that she imagined must look like Senhora Immaculata's hood. She thought about Isaiah now. She had felt sorry for him and the many children like him on the island that were compulsorily separated from their parents. Just like her.

Senhora Immaculata called for attention; she wasted no time in getting to the point.

"The *fazenda* hasn't been profitable for some time. Our sugar has been of poor quality. We've been unable to sell well at the sugar markets in Antwerp." She paused, sweeping an accusatory stare around the gathering, as if to ensure they knew they all shared in the blame of the failing harvest. "My brother's death has made things even worse. I'll need to sell some of his property to keep the plantation for Antonio and Roberto, my brother's only heirs." Her hostile gaze descended on Onaedo. "Fortunately, we have a savior in the person of Senhor Felipe de Toledo who arrived yesterday from Brazil. He has generously agreed to put some money into this *fazenda* by buying anything we need to sell quickly. I'll prepare a list of items for sale by next week."

An anxious murmur ran through the crowd. Everybody had questions. What would she sell? The slaves? And what of the indentured workers that Senhor Diego had promised freedom? Would the Senhora honor those promises? Would families stay together?

But Senhora Immaculata was done with her speech and did not feel the need to share more information with anybody. She ignored the murmurs and went into the house.

ନ୍ଦନ

Onaedo was worried. She wanted access to Senhor Diego's office. She wished she had done this earlier. But she also knew things had been secured and she shouldn't be worried even though Senhora Immaculata had kept the office locked most of the time. But she was gone to the city today on *fazenda* business and Onaedo had found the spare key in Senhor Diego's belongings after turning his room inside out.

She let herself in and looked around. She'd not been inside the office for some time. She thought about how her life had changed since that first day Violante had brought her here many years ago. She ran her hands over the books she had read with Antonio. When she'd learned that he wouldn't return for his father's funeral she'd not been surprised. He was on a different path now.

She walked to the painting of Senhora Helena. The artist had captured her brilliant green eyes and dark hair in exquisite detail. Onaedo reached behind the frame until her fingers felt the cold metal of a key that was glued to it. Only she and Senhor Diego knew of this hiding place. She carefully removed it and fitted it into the keyhole of a hidden false-bottom drawer of the writing desk. She saw what she was looking for. A roll of parchment paper. She breathed her relief. It was there—her *carta de alforria*, her emancipation papers. She'd seen Diego place it there months ago when he'd first prepared it for her. She had asked him for it then, to hold for safe-keeping, but Diego had reassured her that it was more secure in the drawer with his other important documents and he'd showed her the false compartment. She examined the paper, noting its familiar red wax seal and Senhor Diego's signature at the bottom. It was covered with long lines of carefully written script. She had to hurry. Senhora Immaculata would soon be back. She started to roll the document when something caught her eye. Three words.

Three words that spelled out a name that was not hers.

*Violante da Costa.*

Onaedo stared at it for what seemed like an age. Then she tore through the drawer again, searching, but she knew. Her own *carta de alforria* had disappeared.

"Are you looking for something?" Senhora Immaculata stood at the door. Her tired eyes seemed to gleam with renewed energy.

"My *carta de alforria* is missing," Onaedo said, trying to quell the panic that had overtaken her. "Did you see it anywhere, Senhora?"

"Did you have one?" Senhora Immaculata asked. She walked lightly into the room with deliberate steps.

"Your brother wrote one for me months ago. He gave us our freedom."

Senhora Immaculata looked at her. "Are you sure? He never said anything about it to me. Was it registered at the court house?"

"The court house was burned down by an *incendiário* a few months ago. Most of the records are lost, but . . ." Onaedo looked into the open drawer like a malignant, gaping mouth that had swallowed her document. "Senhor kept everything here in this drawer," she said in a low tone, speaking almost to herself. "It must be here, somewhere."

Senhora Immaculata walked to the desk and shut the drawer firmly before she turned to Onaedo, smiling triumphantly.

"There was never any such document. You're a wily one, but your sorcery and witchcraft won't help you this time. Prepare yourself and your children. You're going to Brazil. Senhor Felipe has requested you specially, and I told him that you'd sail with the rest of his purchases." She paused then said mockingly, "It will be a new beginning for all of you."

"But I will be a slave again, Senhora." Onaedo was desperate. She choked on her fear. "Your brother gave me my freedom when he was alive. If I can find the papers, I can prove to you that I'm a free woman."

Senhora Immaculata laughed derisively. "You were never free; you're a slave now and always will be. My brother never married you anywhere but in his head and his loins. Now go. Pack quickly. You sail early next week." With that Senhora Immaculata walked back to the door and held it open for her.

Onaedo stood rooted. She did not want to move. The document had to be somewhere here and if she left now, she'd never have another opportunity to look for it. Onaedo suspected that Senhora Immaculata had something to do with the disappearance of the papers and that she had to move quickly if she were going to save herself and her children from a lifetime of slavery in Brazil.

She would write a petition to the governor. Padre Joao would help. Onaedo looked at Senhora Immaculata as she gloated. She would leave, she thought as she walked towards the door. For now.

CHAPTER

# 43

In a slave barracks that lined the coastline of Sao Tome, a man railed against his fate and his enemies as he waited for the next leg of his journey. Unlike the other wretched souls, he knew exactly how he had ended up in a place like this. And it was all of his making. Woman trouble.

One woman, to be more exact. A woman to whom he'd become addicted, throwing all caution away just to feel her embrace. As his people would say, he could not keep his knife in its scabbard. That was why he was here.

Oguebie had ended his affair with Ideheno's wife when he moved into his own house in the city. His life had been stable until she sought him out again. Oguebie had been unable to resist her, even though it was more dangerous this time since they didn't live under the same roof. But they had managed to meet secretly. For a while.

Then people started to talk about Ideheno's last son. Only a blind man would have failed to see that the boy looked like Oguebie. And Ideheno didn't stay blind for long.

Of course, Oguebie had denied everything when Ideheno confronted him, but he knew that Ideheno was unconvinced. Oguebie had considered leaving town but there was nowhere to go. The elders at Abonani had sent him word that they had at last discovered his activities as a slave merchant, a kidnapper, and warned him in no uncertain terms that he was a wanted man.

"Anybody who sees him should tell him that if he's seen in Abonani, we'll show him how fire consumes a rat's ear." So said the emissary they'd sent to carry the angry message from his kinsmen.

So he had stayed in the Delta City. Maybe Ideheno had believed him in spite of the obvious, especially since months passed and nothing happened.

So the night that Ideheno's men had come for him, Oguebie had been a little surprised, but also resigned.

"Only my years of friendship with you has kept you alive now," Ideheno said to him when he was bound and gagged. He was taken to Forcados and from there put on a ship. Oguebie knew that many men had been killed for much less than sleeping with another man's wife.

Ideheno was more cunning than Oguebie had realized. He'd sold him to Portuguese traders that they didn't know, so that even though Oguebie spoke Portuguese and said that he was a friend of Alvarez and promised them all sorts of bribes to let him go, they were not swayed. They put him in shackles and threatened to whip him if he did not keep quiet.

So he had shut up and endured the journey to Sao Tome. He knew that it was a first step. The final destination was Brazil. He had overhead them discussing it as they brought them ashore and packed them into the *barracoons*.

On the few occasions that they had let them out, still shackled, to stretch and to breathe, he had noticed that there were at least half a dozen ships anchored and waiting to sail. He didn't know which one would be his, but at this point it probably didn't matter.

Whatever boat he sailed, there was only one end; slavery and captivity.

ண

It was time. Onaedo turned to Maria. She had come to the waterfront with Agostinho and two of their three children. It was early morning. Up and down the shore, slave barracks opened to let out the slaves that would board ships bound for the New World. Sao Tome now exported more slaves than sugar.

"*Olisa* will guide you. He is the Almighty, so have no fear," Maria said. She was crying. "I don't know where they are taking you but the gods and ancestors will go with you."

Onaedo nodded. She was tired. She'd spent the past few days trying to find a way out of her predicament. She hadn't found the papers. She'd gone to the courthouse but, as she'd expected, they had no record of it there.

"I met Senhor Felipe," Onaedo said. "He looks like a kind man."

"A kind slave owner?" Maria snorted in disgust. "Now I've heard it all. They're all the same. If he were so good, he wouldn't own slaves in the first place, and he would have believed you were a free woman and given you your freedom in exchange for money. Instead, he's taking you to Brazil. I hear that that place is worse than here."

"He says that he needs a housekeeper there, so, at least I won't have to work the sugar fields," Onaedo said. She sounded hopeful. "Life may not be so bad for me there even though I'll still be a slave. And I've heard that ships go from there to our own country all the time. It may be easier for me to return home to Abonani from there than from here, even though it seems closer from here."

"I know that you'll swim to Abonani if you have to," Maria said. Her attempt to lighten the parting fell short; a depressed mood fell upon them. They had shared a life, no matter how restricted and confined. And it was coming to an end.

"Hurry," one of the crewmen shouted at Onaedo. "You have to board soon."

Onaedo looked at the ships anchored in the distance. When she first saw them a week ago she'd not given them much thought. They were no different from dozens of other ships that stopped at Sao Tome on the way to and from India, Timor, or Macau. She'd been

blissfully unaware of what Senhora Immaculata had planned for her.
Now she knew. She'd hoped all these years that if she ever boarded
another ship, it would be to go back to Abonani. Instead, she was
undertaking yet another journey to an unknown world. Worse, now,
she had children to think about too.

She looked at the twins who were still bleary eyed from waking
so early. Beatriz slept on a mat on the ground beside her. Onaedo
had torn one of her gowns to make a dress for Beatriz and tunics for
the boys. She bent to wrap a shawl around her sleeping daughter.

"Hurry! Hurry!" Someone called out.

She saw shadows in the distance. It was still too dark to see
clearly but she knew that groups of slaves were being led from the
*barracoons* to the waiting ships.

"Look at that," Maria commented.

"Some things never change," Onaedo said. "Thank the Lord
that Padre Joao paid the captain some money so we could have a
cabin. We'll have to share it with another family but it's better than
travelling in the slave hold."

"Tell me again why the Padre Joao could not stop Senhora
Immaculata from doing this to you and the children?"

Onaedo shook her head. She remembered the conversation with
the priest.

"You know that I'd have paid anything to free you and the children." They were meeting in the chapel for the last time. "Immaculata
never gave me a chance. She said that she'd already signed the papers
with Senhor Felipe and it couldn't be undone. There was nothing
that I could do."

"I know, Padre," Onaedo had replied. "She's now in charge and
she's always hated me; this is her revenge."

Padre Joao shook his head. "I will pray that Christ will dwell in her
heart although I see no sign of Him there. Go well, and God be with
you, Aurelia." He had kissed her cheek and turned to hide his tears.

Now it was time to go. Maria snaked an arm around her waist
and squeezed her tightly.

"Goodbye, my sister, go well."

Onaedo lifted Beatriz in her arms and walked to the water's edge. The boys were behind. The boat would take them to the waiting ship. Afonso dragged a burlap sack that contained half of their worldly goods: a change of clothes, Onaedo's gowns, and sheaves of writing paper from Padre Joao.

Alberto's sack had the rest: food to eat on the way, bananas, coconuts, nutmeg plants, hot pepper, and dried pork. The four ceramic cups, her most prized possession had been a gift from Violante years ago. She had wrapped them carefully in layers of dried sugarcane leaves. Alberto heaved the sack into the boat.

"Be careful, Alberto," Onaedo said. She took the bag from his hands as a folded piece of paper fell from his pocket. "What is this?" Onaedo bent to pick it up and unfolded it. She couldn't read it in the faint light of dawn. So she slipped it into her gown.

"Hurry," she said, helping him with the sack. At the ship, they climbed the rope ladder and found their room. It was as cramped as she'd expected. They were sharing with a mulatto woman and her four children. They were going to join her husband who was an overseer and had left for Brazil months before.

Onaedo sat on one of the two narrow beds as they waited for the ship to complete preparations for the voyage. She got up and went to the door. The paper she took from Alberto fell out of her gown again and she picked it up. She read a few lines and felt faint.

"Where did you get this, Alberto?" Her hands shook. It was the missing *carta del alforria*. With her name.

The other passengers watched curiously.

"Irina gave it to me," Alberto said. "She found it in Senhora Immaculata's box. She was cleaning her room when she found it but she told me that it belongs to you. She asked me to give it to you when we arrived in Brazil."

Onaedo was frantic. What should she do? She was already on the ship and it was pulling away already. She rushed to the deck. She saw Maria in the distance standing with Agostinho. She wanted to shout her name. To tell her that she found her papers. She was free. She stopped. It was too late. They had gone past the point of return. The ship was pulling away smoothly, gathering speed.

Maybe it was best that she left Sao Tome. If she stayed, she would have to deal with Senhora Immaculata. Onaedo couldn't possibly live with her at the *casa grande*.

She was a free woman. She would go to Brazil and she would show Senhor Felipe the document and negotiate with him. She would be an indentured worker and demand payment for her services. Eventually, she would save enough money to buy passage back to Abonani with her children. She heard many ships went to her country from there all the time.

"Mama, what is the matter?" Afonso looked worried as he peered at his mother's face. Alberto had already gone to explore the rest of the ship and Beatriz was still asleep on the bed.

"Nothing, my son. Nothing." Onaedo stroked his cheek tenderly.

As the ship set sail, she looked back again and saw Maria and Agostinho. They were gray blurs in the distance.

# Epilogue

MAXINE RANG THE BELL and waited. She read the sign over the door that said Sedona Retirement Community in bold, black letters on a cream background. She heard quick footsteps inside before the door opened.

A middle-aged woman in a pink and white nurse's uniform looked at her, a brow slightly raised. Graying black hair was held back from her tired face. "Ma'am, I'm sorry but visiting hours are over," she said.

"I made an appointment with your supervisor," Maxine replied, digging into her bag for her card.

"Oh, you must be the lady from Philadelphia," she said and stepped aside to let Maxine in. "I'm Grace. Mrs. Wyatt is waiting for you."

The hallway was brightly lit. At its end was a large sitting room where one of the residents played the piano. A half dozen grayed-haired residents were gathered around and sang along. Most of the others were either watching television or napping.

"This way, please," the nurse said, leading the way. "You must be tired, driving all that way to Providence."

"Oh no, I flew in from Philly, and I've rested a little in my hotel," Maxine replied. "How is Mrs. Wyatt?"

"We told her that you were coming. She's waiting for you. Are you a relative?"

"Oh no. Just an acquaintance." The nurse looked like she expected something more.

"It was quite interesting really," Maxine added. "I bought a box of books from her when she lived in Sag Harbor."

"Oh, I see," the nurse nodded sagely.

"They were important papers. She told me then that there might be another box."

"I see," she said again.

They passed the lounge and turned onto a corridor of many doors. They stopped outside one.

"Miss Nathalia, your guest is here," the nurse announced. She let Maxine into the room. The walls were a soothing mauve. The room smelled of lavender that seemed to come from a small pot-pourri oil pot with a lighted candle. The old lady sat on a recliner by her bed with a mauve cellular blanket draped across her knees.

Her housecoat was the same shade of lavender as the dress that she'd worn on the day that Maxine bought the books from her in Sag Harbor. Everything in the room was in shades of purple and violet.

Physically, the old lady hadn't changed much. Her thick head of silvery hair was arranged neatly in a wave and contrasted with her chocolate brown skin. But there was a definite difference. Her memory was not what it had been at their last meeting. She didn't remember the sale and didn't remember that her sister Jacinta had died. In fact, when Maxine mentioned it, she broke into tears as if she'd just heard the news for the first time. Maxine soothed her and gave her the box of chocolates she'd bought at the airport.

"I'm sorry that she wasn't very helpful," Nurse Grace said, as she led Maxine to the front door. "Her family doesn't come often, poor dear. At least she had company when her sister was still alive."

"Her sister?" Maxine asked. "Her sister died in Sag Harbor before she came here."

"That was Jacinta. I was talking about Esther. She died a few months ago."

"Died?" Maxine echoed. She felt her heart sink. Just her luck. This new sister might have been able to help. She wished she had come sooner. This was a wasted journey.

"Did you say that you were looking for some books?" the nurse was still talking to her.

"Yes. Notebooks actually."

"Miss Esther gave me some things before she died. There were two boxes of junk and I kept them in my garage. I can have my husband bring them to your hotel. Maybe what you want is in there."

ତ∾

Maxine sat on the floor of the hotel room with books strewn on the bed, on the chairs, the side table, and the floor. She'd found the rest of the dairies at the bottom of the second box that Nurse Grace's husband had delivered. They were written in the same familiar handwriting as the previous three translated volumes. The ink was a faded grayish blue. The fragile pages were like gossamer and in poorer shape than the previous batch.

The *Bolero* ring tone of her cell phone interrupted her. It was Travis. She'd left him a message about Mrs. Wyatt's descent into Alzheimer's disease and the lucky find.

"I hope it has the missing information," Travis said.

"I think so," Maxine replied. "We'll translate them as soon as I get home."

There was a pause before Travis spoke again. She knew what he was going to ask before he did. "When will you leave for Nigeria to see your father?"

"I don't know."

The meeting with her father had been uncomfortable. He'd been more of a stranger than she'd feared. They'd both tried to bridge the years and the distance, tried to talk about the short time he'd been around before he left, but there wasn't a lot, and the awkward span of thirty years was not easily overcome. She'd been envious of the affectionate way he in which spoke of his other daughter who was married and lived in England with her children. She realized she had three siblings of whom she knew nothing.

"Things might be better if you go to Nigeria and see things for yourself," Travis said to her afterwards. She'd agreed but had developed cold feet and cancelled the trip at the last minute.

"Would it help if I came with you?" Travis asked.

"Would you, really?"

"Yes. I have an assignment in South Africa in a few months. We could go to Lagos first and then go to Johannesburg after."

She said that she'd think about it, wished him goodnight, and hung up.

She repacked all the books, flyers, almanacs, and maps of Brazil. The country was called Terra Vera Cruz when Pedro Alvares Cabral found it in 1500 A.D.

At the bottom of the old box was an old tattered twine with some chocolate brown beads attached to it. Only a few of the beads were intact; the rest were just broken, empty shells. She examined the string and then carefully placed it among the other papers. It was all that remained of Violante's necklace.

She closed her suitcase, leaned it against the wall before she climbed into bed. She telephoned her daughters to wish them goodnight. They were still at their father's. They told her they missed her.

She pulled the blanket over her head and thought about when she was a little girl. She remembered the exhilaration that she'd felt riding on her father's shoulders. She wasn't sure why she thought of that now as she fell asleep.

In her dreams that night, she was already in Africa.

END

# Author's Note & Bibliography

There was an interesting discovery in 1976, of exquisite bronze artifacts in Igbo-Ukwu an ancient Igbo town located in eastern Nigeria. The bronze works were dated around the 4th century and were executed long before the timeline of this story. My challenge was to find a fictional blacksmith, who would be worthy of that kind of talent and who would be the purveyor of such exquisite offerings. Eneda fitted the bill. Although Abonani is not Igbo-Ukwu, it is conceivable at least to me, that a great, talented artist such as Eneda could have learnt his craft in a similar fashion to the great artists and artisans of that region.

The events in the book are loosely based on a lot of traditions of Igbo people of West Africa. The sources that I found invaluable in my research are listed below but I hasten to add that I have taken a lot of liberties in my interpretations of events and customs and therefore all misrepresentations are entirely mine.

Abonani is an imaginary Igbo town from the 16th century. In its various etymological forms—Ebo-itenani or ebo-iteghete—many Igbo towns such as Ogidi, Obosi, Onitsha and Asaba have used variants of this name in describing their town.

The images I have painted of life in the Delta city is based loosely on descriptions of early European travelers to West African cities in the 15th and 16th centuries. Some tried to give an eyewitness account of well organized and planned cities rather than the over the top images of the savage native that came to be the caricature of the African by some writers of that era. Those images seemed, unfortunately, to have gripped the imagination of Renaissance Europe and were to be continually propagated as truth until fiction somehow became transformed into fact.

Events in the real island of Sao Tome would have spanned over a period of at least eighty years or even more but for dramatic impact, I compressed history into a few pages and hurried things along to tell this story.

The influence of the Portuguese on the African coast made me curious and informed my desire to find out more. It was indeed a learning experience to look into the past from the comfort of the present and re-visit the intense drama of the upheaval that accompanied the Portuguese slave trade and the devastation that trailed it.

⚬⚬⚬⚬⚬⚬⚬⚬⚬

Achebe, Chinua. *Arrow of God*. Anchor Books, 1969 edition.

Agbasiere, Joseph Maria Thérèse, and Shirley Ardener. *Women in Igbo Life and Thought*. London: Routledge, 2000.

Cohn, Paul. *Sao Tome: Journey to the Abyss—Portugal's Stolen Children*. Burns-Cole Publication; 1st edition, December 2005.

Davidson, Basil, with F. K. Buah and the advice of J. F. Ade Ajayi. *A History of West Africa to the Nineteenth Century*. Longman, 1993.

Garfield, Robert. *A History of Sao Tome Island, 1470–1655: The Key to Guinea* (Distinguished Dissertations). January, 1992.

Isichei, Elizabeth. *A History of Igbo People*. Palgrave Macmillan, June 1976.

Passos, John Dos. *The Portugal Story: Three Centuries of Exploration and Discovery*. Doubleday, March 1, 1995.

# Acknowledgements

I cannot end this without mentioning the people that have made my story possible. My father Augustine Achebe taught me and my siblings to ask questions and not to always accept the status quo. My mother Matilda Achebe may not know it, but her stories and funny way with words kept us laughing as children; she has inadvertently put words into the mouths of some of the characters in this book. I hope that God will continue to keep them both.

To the following I am also eternally grateful:

My sisters, Adeze, Ifi and Chiko for being my very first draft readers—correcting, encouraging, disagreeing but always championing. I owe you more than I can ever repay. To my brother Chu who continues to hold the fort—*Jisike*. To my children, Jennifer and Nnamdi, for your patience all these years and your belief that one day "Mom will get this done." To my *twin* nieces Kiki and Amy, I thank God for your life in this century. To friends who aided me in their different ways—Anita Remerowski for all those meals and conversations, Linda Myers for wise and invaluable counsel, Anene

Ejikeme for very early advice, Laurie Rockwell photographer extraordinaire and Angela Onwuanibe for just being there.

A special salutation to my aunt, Zinobia Ikpeze, from whom we learned that daughters can sometimes be the custodians of the history of a family or a people. Thanks also to Monica Achu Nzejekwu, our earliest storyteller. To my late uncle, John Achebe, a Heinemann and Thomas Nelson book representative for many years and whose home was a childhood paradise for any self respecting bookworm.

Finally to my greatest inspiration, my other uncle, Chinua Achebe, the world renowned writer, whose early influence on the way I saw literature and storytelling cannot be overestimated.

To you all I say a big thank you.

And to those that were lost, your stories will be told.